CURING
the
Uncommon
MAN-COLD

J. L. Salter

δ

Dingbat Publishing

Humble, Texas

Published by Dingbat Publishing
Humble, Texas

Maxim by Darden Media Group

Mister Potato Head (Mr. Potato Head) by Hasbro, Inc.

Oprah (*O, The Oprah Magazine*) by Oprah Winfrey and Hearst Corporation

Oreo by Nabisco, a subsidiary of Mondelēz International, Inc.

PayPal by eBay, Inc.

Penney's (JCPenney) by J.C. Penney Company, Inc.

Penthouse by FriendFinder Networks, Inc.

Playboy Channel (Playboy TV) by the Manwin Group

Q-tips by Unilever

Sears (Sears, Roebuck & Company) by Sears Holdings Corporation

Shoney's

Snickers by Mars, Incorporated

Sugar Crisp (Golden Crisp) by Post Holdings, Inc.

Super Glue by Super Glue Corporation/Pacer Technology, Inc.

Tasmanian Devil (Looney Tunes) by Warner Bros. Entertainment, Inc., a subsidiary of Time Warner, Inc.

Tractor Supply Company

Trix by General Mills, Inc.

Victoria's Secret by L Brands, Inc.

Vogue by Condé Nast, a division of Advance Publications, Inc.

Dedication

If I dedicate this novel to my wife, people will naturally assume that I'm a big baby when I get a cold. Oh, well, what the heck... dedicated to Denise Williams Salter.

CURING

the

Uncommon

MAN-COLD

Chapter 1

August 10 (Monday)

"I don't think I can hold up…" Amanda's eyes were full. "Jason just left the doctor." Her apartment suddenly felt smaller.

"What on earth is wrong?" Her friend Christine had just arrived and already plopped down on the small sofa. "Cancer? Paralysis?" She probably pictured even worse diagnoses because Christine zealously read supermarket tabloids.

Amanda groaned softly.

Christine grabbed her younger friend's shoulders. "You'll feel better if you talk about it." She moistened her lips slightly. Medical news was known to be among her favorites, along with stories about nasty divorces.

Amanda looked for her nearest tissue box. "It's… a… man-cold."

Christine sighed heavily. "Don't wind me up like that. I thought this was a real *situation*."

"It is!" Amanda had been home from work about twenty minutes and still had her heels on. "I don't know what I'm going to do."

"Just ship that basket case back to his momma." Christine snapped her fingers. "Let Margaret wait on him hand and foot for the next week."

"More likely two weeks. Remember when he was sick in January?"

"I thought he had triple-Nashville-man-ditis or something."

Amanda nodded. "Totally helpless. He could barely use the bathroom by himself."

"Look, Jason was overindulged from the get-go. I bet Margaret nursed him too long. Ship him back."

"I can't." Amanda closed her eyes. "She absolutely won't take him."

"His own momma?"

"The last time a sick Jason stayed at her place, it nearly put Margaret in the hospital." Amanda lowered her voice. "She said Jason moaned every waking hour. Hardly ever moved from her couch for over a week... and he *limped*, for cryin' out loud!" Amanda shook her head. "I can't live with that."

"You can't let him stay here! You won't survive two days with Jason's sick-over." Christine sputtered. "There's got to be somewhere else... somebody else. Maybe he can bunk with a buddy."

"A buddy? Just picture irresponsible Kevin trying to assist helpless Jason who's down with a deadly illness. Kevin would hightail it out of his own apartment so quick you'd think he just spotted a fumigation fog sliding under his door."

"Slow down and rethink this." Christine touched her friend's forearm. "Do you really know this person well enough to nurse him back from near-terminal man-sniffles?"

"Know him? We've been sleeping together since the Halloween party last year. My place *and* his!"

Christine leaned in closer, even though she should have remembered this development. "At his place too?"

"Three times." Amanda was prepared to list the dates.

"Hmm. That is serious, I guess." Christine waved her hand briefly. "Okay. So you do have an investment, so to speak. The issue is how to tend Jason enough that it even registers with him, yet not so much that the effort kills you."

"Now you understand why I'm freaking." Amanda moaned again. "Not to mention these are my Hell Weeks at work."

Verdeville was about twenty miles east of Nashville's Interstate loop. Amanda Moore's current crunch was reviewing applications from every Greene County agency seeking federal grants. Some thought she was too inexperienced, at age twenty-eight, for such a significant role and she was not taken very seriously in county government offices because of her shapely legs and hips.

"Okay, back up. Let's say you were in-the-bed ill, with doctor-ordered bed rest." Christine's hand went horizontal. "Would Jason take care of you at *his* apartment?"

"Are you kidding? He'd tell me he'd been evicted and show me a cell phone picture of a notice on his door."

"Okay, you're catching on. So, tit for tat." Christine Powers crossed tanned arms beneath her augmented bosom. Divorced for about four years, she was financially secure because of her lucrative alimony settlement. Frankly, she had too much free time on her hands: brunette Christine had lots of urges and often followed up on them — she behaved more like a redhead. "In fact, if you were the one sick, I'll bet Jason wouldn't even help you here at *your* place."

Amanda merely shrugged.

"Of course not." Christine showed a satisfied smile. "I'm glad I was able to talk sense into you."

"You realize I've got to help Jason."

"Why? He's obviously not worth it."

"I do actually love him, you know." Amanda sighed.

"Give me one reason." Christine rolled her eyes. "And don't go way back to him rescuing you at that New Year's Eve party. Jason did real good in a scary situation, but you can't let him coast forever on a single night of good ole boy gallantry."

Actually, Jason had been Amanda's very chivalrous knight that memorable evening nineteen months ago, and his rescue was both literal and figurative. However, Amanda loved Jason more for the connection they'd made since then. "Well, right now I can only think of his eyes — they're deep and soulful… and loyal."

"A spaniel has interesting eyes and loyalty. Get a dog." Christine was uncommonly pragmatic at times. "And that's his most endearing quality?"

It was sometimes difficult to ignore Christine's negative attitude toward the man in Amanda's life. *Why does she have it in for Jason?*

Christine frowned. "So you actually intend to cancel your own home life for the next two weeks and baby Jason?"

"Don't really have a choice. I can't totally refuse to help my boyfriend. But I don't think I'll survive his sickness."

"Okay, the only workable option is he stays in his own apartment and you bring deli soup each evening."

"You must be joking." Amanda bent forward until her face nearly met her knees. "He'll be on Facebook and e-mail telling everyone he's been abandoned to die. Somebody would probably start up a blog to raise donations for his cure."

"Yeah. He does tend toward the dramatic. Probably got that from his momma, too. When boy babies nurse that long, they suck in a lot of drama." Christine didn't explain her certainty that Jason had spent more than the typical phase at Margaret's breast. "Plus, I thought guys who played all those team sports didn't get sick. This is weird."

"You know, it is pretty suspicious that he fell ill during the one sliver of August when none of his leagues have any games scheduled."

Christine's mind obviously churned. "I still say there's got to be another solution."

"I've been pulling my hair out, looking for it." Amanda tugged on the longer front tresses of her inverted bob cut — honey brown coloring this year. "I hate guys getting man-sick. If you and I had a cold like that, we'd just keep on going." She moaned again. "I'm in for total misery with no escape. He'll sit around in his jammies all day, contemplating what's inside his jammies. Guess what he's thinking about while I'm at work all day."

"Sex... with you."

Amanda nodded and closed her expressive blue eyes. "One time in that January siege, I was up all night bringing water or pills... or just listening to him whimper. I dragged myself to work, put up with nine hours of B.S. from my boss, and then crawled home. There was Jason — a stupid smile on his face, sprawled on the couch in those ratty jammies."

"Just hand him the December *Cosmo* and tell him you've got a headache." Christine looked into her friend's tear-stained face. "You didn't fall for that old routine."

"I did, back then, but I've wised up. So it's mainly a matter of extra guilt." Amanda recalled the previous occasion. "Don't even get me started about the mucous and coughing... plus he hadn't showered in two days. Yuck."

Christine's expression clearly indicated she shared that characterization.

Amanda slowly toppled over onto the vacant cushion. "I feel sick myself. Maybe I'll go home to *my* mom."

"Arizona? In August?" Christine poked her friend's shoulder. "Just pull up your big-girl panties and tell him no. Jason cannot stay here with you, period. Just break the news quick and steel yourself against his whining."

"I can't. I've been trying to tell you: he's already on his way over. Right now."

Christine quickly began gathering her belongings. "You've got two choices…"

"Suicide is one. What's the other?"

"Seriously. This is the time to decide if Jason's going to remain part of your life. Because if he does, this ultra-high maintenance side of him is going to kill you."

"What's the second choice?" Amanda tried to look hopeful.

Christine shrugged. "Become his nurse, errand girl, and sex slave for the next two weeks."

Amanda's tears gathered again. "Well, there's one thing I won't do. Absolutely will not do."

Christine nodded solemnly. "I wouldn't do that, either, 'specially if he hadn't showered."

"No. I mean I'm not going to call in sick for him." Amanda clamped her jaw shut. "Jason can make his own calls every morning."

"Oh, I thought you meant the other thing." Christine held up her hand, signaling a new subject. "Well, if Jason does stay here, he sleeps on the couch."

"No, too much in my way out here. Back in my guestroom."

"You couldn't fit a sick hamster in there."

"I cleaned it up, a little." Amanda had not intended it to sound so defensive.

"Show me."

Amanda escorted her friend down the short hall to the guestroom. Boxes were stacked along one wall and a single bed occupied a corner. Extending from another wall was a treadmill with a long row of clothes hanging on each handrail.

"I didn't know you also had exercise equipment in here."

"Mom insisted on leaving it here when she and Dad moved to Tempe." Amanda shrugged. "I only use it for closet overflow."

"I did that with Daniel's treadmill for a few years. Works better if you stack bricks under each back corner." Christine pointed. "That helps level out the handrails so the clothes hangers won't slide down to this end."

Amanda fleetingly wondered where she could find some free bricks. "Well, anyway, a human can certainly fit in here."

"Okay, I guess so, since you've got that path through all those boxes. Might need a map, though." Christine obviously didn't approve. "Although now that I think about it, you don't really want him too comfortable. So maybe this hamster nest is a good idea after all."

"It doesn't matter where he stays, really. In this tiny apartment, he'll never be more than about twenty feet away. Coughing, whimpering, calling for whatever kind of attention."

They left the cluttered guestroom and returned to the living space. Amanda crumpled to the couch and curled into a crescent. She knew the dreaded uncommon man-cold was incurable — so nobody even tried. They just gritted their teeth and stuck it out... or they packed up and left. Not many options. "You've got to help me."

"Sorry, there's no cure." Christine started to leave, but stopped suddenly. Her eyes brightened and her fingers twitched slightly. "Unless..." She sat again. "Well, it's a long shot, but theoretically possible."

Amanda straightened slowly and pulled hair from her damp eyes. A few strands stuck in the corner of her mouth where drool had started to collect. "Do you have a plan?"

"Scare him."

"You mean, like… boo?"

"More subtle." Christine lowered her voice. "Remember that movie with Kathy Bates and James Caan in a remote cabin? He's a writer."

"*Misery*? You call that subtle? You want me to scare Jason with a sledgehammer and a stub of lumber?"

"No, I'm still on *subtle*. But you might need the hammer later." Christine nodded. "If this works, you'll get Jason out of your apartment and might even cure him of man-colds forever."

"Okay, I'm on board." No hesitation. "Tell me your plan."

"Fear is a powerful force if properly applied."

Amanda heard a noise outside. "He's here! What's your plan?"

"We're going to give Jason the Scare-Cure."

"The what?" Amanda looked out the window. "Hurry! He's nearly at the door."

"The Scare-Cure." Christine seemed to like its sound even though she obviously had no strategy yet developed to implement that devious term. "I've got some research to do."

"You're leaving me alone with Mister Sick?"

"I'll call you tomorrow at work." As the doorknob twisted, Christine whispered, "Don't feed him anything besides really thin soup and those nasty crackers your mom left last year. You have any other yucky food?"

"There's a soy hotdog leftover from July 4th."

"Perfect. That's Jason's lunch tomorrow. No bun. Hide everything else." Christine opened the door.

Jason Stewart was slumped over like he'd been at hard labor on a chain gang for weeks without food or water. He looked up pitifully, saw who it was, and waved lazily. "Hi, Christine. Where's Amanda?"

She turned her head to indicate the interior of Amanda's apartment. Christine moved down the walk — partly backwards and partly sideways. She noticed how much more debilitated Jason looked when Amanda came to the door.

Scare-Cure. This could be interesting.

Amanda took in the pitiful sight. Jason seemed like an abandoned kindergartener clutching his teddy bear as he looked for Mommy at the house next door. It might have been endearing, except her boyfriend was no longer in preschool. At 32, Jason seemed in no hurry for their serious relationship to grow deeper. He obviously adored Amanda and loved being with her, but his notion of commitment had some leftover adolescent one-sidedness. Could he become a responsible mate? Nobody knew, including Jason… apparently.

Good-looking and leaning toward handsome, Jason had a boyish face and thick, dark hair that would look better combed the other direction. His blue eyes, occasionally dark and soulful, were bright with zeal when he participated avidly in basketball, softball, soccer, and flag football. About average weight for his frame and medium height, Jason's strength and athleticism were belied by a slight paunch, due to his predilection for junk food, beer, and frequent snacks.

She remained in her doorway, blocking his entrance. "I'm sorry you're under the weather. But like I said on the phone, these are my most horrid work weeks all year. Already stretched to the limit. I simply can't deal with anyone staying here."

Jason looked puzzled at why he was still on her threshold. "I won't be in the way. You won't even know I'm here."

"Trust me, I'll know." She frowned. "Even without the bell you auditioned in January."

"The concept was good; maybe the tone was off."

"If you'd rung that bell once more, I would've stuffed it up a… really… dark… place."

Jason's muscular shoulders slumped. "But I don't think I'm well enough to drive."

"You got here all right and your place was closer to the doctor's office."

"But I shouldn't be alone when I'm sick."

Whiny is quite unbecoming in a lover. "It's a cold, Jason. How bad could it be?"

"Doctors miss a lot. I have complications." He coughed to illustrate. "And fever."

"Well, I'm sure this is the worst cold in all of middle Tennessee." She sighed heavily and felt his forehead. No discernable warmth. "Okay. Wait right here and I'll get a thingy to check your temp."

When she returned from her bedroom, Jason was sprawled out on her couch and already had the TV on. She paused to consider *where* to insert the thermometer.

After an hour of channel surfing, Jason entered the hall bathroom. Moments later, he emerged wearing floppy socks, a very old tee-shirt with several holes, and pajama bottoms with a sprung-out waistband. He headed toward Amanda's bedroom.

"Hold on, Mister Germs! Not in *my* bed!"

"Huh?"

"These are my Hell Weeks. I can't get sick with all those grant apps stacked on my desk. The boss would bring files to my hospital room." Amanda ground her teeth slightly. *Why can't you wait 'til after Labor Day to get sick?*

"So where do I sleep?"

"Your own apartment."

No reply from Jason.

Amanda shrugged and pointed to the guestroom.

"All the way over there?"

"It's forty-two inches across this hallway."

Jason peered in. "That's not enough room for a five-year-old."

"Well, stop acting like a five-year-old." Amanda sighed. "You'll be safe enough if you stay on that path."

Supper was a few hours later. As per Christine's instructions, Jason's complete meal was a small mug of chicken-flavored consommé with one stale, generic rye crisp cracker.

It was a long night for Jason. Highlights included: loud groaning, coughing fits, sneezes like backfires from a rusted exhaust manifold, and snoring which rattled the inside wind chimes. On numerous trips to the bathroom he even managed to click the light switch with amplified noise. Beginning around 2:00 a.m., he spent another hour flipping through TV channels.

Amanda netted about three hours of sleep.

Chapter 2

August 11 (Tuesday)

An exhausted Amanda watched from the kitchen as Jason approached from the short hallway around 7:00 a.m. The patient's minor cold symptoms had already improved significantly but Jason looked worse: hair not combed, face unwashed. It was a matter of slight scientific curiosity as to how long his saggy pajama bottoms could stay up with so little spring left in their ancient elastic.

Jason's complete breakfast was a small glass of unsweetened prune juice and two more generic rye crisps. "I think British press-gang prisoners ate better back in the 1700s." Jason groaned. "Tell me again why I can't have real food?"

"Christine is pulling together a special diet. Something from NASA, for astronauts and deep-sea laboratory people."

"Do they work with sea labs? I thought NOAA did that."

"Whatever. Our connection was futzy." Her fingers wiggled to illustrate. "Anyhow, she gave strict instructions for you to stay on liquids and crackers until we get the complete menu in place."

"How well do you know Christine?" Jason's voice lowered. "I mean really know her?"

"Oh, we've been best friends about five years. Since before her divorce. Why?"

"She hates me, you know."

"Why do you say that?" Amanda's mouth was about to smile without permission.

"The way she looked at me, yesterday when I arrived. I think she put a spell on me. Looked like she wanted to cut the brake lines on my car or something."

"That's silly. Christine wouldn't know brake lines from wiper blades. You're just a little paranoid — light-headed because of your illness."

"Light-headed because I've only consumed thirty-seven calories since I got here."

"Look, you're not at work because you're sick. I told you to stay at your place, but you insisted on coming here. Okay, so I'm taking care of you. But I need lots of help and Christine's helping me."

"But I don't want Christine around. Just you and me." Jason resumed his pitiful expression. "You know, my private nurse..."

"Yeah, I know. But we have to focus on getting you healthy again. You can never tell when colds might relapse and turn really nasty."

* * * *

Comfortable on the couch, Jason flipped though channels and scratched his lower belly.

Amanda stopped on her way out the door for work. "Did you call in?"

He nodded. Jason was good at his job, handling the electric co-op's phone customers, but he sometimes viewed himself as the anonymous *Press Six for Billing Complaints* rather than an individual with actual identity.

"So what are your plans today?"

"Plans? Uh, no big plans. Just—" *cough, cough* "—try to get better."

"Well, if you burn up that remote, you're outta luck." She pointed. "No more batteries."

Jason shrugged. "Do you have anything at all I can eat without Christine hexing me?"

"I'm out of almost everything. I'd originally planned to do groceries tomorrow." Amanda frowned. "But since Christine's bringing over that special food soon, we'd best wait."

"I'm—" *cough* "—recuperating. You know, vitamin C and bed rest—" *cough* "—but I need to keep my strength up."

"Well, I'll check with Christine about supper possibilities."

"Oooh. Maybe pizza!" He felt a flicker of hope.

"No dairy for Mister Sicko. Messes with your mucous."

Jason was crushed.

Amanda touched the side of his face.

"Have I still got fever?" He hadn't intended to sound so eager. His skin was probably 98.7 degrees.

"No. I was measuring your stubble. See if you can find a razor that hasn't been up and down my legs thirty times. Bye."

— — —

Mister Sicko's sumptuous lunch was a single soy faux hotdog, minus the bun. His mouth watering, Jason spent five minutes painting mustard from tip to tip and then sliced it into twelve equal pieces. He ate them with a fork, slowly. He tried drinking more prune juice, but it clashed with the mustard.

**** **** **** ****

Among Amanda's normal work interruptions — including several from Louis Erie, her supervisor — Christine called Amanda's cell phone, shortly before lunch. "Hello?"

"You sound awful. Bad night with the desperately ill?"

"I'm dying." Amanda groaned. "He kept me up all night long with his noises."

"I thought he was in your guestroom across the hall."

"He is. But I could've heard him from across the river. I'm so tired I need help holding my coffee cup."

"I'm thinking this will be lovely." Christine sounded like she was smiling into the phone. "Sweet, sweet revenge."

"Uh, who's getting revenge here? Me, for Jason's intrusion? Or you, on your ex?"

"Oh, I'd say revenge is a big enough platter to share, maybe with some left over."

"Huh?" Amanda's antennae went up. "What have you got in mind with this cure-scare?"

"Scare-Cure. Top secret... I'm thinking about getting it copyrighted. I'm starting up a blog, too."

Amanda ignored the blog topic and waited for an answer.

"Well, everything's not fully in place yet, but I think we've got Jason right where we want him. Except in the wrong apartment, of course."

Amanda heard somebody walk past her office doorway. "Look, I've got to go. They're not paying me to chat with a mad scientist."

"Quick question — what time do you get home from work?" Over the years they'd known each other, Christine had asked that question about a thousand times.

"By 5:20 if I hustle."

"Well, hustle tonight and give Jason a triple dose of that special cough syrup I left with you in January. Bury him in that little bed and shut the door. I'll meet you at 6:00."

"Okay, but I'm dead on my feet and it's only been one night. I hope you've got some really powerful magic."

"Magic! Hey, that's an angle I hadn't thought of." The wheels inside Christine's brain clicked almost audibly. "See you this evening. Do not feed that patient! Okay? Make sure he's out of it. Bye."

Amanda briefly stared at her phone as though further information might remain inside. *Nope.* She flipped it shut, closed her eyes, and mulled the bizarre possibilities for the days ahead. She realized Christine was in a turbo-charged manic phase. They were headed together into uncharted territory with this complicated campaign, but Amanda was not terribly frightened as long as Christine's throttle had some sort of override. Right now, Amanda was the only governor; otherwise, Christine's engine ran at flank speed. With such momentum, it was usually best to stay out of her way if possible.

Amanda's eyes were still closed as her ungainly boss entered and plopped down on the chair in front of her desk.

"Late night?" He sniggered.

"Hi, Louis." She was unable to disguise her dismay.

Louis Erie was roughly average height but nearly double normal weight and wore an awful toupee. No one knew exactly what part of New York State Louis hailed from but many assumed it was near the historic lake that matched his surname. His Yankee accent was quite grating to middle Tennessee natives. "You making good progress on those grant apps?"

"Yeah. Pretty much on schedule. But I could use some clerical help."

As usual, Louis ignored the request and just stared.

Grizzled gonads. Amanda stared back as long as she could stand it. Then she shuffled the unread grant applications until her boss seemingly lost interest.

After Louis finally left, Amanda looked at her office clock: 11:55 a.m. She was barely functioning and still had four hours at work. If she skipped lunch and took a nap she might narrowly survive Day Two of her Hell Weeks.

* * * *

"Shoo, cat!" Amanda waved her hand at the mature nineteen-pound black cat on her doorstep. "You don't live here any more. Go away!" The feline glared disdainfully for a moment and then hopped, nearly sideways, into the grass bordering the short walkway.

Amanda had just hurried home from work and found Jason napping in the guestroom. *Good.* She'd been prepared to dose him with Christine's heavy-duty cough syrup from who-knows-where, but it wouldn't be necessary. That was a relief; she didn't really want to poison Jason. Not yet, anyway.

Her apartment was a mess — newspaper pages all over the place. Tissues were on the floor, tucked between couch cushions, and even in the potted plants on either side of the television. A water glass had formed a ring on top of a low bookcase. On the table: a half-empty bag of chips and an open box of cereal. It even looked like Jason had drunk prune juice from the container. *Yuck!* There was a huge wad of mucous in the bathroom sink — she'd probably need a putty knife to scrape it up.

Shortly after six, Christine bustled in with two large empty trash bags. "Is he down?"

"Sound asleep in the guestroom. I'm surprised you didn't hear him snoring from the parking lot."

Christine noticed the chips and cereal on the table. "He's been snacking all day?"

"Afraid so. I thought I'd hidden everything last night. Must've been up on a top shelf." Amanda hugged her friend. "You came back! I was afraid you'd abandoned me."

"Not only back, but I'm launching Phase One of our Scare-Cure. Armed... and... dangerous." Christine held up a tube of Super Glue.

"What are you going to do to him?"

"This doesn't go on him. It's to glue down the toilet seat. We're going to make him sit to pee, like normal humans."

Amanda frowned. "I'm going to lose my deposit if you cement all the fixtures."

Christine dismissed that concern with a wave of her hand. "We're going to fill this place with estrogen 'til it's oozing from the walls. We're cutting him off from everything male." She held up one empty plastic bag.

"What's that for?"

"Food, to start with. Everything but staples. What all have you got?"

"Other than these chips and cereal, hardly anything. I don't really cook, you know. And I haven't been to the store in a week."

Christine had already shifted focus. "Whatever. Edibles in one bag. In the other bag, we gather up every magazine with a sexy girl on the cover. *Cosmo, Vogue, Oprah,* whatever."

"*Oprah?*"

Christine ignored the interrogatory. "Catalogs, too. Got any lingerie mailers?"

"Uh, just Victoria's Secret, as far as I know."

"Ah ha!" Christine sounded like Sherlockella Holmes solving a dastardly crime. "Prime example. Get it." As she looked around, her eyes were wild with the excitement of a case. "Does Jason keep any girlie mags here?"

"Here?" Amanda held out her hands, palms up, like they might hold some clues. "I don't think so. Why would he keep nudes in my apartment?"

"He's a man. Check the garage."

Of the fourteen apartments in the complex of duplexes, only six units had private garages… for thirty dollars more each month. Amanda needed that space for things left by her downsized parents, so her car stayed outside in the parking lot. "Why the garage?"

"Prime hiding places: toolboxes, high shelves, places you wouldn't normally look."

"I don't have any toolboxes." Amanda sighed heavily. "Tell you what, I'll collect what little food's in the place. You go look for dirty pictures."

Christine rubbed her hands together. "Thought you'd never ask. I'm an expert at this."

Amanda could tell. And it scared her a little.

Both searched for nearly fifteen minutes.

Christine came back empty-handed except for a small notepad with a Gil Elvgren pin-up on the cover.

"One of my dad's old tablets, from a tool supply company. This thing's over fifty years old." Amanda checked the calendar inside.

"Can't be too careful. We're confiscating all of Jason's visual stimuli."

"He'll just turn on TV."

"Not after 7:00." Christine checked her watch. "In about thirty minutes I've got a cable guy coming to disconnect."

"Disconnect my cable?"

"Relax. It's only my sister's husband."

Amanda clutched her friend's forearm. "Do your sister and her husband know about our secret cure project?"

Christine shrugged. "Just enough for them to cooperate with this particular phase."

"That's way too much for anybody else to know! This was supposed to be just between us. But now twice as many people are in on it!"

"Not a problem. My brother-in-law only talks about sports. And my sister doesn't even know you. Besides, who's she going to tell?"

Amanda tried to recall the statistical maxim about how fast information spreads when each person learning a secret tells just one other person. It was roughly equivalent to the bubonic plague epidemics in the Middle Ages. Then she realized her friend had already moved on, so Amanda shifted to more mundane matters. "But there's a big fee to get my cable service back!"

"He won't really disconnect anything… just disable it."

"How?" Amanda looked puzzled.

"Never mind. Check our blog later this evening and I'll try to post our Phase One efforts." Christine snapped her fingers. "Oh, your laptop. Keep it with you at all times. Lock it in the trunk of your car while Jason's awake. Never let him near it."

"Okay, I'm ahead of you on this part: no Internet or video games. But how do I explain where my laptop is?"

"In the shop. Tell Jason he spilled coffee on the keyboard and it stopped working. That way it's his fault."

"But he didn't spill anything." Amanda shook her head. "He won't believe that."

"What he won't do is remember… either way. Men are always guilty of something, so it feels pretty natural to be accused of just about anything. You watch. If it's necessary to tell him about the bogus coffee spill, he'll look like a third-grade boy caught putting tadpoles down a pretty girl's blouse."

Amanda sat at the table with a loud sigh. It was like hunkering down in the middle of a whirlwind. She wondered what else was involved in Phase One but was too frightened to ask.

No matter. Christine was bubbling over to tell. "I'm taking all the booze in the apartment. Hot, cold... open or not. No alcohol whatsoever. Not a drop." She also produced a handwritten list of her strategies, arranged by category. "It's still a work in progress."

Amanda scanned the page and smiled. She was beginning to see the kinky wisdom in her friend's manic plan — take away all Jason's creature comforts. "You know he's going to freak without his beer."

Christine nodded with a cheesy grin.

Amanda retrieved four bottles from behind the microwave. "Hid these last night."

"Are you sure that's all the booze? Just four beers?"

"Jason drank the other eight this past weekend, shortly before he was struck ill." Amanda felt a bit defensive. "It was on my shopping list."

"Let me see that list."

Amanda reached for the magnet-backed tablet on the refrigerator door. It wasn't really much of a list because Amanda didn't bake, either.

"Okay, scratch this, this, this... and definitely that." Christine made those motions with her finger. Then she eyed her friend narrowly. "I can see why Jason gravitates to your place when he seeks primal comforts. His momma wouldn't buy all this junk. You've been catering to his cravings: sweets, chips, beer, ice cream. If I was a lovesick man with a big appetite, I wouldn't go home, either."

It felt like Amanda was being chewed out by her fifth-grade teacher.

Christine obviously noticed. "Hey, after we cure Jason of this syndrome, you can buy him some treats, if you want." It sounded like Jason was a recalcitrant Yorkie. "But maybe you should think about scaling down the magnitude. Looks like half your grocery budget goes to Jason's sweet tooth and his spare tire."

Amanda shrugged. "I didn't realize it had gotten that bad. Jason would look around like something was missing, so I'd buy it. That way he didn't have that lost expression on his face."

"He pretty much always looks lost to me. Don't focus so much on his face and stop feeding it so much." Christine sounded too stern. "I'm not trying to meddle, Amanda. I mean not beyond this experiment and quest for a cure. But I am concerned. It's easy for some women to become doormats under men's feet. In a relationship, the position you want is on top."

Amanda pondered that image, but didn't inquire how literally her friend intended it.

Christine halted her train of thought like she'd suddenly noticed a completely incongruous tollbooth along the tracks she'd been traveling for years. "How on earth did you and Jason ever hit it off to begin with? I mean, besides his sad, loyal eyes… and that he rescued you, once upon a time."

"I don't know. He was cute, a little rumpled, and slightly confused." Amanda realized that description also fit most Guinea pigs.

Christine rolled her eyes and started to interrupt.

Amanda quickly continued. "And he makes me feel good."

"You mean in bed?" Her older friend edged closer.

"That, too. But I mean he makes me feel *valuable*. Sometimes when we're out, I sense that he's practically guarding me, like a security guy walking to the bank with a big payroll bag."

Christine apparently ignored the imagery. "That's it?"

Amanda smiled softly. "Plus, he seemed so uncomplicated. I like that. My life is very complicated, so there's a comfort level in a boyfriend with predictability."

"You can get that kind of comfort with a plush blanket from Sears. You two are about as opposite as could possibly be... within this species, that is."

"Is it wrong to want a boyfriend who's uncomplicated and predictable?"

Christine considered. "Well, it gives you the upper hand, which you seem to need."

"I'm not sure how to take that, Christine. To me, it's more like Jason needs directions and I already know where I'm going." *Hmm.* Truly, it sounded about the same.

"Whatever. Now back to the alcohol situation. Do not get him any more." Christine raised her hand for emphasis. "Check his friends, if anybody visits. They're quite accomplished at sneaking in booze."

"I don't really expect any of his buddies to visit here. But if they do, you want me to pat them down as they enter?" Amanda considered it might be enjoyable to pat down Big Ernie. She suspected that nickname represented more than his height of six foot seven.

"Use your discretion, but don't let them bring any contraband, especially booze."

Amanda pointed to a third, smaller bag in the top of her friend's purse. "So what's in there? Or do I even want to know?"

Christine smiled. "What's one thing guaranteed to scare away men as efficiently as wolfsbane and garlic runs off all the vampires?"

A light bulb blinked on in Amanda's brain. "Potpourri!"

Christine nodded vigorously. "Got a ton of it. And more where that came from." She handed over the cellophane bag like it was a treasured secret known only to Professor Vanella

Helsing. "We'll have this sick puppy up and out in three days, tops."

"Maybe sooner, with no beer in my apartment."

"Check our blog tonight and watch the donations pour in."

"You mentioned some blog stuff before." Amanda frowned. "I don't understand."

"I'll explain later. Right now it's just theory, but I think I can combine what we're doing to Jason with a cosmic act of charity."

That made no sense at all. "Wait, Christine, I need to ask you. This is a lot of thought and effort on your part. Why are you doing this?"

"Girl, I suffered through at least one man-cold every winter for fourteen years with my Daniel." She turned her head and spit dramatically — though it was dry. "I hope that young hussy he took up with gives him a bad dose of the clap." Christine looked like she wished for even worse maladies.

"You're still smarting from that divorce, aren't you?"

"The hurt doesn't end when your lawyers shake hands at the courthouse. Every time I see him, or that witchy bimbo who stole him, I get upset all over again."

"I'm sorry, Christine." Amanda had wanted to ask this before but it never worked into a conversation until now. "Did you and Dan *ever* love each other?"

She smiled. "Oh, yeah, 'specially at first. Lots of love. But he's older than me — I was his second wife. After about seven years, he got the itch. Then he scratched it… a lot."

Amanda touched her friend's forearm.

"But, hey, at least I got these out of the deal." Christine thrust out her bosom. "For our tenth anniversary, he sent me to the plastic surgeon."

Amanda had heard the story numerous times. "Well, they are quite impressive."

"The other day, I thought I'd lost the pendant from my favorite necklace. The chain clasp had broken at some point and I didn't realize it 'til I was buying stamps at the post office."

"Isn't that your favorite pendant?" Amanda pointed. "The one you're wearing?"

"Yeah, I found it that night while I was getting ready to bathe." Christine giggled. "It was stuck down in my cleavage."

"On me, it might keep sliding." Amanda's hand reflexively went to her breast. She preferred to remain natural, but would be delighted with one cup size larger.

"The funny part is the postal clerk who helped me search for the pendant kept looking at my chest. I think he knew that's where it was!"

It seemed like a lot of responsibility, carrying around such pronounced upper attributes. "Maybe they'd require less maintenance if you kept them contained a little more."

"Why? I might be in the mood to try out another husband one day." Christine cleared her throat suggestively.

"Well, I don't think I'd want to cope with boobs that capture cookie crumbs and loose jewelry."

Christine didn't react. "I'm pulling together a complete dietary grid for your sick boyfriend." She waved a writing tablet. "But it'll be tomorrow before I can collect everything and get it over here. For the time being, here's a box of crackers I want you to use on him."

"*Use* on him? What are they?"

"They're similar to rice cakes, but smaller and flatter. Plus, the manufacturer found a way to make them taste even more awful."

"*You* eat those?" Amanda was skeptical.

"Well, I tasted them. Bought these back in the spring when I briefly contemplated wearing a swimsuit this summer." Christine looked as though her younger friend should already know that. "Anyway, I'll get the really healthy stuff over here tomorrow."

Amanda examined the box. "I can't deliberately starve my boyfriend, even though I do wish he'd go home."

"We're not starving him. That's the beauty of our plan. He's going to starve himself."

"How do you figure?"

Christine acted like she was explaining civics to a child. "We're providing legitimate, nutritionally healthy foods, along with other items that sound yucky but actually are perfectly fine to eat. But here's the key — everyone knows men won't eat stuff like that."

"None of them?"

"Okay, 85 per cent of American men won't eat healthy stuff." Christine had to close her eyes to manufacture that statistic. "It's his own mind that defines things as inedible... and he'll refuse to eat most of it. So it's not that *we're* starving him. We're feeding him, but he won't eat. Ergo, he's starving himself. Satisfied?"

"I don't know."

"Amanda, this is a win-win situation. Pay attention. We know he won't eat much of this, if any... so he's got two choices. One, he leaves. You win — your apartment is yours again and you can concentrate on surviving your current problems at work. Two, he stays several days and eats healthy food for the first time in his life. You win again — he'll lose that spare tire and you'll have a more proportioned boyfriend." Christine paused. "Speaking of... with him playing all those sports, he shouldn't be growing a belly." She seemed oblivious to all the bulky professional football and baseball players, many with considerable stomach girths.

Amanda ignored that familiar observation about Jason's paunch, but she was coming around about this cutting-edge diet. "What about some of those truly awful things, like tree roots or whatever you had on that list?"

"I didn't list tree roots, but it's not a bad idea." Christine added a note to the tablet. "Look, this is about illusion. Jason wouldn't know arugula from coyote weed. We tell him something's a tree root and he'll believe it. We simply produce the illusion of tree root. In reality it's just asparagus tips or something. He'll never know. Illusion. Men are suckers for it."

"Christine, you seem to be banking on my boyfriend being quite ignorant about non-traditional food. What if Jason isn't as stupid as you think?"

"You probably don't want to hear my answer. Suffice it to say that men, in general, are pretty dense about food details and most have remarkably unsophisticated palates."

"Okay. You've convinced me Jason won't be poisoned and he won't be starved. But I still feel awful about ganging up on him — two against one."

Christine smiled. "It's actually three against one. You, me, and his own mind... all working together to cure Jason and get him out of your apartment. When a man won't use his own brain for the good of womankind, it's perfectly allowable for us to use his mind for our own purposes."

"Sounds like Jason's going to be an unwitting brain donor."

"A mind is a terrible thing to waste."

Amanda remained fretful. "You're probably right that Jason won't eat stuff like this." She pointed to the tablet. "But why are you restricting his intake quantities so drastically?"

"Feed a fever, starve a man-cold."

Amanda started to correct. "I don't think..."

Christine waved her manicured hand.

In the language of manic individuals, that signaled the subject was dead. *Don't waste any time trying to get back to the matter.*

Over the next several minutes, Christine explained a bit more about her intentions with the blog and they discussed some of the possible strategies to keep Jason off balance. The goal was not to evict him outright, but to make him so uncomfortable that he would leave on his own.

Amanda had asked as many questions as she could formulate. Finally, she repeated her gratitude for the assistance.

"You're welcome. I wish I'd had a wise friend to help me cure Daniel." Christine sounded wistful. "So this is something I'm giving back… to the community, so to speak."

"Which community is that?"

"Wives and girlfriends of males struck down with this incurable disease. Only now we're finally close to a cure and women will beat a path to our blog to get it. Give me a couple of hours to get everything entered and then you log on this evening. Here's the web address I'm using." Christine left in a blur, smelling heavily of potpourri. The beer bottles clinked loudly in one of the two large bags she carried.

Amanda reflected on her occasional crises; she'd often been resigned — possibly even content — to have a bossy older sister take care of things for her. Her real sibling Kaye, eight grades older, had practically raised her until leaving for college when Amanda was ten. For the past five years Christine, a dozen years older, had played that big sister role. Being occasionally dominated by an older female, whether sibling or friend, affected Amanda in two distinct ways. It often made her furious, so she'd snap or growl or fume until the takeover attempts subsided. But it was sometimes comforting, on a complex and confusing journey, to be able briefly to let go of the wheel. With an experienced elder steering, Amanda wasn't as responsible for the incidents if her *vehicle* careened into people or things.

Through the still-open doorway, Amanda watched her mentor depart. Some friends stay with you in the hospital. A few will keep your kids when you've reached the absolute end of your rope. Some buddies will loan a car when yours is in the shop. But it takes a very special girlfriend to launch a full-scale campaign to cure your significant male's desperate illness. Amanda thought she might even cry.

But that moment was interrupted by Jason bellowing from the guestroom. The creature was awake!

After assessing Jason's dire situation, a half degree of fever, Amanda left for the pharmacy at 6:55 p.m. It was an aspirin emergency but she only had the three other common non-steroidal anti-inflammatory drugs.

Chapter 3

Shortly after 7:00 p.m., while Amanda was resting, a panel truck drove up and parked one duplex over. The bogus cable technician arrived at Amanda's apartment and rang the bell six times.

Jason trudged to the door and opened it. The technician burst in, took the remote out of Jason's hand, and toweled it down with a disinfectant wipe. Then he turned off the television.

"Hey! I'm watching that show. They're going to vote somebody off the island tonight."

"Maybe so, dude, but you ain't gonna be there. We're converting your street from digital to analog. This whole neighborhood's down 'til they work out the bugs."

"Analog again?" Jason looked perplexed. "Uh, why would they go back?"

"Bugs, dude. Digital systems have bugs — those chips the government put in all the new TVs to monitor what you watch. Somebody keeps track of all that. Goes on your record, dude."

As he explained these matters, the would-be technician tinkered around behind the television.

"The V-chip does all that? Keeps track? Goes on my record?"

The faux tech gave him a look like Jason was the last human to receive the briefing. "Where have you been, dude? When you apply for a job or a truck loan — whatever — they look that stuff up. They know exactly when you watched the shopping networks and how many times you looked at porno channels."

"What if you just flip through the channels and it lands on porn by accident?"

"Dude, try that story on the creep holding up your truck loan and see if he's convinced."

Jason was so worried he didn't stop to consider that the government agency allegedly monitoring this particular TV's use would be keyed to Amanda's records... not to his. "Uh, how long did you say it'd be out?"

"Nothing but snow for couple of weeks. Maybe longer."

"How about the local channels?" Actually, of three area affiliates, Jason watched only the station with the island survival show. He specialized in the other 95 channels.

"Sure, if you can travel back in time and find some rabbit ears." He thrust forward a clipboard. "Sign here, dude."

It was a brilliant performance.

* * * *

Amanda walked back down the hallway seconds after the phony cable tech left. Already awake from her short nap, she'd been waiting just inside her bedroom door.

Jason stared at the TV snow for a few minutes and tried the full range of channel numbers three or four times. One experiment involved clicking the numbers in reverse order.

Apparently he somehow hoped that could bypass the problem. It didn't. He tried clicking all the channels quickly, and then tried the same thing slowly. Still only snow. Jason gave up and dropped the remote like it was obviously defective.

In the kitchen, Amanda attempted to open the aspirin bottle. She'd selected the cheapest generic brand available, the kind so chalky it melted the instant it touched a human tongue.

Jason trudged over to the kitchen and exhaled through his mouth. His breath smelled like larvae-eating creatures that dwell in muddy water.

Amanda turned away from that noxious odor, finally wrestled open the bottle, removed a half-pound of cotton, and plunked two tablets on the counter. Enough dust shook loose to comprise almost a third aspirin.

He frowned at the bottle's label and poked both pills with his forefinger. "They didn't have the good ones with special coating?"

"All out. Evidently the community is on the verge of an epidemic. Man-colds have every woman in this county flocking to drug stores."

"Dang, I didn't know it spread that fast. The doc yesterday didn't seem all that worried."

"They're trained to control the panic. If word got out, people would be hoarding vitamin C and Kleenex."

"Yeah, I guess."

Amanda was amazed that Jason's critical virus included a deflector shield for sarcasm. Normally he would pick up on such a response and attempt to formulate a tart reply of his own.

When Jason poked the tablets again, more of the contents flaked off. "I'm going to need something better than prune juice to wash this down."

"Tap water is on the Christine-approved list. No calories, no carbs."

"But I can't stand the taste." Whiny.

"There is no taste. It's water."

"My sensors crave flavor, Amanda."

"Sensors? I figured that ghastly halitosis had already neutralized your delicate sensors."

He missed that one also. "Okay. Taste buds, whatever." Jason stuck out his tongue. It was coated with regularly awful evening breath plus bitter and corrosive post-nasal drip.

She handed him a disposable plastic cup.

He filled it to the brim and then placed the cup on the counter. With a paper napkin, he brushed both pills — and as much residue as possible — onto his dry right hand. Then Jason picked up the cup again in his left. He eyed the contents of each hand as though the timing would be infinitely precise.

"You going to juggle those or swallow them?"

Jason grunted. He threw the tablets — not a gentle plop like some people use, but an actual toss — all the way to the far regions of his throat. Then he slapped his right hand on the counter and raised the cup to his mouth. Each time he quickly ingested a large swallow of water, his Adam's apple moved over two inches. Then he made sounds like "*gerrh... kahh*" and slapped his hand on the counter again. Then three more big swallows of water. Finally the aspirin had seemingly reached his gullet. Jason clawed at the outside of his throat for a moment, as though that might help the dissolving descent.

Amanda watched all this with considerable curiosity. She'd never imagined a person could incorporate so much theater into taking two uncoated aspirin.

Jason took a final sip and put down the water. Then he turned, stretched his throat, and extended his streaky tongue. He made the *kahh* noise again. "The coated kind's a lot better."

Later, Amanda served up another lukewarm mug of consommé and three generic rye crisps. She decided to save the new rice cake crackers for the next day.

With television out and no catalogs to leaf through, Jason decided to return to bed. He slowly trudged down the hall... limping.

Amanda was very curious about Christine's blog but hadn't had a chance to check it yet. Her instructions were to keep her laptop hidden while Jason was awake.

It was a little after 9:00 p.m. when the window-rattling snores assured Amanda that Jason was asleep. At that hour, she didn't feel like piddling in the parking lot to retrieve her laptop from the trunk of her car, so Amanda called Christine at home. "I've been thinking. Doing all this stuff sounds awfully complicated and expensive. I don't have any money to speak of."

"Not a problem, really. I've got some mad money. Plus, like I said, I've started a blog and expect lots of donations."

"Donations? To us? Because Jason has a virus?"

"Sure. In return, the donors can access the results of our efforts." Christine acted like everybody knew this. "I think you'll find the sisterhood is very generous."

"You make it sound like a coven."

"Not those kind of sisters. I mean the poor schlubs like you and me who've had to endure a husband or boyfriend with a man-cold. Those sisters."

"Well, you'd mentioned a blog at least twice but still haven't explained." Amanda sat on the couch and put her feet up. She switched the phone to her other ear. "What's on this new blog?"

"I'm posting daily updates, so our grateful readers can see what works best."

"You don't mean with our names and everything. Uh, I don't thi..."

"Relax. I'm just using pseudonyms." Christine began whispering. "You're *Missy* and he's *Marty*." She returned to normal phone volume. "Besides, there's no pix and nobody even knows where we are."

"Slow down. Nobody knows... *Who* nobody?"

"The World Wide Web, doofus. Our blog is going continental. Might even be global, except I'm not doing any translations."

"You mean you're writing stuff about Jason's sickness and what we're doing to blast him out of my apartment... and posting it on the Internet?"

"Amanda, what the heck did you think I meant by *blog*?"

"I wasn't thinking. My brain's fried from grant applications out the wah-zoo and my boss breathing down my neck for assessments, even though he won't leave me alone enough so I can prepare them." Amanda made a noise that was a combination sigh and groan. "I guess I figured you meant *blog* in a figurative sense — e-mailing some buddies or something. Maybe have them forward it, like a chain. I don't know."

"No, girl, this is major. Like I said, we're giving back to the community. In this case, the Internet community. Look, every woman reading our blog can identify with your situation — they've all had to baby a sick man at one time or another. Some are worse than others, of course. Judging from your January experience, it seems Jason has his own category of extreme disability. By sharing his pitiful story, we cover all the bases of everybody else in the country, or world. Whichever."

"You're missing my main concern." Amanda sputtered slightly. "These are our personal lives you're broadcasting. And what we're doing — while totally necessary for my sanity — is borderline persecution. This might even be a hate crime."

"You don't hate Jason. You just hate his man-cold... and everything it puts you through. Besides, no female jury would convict you. We're not actually harming him, anyway. We're just giving him turbo-charged incentives to get on his feet and out of your apartment."

"But some of what you've already told me sounds inhumane, and I don't think you've even explained the worst stuff."

Christine chuckled. Knowing her, it would taste sweeter to keep the worst components as surprises. "Not to worry. If he ever feels endangered, all he's got to do is get up off your couch and walk out that door. He's not a tied-up prisoner, you know."

"I know. But you've got to remember, I do actually love this idiot." She thought for a moment. "At least I love him when he doesn't have a cold. At this specific period of our relationship, I guess I'm just tolerating him. But that's because I love him."

"Well, you keep working on that cover story. I understand, you don't want to harm him. Fine." Christine sounded bored. "Like I said, he's free to man-up and walk out at any point. But in my theory, men will endure a lot of discomfort just to be given a little extra attention. Must be some gender-trauma-recovery syndrome."

"Christine, you just made that up."

"Well, maybe the name. But the syndrome is real enough. Men truly crave the babying they get when they're sick. Reminds them of those good ole times at momma's breast. That's precisely why man-colds are so exhausting for us. When children get sick, they basically *want* to get better as soon as possible so they can go outside and play. But men don't care if they get better or not. They don't want to go back to work. Why would they? Especially if they get paid sick leave. So if they can squeeze two weeks out of a cold, and get pampered in the meantime, they're completely *with* that program." Christine tapped her phone with a long fingernail while she paused. "That's why we're replacing the standard protocol with our

Scare-Cure. When we get through with Jason, he's going to be glad to return to his own residence and go back to work. And you'll finally get back the serenity of your own place."

"That sounds real nice, but I've never had any serenity here. The neighbors in the next duplex have nineteen screaming kids. The lady in my own duplex spends most of her waking hours yodeling. So, what serenity are you talking about?"

"Work with me, Amanda. I'm sugar-coating it just a little bit, for the blog. Our readers don't need to know that you don't have any bliss."

"Let's get away from my bliss — however imaginary — and back to the extreme loss of privacy that we're exposed to by you posting all these details on your blog."

"Our blog. You're the subjects. I'm just the facilitator."

"Well, you're going to facilitate us right onto one of those confrontational reality shows."

"I hadn't thought of television." Christine apparently mulled that possibility. "Nah. Too physical. They all slap and claw each other. Our stuff is more dignified."

"Dignified? Your list indicated you're planning to have his colon cleaned!"

"Jason doesn't know about that yet… it's just in reserve. I don't think we'll even use it. But if we do need to keep him under control, dangling that colon threat could be very useful."

"Well, don't mention that unless you absolutely have to. I think Jason's kind of skittish about his back door." Amanda caught her breath. "Look, I appreciate everything you're doing… trying to help. I really do. But I'm nervous about having all this detail posted on the Internet where our lives are suddenly the sport, or whatever, for hundreds of voyeuristic blog-readers."

"Hundreds? Ha! Girl, this is gonna take off! We'll have thousands of hits by the end of the first day. Stuff like this is viral. We'll be on every significant blog directory within 48 hours. Or 72 hours, tops."

"Precisely. You keep making my point for me but you seem to keep missing it yourself." Amanda was getting too tense, so she tried to calm down. "Security, confidentiality. Safety. Privacy, for cryin' out loud."

"Got all that covered. I've been trying to tell you. No town listed, no state. Not even a region of the country. A studly FBI agent couldn't track you down. This is accessed by subject: *man-cold*. We're going to be listed in bo-coodles of blog indexes. But it's topical. Nobody sees your name, address... nothing. We're not posting any pix. You're just a woman with a sick boyfriend you refuse to dump temporarily because you love him too much... or think you do. And your boyfriend is the biggest wuss in the world when it comes to sickness."

"He's not really that much of a wuss, is he?"

"Your male significant other is off work, in his way-too-saggy PJs, in your guestroom, hasn't shaved — and probably won't — and likely hasn't bathed." Christine sounded like she was telling a slow-witted niece to run tap water while grinding the garbage disposal. "And all this is because he has a sniffle and slightly over 99 degrees of temperature. He probably got his alleged fever that high by holding the thermometer near a light bulb. He's a wuss and a faker. Not even a good faker. I noticed how he slumped over that first evening, right before he saw you. He put on the oh-poor-sick-me thing like it's a worn-out bathrobe. He's a wuss, all right."

"Okay, okay. Enough. Yeah, he's a baby about the sniffles. But I do love him. You know, beyond the mucous and that awful breath from post-nasal drip."

"Beyond the mucous and the drip — now that's a sentimental image." Christine paused "And you'd like to see him get past this. Right?"

"Of course."

"We're going to cure him and the whole world wants to know how. We owe them the explanation, the plan, the details. The results! It's our obligation to the sisterhood of caregivers all over the universe…"

"It grew from globe to universe in the last ten minutes." Amanda felt like she was chasing a runaway train.

"Like I said, it's viral. Our blog is taking off. While I've been yammering with you, we've had 78 more hits. Some of them are even donating."

"You're kidding."

"I'm looking right at it, as we speak. We're hot, girl. This is virgin stuff. Nobody else has attempted to cure the uncommon man-cold and we're already making progress. We're creating history. We might have a grassroots movement here that could eradicate the man-cold as we know it." Christine took a breath. "Could make a little profit, too. Might be a book in this. Movie deal… who knows?"

"Uh, maybe this has already gotten out of hand. We started out trying to get Jason out of my apartment. Can't we keep the focus on him, for now, and skip the rest of the world?"

"Too late. We've had sixteen more hits while you've been trying to talk me out of this."

Amanda sighed heavily. "Oh, heck, Christine. Blog it if you want. But keep our names out. Promise me nobody will ever know the *Missy* and *Marty* in your blog are me and Jason. That includes your sister and her cable-guy-impersonating husband."

"Not to worry. The only blogs my brother-in-law reads are the *Penthouse* online forums. My sister knows about our blog, because she helped me set it up. That's it… nobody else. Trust me. No way anyone else could find out. It's foolproof."

That final word sent chills down Amanda's back. The last time she'd heard *foolproof,* a chicken with a beer can up its butt exploded inside her back porch grill. *Nobody told me to open the can first*. "Remember, this is about getting Jason out of my apartment."

"Right. We're starting with him, but this could change everything." Christine's voice sounded like she was smiling. "I think I know how Madame Curie felt."

"Or at least Kathy Bates in that movie."

"We won't likely resort to maiming, but it's still on the table, as far as I'm concerned."

Amanda peered into the phone as though she could see how much of Christine's reply was in jest. *Can't tell.*

"Oh, two more things." Christine probably held that many fingers near the phone. "Keep his car keys and britches hidden at all times."

"Why hide his pants?"

"When you've got a man's britches, he's basically paralyzed." Christine paused. "It's like rubbing the stomach of an alligator."

"I think you're making this up as you go."

Christine likely shrugged. "We can't have him roaming the neighborhood looking for unsanctioned food." Short pause. "So where do you figure to conceal his things?"

Amanda didn't need to think. "A place he'll never look."

"Now you're catching on."

"Uh, what about his wallet? Should I hide that with his pants and keys?"

Christine thought for a moment. "No. Better not. Most men have ultra high anxiety when they're separated from their wallets. We're just trying to run him off; we don't want him committed to the hospital's fifth floor. Uh, leave his wallet out on one of those boxes near the guestroom door where he can easily find it. He'll think *he* put it there." She snapped her fingers into the phone. "Oh... but you'd also better hide his credit cards and any cash over about ten bucks."

"Okay, I know this one — to keep him from ordering delivery food."

"Correct." No doubt Christine smiled proudly with the realization her protégé was slowly learning.

Amanda was not smiling, however. "Won't Jason notice his wallet is nearly empty?"

"Only if he tries to use it." Christine snapped her fingers. "And if he asks you about it, just tell him he probably left his cards and big bills on the dresser at his own apartment."

A frown clouded Amanda's face. "You sure about all this?"

"Positive." One of Christine's most alarming characteristics: she was always certain.

Later that night, Amanda read the instructions on the Super Glue package and tip-toed into the hall bathroom like a novice jewel thief. She closed the door quietly and went to work.

Chapter 4

August 12 (Wednesday)

Amanda watched as Jason exited the hallway bathroom with a puzzled expression, and scratched his rump inside the sprung-out waistband of his saggy pajama bottoms.

He trudged into the kitchen, wearing the same stained tee-shirt as the day before. Jason looked awful, but it was nothing that a shower, shave, and clean clothes wouldn't fix. He seemed healthy enough, but his clothing and grooming made him appear terribly ill.

Amanda suspected Jason was using this as a costume. *If you want to look sick, just wear sick clothes and eliminate all signs of normal grooming.*

Jason lifted his hand slightly and spoke a single word. "Morning."

He'd also foregone normal dental hygiene. *Yikes.* "You know, I'm willing to wash those rags you're wearing before they get a mind to run away. You said you'd brought one extra set in that little grocery bag. Right?"

"Naw. These feel comfortable. And my skin's real tender. You know, fever and all."

"True." Amanda nodded. "Once you break that barrier of 99 degrees, the flesh can practically fall off your bones."

In his weakened condition, Jason evidently still could not differentiate medical science from sarcasm. No response. But he obviously remembered something unrelated. "Did you know somebody yodels in your neighborhood? Hours at a time."

"Lady next door. Other side of the wall in this duplex. I think she's practicing for some international competition."

"Somebody actually competes in that?"

"People compete in lots of things. I once watched a hog-calling contest at the state fair." She hadn't remained very long, however.

"Yeah, but that usually ends at some point. Presumably, the hog eventually shows up. But whoever this lady's calling... he ain't coming. Not ever."

"You get used to it after a while. I hardly notice any more unless I'm outside, or if my windows are open."

He looked back toward the bathroom door. "Uh, Amanda, I think your hall toilet is busted or something."

"What do you mean, busted?"

"Jammed somehow. Couldn't get the seat up."

"Just sit down to pee."

"Sit? Aw, no. The perspective is all wrong. Besides, I wouldn't have anything to do with my hands." He wiggled his fingers.

"Take up knitting."

"Very funny. It's like shooting a gun. You've got elevation and windage to consider."

Amanda didn't even look up. "Encounter a lot of cross-breeze, do you?"

"Har har. You know what I mean."

"So you're not one of those guys who unzips and stands there with both hands on his hips and just lets it fly?"

"Huh? Oh. I've seen a couple of guys do that. But it's pretty rare. Besides, I think they're just showing off. Most of us need some directional guidance." Jason paused. "So, where did you see a guy whiz like that? You didn't grow up with brothers."

Amanda chuckled. "Can't remember. Maybe it was a joke I heard. Or, no, it might have been a scene in a movie."

"Hmm. It's a little weird for females to be that familiar with a man's whiz positioning."

"I'm a student of human nature. Sue me."

"Well, anyhow, your hall toilet. Seriously. Seat's jammed." He pointed toward the bathroom again.

"Okay, out of service — seat's down in a fixed, locked position." She folded her arms.

"Never seen a toilet seat hinge freeze up like that. You got any WD-40?"

"It's not frozen." Amanda sighed heavily and paused before explaining. "It's glued down."

"How come? The hinge broke off?"

Although tempted to go with that serendipitous explanation, Amanda was supposed to stick with the scripted cover story. "Interestingly, Christine did some research and found that male disorientation increases dramatically — up to 65 per cent higher in your age group — when congestion flirts with the inner ear and the patient has half a degree of fever. If you got zoinked suddenly with vertigo, you'd keel over like a scared possum. Some guys spend several hours curled up on the grungy bathroom floor before anybody even discovers them." She had embellished the script. "Plus, it affects things like balance, focus, and aim."

"Where does Christine get all these studies? I've never heard of this crud."

"You should read more." She waggled her forefinger. "Anyway, I don't want to put down a drop cloth just to protect my floor and walls from all that collateral splatter. Plus, it's a health issue: your urine currently has acidic virus molecules which contaminate the bathroom's oxygen. You breathe in that toxic mixture in such a small space and you'll drop like a fly."

"Hmm." He scratched the back of his head.

Amanda scrutinized his face and could tell some brain event had just occurred. "In case you have the misguided assumption you can completely avoid hitting the seat and you intend to use that toilet while standing, I've got two words for you."

Jason likely imagined two words spoken by some crude team buddies.

"Antibacterial wipes." Amanda reached under the counter for a plastic container. "After every single incident, you'd have to wipe down the seat." She knew no man would actually expend effort on any task related to household cleaning if there was any other option at all. In this case, the option was to urinate from a seated position. "If I find one drop on that seat, I'm getting out a noose."

Jason possibly wondered which part of his body would be noosed.

"Understand?"

He nodded slowly. Jason clearly understood; it was checkmate. She'd placed her queen where his king couldn't urinate properly.

"Uh, I could use the bathroom off your room…"

"Don't you go near my bathroom!"

"Cheese Louise, all right." He looked deeply offended. "I thought I was a pretty good shot. Lots of practice, you know."

"Maybe so, but that was before you got so sick and all."

"Oh, yeah—" *cough, cough* "—good point, I guess."

This meek patient was nothing like the competitive athlete on the court or field. *Very puzzling.* "And don't even think about peeing off my back porch into the yard!"

* * * *

Right before Jason had awakened that morning, his dream featured a sexy nurse who fluffed his pillows and served him a large plate of bacon, eggs, grits, and toast with plenty of jelly. He couldn't get any of those images out of his mind as he shrugged himself onto a chair at the small table.

However, Jason's complete breakfast was leftover consommé and two of the newly-arrived rice cake crackers, courtesy of Christine. "What's this? Flat dog biscuits?"

"They're very healthy. Think of them as cousins to regular crackers." Amanda seemed completely unconcerned for his welfare.

"More like a redheaded step-child." He poked both rice items as if one might try to jump away. The cracker cousin seemed to have been produced by flattening a rice cake in a bench vise and trimming the result with ragged tin snips. The box it came in would have tasted better.

Though Jason was hard pressed to think of these spare offerings as meals, this was his fifth meal observance at Amanda's apartment since he'd gotten sick. The combined total of all five did not likely exceed three hundred calories. Had his mind been a bit sharper, perhaps Jason would have realized he'd acquired a one-way ticket out of the Culinary Zone.

Even as he groused about the stingy fare, Jason wondered which dream image he missed more: the sexy nurse or the plate of food. His stomach grumbled urgently. *Right now, the food.*

* * * *

Amanda got to work early and logged on. She typed in the blog address she'd been provided and read Christine's introduction.

Welcome to the only blog on the newly developed Scare-Cure! Here, you'll learn how to treat (and cure) the dreaded and uncommon man-cold.

You've always thought it was inevitable and hopeless. You figured you'd have to do triple duty for a week or two while your male lounges around, naps and snacks all day, and then watches TV all night long while you're trying to sleep.

Ladies, you've all been through it. Your male — whether husband, boyfriend, or even still-at-home son — has the sniffles. But to him, it's like a crippling disease. He wants to be waited on hand and foot.

What you're reading here is an actual ongoing case, where only the names have been changed. Now, all these activities cost money. So if you'd consider making a donation, send it to the e-mail address below, using PayPal. This is non-profit. After my expenses are reimbursed, I pledge to put the remaining funds into the publication of a print version of this handbook.

Today was Day Two and we've already seen dramatic changes.

<Click here to learn about Day One's strategies.>

Here, you will learn more than you ever imagined about how to cure the illness and get the male back on his feet… like you and I would be.

Check again tomorrow for more updates.

Donations are not required. You may make free use of these nonproprietary strategies. But loosen your purse strings if you can.

Thank you for yesterday's donations.

<Click here for the latest total collected.>

Amanda clicked. *Forty-seven dollars.* "Wow! Christine might be on to something." Then she clicked on the first main narrative — for Day Two. The blog hadn't been up on Day One.

Curing the Uncommon Man-Cold
Day Two

My sister's husband drove up this evening in a borrowed panel truck and pretended to be the cable guy. He wore regular jeans and a shirt he borrowed from a mechanic friend named Ralph. *Marty* didn't seem to notice. He just sat on the couch in his saggy PJs with his mouth open and snot dripping from his nose. His main response was to repeat: *You mean it can't be fixed tonight?*

All this technician actually did was snip off the end of a Q-tip and put it inside the metal housing of the coax cable end. It keeps the pin from making contact, but still allows the fitting to be partly screwed-on. No way *Marty* will figure that out.

No TV means no entertainment. And you know men don't read books.

Missy and I confiscated the racy catalogs, so Victoria still has all her secrets. Also took all ladies' magazines with anything remotely provocative on the cover. No visual print stimuli at all, not even the JCPenney flyer with the huge sale on bras and panties.

All the booze is gone. Not a drop remains.

If the absence of booze, TV, and pretty girls doesn't kill him, this healthy food diet will surely run him out. More food surprises coming up tomorrow!

* * * *

Christine arrived at Amanda's apartment a few minutes after noon. Today was the first scheduled alternative therapy session with Jason. She let herself in with a borrowed key and found Jason on the couch snoring with his mouth open.

This was only the second time she'd actually been alone with Jason. Christine paused to take in this unusual specimen. He was actually good-looking, way underneath that uncombed hair and three-day beard. But he needed less beer and more stomach crunches if he wanted to keep that belly from blooming. Of course, right then he looked positively horrid: unshowered, snoring, and wearing those awful saggy pajama bottoms. Even highchair babies kept cleaner shirts!

Speaking of babies, if Jason didn't have the apparent need to be babied through his minor sickness, he might possibly make a good partner. From what little detail she'd squeezed out of Amanda, Christine concluded that Jason was a pretty good lover. Not toe-curling great, probably, but good enough. Selfish like most men, but occasionally attentive. Clumsy like most men, but he tried. Christine wouldn't necessarily settle for that, but she figured Amanda would.

Christine wore her usual type of blouse, which showed just enough cleavage to keep men interested but not so much that women overtly despised her. Her skirt was the ideal length for very nice legs and the right cut for curvy hips. Christine wished she had legs and hips as perfect as Amanda's. Of course, she would not wish for Amanda's bust… nobody wants to move back down to a B-cup.

She cleared her throat loudly and Jason's head bobbed up, his mouth still open from the current snore.

"What the crud?" His lower face had drool streaks.

"I'm here for your first treatment."

"Treatment?" He was still fuzzy.

"Surely Amanda already briefed you on our schedule of alternative remedies to help get you past these crucial days of the illness. Remember?"

"Uh, maybe. I guess. Well, I heard her talking about something. Not sure what."

"Yes, that was it. Good. I'm glad you remember clearly. During sickness like yours, it's important to keep mental clarity." Christine motioned for him to move his feet.

He did, very slowly, and groaned a bit. It sounded fake.

Christine took a section of newspaper and whapped the couch cushion twice. Then she folded the paper, placed it on the footstool, and sat on the newly-available seat. "Now, you know the natural health food diet I've researched is just part of the equation. The other major portion is therapy, and for that I've had to reach far beyond conventional modern medicine. Some of these treatments go back centuries."

"You're not talking about leeches and stuff." His eyes showed logical alarm.

"Not that far back. Just a couple of generations, actually. Now, a key to your recovery is to flush or draw impurities out of your body."

"Uh, I'm not sure I like the sound of that." Jason leaned away slightly. "I think Amanda can handle my impurities okay."

"Nonsense. Amanda hasn't done the research and she doesn't have the constitution for it. Plus, she's at work." Christine figured that covered the bases. "So it's up to me."

"What are you talking about doing?"

"You'll need to peel off that filthy shirt." Her nose wrinkled as she pointed.

Jason looked around the room like he expected a hidden camera. He slowly pulled the soiled shirt over his head and sniffed it before he tossed it on the footstool.

Christine knew he'd put it back on later. Men liked their clothes to smell broken in. "Now, as everybody already knows, the blood flowing through the heart exits over the arterial system and reenters through the veins. Some of the organs help filter the blood before it returns to the heart. But there are also indicators — mostly in overseas research, so far — that certain glandular actions may have beneficial effects on the body's overall system by trapping particular impurities. Not those directly within the bloodstream, of course."

"Sounds about right." Jason probably wasn't used to being around nicely dressed, attractive women with his own shirt off. He looked like he wanted to cross his arms, but didn't.

Christine noticed Jason's nipples were erect. *Must be nervous.* Most of what she was doing in this entire course of the Scare-Cure was extemporaneous, a bit like improv. But seeing Jason's nipples, and his obvious discomfort at being barechested in front of her, gave Christine an idea. So, like a good scientist, she altered her course. Well, maybe that's a bad scientist. *Whatever.* She continued her build-up. "But this concerns auxiliary impurities within the body, specifically related to airways."

"Don't the lungs handle that?"

"Correct. Good, Jason." She reached over and patted his bare shoulder.

Jason flinched.

"But lungs only do part of the job. There's a growing body of research on the auxiliary part played by the glands." This was where Christine veered from her original plan to put the poultice on his back. "Especially the mammary glands."

When Jason heard the word "mammary" he perked up considerably. Two of those were peeking out over the top of Christine's low-cut blouse as she leaned forward slightly.

She noticed him looking but didn't mind. In fact, Christine more or less invited such scrutiny. But she also liked to ration it, so she put her hand daintily to her bosom and continued, "So the way to bolster this natural auxiliary system is to periodically drain those impurities which have collected in this glandular network, centered over the frontal lung region, specifically the mammary gland. I'm sure you've seen this in the medical news."

"Maybe. Well, yeah, I think the news. Or might've been a TV doctor."

"Whichever. So anyway, I've prepared a poultice which I'll apply over your right chest region. This is purposefully away from your heart, so there's no direct interference with the blood-pumping system."

With the word "mammary" still in his brain and Christine's fulsome cleavage right in front of his face, Jason seemed unable to focus on the rest of her explanation. Most likely, he didn't truly appreciate the particulars of this therapy until Christine gently prodded around his right nipple with two long, manicured fingernails.

"Now the first part of this therapy will be soothing…"

Perhaps Jason wondered vaguely about the second part, but it was difficult for him to focus.

* * * *

After the procedure was complete, Christine left the apartment quickly. She was in a hurry to post a description of Jason's treatment on her blog.

Curing the Uncommon Man-Cold
Day Three

Marty's special therapy for today was what I call "gauze shock".

I told him it was special ointment that would draw out male mammary contaminants as effectively as black salve, but without that awful smell.

So, I poured white Elmer's Glue on a 3x3 gauze pad and applied the compress over his right nipple. I left the pad on for about eight minutes... just long enough to partly dry. Then I told him to brace for the impurities to be drawn out by this special poultice.

This particular virus has definitely slowed down the energy transfer of synapses in the male brain, because he was actually watching to see what color the impurities would be. In his confused state, he forgot all about the coarse hair on that part of his chest. Hmm. Maybe instead of the word "drawn" I should have said "yanked" — because that's what I did. In the resulting shock, moans, and curses, he forgot to check on the color of those nasty mammarial germs.

A large square patch of hair was gone from the vicinity of his right nipple. "Oops," I said.

His reaction: "Yow! You're killing me!" Then he called me a witch... or maybe a different noun. Not certain. He didn't stop to question which impurities had been lurking.

He also forgot to thank me for stopping by to administer this healing remedy. Ha!

Log in again tomorrow evening for the results of Day Four's Scare-Cure.

We're curing the uncommon man-cold, one man at a time.

Chapter 5

Amanda needed to get away from her office. If she kept working while eating at her desk, which was frequent during Hell Weeks, King Louie would probably wander in. He'd plop down on her guest chair to watch her chew and would ask if she was finished yet.

So she worked until 1:00 p.m. and then left the building for the next hour. She decided to grab a quick burger and zip over to her own apartment to check on Jason.

On reaching her residence, Amanda let herself in quietly.

With the volume on, Jason was staring at the TV snow and obviously intent on his inexhaustible experimentation. He seemed to remain convinced there was a way for the remote to bypass whatever problem the receiver had. Judging from the exertion and movement in his shoulder, that day's test dealt with the amount of pressure needed on the up channel or down channel buttons. No doubt a new device would be necessary when Jason finally cleared out.

When Amanda put down her purse and keys, Jason turned around. "Oh, hi. Didn't hear you come in." He pointed toward the screen. "I thought I had something about half an hour ago. Looked like a flicker of a regular TV image. I'm trying to remember how hard I pressed the button that time." He shrugged. "I also forgot which channel it was."

"Maybe you just blinked and were having a flashback to the good ole days when the cable was functioning."

No reply. He was clearly too intent on his riveting investigation.

"Didn't the cable guy say the whole street was down because of some retro-conversion thingy?" Amanda sat in the rocker near the couch. Her shapely legs had a light summer tan and were even lovelier when elevated with her office heels.

"So he said. But the neighbor lady had her TV on earlier. I heard it about 10:30."

"Missus Yodel stopped practicing long enough for you to hear something else from her apartment?"

"Yep. For about fifteen minutes. Must've been on the john or something."

"Any reason to think you couldn't hear yodeling from her bathroom?"

"She stopped is all I know. I don't know where the heck she was. Don't care why, either. My ears were so relieved to have that noise barrage lifted, they practically twitched."

"I don't see any twitching." When Amanda leaned closer, her skirt rode up slightly.

He obviously noticed the enticing view. "Can't do it now. She's still practicing. Listen." Jason turned down the volume of the snow. "Hear it?"

"Uh, yes, I do." She pointed to the television. "So that's why you have the volume so high? To mask her serenade?"

Jason nodded. "White noise. The more, the better. Without this buffer, I'd be stark raving mad after eighteen hours of yodeling each day." He exaggerated; Mrs. Yodel didn't practice more than about seven hours daily.

"I doubt there's any yodeling near your apartment. This might be a good time to make the switch, since you've got your strength back after exercising on those remote buttons for three days."

Jason shook his head. "Nah. I'd be all alone over there."

"You're alone *here*, you know, for most of the day."

"But I'm still—" *cough, cough* "—sick, you know."

"Yes, of course. It's written all over you." Amanda crossed her legs and noticed his fascination. She wondered if his desire could somehow be used to get him to leave. Maybe with implied promise of intimacy at his place... later, when he cleaned up. *No!* Amanda abruptly dropped the desire angle — too risky. It might get her in bed with him here... now. *Horrors!* She shifted. "I don't think you've been getting much rest here. You look kind of haggard."

Jason probably wished he had a mirror so he could see what "haggard" looked like, in case he needed to employ such an expression later.

"We got sidetracked. I doubt Missus Yodel has her cable working. I'll bet that was a radio you heard."

"Radio? Do they have game shows on radio?"

"Sure. Satellite radio. They've got everything. I'll bet they've even got porn on the radio now."

"Porn on radio? How... what... ? Hmm. Wonder what station?"

Amanda shrugged. "Or maybe not. I don't know. Who has time to listen to radio porn?"

Possibly Jason could work it into his schedule.

"So you still believe you can get a TV station, without an antenna, even though the system is down for their analog thingy? How do you figure?"

"Yeah. Those cable guys don't know everything. When I was a kid, I could get the Playboy Channel by pressing two particular buttons halfway down, at exactly the same time." He obviously meant the old remotes with wires and about forty numbered buttons. "Pretty fuzzy, but I got it!"

"I can see why you'd keep trying."

Either he ignored the dig or didn't catch it. "So are you off for today? Come home to make some real lunch? Want to zip down to the rib place and bring home a rack?"

"Slow down, Mister Sicko. You can't eat anything but that healthy stuff on Christine's NASA diet."

"I don't think astronauts eat that junk. They eat tubes of goo. Not undersea lab people, either. In fact, I don't think there are any undersea labs. Christine made up all that stuff just so she could punish me."

"Punish you for what?"

"Not sure she needs a reason... she might just like inflicting misery. Besides, she's a witch."

"She's not a witch. Christine is my best friend and she's helping both of us. Helping you recover from debilitating illness and helping me survive your recovery."

"I told you yesterday I thought she'd put a spell on me." Jason moaned. "Well, witch or not, I think Christine wants to kill me."

Amanda laughed. "Why would she want to?"

"I was hoping you could tell me. But she does. Witches don't need motives to kill anybody. Sometimes it's just for practice."

"Don't be ridiculous."

"No, I mean it." He nodded several times. "Just observe her closely — Christine is a practicing, broom-riding witch. And she enjoys tormenting sick people." He looked at her earnestly. "I've been explaining this since the second day I've been here. Don't you remember?"

"I don't recall hearing any details of your theories. But Christine's not a witch. Your imagination is more vivid because of your illness."

"She was here, you know — today, about noon. I thought she'd brought me something to eat, but she just came to put a hex on me."

"Christine was here? While I was gone?"

"Yeah. She said you knew all about it. She called it poultice therapy." He lifted up the front of his stained tee-shirt.

Amanda peered closely. "Yikes. When I told you to shave, I meant your face! What happened?"

"She maimed me!"

"Christine shaved you?"

"Not a shave. That witch ripped away my chest skin and nearly plucked my nipple clean off!"

"Wonder why she picked that spot?" Amanda touched the area gently. It was still red and inflamed.

"I think she needed some of my chest hair for her witch's brew. Or to cast a spell. Probably trading my soul to the devil right now."

"Oh, I doubt that. Wouldn't get much in trade... you being sick and all."

"True—" *cough, cough* "—the devil mainly wants healthy bodies."

Amanda sniffed several times. "What's that on your breath? Smells much better than your regular halitosis."

"Toothpaste. It's the only thing around here I can stand the taste of."

"You're eating toothpaste?" She shook her head as though it would loosen some logic onto the situation. "That's not food! It's just abrasive cleaner stuff."

"Well, I've been eating an inch every hour, just to keep myself alive."

"You're serious?"

"In survival situations, a man's gotta do…"

"Yeah. Whatever." She stared at him intently. "I just hope you don't get a notion to sample my dad's hemorrhoid cream."

Jason looked toward the bathroom. "Does it come in flavors?"

Amanda rolled her eyes.

"So what's on Christine's diet for my lunch?" Jason looked hopeful. "I was afraid to go read it on the fridge."

Amanda rose from her chair and checked in the kitchen. "Sandwich today. Well, kind of a cousin to the typical sandwich. But healthy."

Jason was thinking. "Something like whole wheat and turkey?"

"Nope." *Not even that good.* "No bread. Can't have gluten, remember?"

"Then I'm afraid to ask."

Amanda pulled out the same rice cake crackers and loudly opened a tin of oily sardines. "The sardines have some omega stuff that Christine says will sharpen your antibodies."

"They're already sharp enough. The problem is, I'm starving!"

She'd once seen crackers and sardines served in a Tom Hanks movie. It sounded edible but looked thoroughly revolting.

It was.

Smelled awful, too.

* * * *

Late in the afternoon back at her office, Amanda phoned Christine. "I read your blog entries today from what you're calling Day Two. Lively stuff. Some embellishment, but definitely entertaining."

Christine nearly squealed. *"Our* blog. I'm glad you like it."

"Also read the first entry for Day Three. Why did you yank out all his chest hair?"

"Your Jason squealed like a little girl." Christine chuckled. "It was just the right nipple area, however. I was originally going to put the poultice on his back."

"You missed."

"Changed my mind when I saw his nipples. They were decidedly erect. My Daniel always had flat nipples... just lay there like flabby quarter dollars. But Jason's nipples looked like they had something interesting to say, and I found myself wanting to listen." Christine sighed into the phone. "Whatever. The funniest part was that he actually thought white glue would suck impurities from his mammary gland."

"Do men even have mammary glands?" Amanda had not paid much attention during high school biology. "I thought their nipples were just stuck on the pectoral wall, a bit like Mister Potato Head."

Christine likely rolled her eyes. "Potato toys don't have nipples. Do they?"

Amanda ignored the question. "Remember, I told you up front I didn't want Jason being harmed. You agreed. But this glue thing is over the line." Long pause to emphasize the seriousness. "No more physical duress. Okay?"

"Got carried away. Sorry." Christine probably shrugged.

"No more mutilations, whatsoever. Promise?"

"Define mutilation." Christine paused. "Just kidding. Okay. Promise. I guess I was caught up in the science. But we are gonna scare him into *thinking* mutilation. Wait'll you see what I found at an obscure market on the east edge of town."

"Don't even tell me. I'll probably have nightmares." Amanda wasn't certain how to say this next part, so she used a serious tone and just blurted it out. "By the way, I don't want you visiting Jason when I'm not there."

Christine paused before responding. "Uh, I'm not sure if I should be offended..."

"Men act funny around you, 'specially when their girlfriends aren't present. I just don't want anything to get complicated. So, no private sessions."

"I figured you'd be thanking me, Amanda."

"Maybe I'd thank you if I had been there. But you're tugging on his nipple when I'm not around... and I worry."

"Okay, no more day visits." Christine sighed. "I wasn't thinking of that other stuff."

Amanda was a bit rattled that Christine would visit Jason, alone, even if her professed purpose was to energize this bizarre cure. But Amanda wanted it clear that Jason was off limits. She'd made her point, and she was glad it had been by phone. In person, Christine intimidated her slightly more.

"And I promise I won't apply any more overt punishment." Christine sighed and then continued her main point. "If we can understand how the male mind suspends rational reasoning during the progression of his debilitating disease, maybe we can replicate it in laboratories. This new program of ours has the potential to eradicate the uncommon man-cold as we know it."

"That's something else I wanted to talk about." Amanda frowned at the phone. "Don't you think this is going overboard a bit? I mean, these bizarre experiments, and posting all that stuff on the Internet?"

"Look, there's about 152 million males in the U.S. Let's say half of them are over twenty-one — approximately 76 million men, give or take. You know some men never get sick... period. Never walk inside a doctor's office. And the last needle they saw was on a sewing machine." Christine must have thought this out in advance. "Let's estimate 10 per cent, but it's hard to pin down that number because no doctor's ever seen those guys."

Amanda was skeptical. "You mean, since their births."

"Most of them were born at home and maybe even out in their backyards." Christine sounded very grave. "No doctor's ever laid eyes on them."

"Completely off the radar."

"You should take this more seriously!"

Amanda looked sheepish, even though her expression didn't transmit through the phone signal.

"That's nearly 8 million disgustingly healthy males." Christine likely calculated with her fingers. "Which leaves 68 million men who *do* get sick some time or other."

"Okay, to make this a good statistical curve, let's say the opposite 10 per cent are constantly sick. Always at the doctor, they know first names of the hospital staff, and they can cite chapter and verse on their operations going back fifty years."

"Chapter and verse. I might use that on the blog." The audible scratching suggested Christine had paused to write a note. "So, that leaves 60 million in that general core. There's another 10 per cent who occasionally get sick — like most people — but they pop a few pills, slurp some chicken soup, and get on with their lives."

"True, but I wish some of those guys would stay home. They bring their nasty germs to work and get everybody else sick. My boss is one of them. Listening to King Louie snort up gallons of snot all day long just drives me bonkers. You know he's got to be swallowing it all. Never gets rid of it... a really vile form of Yankee recycling."

"Vivid image and good point. Maybe we'll strategize on them after we fix Jason's wagon. But stay focused. We just subtracted another 8 million males who occasionally get sick, but just shake it off."

Amanda did the math this time. "That leaves 52 million men over age twenty-one."

"So, in a regular curve, near the bottom — next to the chronic sickies — is another 10 per cent who are sick a lot, but not like the unfortunates who stay sick all the time."

"I'm not sure you've adequately described them, but yeah — more sick than the norm, but not chronically ill like the bottom group. So subtract those and we're left with 44 million men who are neither extreme."

Christine's eyes certainly lit up, even though it was not visible during this phone call. "Exactly. That's the middle of this curve, the normal 60 per cent of adult American males."

"Define *normal*."

"No men are actually normal." Christine sighed heavily. "For the purposes of our study, I mean the normal amount of being sick."

"Had you considered shaving off the men in prison, the ones on heavy drugs, and those not in hetero relationships? I mean, since our new mission is to help the *women* mired in these tragedies."

Evidently Christine considered it briefly. "No, we're going for round numbers here. So stop being snide and work with me. We've got 44 million American males in regular health. How many do you figure catch debilitating colds that put them out of commission while their mommas, wives, or girlfriends wait on them hand and foot?"

"We'll be hard pressed to locate any studies on this. Let's see. In the interest of simplicity, let's just say a third hardly ever get a man-cold, a third are afflicted constantly, and the middle third — roughly 15 million — get sick at least once a year."

"Exactly!" Christine said it like she'd just found the verifying scientific citation. "Those are the 15 million in our target group."

"Nice small test group." Amanda didn't care that her disapproving tone went through the phone. "Okay, let's inject some reality into this grand scheme. When you start talking about millions of man-colds, that's a gigantic leap from getting Jason out of his sagging jammies."

"Our strategies are designed for women with some backbone, females still willing to fight the oppression of this stranglehold."

"Oppression? Stranglehold? Christine, sometimes I think you're leading a proletariat revolution instead of helping me get Jason out of my apartment."

"Think about it. When a man is cowed into pretty complete submissiveness and passivity, we call him *whipped*. Right?" Christine sounded smug through the phone.

"Yeah, some dolts are supposedly *managed* by the woman withholding or rationing sex. But what does that have to do with man-colds?"

"Turn the tables and you have a woman whose entire life is dominated by the excessive demands and exponentially increased workload of her significant male, who schedules a cold for every season. She's man-cold-whipped."

"Uh, I think the analogy falls apart, though I do get your convoluted point." Amanda sighed. "But I'm getting confused. Too many numbers."

Christine summarized like a bored substitute teacher. "We were down to approximately 15 million adult American males who get at least one cold, and occasionally two, each year. Maybe winter and summer. During these debilitating illnesses, they cause total chaos and horrible disruption in the lives of their significant females."

"Sounds like you want to have them rounded up and imprisoned."

"You mean like a quarantine camp. Yeah, good idea! But we'll hold that for the second or third tier."

Amanda could never tell whether her zealous older friend literally meant what her words described. "I'm not sure I agree with your mathematical breakdown, but let's say I agree there are about 15 million of these guys hacking, sneezing, moping around in saggy PJs, and leaving used tissues between the cushions. You can't cure all of them."

"Precisely. *We* can't cure them. But by perfecting the Scare-Cure on Jason and blogging it for the sisterhood, we'll provide a tiny glimmer of hope for those 15 million females who otherwise have to endure the collateral damage of this dreaded illness."

"We all light just one little candle..."

"And the whole country will blaze up!" Christine sounded like she was practicing her acceptance speech for the Nobel Prize. Special new category, *Curing the Uncommon Man-Cold.*

"You seem pretty confident of these numbers. They sound high to me. I'm not even certain 15 million American guys have at least one man-cold each year."

"The medical journals don't get the word." Christine replied with authority. "It's underreported."

"Underreported?"

"Sure. Like crotch rashes, bowed legs, and webbed toes."

"Webbed toes?" Amanda scoffed.

"Of course. That's just a partial list. Infirmities like those are not reported because people would rather hush them up. Besides the social stigma, think of the lost hours at work."

"You're saying this disease goes underground because people are ashamed?"

Christine evidently reconsidered. "Well, that's only part right. Men really aren't ashamed... because they all think they're truly dying when a virus hits. However, the women are ashamed because they let their guys get away with it!" She grumbled briefly. "But that ends now — the beginning of the end of the uncommon man-cold. We're making history."

Amanda wondered how much of this Christine actually believed and how much was generated by her background in college theater. Whichever it was, Christine seemed totally devoted to the interactive strategy she'd deviously concocted.

"Oh, almost forgot to tell you. Somebody's already provided a link to a new blog, based on ours."

"What's on that other blog?" Amanda was not truly interested.

"Its tag is Kick-Marty." Christine clicked. "I stumbled on it earlier today. Somebody's started a serial or something. In among the comments about our blog, on this different blog, somebody started a tally on the slogan *Kick Marty Out*."

"Don't I wish. How many people agree so far?"

"They're numbering as they add their sentiment. Let's see, the most recent one is *Kick Marty Out* — 11. Wow. Eleven people already agree with us!"

"Cool."

Chapter 6

August 13 (Thursday)

As usual, Jason entered the kitchen wearing his stained tee-shirt and droopy pajama bottoms. While yawning, he scratched his front and back at the same time. He smiled as he inhaled the aroma of something brewing. "Oooh. Is that java? I'm dying for a cup of coffee."

"Well, it's a coffee cousin."

"A what?" He moved closer to the brewing appliance. It looked hot and its color was... well, actually, fairly light.

"It's kind of a cousin to coffee." Near the stove, Amanda was stirring something in a bowl. "Some people call it *ersatz*."

"Well, house brands are pretty close to the good stuff. Coffee is coffee."

"I said it's a cousin to coffee. This is made from crushed acorns. Then they're ground, just like coffee beans. Only it's not coffee."

"Acorns? Do I look like a chipmunk?" As he said it, his bearded cheeks puffed out and for that moment, he actually did resemble a larger version of those tree creatures — though not quite as furry.

"Ersatz coffee. They've made it from just about anything you can grind up — bark, leaves, whatever. But acorns give it more of the body you're looking for with coffee." Amanda pulled a frying pan from the cupboard and placed it on the range.

"This was Christine's idea, wasn't it?"

"We've both gone to a lot of trouble to locate this special diet, including ersatz coffee. A lot of expense and time to collect all these healthy food items for you, to help you through this illness. I'd think you could show a little appreciation."

He just shook his head. "Acorns." Jason sniffed the still-brewing concoction and wrinkled his nose. "Look, I'm going along with most of this stuff while I'm sick — you know, putting up with Christine's craziness — but you've got to promise me one thing. It's important."

There was a loud sizzle as Amanda poured the contents of the mixing bowl into the hot frying pan. She stirred briefly and then faced him. "Promise what?"

"Not to tell anyone I know, or anyone who knows me, that I ate and drank any of this junk Christine has been trying to feed me from her cauldron."

"Okay, I promise I won't tell a soul about your healthy diet. My lips are sealed." She returned her attention to the pan.

Jason spent the next five minutes watching her every movement. He was fearful the meal would disappear if he didn't monitor it constantly.

"Okay, hold out your plate."

"At least we've got scrambled eggs." Drool had formed at the corners of his mouth.

She plopped a large spoonful on his plate. "I guess I should explain these aren't actual eggs. Think of them as egg cousins."

"Cousins again! Don't tell me you scrambled some ground acorns."

She chuckled. "Good grief, no. You can't scramble acorns."

"Whew! You had me worried for a minute." It looked okay... kind of. Though slightly pale and thin. *No matter.* His intense hunger outweighed his normal investigatory precautions. "So what kind of egg cousin is this? The kind with no yolk?" He put a large forkful into his mouth.

She paused long enough for his mouth to comprehend that inaugural sample. "Tofu."

The spray from his immediate expulsion occupied a radius of six feet or more. Some of the tofu fragments made it as far as the couch. Jason rushed to the kitchen sink and shoveled water into his mouth. His reaction was much like the aspirin sounds: *gerrh... kahh.* With a paper towel, he rubbed the surface of his tongue for about thirty seconds. Then he rinsed and gargled. He began sputtering before he'd finished spitting out the remaining water. "Scrambled tofu! Are you kidding me? It tastes like fried phlegm. You think some grease that comes from a pig's hoof is a cousin to eggs?"

"Tofu has nothing to do with pig's feet, or any other animal. It's a by-product of soybeans. People use tofu in lots of ways — it's very amenable to whatever it's cooked with. It mimics the flavor of the other stuff in the pan."

Jason tried to extend his tongue far enough to examine it. He couldn't. "Well, I guess soybeans can mimic bird vomit, but that doesn't mean I want to eat any."

Amanda still held the pan and the scooping spoon. "So you're saying you don't want any breakfast?"

He shook his head sadly and rubbed his stomach. "No. I think I'll just go brush my teeth a few times."

"Well, first you've got to clean up all that tofu you spit into my living room." She put down the frying pan and reached under the counter for moist towel wipes and a spray bottle. "I don't want to find a single speck of tofu except on your plate and in this pan."

"Look, I'm too weak to clean up soybean fragments." Jason paused to add his hangdog expression. "Besides—" *cough, cough* "—I'm sick."

She shook the large plastic spoon as she moved toward him. "You may think you're sick now, but if you don't clean up that mess you just made, you're going to wish you were in the hospital." Sometimes Amanda sounded like somebody's stern mother.

Even as he cowered, he wondered why. Because he was so weak from hunger? It was partly because he'd never seen Amanda that severe before. Jason took the cleaning items and spent fifteen minutes collecting every shred of tofu he could find. He began to imagine he could smell it, even though the wily tofu was obviously mimicking the odor of couch cushions and draperies.

— — —

Amanda monitored Jason's cleanup carefully. While Jason was occupied with that endeavor, she got a clean fork and sampled the scrambled tofu. She rolled it in her mouth a bit, chewed slightly, and then decided it needed more of a sluice action than a chew. So she sluiced down a little. "Ack!" She turned quickly and spit the remainder into her hand.

"What'd you say?"

"Back. I said *back*. Back behind you is some more tofu to clean up."

"Oh." Jason returned to his duties like a prisoner forced to mop his cell before his own execution.

Amanda discreetly dumped the remaining contents of the pan into the trash and covered it with two paper towels. She found herself making the *kahh* sound, though much quieter than Jason's rendition.

She grabbed her purse. An egg sandwich would be nice this morning on the way to work. Maybe with a fried potato patty. And freshly brewed coffee. *Ha.*

* * * *

When Amanda got to work, she phoned Christine and reported on her enterprising breakfast.

"Where'd you find acorns? And how on earth did you grind them?"

"I took a page from your plan — I made it up. It was just weak tea with a little salt added."

"Well, necessity caused mothers to invent things. I'm in traffic. Gotta go. Bye."

The call ended before Amanda could correct her friend's mangled quote. All of a sudden, she didn't remember how it really went. *Sheesh.* Not enough sleep.

In the middle of Amanda's lioness yawn, Louis walked in, plopped down, and started talking about how far behind he was because he didn't have her evaluations.

The pressure at her office was intense. The other workers — all female except the boss — were civil, but not really friendly. No one was assigned to assist her and nobody voluntarily helped. Some, including her Yankee supervisor, actually hampered Amanda's productivity. His frequent drop-ins were very distracting and nearly 90 per cent were pointless. During most of the usual year she could cope with these typical circumstances, but during Hell Weeks everything bothered her. Especially King Louie.

"Well, Louis, I'd be farther along if you could carve out a couple hours of clerical help for me during these grant reviews. Gayle or Joan probably wouldn't mind helping if you'd let them. Or one of the other ladies."

He was already shaking his head. Sometimes when he shook his head with particular vigor, Amanda thought she could see his toupee shift slightly.

"And I could get more done without all the interruptions."

"You mean like phone calls to and from your darkly tanned friend?"

Amanda yawned again. It was either that or scream at King Louie.

Later, during an afternoon break, Amanda quickly checked the blog and scanned Christine's update — very little posted. There were more comments, however, from blog readers. Most were excited and optimistic that someone was finally undertaking a cure for the uncommon man-cold. A few predicted the project's total failure. As one blogger — presumably female — wrote, rather pithily: *'A man's a man. You can thump 'em, but you never really know what you're getting. When a melon goes sour on you, only thing to do is toss it out.'*

One comment, presumably from a male, in a different vein: *'What you two are doing to that guy is hateful. Somebody ought to slap you silly!'*

She clicked on the link to Kick-Marty, the adjunct blog discovered yesterday. The new tally was *Kick Marty Out — 15…* an overnight increase of only four.

Back to work.

* * * *

Possibly worse than her office stress was that which waited in Amanda's apartment. Since Jason's invasion, she'd lost all her solitude and was getting hardly any rest during the night. Until Monday evening, he had been her sweet and comfortable — but not always remarkable — lover. Now he was her noisy, uninvited leech. That image bothered her, but it was accurate: Jason stuck to her, sucked out her resources, and wouldn't let go.

Amanda was near complete exhaustion as she dragged herself into the apartment. She stood in front of her couch and dropped like a rag doll. Her purse remained in her hand and she stared straight ahead without speaking.

Jason wandered in from the bathroom with a tube of toothpaste in his hand. It was 5:30... he was cheating. He waved lamely and coughed just to remind her how sick he was.

Amanda studied him as though he were a pesky ghost after an unsuccessful exorcism attempt by a seminary student intern. "So how was the patient's day?"

"Some kid tried to sell me a magazine subscription so he can go to Paris or something."

"You buy any?"

"Thought about subscribing to *Maxim*, but he said it'd be at least ten weeks before the first issue arrives. I figure I'll be gone from here by then."

Amanda figured ten *days* of live-in Jason would kill her.

He changed the subject. "You think I could have a normal breakfast tomorrow?" Jason briefly scraped his tongue with two fingernails. "I can't handle scrambled tofu again."

Amanda sighed very heavily and put down her purse finally. "Well, it depends. What would the patient like?"

"The Shuney's mega-breakfast buffet." Shuney's was locally owned by an investor who'd bought the facility and property from a former holder of a well-known national franchise. To keep existing customers and save money on remodeling and decor, the new owner simply altered one letter in the name. "But, if that's out, I'd settle for some ordinary, normal cereal. Lucky Charms, Froot Loops... any of the standards."

"Cereal might be possible. I'll call Christine and have her bring some when she comes over."

"No!" His voice was shrill. "I mean, not Christine. She'll just find some rat poison in a box. Can't you call somebody else?" He paused. "Wait, who's coming over?"

"Some girlfriends." Amanda wasn't really up for any kind of event that night, but this was all part of Christine's elaborate plan to render the apartment inhospitable for a man. "We're having a crop."

"A what?"

"Crop." Amanda rolled her eyes. *Where has he been?*

"Crop what?" Still standing, he trembled slightly. "Not... me?"

Amanda touched his arm reassuringly. "Crop *you*? Of course not. Why would you think that?"

"Well, after that witch yanked out half my chest hair, I thought maybe she was going to practice some more black arts or something, with some of my body parts."

"Which body parts were you thinking about?"

"Uh, never mind." Apparently without realizing it, he pressed his legs together tightly. "So what are you going to crop, and when?"

"It's for scrapbooking. We crop pictures, photos, artwork, headlines... stuff like that. I guarantee there's no bodily harm for you."

"When?"

Amanda looked at her watch. "About half an hour. I'd better call somebody about that cereal. Sunny lives near the Verde Grocery. She probably won't mind."

— — —

Jason's brain had already shifted to the crop party. He knew whenever women gathered to talk and conduct some kind of activity, there was always food. Usually, good food. Of course, in this case — as desperate as his stomach was — even bad *real* food would be better than the health diet items he'd been nibbling on. He thought of something else. "Uh, can you ask Sunny to bring me another tube of toothpaste? Maybe something with spearmint flavor."

Slightly less than ten minutes later, Christine arrived at the apartment with a flourish and a large canvas tote bag. She motioned for Amanda to remove the slightly gaudy floral tablecloth and then plunked her bag on the table. Amanda folded the material and draped it over the back of a dining chair.

"Amanda says you're starving." Christine looked at Jason. "You're in luck. I downloaded this diet from a website I got from my nephew who's on staff at Johns Hopkins Medical School. He's a nutritionologist…"

Amanda interrupted. "Uh, I believe that's nutritionist."

Christine waved her hand. Small details didn't typically concern her. "Anyway, he highly recommends this. Perfect balance, all natural. Zero carbs. Astronauts use this during their training phase. It's truly the right stuff."

Jason was already drooling. He'd been without real food for parts of four days. After the doctor visit on Monday, he'd grabbed a burger, fries, and shake. For the time, so far, at Amanda's apartment, the staple had been dry, unsalted crackers. *What's in those crackers?* They tasted like dog biscuits going down but had the aftertaste of the earliest supplemental fiber liquids. Added to the crackers had been small mugs of bland, thin consommé, tiny glasses of unsweetened prune juice, a soy hotdog with no bun, and some of the nastiest sardines ever caught in a mildewed net. He was not counting the tofu since he'd so thoroughly excoriated the inside of his mouth afterwards. He'd barely tasted the acorn coffee brew. Had it not been for his hourly — and sometimes half-hourly — inch of toothpaste, he was certain he would have expired at least 24 hours ago. He was starving… and had to restrain himself from diving into the canvas bag.

Though he did not like her or trust her, right now Jason viewed Christine as a buxom Red Cross worker visiting his refugee camp. "You know, this *starve a cold* thing is pretty austere. I'm so weak from hunger I can't even take a dump."

"Too much information, Jason." Christine held out her vertical palm. "Anyway, I'm on duty... to the rescue. This stash here will keep you going for at least four more days... unless you decide to go home, of course. By then I'll have located the second stage of this special NASA diet. That's important, because it prepares your intestines for the colonic bath next week."

"The what!" Jason's voice cracked like a fourteen-year-old boy's.

"The solution bathes the insides of your colon for forty-five soothing minutes of purification. The pure natural extracting herbs literally suck all the impurities from your colon." Christine acted like she sold the procedure door to door.

"I don't want my colon sucked! And I'm not getting an enema from some fat-fingered lab technician." Jason looked at both women. "You're nuts!"

— — —

Amanda had predicted a reaction like that. "Now, that's no way to speak to the lady who just brought your meals for the next four days." Amanda nodded deferentially toward her older friend.

Jason's drool seemingly overtook his sensibilities about the threatened colonic procedure. "Okay, sorry, I guess. I'm light-headed from no food. Anyway, you can cancel that enema thing. I'm positive I'll be up and around by... uh, when did you say it was?"

Christine waved her hand. "Apology accepted. I understand how a sliver of fever can affect your brain. They say half a degree is the worst kind. Most doctors miss it and it can go untreated for who knows how long."

"Right. So, let's see what's in the bag." Jason actually rubbed his hands together.

Amanda had to step back slightly because she already knew some of the contents and didn't want Jason to see the grin she was trying to control.

Christine continued her introduction. "Now, there can be some variation on the order of these meals… you know, in case you want to swap tonight's supper for tomorrow's lunch. And so on."

Jason rolled his hand sideways. *Hurry up.*

Christine reached in and pulled out some celery stalks. "These are wonderful dipped in hummus." With a minor flourish, she produced a small plastic tub.

"Hummus!" Jason looked like he'd been poleaxed. "That's, uh, that's…"

"Correct." Christine could have been a game show hostess. "It's ground-up chickpeas, made into a paste. But this is a special brand that takes out some of the gritty texture. Some people think it feels a little slimy, but they say you don't notice the consistency as much if you spread it on a rice cake."

"Hummus? Chickpea paste? Gritty? Slimy?" Jason sputtered for a moment. More syllables slipped out occasionally but no recognizable words. "Why, that's practically poison! I can't eat crud like that."

Christine put the celery and hummus back in her bag. "Very well, you may be right. Sometimes an out-and-out fast might be better for you anyway. As sick as you are." She turned like she was about to leave.

"Wait. Uh, hold on." Jason sounded pitiful. "Let's see what else is in there. Maybe I can eat that celery if I douse it with sugar and microwave it for a minute."

Christine looked toward Amanda. "Absolutely no sugar for this patient. Nothing that's been processed. I thought you knew that."

Amanda pretended to be chastened. "Sorry, I thought I removed all the sweeteners."

"Not all of them." Jason spilled his sweet secret before he could stop himself. "This afternoon, I found several little packets — pink, blue, and yellow... I think. Had 'em for a snack."

"You did what?" It was not easy to shock Christine.

Jason looked a little sheepish. "Little packets of pretend sugar. I found them in the back of a drawer. My head was pounding from sugar withdrawal. I figured, what the heck."

Amanda was equally startled. "You swallowed a packet of sweetener? Dry?"

"Well, that's the thing. I took one and just poured it into my mouth at first. Some melted, but a bit of it clotted and formed a lump. So I took a sip of water and swished it around. That pretty much chased it down."

"I don't have words." That was rare for Christine. "I think half a packet of that stuff will sweeten a full quart of tea. What on earth did it taste like?"

Jason closed his eyes and licked his lips trying to remember. "It's a rush. You can't see anything for a few seconds and your mouth puckers up."

"This is interesting." Christine looked around like she wanted something to write on. "How many packets of sweetener did you eat? Science may need to know."

Jason thought for a second. "Oh, not more than half a dozen, I guess. One pink, two yellow, and three blue. Awful rich. Plus they've made my pee turn a funny color."

"What color?" Amanda didn't want to be surprised when she ran a brush inside the toilet rim.

"Well, it's nothing like you'd expect from the color of the packets. You know, I figured blue and yellow would make green." He shook his head. "Nope."

Again Christine held up her vertical palm. "Too much information again. Ab-so-lute-ly too much. You can discuss his urine after I'm gone." She pulled the remaining items from her canvas bag and arrayed them neatly on the small dining table.

Jason surveyed his unorthodox diet: Dairy-free cheese, made from soy. Flourless and sugar-free brownie mix made with black beans. A jar of sprouts, a block of tofu, and a container of bean curds. He probably figured the hummus was looking better and better. "Hold on! Where'd you get all this junk? Didn't they have any *real* groceries in that store?"

"These groceries *are* real." Christine seemed offended. "Everything's natural, organic, and without carbs, fats, sugars, et cetera."

"Without any taste, either! This is the stuff those militant vegan freaks eat!"

Christine nodded. "Correct, Jason. I can see you're already on board with this diet. The vegans are among the healthiest humans on our planet."

"They only weigh 86 pounds a piece. And that's their largest men! A stiff wind will blow them away. Their skin's made of tissue paper and their blood's green from malnutrition. I can't eat this vegan junk for four days! It'll kill me!" Jason slumped down in the dining chair nearest him. He was clearly exhausted from the effort of his impassioned speech.

Christine spoke earnestly, in the stiffest face she could apparently muster. "This early stage of your illness is the most crucial for your nutrition baseline to be established. If you were eating all that junk food you ordinarily consume, your system would have to work three or four times as hard to beat this disease. But with the purity of this diet, your body can focus all its energy on defeating those defiant cold germs." She covered her smile, but Jason wasn't looking at her anyway.

He stared at the alternative grocery items on the table. "If this is health food, I'd be better off dead." He grabbed a celery stalk, turned, and trudged toward the cluttered guest bedroom. On the way down the hall, he paused at the bathroom and probably wondered if a dab of toothpaste would give celery any discernable flavor.

Both watched closely as Jason retreated down the hall. His pajama bottoms slid the final stretch just as he reached the guestroom door. Jason was able to catch the waistband right before it reached the bottom curve of his buttocks.

"Pretty good reflexes, for such a sick puppy." Christine likely wondered if she should research the issue of bodily reflexes in the scientific part of her illness therapy protocol.

After the guestroom door closed with a soft click, Amanda turned. "Wow! I've never before seen a grown man so close to tears… over food."

"You know, I never noticed before." Christine sighed. "He's got pretty nice buns for a man his age."

Amanda nodded her head slowly. "But what is it with men and PJ waistbands? Does elastic automatically disintegrate when it's worn near a testosterone factory?"

"Not sure about that. But you're lucky Jason even wears PJs at all. My Daniel," she turned her head and spit, "just schlepped around the house in his boxers. No button on the fly, either."

Amanda made an exaggerated grimace. "Tell me about the elastic on his boxers. Did all his waistbands look like they'd been used to tie down a load in his pickup truck?"

Christine mulled that image. "Well, men's underwear is probably the longest-used, rattiest article of clothing in the wide array of humankind's effort to conceal nakedness. Consider this example: on the very same day, a man buys a pair of briefs and a woman buys a pair of panties. The woman tosses the panties in about one year, if not sooner, because the elastic is shot and they've probably gotten stained or lost their color. Seven years later the man still wears his briefs, even though they've given their all — way above and beyond the call of duty. But if his wife, sometime in the ninth or tenth year, happens to discard those same briefs — with busted seams, sprung elastic, and multiple holes in the fabric — the man will scream like his best friend was murdered. It's insane. For Christmas, you give him a brand new three-pack of briefs — about five bucks at Discount World — and a man just puts the new package in his dresser drawer. Won't even open them. You ask him why and he says, 'I already got some skivvies.' Insane." The length and intensity of Christine's monologue was surprising. "Uh, why do you ask?"

"Oh, I don't know. Guess I'm just thinking ahead to when — well, if — Jason and I ever get married. I wonder if I'm always going to see his crack when he walks the other direction."

"Good point. I think every man ought to be given two mirrors that line up exactly so he can see how truly awful that view is. They probably think it's sexy." Christine rolled her eyes.

"I don't have the words. But definitely not sexy."

"Just buy a safety pin and take up a couple of inches in the waistband. Think low-tech occasionally. That's how we used to handle elastic emergencies in the olden days."

"Don't give me that olden days B.S. You grew up on *Sesame Street*, not listening to Edward R. Murrow. Olden days... ha!" Amanda eyed her friend narrowly. "Do you really have a nephew at Johns Hopkins?"

Christine nodded. "Sure. He works in the maintenance department."

That's about what Amanda had figured. "Does he actually eat any of this stuff?"

Christine laughed. "Are you kidding? He eats cheeseburgers and pizza, like every other guy... you know, ice cream and beer."

"So you made all this up?"

"No, people really do eat this."

Amanda shook her head. "You don't actually know any people who eat like this, do you?"

"I'm not personally acquainted with any Eskimos, either." Christine seemed indignant. "But I know they exist... somewhere."

There was movement behind her.

"What the heck is *that*?" Christine pointed as she jumped partway behind her friend.

Amanda turned as the creature entered from the utility room. "I think they're called housecats." Blasé.

"You don't have an enormous black cat!"

"True. But the neighbors down the street do." Amanda rolled her eyes.

"What's it doing in here?"

"I thought I told you about the big cat that can't get over its relocation."

"Huh?"

"The couple who used to live in this apartment own a cat. That cat. They relocated to a house two or three streets over, right before I moved in here."

"I understand real estate. Explain the cat."

"I've been here about three years and I'd never even seen her. But about two months ago, out of the blue, this cat started popping up. In my garage at first, but later she'd show up inside the apartment."

"How does it get inside?"

"Beats me." Amanda shook her head. "I've never let her in. Every time I see that cat inside, I shoo her back out. But she keeps returning. I think she's even stayed here overnight a few times. Seems to like the guest bedroom best."

"Oh, my." Christine's brain wheels were clacking almost audibly. "This could be useful. You say this cat likes your guestroom?"

Amanda nodded. "Must've been where she slept when this was her actual residence."

"What's its gender again?"

"Female. Neutered, I believe."

"Perfect! I've just had another brainstorm." Christine smiled. "What's this giant pussy's name?"

"You'll think I'm making this up."

"Try me."

"Diabla."

Christine squealed with delight. "Ohh. That's lovely! Now we have a large neutered puss named Diabla on our team."

Amanda was worried. "Now, you cannot skin this cat or boil it... nothing like that."

"Oh, no. No harm for the cat." Christine waved her hand. "But Jason might have second thoughts about staying here." She went to her purse for a small notepad. "Tell me what else you know about this giant puss."

As Amanda recalled everything the former occupants had told her about Diabla, Christine scribbled and cackled. Amanda had never heard her friend cackle like that before.

Then Christine explained her half-baked plan for enlisting the cat.

* * * *

Jason's supper that evening was celery smeared with toothpaste. No time for anything more elaborate, had he been willing to consume it. There were barely five minutes between Christine's departure and the crop party's beginning.

Scrupulously holding up his pajama bottoms, Jason ventured into the hallway. He knew Maria Perry from a few double dates with her and Roger the fireman. Maria was pushing thirty. Shorter than Amanda and not quite as curvy. She had a gorgeous face with a dusky tone — as lovely as her mother, who'd been a movie star in Mexico City. Beautiful, lush black hair.

Jason also recognized Sunny Cannon, who'd been tasked to bring different cereal and more toothpaste. The nickname "Sunny" was short for "Sunshine" — her parents had been devout hippies, more than a decade after it had already become mostly passé. Sunny was about twenty-six, hardly over five feet tall, and wore long blonde hair, very straight, with no facial makeup. She typically wore long peasant skirts, didn't shave her legs, and never had been seen in heels.

There was also another woman he'd never seen before.

Jason stayed as near the small gathering as he could without being seen. There was a lot of chatter, noise, and movement. All four women seemed completely oblivious that he was even in the apartment. He could smell several snacks and could hear them being eaten.

His mind raced with visions of the leftovers they might leave behind. Even if some had a bite out of them, he could live with that flaw. He drooled for nearly two hours while they cropped and laughed and snacked.

Maria, Sunny, and the other woman finally left about 9:30 p.m. Jason heard Amanda go to the bathroom inside her bedroom suite. He hustled to the kitchen to survey the prizes he was sure they'd left behind.

Nothing on the plates. In fact, no plates. He knew they'd used dishes — he'd heard the forks clinking. But those three devious women had rinsed every dish, swept up every crumb, and even taken the trash bag outside to the curb before they departed.

Witches!

The single consolation on the counter: Sunny had left a new tube of toothpaste, the brand with three stripes.

He opened it immediately and sucked down about two inches.

Chapter 7

August 14 (Friday)

Amanda was up slightly earlier than normal and already busy in the kitchen.

As was his new habit, Jason trudged in, yawning and scratching. Those two activities consumed nearly fifteen minutes each morning. "Might as well skip the acorn allshitz brew. Don't want any."

"Ersatz."

"Whatever. I spent yesterday belching like a squirrel."

"I didn't know squirrels belched." Amanda suppressed a smile. "And I didn't realize you'd even tasted yesterday's coffee cousin."

"I tasted it, all right. A complete teaspoonful. It was a bit like dishwater, but not nearly as agreeable. Plus, those acorns are way too salty."

"Okay, I'll skip the coffee and put on some herbal tea instead."

"Don't bother. Herbs make my windpipe quake."

That image puzzled Amanda, but she didn't inquire. "New breakfast offering. Last evening, Sunny brought some generic shredded wheat for you. Along with that toothpaste which I notice is already nearly a quarter gone."

"Yeah, tell her thanks for the toothpaste. Those stripes really help with the cavities and stuff."

Amanda busied herself with minor meal preparation.

"Haven't had shredded wheat in a good while. Is this the frosted kind with loads of sugar? I like those little mini-squares."

"No, these are the large pieces." They were actually huge, with nearly the weight and dimensions of small rectangular paving stones. The texture was a bit like highly compressed straw. "And no sugar — Christine's orders."

"Aw, man!" Jason slumped almost completely over while standing. Tricky maneuver.

"You might want to let them soak a while, to loosen up those fibers some."

He peered closely. "You got a chisel around here?"

"I believe most people use a sturdy spoon."

"What about milk? You can't expect me to eat that gigantic Brillo Pad without milk."

"Sorry, no milk. No dairy of any kind. Congestion, remember?"

"I can't handle any more unsweetened prune juice. I've been spending too much time on the john as it is, just for Number One. With all this prune toxin, my intestines keep telling me it's time for Number Two. But since I haven't eaten anything but toothpaste, there's nothing to empty out. I'm dying here!"

"Well, you could try water, I suppose. But it's bound to taste a little thin." Then she looked at him pointedly. "And, of course, you could find other lodgings where they serve less healthy food." She made ready to leave.

— — —

Jason ignored both comments and waved silently as Amanda left for work.

He carried his new tube of toothpaste almost all day long. An inch every hour. The stripes were delicious. Every half hour, he cheated.

By late morning Jason had noticed the warming inside air and called Amanda at work. "I think your thermostat's busted. It's really hot in here. Apparently set for 72. But it's about 80 degrees inside and not even noon yet."

"Well, I meant to tell you a repairman was coming out today."

"When's he coming?"

"He's already left." Amanda probably checked her office clock. "He called me half an hour ago."

"I didn't see anybody." Jason looked around the room. "Are you sure?"

"He said he ran the diagnostic outside at the compressor. Didn't need to come inside."

"Never heard of that. I thought they always came inside."

"These are the new systems with that advanced refrigerant, R-700. You just plug in a gizmo like they do for vehicles."

He'd heard of R-Something. "So what did he say the problem was?"

"A broken controller thingy."

That diagnosis seemed pretty general but he knew Amanda was no HVAC specialist. Neither was Jason. "When did that break? It was running okay this morning."

Amanda paused. "It broke while you were griping about breakfast. I'd noticed before I left the apartment, but didn't have time to call right then. So I called when I got to work. The tech happened to be three duplexes over. So he was able to get there quick."

"Uh, I think it's still broken, Amanda. Don't believe he fixed it." Jason fanned his face.

"Couldn't. The part he needed is on back order." Her voice sounded funny.

"You're kidding! This is the middle of August! I can't survive oppressive summer heat with no air conditioning."

"You should check the unit at your own apartment. Maybe the controller thingy works just fine on yours."

If that was a hint, it went over Jason's head. He just groused a bit more.

"When it gets really hot, just open a few windows."

"It's real hot already." Jason switched back to whining. "And if I open the windows, that lets even hotter air come inside. Plus, I have to listen to constant yodeling from next door. Creepin' crud!"

"Look, Jason, I've got to get back to work."

"Wait. One more thing. Do you have a cat?"

"You know I don't own a cat."

"I've been hearing something meowing off and on today." He paused to check again. Nothing at the moment. "Earlier, it sounded like a giant cat."

"It's probably your imagination. Or maybe Missus Yodel is practicing some different nuance in her competition routine."

"Never heard anybody meow while yodeling. Not sure it's even possible, Amanda. Different throat muscles, I think."

"Well, I'm glad you're becoming such an expert. It'll broaden your horizons. Now I'm resuming my work. Bye."

* * * *

Amanda ate lunch with Christine near Amanda's office downtown.

"You should have told me the A/C guy was coming today. Jason called and squalled and I had to make up some convincing lies out of thin air."

Christine did not look the least bit apologetic. "Did he accept your explanation?"

"Surprisingly, yes. He bought it completely."

"Good lying just takes a lot of practice." Christine nodded. "Before you know it, you'll be running for political office."

"So who deactivated my air conditioner this morning?"

"I did." Christine looked distinctly proud. "Drove over about 10:00."

"What did you do to it?"

Christine tore a page from her small notepad. "Here's a diagram. It shows what to do and where it is on the unit. Oh, when you get home tonight, be sure to close the A/C vent in the guestroom."

Amanda turned the crude drawing upside down. Then back again. "Blistered butt-rash! You know, this project could get out of hand."

Christine's hand waved slowly and apparently erased all of her own concern, though it didn't delete much of Amanda's worry.

"Jason also said he heard a big cat meowing."

"Excellent!" Christine clapped briefly. "So the cat food I put out is keeping Diabla nearby?"

"Apparently. But I still don't understand the next step."

"We've got to get that cat into his room. I'll explain on the way out. Don't want to tip off anyone here who might be listening." Christine looked around suspiciously.

There were only three other diners in the sandwich shop and none within hearing distance.

As they continued eating, Amanda whined a bit about her job — a daily ritual. Then she shifted slightly. "I'm completely flagged out by the time I get off work, and I don't even have a weekend to look forward to. During my Hell Weeks, which is looking like nearly three this year, I'll be working all the Saturdays and Sundays on grant reviews." She sighed heavily. "Why all these evening activities scheduled for my apartment?"

"I already covered this. Two very distinct reasons to have evening *girl* events at your place while Jason's camping in. One." Christine held up a finger. "Men hate having their turf invaded by a hen party."

"It's not even his turf, it's mine!"

"Exactly. And this is another way to subliminally convey our core message to him: *go home.*"

"What's the other reason?"

"To keep him from seducing you."

"Ha! Like I'd jump in the sack with a guy in his getup! No appreciable grooming or hygiene, and all that additional mucous. No way!"

"But you already admitted you've fallen for it before. And you know most men have some little trick to melt a woman." Christine looked around the restaurant and lowered her voice. "There's a special school where men go to learn how to counter any objections about sex. They learn how to keep at it until the woman just says, *Whatever…* figuring ten minutes of sex will be less exhausting than thirty minutes of argument."

Amanda rolled her eyes and then looked at the time on her cell phone. "Time flies when you're talking about sex."

"Sex flies when you're talking about time."

"What does that mean?"

Christine shrugged. "Saw it on a billboard or somewhere." She paused to let that sink in. "This sure beats whatever Jason is having for lunch." Christine smiled as she chewed. "Speaking of… what is he having?"

"Not certain. He threatened to steal some dog food from the back porch of the duplex next door, but I think that was for exaggeration." Amanda adjusted the grip on her BLT. "He's still limping along with consommé and those horrid rice-based wafer thingies. Have you actually tried those?"

"Indigestible. He'd be better off with the dog food." Christine poked at her chicken salad. "I'll have to tell you, I'm a bit surprised your Jason has stuck it out this far. In my original premise, the shock of not getting his munchies, booze, porn — and none of the TLC from you, of course — would get him out the door pretty durn quick. This is Day Five and he shows no signs of giving up."

"Yeah, kind of surprises me, too. Of course, I didn't truly comprehend all the horrors you'd planned for him. But he's pretty much just rolled with the punches. I'd halfway expected him to show a little initiative — like stealing a box of cookies from a passing student salesman or something. But he just mopes around my apartment, sucking on a toothpaste tube." Amanda took another small bite of her sandwich and chewed thoughtfully. "Once we took away all Jason's creature comforts, it's been a bit like *Gulliver's Travels*: he's out of the male-centered universe as he knows it. He's not able to grapple with the enormity of this upheaval, so the smaller manifestations simply waft by him and he just watches like a stoned hippie."

"Can you write that last part down? I'd like to put that on the blog." Christine handed her the notepad. "I think you've hit on the key to this case. Normally a man would bristle at any *one* of the setbacks Jason has experienced. But facing all of them at one time, with our unified front, he's just as disoriented as a dazed bird, trapped inside a greenhouse, that keeps bumping into windows."

"Put that on your blog also." Amanda slid the pad back over.

Christine made a note. "Oh, does Jason speak any Spanish?"

"You must be kidding. He can barely order his own meal at the Mexican restaurant."

"Good. I've got a surprise for him tomorrow. Want to hear about it?"

"Probably better if I don't know." Amanda sighed. "I'll just read about it on the blog like everybody else."

"Suit yourself."

"Remember, no physical harm."

"Not a hair on his body." Christine smiled.

Amanda checked the time again. "Only have a few more minutes. I wanted to ask you more about that handbook, or whatever you talked about publishing. Were you serious about that?"

"Sure. Think about it. Our core group is 15 million American males who have about one man-cold a year. Right?"

"Yeah, but that just came out of your own head, Christine... it's not a real number."

"No matter. My brain is plugged into this."

"Your brain's plugged with something."

Christine seemed to dismiss the comment. "So we figure these sickies have 15 million females tending to them, and they're all desperate, frazzled, overwrought. Like you were."

Amanda nodded. "Still am."

"Well, cut off a third who probably can't read. That leaves 10 million. Then knock off another third who never buy a book — they just borrow somebody else's copy and never bother to return it."

"That leaves the final five million desperate women who can read and are willing to buy a book." Amanda helped move the arithmetic forward.

"Exactly. We've practically already sold five million copies. Bestseller — top of the Amazon rankings. There'll be interviews, maybe a makeover… for at least one of us. They'll probably fly us to New York for a nighttime talk show."

Amanda shook her head. "Don't buy your interview dress just yet. You haven't even written the dang book."

"It's writing itself on our blog. We're getting feedback from all over the globe."

"Now that's a scary thought." Amanda had already seen some of the posted comments. "Absolutely terrifying."

"Don't chicken out about our book. Like I said, it's already a guaranteed bestseller. We've got practically automatic sales to five million women who are slaves to these once-a-year man-cold perpetrators."

"Perpetrators? You make it sound like a crime."

"It ought to be criminalized. But I project that to be addressed in the fourth or fifth tier. You can't get new legislation just because the grassroots demand it. You need lobbyists and celebrities on your side, pumping up your message."

"Hold on. Grassroots? Lobbyists? Celebrities?" Amanda's eyes grew large. "What celebrity is going to be a spokesperson for the women combating man-cold perpetrators?"

"Hey, those are some of the words we might use, but it's got to be a flashy acronym." Christine thought for a minute. "What about D.A.M.P.? Defense Against Man-cold Perpetrators. D.A.M.P. I love it!"

Amanda pinched her friend's forearm. "Forget D.A.M.P. Just name me one celebrity who'll help us with this. And it's got to be a female celebrity who's married to, or living with, some schmuck who acts like a baby when he gets the sniffles."

Christine closed her eyes briefly. "Well, I'm drawing a blank at the moment, but I'll come up with somebody. Like I said, the political action committee aspects of this would be way down the line."

"Wait. Maybe we're looking at the wrong gender. How about a male celebrity? You know, some washed-up actor who can't get any decent roles." Amanda might already have a short list of names. "We'll get him to say he used to be a man-cold perpetrator, but now he's reformed. Saw the error of his ways, et cetera."

"Great idea, Amanda! But we still need a name. Know any male actors with a troubled past of man-cold perpetration?"

"Irrelevant. Actors are paid to say the lines provided in the script and make it look convincing. Take an out-of-work actor and pay him the S.A.G. scale, and we've got our celebrity endorsement. Our mouthpiece, our poster male for the legislation."

Christine squinted. "A few days ago you told me that you don't know when I'm kidding and when I'm serious. I think I've just reached that point with you. Are you serious about all this stuff you just blurted out? Or are you just humoring me?"

Amanda took another quick look at her cell phone clock and jumped up. "Oops. Gotta run. Later."

* * * *

Shortly after lunch, one of the other workers entered Amanda's office with two additional grant applications.

"Just got these apps from King Louie," Joan said, whispering the boss's name. "He told me to bring them in." She handed them to Amanda. "Sorry."

Amanda glanced over the top document. "Any idea how long he's been sitting on these?"

Joan shrugged. "I didn't see them come in, but he just now made a point of telling me that they did beat the deadline."

"Deadline was Friday a week ago." Amanda double-checked her calendar.

"Don't kill the messenger." Joan rolled her eyes.

"Sorry. My frustration quotient is through the roof." Amanda sighed heavily. "Not aimed at you."

Joan nodded and departed.

* * * *

During late afternoon, Jason called his buddy Kevin Haywood at the electric co-op. A year older and already divorced twice, Kevin's sole avocation was to cruise the numerous conventions, conferences, and other events which gravitated to the Nashville area. About half of these had women attendees, and about a quarter of the events were mostly aimed at females. Women visiting Nashville without their usual male partners were juicy targets, and Kevin almost always got a hit.

At the apartment, Jason finally realized he'd had enough deprivation and was eager for rescue. "Kevin, you got to come get me. I'm at Amanda's on Melrose. I'm sick and I'm starving! No TV, no Internet, nothing! The most exciting thing around here is watching some kid with no neck who keeps banging a tennis ball against the side of the community laundry house. And after the first hour, even that excitement wears off. I'm a prisoner! When can you get here?"

"Are you kidding? You've got it made. A foxy nurse like Amanda and you're off work all week. What's to rescue? Has she given you a full body massage yet?"

"No, I'm serious, Kevin. Everything's upside down. Amanda's hardly here at all and these other women keep coming over."

"Other women. Hmm. How many? This sounds interesting. Who are they? Nice looking?" Kevin theatrically faked a cough. "Maybe I'm feeling a little sick, too."

"No, no. It's horrible. They're killing me over here. Starving me!"

"Jase! If you're hungry, just order a pizza delivery."

"Yeah, good idea." It had not even occurred to him. But his friend was missing the big picture of punishment and isolation. Jason tried to explain.

Kevin just sounded bored.

"You don't seem to realize how serious this is." Jason sputtered. "Here's just one example. Yesterday, a kid came to the door selling magazine subscriptions. So I say I don't live here, but ask if he's got any food on him. He acts like he doesn't understand the concept. So I say, 'Anything at all to eat. I'm starving. I'll pay.' So he digs down in his pocket and comes up with two gummy bears and an old piece of butterscotch."

"Uh, don't tell me you bought them."

"It was a bargain at a dollar apiece, even if I did have to scrape his pocket lint off the bears. Fortunately the butterscotch morsel was still wrapped, but it was dried up and stuck to the wrapper, so it took me nine minutes to peel it." Jason sighed heavily. "Where are all those kids who sell boxes of candy bars to raise money for schools? I used to see them by the busloads before I was imprisoned."

Kevin didn't respond. Desperation in a buddy probably made him uncomfortable.

"I'm desperate, Kevin. Plus I seem to be out of cash."

"I don't know, Jase. If you're off-work-sick, I think you need to stick it out."

Jason wailed pitifully. "Save me. Please! You know I'd come for you."

"No, you wouldn't. You'd head for the county line." No sympathy from Kevin. "You're on your own, buddy. Besides, I know you're exaggerating. It's a cold. How bad could it be?"

"I don't even have any pants!"

"Now, that's what I'm talking about!" Kevin laughed. "After you finally come back to work, I think I'll catch a cold for the next week."

"Kevin, I'm begging…"

"Sorry, buddy, you're on your own with an apartment full of attentive women. Gotta go. Let me know if I can help."

"I *am* letting you know. I *do* need your help! Come rescue me!" Jason's call was not going as planned.

"What a kidder! Bye."

Jason stared at his phone in stunned silence. His best buddy wouldn't even take him seriously! But at least Kevin had offered a useful suggestion and Jason called the pizza place.

After nearly ten minutes, he flipped his phone shut with total disgust. "Pizza nazi! You just lost my business forever!" Then he sucked down another inch of striped toothpaste.

Chapter 8

Amanda checked the blog before leaving work. The comments reflected about the same proportion of supporters and detractors. She clicked on the Kick-Marty link they'd discovered on Day Three. Current tally was *Kick Marty Out — 24*. More than double the number from two days ago.

There was a new link to a second adjunct blog. This one was tagged Free-Marty and the first-day tally was *Free Marty Now! — 5*. It would be interesting to track these two opposite viewpoints: one group understanding that Jason was an intruder and the other group assuming he was a prisoner.

Amanda clicked back onto the central blog's main page to see Christine's newest posting.

Curing the Uncommon Man-Cold
Day Five

Lunch for our patient was right on the very edge of edible. *Marty* took a couple of those compressed rice cake cracker things and actually spread toothpaste on them.

Cheez Whiz is off the list — dairy, of course — so he must have figured anything that's gooey could be substituted. I'm tempted to try this myself. He insists the striped toothpaste will go with anything.

Marty had barely finished his meager lunch when the two female insect sprayers I'd arranged came in and doused the apartment. Of course, they were bogus… which is the whole point of these disruptions. In any normal week you wouldn't have a technician visit every day and a hen party every evening. Remember this, ladies, when you plan your Scare-Cures. Pull out all the stops!

Oh, back to the pretend sprayers. They did most of their work right around *Marty*. Both his feet got dosed liberally. Apparently our patient had discovered an old peppermint nearly buried on *Missy*'s dresser. The sprayers told me he'd just spent five minutes carefully unwrapping this dried-up mint. So, right when he was about to plop it in his mouth, one of them zapped it with the pretend bug spray.

Sorry, thought I saw a bug, she told him.

Important hint: don't use real bug spray for this part of the treatment. You don't want to go to jail for poisoning. All they were spraying was water with a quart of dime store perfume dumped in.

Oh, final note about this: The sprayers were friends of my sister. You can use any relatives or friends the patient has never met.

Almira Gulch

That signature sounded vaguely familiar but Amanda couldn't place it. Maybe a teacher she'd had in elementary school?

She reread the part about the insect sprayers. No idea who those women were, but clearly they represented two more individuals who now knew about the Scare-Cure that Amanda and her bossy friend were perpetrating against an unsuspecting Jason. At least six people now knew that Amanda's life was being played out on a blog.

* * * *

Dead tired, Amanda arrived home from work about 5:35. First stop was the air conditioner's outside compressor, where she followed Christine's instructions. The unit cycled on and began moving the afternoon's stale, hot air through the duct system. It would take at least thirty minutes to cool off sufficiently.

With an overall body expression of total exhaustion, Amanda entered, dropped her purse, and kicked off her heels. She stared at the inside of her own apartment for a moment as though she wasn't sure it was the correct address. She left the door mostly closed, but it would take too much effort to push it until it latched fully.

It was jungle hot inside! She pulled her skirt halfway up her thighs and loosened two extra buttons on her blouse. Since she didn't possess the energy required to reach the couch in the living space, Amanda just sank into the chair nearest the door and closed her eyes.

About six minutes after she fell asleep, Jason trudged in and pushed the front door until it clicked. Amanda woke immediately with a feeling like she'd just landed in the middle of a 1950s horror movie. She had. Directly in front of her was the *Creature from the Guest Lagoon*.

"Hi. Didn't hear you come in." Jason obviously noticed how much leg was revealed by her disheveled skirt.

He approached and apparently attempted to negotiate an embrace, but the positioning was all wrong. Plus she was not remotely in the mood for embraces with a man who apparently hadn't showered in at least four days. Amanda held him at arm's length and didn't even rise from the chair. "Get in the bathroom and take a shower, for cryin' out loud." She pointed sternly. "You positively stink! And you still haven't shaved!"

Jason's apparent ardor cooled significantly. "I haven't been doing anything but sitting around... haven't been anywhere." He inhaled deeply at his own armpit. "You don't get smelly unless you do stuff and go somewhere."

"I don't know which farm school taught you human hygiene, but if you're going to stay another minute inside my apartment, you're going to take a shower." She jabbed her pointing finger in the appropriate direction. "And throw those filthy rags outside the door. If I can chase them down, I'm going to wash them."

"Cheese Louise, what a grouch. You used to be fun to be around."

"Don't get me started, Jason!" She sounded like her own mother. Amanda took a breath. "You brought one change of sick clothes. I'll bring them to you. Now shuck those filthy things and get yourself washed. Missus Yodel can't even practice with the smell coming from this apartment."

"It sure didn't bother her the rest of today." Jason hurried into the bathroom before Amanda could reply.

About fifteen minutes later, Amanda saw Jason emerge from the hall bathroom — presumably clean. Except for damp hair, however, he didn't look much different than before.

Clearly, he noticed the interior climate change right away. "When did the A/C guy come and fix your unit? Whew! I was dying in here today." Jason wiped his brow theatrically. "With the windows open, I had to listen to Missus Yodel practice for seven hours straight. Today she didn't even take a fifteen minute break."

"The air's not really fixed."

"It's running right now." Jason held his hand up near the ceiling vent. "Feels great. Thanks, whatever you did."

Though Amanda enjoyed hearing his gratitude, she had to break the news. "Just temporary. That part the technician ordered hasn't come in yet, but I told him I had a meeting tonight."

"Another meeting?" Jason let out a string of curses, some of which were new to Amanda.

She ignored his interruption. "So he brought over a loaner part from his shop. But it's got to be on his shelf again in the morning. I'm afraid you're back in the tropics tomorrow."

"We get *temporary* use of an A/C part? If he's got it in his shop, why can't you just buy that one? We don't need one imported from Osh-Kosh. The local part will be just fine."

"You don't understand. This has to do with my landlord — the geezer who owns these fourteen apartments... seven duplexes. He has an exclusive contract with Spiros Brothers Air, and they're closed down for a funeral in Greece."

"The entire shop closes down 'cause somebody died in Greece? You can't run a business that way!"

Amanda nodded. "Good point. And I think Mister Geezer is coming around, as well. But he's got to wait until the Greeks get back in the States to see if that contract can be amended, or if he'll have to get a lawyer to run interference."

"Look, I don't give a frying flog — um, a flying frog — about the Geezer, the Greeks, or the lawyer. I spent this entire day suffocating in here and listening to the female Slim Whitman next door. I'm going nuts! Another day like today and I'll be running in the streets screaming."

Well, at least he's identified the correct direction. "Look, no need to get agitated. Just enjoy the cool air while we have it. Maybe this particular Greek funeral will be short and sweet."

"It'll probably be the start of a new Grecian civil war and they won't make it back to the States for months!" Jason sputtered a lot when he whined. He also exaggerated.

"Well, at least we can hope they'll be back in time to light my furnace for winter. Think positive."

"I already am positive. I'm positive this whole situation is totally insane! And it's all Christine's fault. Couple of days ago, I only suspected she's a witch, but now I'm certain. If you cut her, I bet she won't even bleed."

"Don't witches bleed?" Amanda raised her eyebrows.

"Well, whatever the test is. Maybe you have to dunk them under water and see if they drown."

"I don't think she'd appreciate that." She peered into his rather frantic eyes. "You used to like Christine."

He shook his head slowly.

"Well, you certainly paid attention to her. I thought you were being friendly."

Jason's head continued to move slowly side to side.

"Oh, I get it. You only put up with her because she has such forward attributes."

"I can't deny I've noticed Christine's rack. But that's partly because she showcases those very healthy melons."

"Melons?" Amanda looked wistful. "I would have calculated grapefruit as the proper comparison."

"Whatever. Anyhow, now that I'm certain she's a witch, I bet Christine's boobs are solid ice. You'd get frostbit if you even touched them."

"Yet you'd still be tempted, wouldn't you?"

Jason paused while he obviously reflected on the flesh he'd seen over Christine's low-cut blouses. "Probably so. But not for long. Your fingers turn black if they stay frozen more than a few minutes."

"Better rewind that Arctic documentary. I think it requires several hours of exposure."

Jason seemed to contemplate a longer exploration of Christine's bosom. "Whatever."

"Well, regardless of your feelings for Christine, or if you're just bewitched — ha! — by her cleavage, you'd better not make her angry. If she gets upset, she might reschedule that colonic tonic."

Jason started to waggle a finger in her face, but quickly stopped. His finger still extended, he just stared into her eyes for a long moment.

Amanda could see his frustration, exasperation, and disappointment. But she could also see Jason was clearly no longer sick. He was already completely over his cold, but was stubbornly holding out for the *owed* TLC he had manufactured in his mind.

Sorry, 'Marty'.

"Since your slacks are still at the cleaners and all you have is sagging jammies, you'd better stay in the back room while my guests are here."

— — —

Jason felt like a fourth grader sent to the chalkboard to write disciplinary lines. "More guests? Creepin' crud! How long are they going to be here?"

"Probably not much more than two hours. Now scoot. I think they're arriving now."

They were.

From Jason's listening post in the guestroom, it was difficult to imagine the purpose or function of this gathering. He thought he recognized Sunny's and Maria's voices and was positive he heard Christine's. With that combination, this could be a meeting of their secret coven.

However, it didn't sound sinister. There was laughter, oohs and ahhs, and somebody even clapped briefly. What could this be? There was a fifth female voice not recognizable. Jason strained to hear. He discerned snippets about color and shade and tone — perhaps the fifth woman was an amateur artist painting a portrait of one of the guests.

No, not quite that, but it had to be related somehow to artwork. In fairly short order, she had apparently painted pictures of all four attendees. *Hmm.* More laughter; also excessive flattery which sounded enthusiastic but insincere. *What the heck are they doing out there?*

Jason didn't know. But they also ate a lot of snacks, which, of course, interested him considerably more than the portraits, or whatever. During their two-hour stay, they evidently gorged themselves on what sounded or smelled like nuts, cookies, and nachos, among other indistinguishable edibles.

Sound traveled well in that apartment. At the guestroom door, as he savored the sounds of distant food, Jason wondered how things had come to this. Something was wrong with this picture, terribly wrong. But he couldn't put his finger on it.

He was banned from hen-party sessions which did not interest him anyway. He had no accessible street clothes, couldn't find his car keys, considerable cash and his credit cards were missing, and his girlfriend had just ordered him to shower. *Crud.* He'd come here to recuperate from illness. But Amanda had basically imprisoned and then abandoned him. The evil witch Christine had administered torture and probable poison, and his buddy Kevin flatly refused to rescue him. Everything was off kilter!

Tonight would be his fifth night at Amanda's apartment and there was absolutely no sign of impending sex. *What's the point of being sick if you get absolutely no TLC at all?* He couldn't answer that. In fact, Jason could barely formulate the question. He began to wonder if they were also drugging him with some mind-altering serum — some exotic elixir that fogged the brain and turned normal men into zombie convicts. Maybe he would become a mindless prisoner who'd bounce a tennis ball off a brick wall for hours on end, like the irritating no-necked kid.

Jason felt like a zombie. Why couldn't he just walk out? *Zombies aren't allowed to leave.*

What would break his evil spell? *Probably need magic stronger than the witch's.*

Was he truly one of the undead under a spell? Or was he still so sick that his fevered brain imagined most of this? *Hmm.*

Time passed. Jason might have dozed briefly while sitting on the floor with his ear to the door. *Not sure.* He listened for sounds from the art meeting. Silence in the main rooms. He got up stiffly, opened the door, and crept down the short hallway to check the kitchen.

"Dang it! They took all the food scraps with them!"

Witches... again!

Jason peeked inside a decorative bag left on the table. Makeup! The *art meeting* was a make-over party! A receipt was underneath the bag. Over $48 for that little bag of cosmetics. The other women probably bought at least that much. At least $200! That fifth woman was an artist, all right — a con artist! She'd bilked Amanda out of nearly fifty bucks for two hours of laughter and insincere flattery. Jason and two buddies could duplicate that with a twelve-pack of beer! *Would've saved a lot of money.*

He peered more closely inside the little bag. Interesting colors. Jason wondered if any were edible.

* * * *

Curing the Uncommon Man-Cold

Day Five

Just a very short addendum.

Our patient suffered through a full day of no A/C in this August heat.

Why would *Marty* put up with these discomforts? Inquiring minds want to know.

Ladies: this portion's lesson is that a man will believe almost any lie... provided it's unbelievable enough. The key is to go boldly where no prevaricator has gone before and come up with a fantastic lie. The little, simple lies are fairly easy to disbelieve. But the whiz-bang whoppers just swoop away these guys and carry them off for a marvelous ride.

I gorged myself on snacks tonight at the make-over... couldn't leave them for *Marty*. In addition to everything else, I ate four Southern Lassies and took home three more. That's nearly half a pecan pie!

Log on tomorrow for more updates on the Scare-Cure for the man-cold.

Almira Gulch

Chapter 9

August 15 (Saturday)

In the coffeemaker Amanda brewed some very weak green tea, which made a nice sputtering sound. But she knew Jason wouldn't drink any because it smelled vaguely like potpourri.

Shuffling slowly from the short hallway, Jason appeared in those awful clothes. Since his other set was still in the dryer from yesterday's wash, Amanda knew these were different items. But they looked identical to what he'd worn for the previous five days.

"Do all your pajama bottoms look exactly alike?"

"Uh, what do you mean? The style?"

"Don't get me started on *style*. I'm talking identical — color, pattern, everything. Right down to the sprung-out waistband. Why do you wear them so dang loose?"

"Blood flow to my lower extremities. Cuts off the blood supply if the elastic's too tight."

"Well, you've got at least six inches there." She pointed.

Jason seemed caught off guard by her observation, but then he looked distinctly proud.

She sighed through her nose. "I'm talking about your waistband. You've got six inches of slack from that sprung-out elastic."

His face showed immediate disappointment and he raised his pajama bottoms up about an inch. Now they were temporarily about four inches below his navel.

"I can't believe these jammies sag as much as your other ones. Maybe worse!" Sometimes Amanda couldn't drop a subject. "I'm bringing home a set of suspenders."

He shrugged. Most likely, after he'd realized his favorite topic was not even in the conversation, Jason had lost interest and shifted to something new. "I had the strangest dream last night." He didn't even pause to see if she was interested. "Dreamed I was asleep. I woke up, in my dream, with a small panther on my chest. Purring and digging its claws into my pecs."

"Not many panthers this close to Nashville. I think you have to go further north toward the Kentucky border for cougars and mountain lions."

He ignored her nature lesson. "I think this dream panther escaped through the window, because I heard the blinds rattling, like the animal was whacking them or trying to tear them down."

"You must have been sleeping somewhere else. No blinds in my guestroom. Those are curtains."

"Well, it sounded like blinds. Maybe the panther was on your treadmill, rearranging those two hundred clothes hangers."

"Panthers don't tend toward domestic chores... they prefer hunting and killing." Amanda wondered how long this conversation could last before she'd burst out laughing.

"I'm telling you, this dream was so intense I could even smell the panther's breath."

"What does panther breath smell like, in dreams?"

"Pretty much like stale cat food." Jason scratched his uncombed hair. "What do panthers eat?"

"Sick humans, I expect."

He seemed to ignore the near-miss from such danger. "What do you figure my dream means?"

Amanda thought for a moment. "The panther symbolizes your illness and it's telling you with its breath that you're all recovered now. With its claws, it's saying, 'Go back to your own apartment.'"

He studied her face briefly, evidently trying to determine whether that interpretation could possibly be correct. "Not sure. If the panther represents my illness — and it was lying on my chest — then that could mean I'm still sick. Still under the influence of the cold virus."

"Nah. My version's better."

"Well, there's something else. When I woke up this morning, there were black hairs all over my shirt, right where the panther was lying during the dream."

"I think they call that *vivid* dreaming — when images of the dream realm actually manifest themselves in the real world." Amanda hid her smile.

"I've never dreamed any animal hair onto my shirt before."

"Okay, find another dream therapist." Amanda sighed heavily. "And see if she's got a spare bed in *her* apartment."

When Jason shrugged, his stomach grumbled like the earliest beginnings of Krakatoa. "Please tell me there's something edible in this place. I'm so weak I had to crawl down the hallway." Jason's exaggeration hadn't faltered.

"You're in luck. I found some great stuff in the nutritional aisles at the grocery yesterday. It'll put the rose back in your cheeks."

"I don't want any roses. I just want something to gnaw on that doesn't terrify my taste buds."

"Well, I've never tried this myself, but it's a highly recommended cereal."

"Frosted Flakes? Franken Berry? Anything but the shredded wheat bricks from yesterday. That junk tasted like rusty steel wool." He was drooling again. "Hey, how about Trix?"

"Silly rabbit. Trix are for… healthy men." With measured ceremony, Amanda placed a box near him on the counter. "This is organic hemp with granola."

"Hemp! You expect me to eat pieces of *rope*?"

"It's not rope. Though I guess you could make some rope from it. This is an organic plant… substance. Besides, it's mixed in with granola."

"You could mix dog turds with granola, but I wouldn't eat that, either." He stared at the box.

"You seem awfully picky for someone so ill. I thought you'd be grateful I was providing nutritional foods instead of over-processed junk that would retard your recovery." Amanda poured a few ounces into a bowl. "Here, try it. You might even like it."

"I'm not going to try it." It was beginning to sound like a famous TV commercial from several decades before. Jason peered into the bowl and poked its contents with his forefinger. He picked up one small cluster and sniffed it. "Smells just like a piece of rope." He touched the cluster to the tip of his tongue. "Tastes like rope, too."

"Well, enjoy your rope cereal, Jason. I've got to go earn a paycheck. Bye."

"But today's Saturday! I thought you'd be home at least today. You know, to take care of me a little... or something."

"Sorry. I've lost a lot of time already this past week and this is our crunch period, with decisions coming up at the end of the month on all the applications for next fiscal year. If I don't get them read and assessed, my boss doesn't have anything to go on about who gets funded. Not that he pays much attention to my recommendations anyway. There's a lot of politics involved and quotas of various kinds. Demographics... whatever. I might as well weigh them and just recommend he fund the heaviest ones." Clearly, Jason had tuned out during her first sentence of complaint... and that peeved her. Amanda turned to leave.

"Quick question before you go. Was it cooler in here last night, to you?"

"No, pretty hot, actually. August, you know. Why?"

"Well, when I got up last night to use the bathroom — and had to sit, by the way — I felt definitely chilled in the hallway." Jason pointed that direction. "Maybe that hall's a cold spot. Hauntings or something."

"Or panthers. But if my apartment is haunted, it's by the ghost of the man-cold."

Either he ignored the dig or didn't get it.

Amanda rolled her eyes discreetly. "Well, chills alternate with fever during a man-cold. Like a pendulum — half a degree hot, half a degree cold."

"Felt like ordinary apartment air conditioning to me. Felt good. I even considered sleeping in the hallway."

"Better not. Sometimes I'm way behind schedule in the mornings and I hit that hall running. I wouldn't want to accidentally stomp on your pills with these heels."

Jason moved his knees together without apparently realizing it. Instinctive.

She started to leave a second time, but Jason stopped her again. "Any chance you'll be home by lunch? I sure could go for some Chinese take-out."

Amanda shook her head. "Too much MSG."

"I don't care how much it costs. I'll pay. I'm starving!"

"Monosodium glutamate, I think. With an illness like yours, that stuff is lethal. They'll take you straight from the restaurant to the morgue." *Sorry, 'Marty'.*

On her way to work, Amanda stopped at a convenience store for gasoline, and bought a sausage biscuit with a sixteen-ounce coffee. And a Hershey bar to snack on later.

* * * *

The municipal building where Amanda worked had been originally on the square facing the courthouse, but had moved three-quarters of a mile east as the city had slowly conformed to the new dominant geographic feature — I-40. At one time that interstate was on the southern edge of the city, but now it was the relocated center. Most of the once-thriving retail businesses had drifted away from downtown and moved to the frontage roads, leaving many buildings vacant near the courthouse. Some of these had been razed to create parking lots for the numerous law offices which moved closer to court. Verdeville's current downtown was mainly law, banking, and — at its eastern edge — city/county government. In the other direction was the county hospital, so that western half of old downtown had become doctors' offices and diagnostic clinics. As such, reconfigured downtown thrived and parking was premium.

When she reached her building, slightly east of old downtown, Amanda entered with a punch code. It was closed on weekends, but HVAC systems were running. The elevators were also operable, but Amanda didn't use them when she was possibly alone in the building. If anyone got stuck on a Saturday, it might be Monday before they were rescued.

She often took the stairs anyway, even on regular days. It helped exercise her legs and tighten her buns. Also worked off the chocolate bars. Plus, whenever King Louie irritated her to boiling point, those stairs helped release excess stress.

Her floor looked empty. In her office section, Amanda was by herself. *Good! No Louis.* Maybe she could get some work done this Saturday. She checked the blog first, however.

Predictably, men's comments were still almost a hundred per cent in support of *Marty*. Several still wanted to smack *Missy* and *Almira*. Some protested that colds hit men harder because of their hormones. Some openly wondered how hard could it be to take care of a sick man? *Ha!*

Just as predictably, women's comments were mostly on the side of *Missy* and the blog-creator *Almira Gulch*, a name Amanda still didn't recognize. Most were rooting for them to cure *Marty* of this cold syndrome, for the betterment of all womankind.

A third large group seemed to be more speculators than spectators: They had links to a different blog running bets on how many days *Marty* could survive before he fled *Missy's* apartment.

So much for their own blog. Next, Amanda clicked on the adjunct threads which had sprung up through links from the comments in their blog. She returned to the first they'd discovered, nicknamed Kick-Marty. That had gained over a dozen: *Kick Marty Out* — 37 was the most recent post.

She returned to the primary blog and clicked on a link to the Free-Marty serial which she'd just noticed yesterday, with a first-day tally of five. The newest chorus was *Free Marty Now!* — *19*.

Back to the main blog. Apparently in response to that loosely knit thread, another blogger had turned attention on

Missy. In the comments, this link to a new blog was tagged Lighten-Missy. The first-day tally was *Lighten Up, Missy! – 03*. Amanda wondered which thread would garner the most running votes.

She didn't think about it very long, however. There were grant applications to wade through, so Amanda went to the staff lounge to make a pot of coffee.

She returned to her desk and kicked off her sneakers. No heels when she worked on weekends; she wore jeans and a golf shirt.

As she reached for the stack of unread grant proposals, Amanda paused to examine the two small frames on her desk. In one were two family photos: Amanda, her sister Kaye, and their parents in a candid pose, and a studio shot of Amanda's only niece. The other frame featured two different views of Jason. One was a candid shot of Jason alone as he looked up from opening a gift. His eyes showed surprise at the flash and delight at the present, a gift certificate for the steakhouse buffet. Also obvious was Jason's pure enjoyment of the moment, alone with Amanda for their first Christmas together. In the final photo, Jason's arm around Amanda and Amanda's hand lovingly on Jason's chest. They both looked like they'd just arrived in Heaven.

Back when Jason was healthy.

* * * *

Jason sat on Amanda's couch and stared at the late morning TV snow. That day's experiment was holding down channel buttons for up to a full minute each. Good thing the wall clock had a second hand. He also clutched the unauthorized candy bar he'd very recently acquired at great expense. Jason figured he'd fantasize and drool for a few moments before savoring the chocolate treat.

But watching television snow was too boring, even for Jason. With no actual programming to click through, he tried looking out through the open windows while fanning himself with an issue of *Oprah,* curiously missing its cover.

It was about 86 degrees inside the apartment. Outside the window was a blooming crepe myrtle. Logically, little birds would perch in those branches and sing contentedly, which would provide at least some type of entertainment for a man recovering from grave illness.

"That constant yodeling probably chased all the birds away." Jason looked around and realized he'd spoken out loud. "Not a good sign, Jason, old boy. Not a good sign."

Just as he'd torn open his contraband candy bar and taken a single drooling bite, Jason heard voices outside the door. Then a key slid into the lock and turned the bolt. The door opened!

Two women entered noisily, chattering in Spanish. They had a small vacuum cleaner, plastic pail, mop, and a tote tray with cleansers, sponges, and rubber gloves. They wore smocks that looked like clothes for hospital ward staff.

Jason stood. "Uh, hold on." He waved the candy bar in his right hand, while holding up his pajama bottoms with the left. "Amanda didn't say anything about a cleaning crew. I think maybe you've got the wrong apartment."

Cleaner A looked puzzled at first. Then she said "Ah..." and spoke in Spanish to Cleaner B. The second woman held up a key and smiled eagerly.

Jason sputtered a bit, but moved out of the way to keep the vacuum cleaner from rolling over his bare toes.

Cleaner A looked him over carefully as she put on her heavy rubber gloves. B said something in Spanish and both laughed.

Jason didn't like those yellow gloves at all. He sat down again and peeled back the wrapper of his candy treasure.

Cleaner B hustled over and sprayed it with a bottle of blue liquid. Then she rattled off something in Spanish. Her companion shook her head and made disapproving sounds. "Tsk, tsk, tsk." Or the Spanish version, anyway.

Jason looked at his candy bar, intact except for the single bite he'd previously taken. It was now covered with blue liquid. He started thinking, *How toxic could this cleanser be?*

Cleaner A pointed to the candy bar and waggled her gloved finger. Then a stern warning in Spanish.

Jason trudged into the kitchen — candy bar in one hand and pajama waistband in the other. Instinctively, he realized he just needed to sever about half an inch from the exposed portion of the candy, then discard the contaminated part and eat the rest. But in his compromised health, Jason's brain ran on fewer cylinders, so that possible salvage operation seemed too complicated. Plus, he'd have to search for a sharp knife.

At the sink, he ran a tiny stream of tap water and cautiously peeled away more of the wrapper. Then he slowly rolled the candy bar under the water, taking care to wash every part of the surface.

Cleaners A and B watched with obvious fascination and considerable commentary in what sounded like pidgin Spanish. One of them held up a dollar bill and the other dug out a bill to match it. They'd just made a wager!

As Jason became satisfied the blue liquid was completely cleaned from the candy bar surface, he realized in horror that most of the candy bar was also gone! *You can't wash chocolate!* He hurriedly peeled back the rest of the wrapper to see how much might be salvaged. In his haste, the candy slipped from his wet fingers and scooted around the sink basin for almost two complete laps. He grabbed for it, but that effort only nudged it down into the discolored drain.

Cleaner A handed B her dollar. B had won the bet — he'd washed it!

Now Jason had a tragic dilemma. He retrieved the soggy candy bar and examined it carefully. There was probably enough remaining to eat, if he squeezed it back into a rough ball shape. But it was basically a soggy mass, distinctly resembling the wretched deposits of the old, fat Dachshund from two duplexes over. What worried Jason even more were the horror tales he'd heard of bacteria in kitchen sink drains — supposedly more germs than the entire state of New Jersey.

Seeing how much deliberation was in play, Cleaner A pulled out another dollar bill and chattered something in Spanish. B held up one of the two bills already in her hand. Another bet!

Finally, Jason emitted a loud, anguished moan and then threw the entire disintegrating mass of nuts, caramel, and — formerly — chocolate coating into the open trash can. He flung it with such intensity that he wrenched his right shoulder.

Cleaner B handed over her dollar — A had won the second wager. B looked disappointed, since she'd evidently bet that Jason would still try to eat it.

Their wagers being even, the two chattering cleaners set about to perform household duties. Curiously, to him, they didn't work in any of the other apartment rooms. Both hovered around Jason, vacuuming under his feet, spraying things near him, dusting the television screen, et cetera.

It was a long cleaning appointment. Jason couldn't even concentrate on his latest test with the TV remote.

Chapter 10

Amanda got a call shortly before noon — Christine, bearing lunch, was on the curb outside her workplace. Since the building doors were locked, Amanda had to put her sneakers back on and make another round trip in the stairwell to let her friend inside. *Sheesh.* "Hope you brought something good. I'm starving." She held the door.

"Two baked potatoes with the works." Christine also held up two diet drinks.

"Sounds a lot better than potpourri tea."

When Amanda headed toward the stairwell door, Christine pointed. "Is the elevator broken?"

"No. It runs, but I don't use it on weekends. Hangs up a lot during the regular week and the building super cusses a blue streak every time." She looked at her visiting friend. "It's only three floors." Amanda also re-explained how she used it often for exercise and stress relief.

"You sure are a contradiction. You have a perfectly good treadmill at home that you use for a clothing rack, but you sprint up and down office stairs for exercise." Then she poked Amanda's derrière, which preceded her up the steps. "Though I'll have to admit, this climbing seems to keep your butt pretty tight."

"Don't watch my butt... that's weird. Plus, it wouldn't hurt you to skip a few elevators." Amanda had noticed Christine eating a lot of extra snacks just to keep Jason from having them. She stopped on the landing and turned. "Uh, sorry, that didn't come out right."

Christine shook her head. "No, you're right. Next time I visit my lawyer downtown, I'll take the stairs."

"What floor is he on?"

"Sixth."

Amanda wasn't sure what to say. "Uh, maybe..."

"Yeah. I'll walk up three and ride the other three."

When they reached the third floor, both were breathing heavily, Christine more than Amanda. Amanda let her friend catch a breath before they proceeded.

Between panting breaths, Christine's natural curiosity compelled her to keep talking. "What's the latest with Jason, besides finally getting him to shower last evening?"

"Pee-yuu! Do you realize he actually stuck his nose deep in his own armpit and didn't detect anything disagreeable? I could smell him from six feet away."

"Men can't smell their own B.O. Scientific fact. If they could, you'd see a lot more men fainting."

"Don't men faint?" Amanda couldn't remember. Her mind had lost a lot of cognitive power since the previous Monday evening.

Christine merely continued her science lesson. "Something about selective evolution or survival of the fittest. The male species has developed unique sensory blockers that keep them from smelling themselves. These highly specialized sensors allowed disgustingly stinky cave men to detect a wounded sabre-toothed tiger half a mile away, but they couldn't smell themselves. Of course, most of the cave women swooned when those revolting bums got back to the home cave."

"Those cave guys probably thought that was all about adoration and romance. Ha." Amanda began moving toward the staff room on the half of that floor occupied by her section.

Before following, Christine raised the warm sack and inhaled the baked potato aroma. "A minute ago you implied you'd added potpourri to the tea leaves this morning. For real?"

"No, not real potpourri. That stuff's probably poison, like poinsettia. This was a special herbal blend of tea that's supposed to taste like potpourri smells."

"Guaranteed to ward off the male species."

Amanda nodded. "He didn't get near it."

"You got a lot done so far today?" Christine looked around the empty spaces of that office section as they passed through.

"Yeah, without King Louie hovering, I can actually concentrate."

"Think we'll have enough time, after we eat, to look at our blog for a minute?"

"Sure. I haven't checked it since first thing this morning. Might be some new comments." Amanda held open the lounge door. "By the way, who is Almira Gulch? I noticed that name below the last couple of blog entries."

"Remember the actress Margaret Hamilton, in *The Wizard of Oz*? She played two characters: the Wicked Witch and the mean neighbor who threatened Dorothy's dog. Well, the name of that nasty neighbor was Almira Gulch."

"Your grasp of movie trivia is astounding. Did you pick that name because Jason has been saying you're a witch?"

Christine smiled. "Maybe I am a witch." Then she cackled.

In the otherwise vacant staff lounge, Amanda and Christine ate their potatoes and then retired to Amanda's office with what remained of their diet drinks.

"You said something the other day about this publication you're planning... that the book is writing itself on your blog." Amanda looked puzzled. "Now that we've got a minute, tell me how a book writes itself."

"Our blog. It's not *my* blog, it's all about you and Jason and whether you'll survive his sickness."

"You mean *Missy* and *Marty*. Confidentiality, remember?" She was still rattled by how many people already knew about their secret project.

"Sure, sure. Got it covered. It's foolproof. The CIA couldn't find out your identities." Christine waved her hand. "Well, back to the book. After reading what I'm posting, we're getting comments from other bloggers. There's heartfelt gratitude, weepy commiseration, even additional recipes for really cruddy-tasting health food. It's writing itself. I just need to copy the threads, paste them into a document. Boom." She pointed to the desk as though a monograph had just appeared. "Book. Bestseller."

"Boom? The book just appears like magic?"

"Well, it'll need a little editing."

"A little?" Amanda the skeptic. "From what I've seen on those comments, you'll need one full-time editor just to clean up their language."

"Ah, small matter. They're just blowing off steam. See, our blog is the first opportunity they've ever had to vent. That's the groundbreaking part of what we're doing."

"Well, the gratitude and sympathy crowd aren't the only ones venting. A lot of the comments are basically of the theme Oh-poor-*Marty*-who's-a-prisoner-of-that-witch-*Missy*."

"Better still." Christine nodded. "That gives our book balance. We'll give one whole chapter to the men whining about mistreatment."

"Glad you're keeping it balanced."

Christine apparently ignored the dig.

"By the way, you portray *Marty* in an awful light." Amanda frowned slightly. "You don't show any sympathy at all. After all, he does feel bad… kind of."

"Sympathy? That's the last thing we want anywhere near Jason. He got way too much sympathy while he breastfed those extra five years."

"You don't know that. Not even possible."

"Well, I wasn't in his nursery, but he's got all the markings of a boy with too much of momma's milk." Christine sometimes tried to look like a professor pointing out proven scientific facts. "No sympathy for your sniffle baby. Sympathy just feeds the pathology."

"Pathology? Where do you come up with this stuff?"

"Like I told you, my brain's plugged in."

"Yeah, and your nephew's a janitor at Johns Hopkins." Amanda paused. She needed to regain focus, since her vital role was to be the throttle governor for this manic extemporaneous therapist. "In some of the posted comments, I've seen links to other sites. How do we control what appears on those other sites?"

"We don't… can't. We control our blog, except for the comments." Christine's face scrunched up briefly. "Well, we can delete offensive comments and block nasty bloggers, if we want." She waved her hand. "Anyway, our blog spawned those other blogs. And they link back and forth. It's a parallel universe with connections, sort of."

"And we have absolutely no control over those other universes?"

Christine shook her head. "Let me show you."

Amanda got up from her chair so her friend could demonstrate.

"Okay, here's my post from yesterday." Christine moved the curser down. "Here's the new comments. See, one of them links to another blog."

"What's in the other one?"

Christine sighed. "More comments, I guess. They probably wish they'd thought of this therapy protocol themselves. Uh, let's see." She clicked. "Oh!"

Amanda peered closer. "Yikes. I thought the language was bad on our blog comments."

"Well, these aren't all bad. Look, here's one." Christine began reading. "Uh, '*Marty ought to get off the couch and jump Missy's bones.*' See, a romantic. And here's something unrelated... they jump around a lot: '*Marty ought to hitch up his big girl panties and leave.*'"

"I looked at the links to those other blogs today. I saw a new one: *Lighten Up, Missy!* Tally was up to three when I first noticed it. Click it." Amanda pointed.

Christine clicked. "Uh, you've doubled. It's now at *Lighten Up, Missy!* — 6."

"When I looked earlier, Kick-Marty was nearly twice as popular as Free-Marty."

"As it should be." Christine nodded. "Wonder if it will hold?"

* * * *

Jason's right forearm rested in the sling portion of a huge, garish bandana around his neck when he greeted Amanda that evening.

"What on earth happened to you?" She'd just walked in the door.

"Hurt my shoulder throwing something."

"You been playing ball with little No-Neck? You're not supposed to romp in your condition." She eyed him closely. "You're supposed to rest and recuperate, unless you're well enough to go home to your place."

Jason shook his head and coughed twice. Then he shrugged. "I don't think I could explain it." He didn't want to clarify because he hoped he'd be able to wrangle another candy bar out of the neighbor supplier — he'd finally found a pusher.

His next fix was tomorrow after Amanda left for work.

Amanda put down her purse and keys and kicked off her Saturday sneakers. She walked over to the couch and sat, wiggling her toes. "What's this stuff?" She pointed to a sprinkling of tiny black crumbs on the cushion beside her.

"Don't know." He'd forgotten it was there. "What does it look like?" Jason hoped Amanda would come up with something.

She licked a finger, dabbed it on the crumbs, and held them near her face, like they did in movies. "Have you been snorting black cocaine?"

"Huh? Does it come in black?"

She examined it closely. Then sniffed it, very tentatively. "Not enough material to generate a specific odor."

"Uh, I think that's been here the whole time." He shrugged.

"Nope, you'll need a better story than that. I vacuumed this couch shortly before you invaded."

Jason just looked around the room. Maybe something in sight would give him a hook to hang on. "Sorry, I got nothing." He rechecked the walls and ceiling.

"Well, I don't know what that's from and I can't figure how else it got here. But I'll bet it's something edible, and probably tasty. Which means you've been cheating on your diet. Which means you're deliberately scotching your own recovery. Which means you're prolonging your stay in my apartment. Which means you're headed over to my dark side, since these are my Hell Weeks at work."

"Uh, mold!" He'd finally thought of something as his eyes moved upward. "Black mold from the air vents. Since the A/C is off all day, that mold has a chance to creep down to the duct opening to take a look around. You know, wondering why the unit isn't running during the daytime in August."

— — —

Amanda turned her head to keep him from seeing her smile. *Actually a very creative effort.* She'd have to remember to tell that whopper to Christine for the blog.

Amanda went to her bedroom to change clothes. She emerged with shorts and a tee-shirt, since it was still so warm inside, even though she'd reactivated the compressor earlier. Coming back to the main rooms, she stopped in the kitchen for a drink of juice. "Jason, I see a candy wrapper in this trash can. Where'd that come from? Not on your diet." She waggled her forefinger.

"Uh, I found it… or something." He squirmed on the dining chair.

"Hmm. Found it, huh?" She eyeballed him closely. "Men are usually pretty good liars, but during this debilitation, your lies are very transparent. You didn't *find* a candy bar. Where'd you acquire it?"

He shook his head slowly and watched her warily.

"Jason!" Again, she used her mother's tone, though the name was different.

"I can't say. I'm protecting someone else." He acted like a captured spy undergoing interrogation.

She circled him slowly, a bit like a sinister interrogator. "So, you won't reveal your supplier. Very well. We have ways of making you talk."

Secret agents are trained to resist the most heinous tortures for up to twenty-four hours, to allow their colleagues to escape. Jason likely wondered how long he could hold out.

Amanda continued pacing. "We've found our hemp is very persuasive…"

Jason lasted about two minutes. "No, no, not the rope cereal again! Okay, I'll talk. It was No-Neck, from five doors down, I think." Jason's head sagged against the back of the chair as though he'd just endured a terrible beating.

"I know him. He actually does have neck bones, you know. It's just that his neck is shorter than normal and nearly as thick as his skull. He'll probably be a good lineman someday, *if* he grows up." She wanted it to sound sinister. "So, what's the going price these days for black market candy bars?"

Jason groaned. "I paid three bucks for that Snickers bar and it was at least a year old. I checked the lot number."

"This no-necked supplier — is he planning to return?"

"He said it'd be at least four bucks tomorrow. What a crook, and not even in sixth grade."

"Well, we shall have to cut… off… that… supply." She spaced it out like a Hollywood Gestapo agent.

"What are you going to do to little No-Neck?"

"I'll make him an offer he can't refuse." It was a shame to mix the movie images, but the first *Godfather* film had such a wonderful archetypal line and one rarely ever has a chance to use it.

"Look, there wasn't really a crime anyhow. I only got one bite before Rosita sprayed it with Blue-Glow cleanser."

"Rosita?"

"Those cleaning ladies you hired… they came today."

"Oh." Amanda hadn't known any particulars about the cleaners' visit, except as part of the general outline Christine had rushed past her on Day Two. "I forgot their schedule.

Wonder how they missed those black crumbs." Two cleaning ladies arranged by Christine meant there were now eight individuals in on their secret plan. Plus Maria and Sunny from the crop party — that made ten!

Amanda checked her watch and groaned. In preparation for the upcoming card-and-game night, she began cleaning the dining/kitchen/living spaces.

Jason watched. "What's going on here tonight? Rotary Club? International Order of Oddfellows?"

She sighed. "Just a couple of my friends coming over to play cards and such. It needn't concern you. You know Maria. Sunny has her young niece in tow."

"Are they bringing any food?"

"Probably. Somebody usually brings something. I would have picked up an already-baked pie or cake at the grocery, but I hustled home to check on you."

He didn't thank her. Jason noticed something and held his hand up near a vent. "Hey, the air's on again! Cool!"

"Oh, yeah, meant to tell you. The technician brought that borrowed part back over and said I could use it for a couple of hours this evening."

"When? I've been here all day and I didn't see anybody."

"He was arriving about the same time I did. I guess he just installed the thingy and left." She held up her own hand. "Yeah, it's working."

"How come the air conditioning only runs when you and your friends need it? It's off all day while I'm here sweating and dying and listening to Missus Yodel through wide open windows."

"Well, I've already told you all I know about her yodeling, and I did explain about the problem with the broken part on my unit. He's not allowed to sell the last one, the new ones haven't arrived yet, and the rest of the Spiros outfit is in Greece for the funeral."

"Yeah, yeah, I've heard all that, but something's fishy about him loaning you the part several different times. He's not looking for any, uh, fringe benefits from you… is he?"

"Jason! I'm offended and shocked! Do you really think I'd trade sexual favors to an A/C tech for the temporary use of a part he can't sell me?"

"Well, when you put it like that, maybe not. But something smells funny."

"It's probably you, Mister Sickie. Have you bathed since Thursday evening?"

"Can't remember. But I want to talk to this guy next time he's here. Maybe I can bribe him to leave the part here. You know, he could pretend like he just forgot it somewhere."

"Well, you better find a belt for those PJs. If you offer him money with those jammies hanging down around your pubes, he's liable to deck you. Hard to recover from an illness like yours with a busted nose."

Amanda straightened a few more things. "My company's coming soon. You'd better head back to the guestroom since you're not dressed. There's a little girl in this group, you know.

"Any supper plans for me?" Jason held out his lands like a beggar. "Or do I have to suck on my toothpaste tube all evening?"

"Ever tried baba ganoush?"

"What? Sounds like that kooky uncle on those *Danny Thomas* reruns — Uncle Tonoose. Is it Lebanese?"

"Not sure. Middle Eastern, I think. You start by roasting some eggplant…"

"Hold on." He shook his head. "Anything that starts with eggplant is definitely off limits. I'll stick to the toothpaste." His stomach was evidently shrinking as a result of six days on that involuntary diet.

"You don't even want to hear about the tahini paste? What about the khubz bread or pita points?"

— — —

Jason raised his hand like a stop sign and turned slowly. Then he trudged down the short hallway while barely holding up his pajama bottoms.

It was only a few moments before they arrived. As he had on the other evenings when banished to the guestroom during a hen party, Jason sat on the floor with his ear to the door.

He heard female voices; they were playing a card game of some kind. Christine, Maria, and Sunny. Sunny's niece had brought a volleyball — or something similar — which rolled down the hallway and smacked the linen closet door several times.

The card players were just about to start eating and Jason strained at the door to hear the food being consumed. It was a bit of self-torture.

Suddenly... Boom! The ball bashed into the guestroom door right at his ear! He thought he was in a submarine being blasted by depth charges. He slowly shook his head to loosen the cobwebs.

He'd never strangled a child before, but he certainly would have punctured her volleyball if he'd had a knife accessible. On second thought, Jason realized if he did have a knife, he'd probably just slit his own wrists. *Creepin' crud.*

* * * *

Curing the Uncommon Man-Cold
Day Six

Marty's supper was spare, as usual. More rice cake crackers and another stalk of celery spread with toothpaste.

Two of *Missy's* other friends came over to play the lively card game golf and dice game farkle. One of them brought a niece.

We all brought snacks, of course, but carefully removed every excess crumb so *Marty* couldn't have any. After all, if we feed the creature, he'll never leave! I ate an extra couple of cheesecake tarts that I didn't even have room for. Can't leave anything for *Marty*!

I've noticed there are lots of bets on a side-link about how long he'll stay in *Missy's* apartment. You won't get any help from me. I would have put good money that the bag of unusual groceries I brought over on Day Three would have run him off. But it didn't. He's managed to survive somehow. Must be sneaking in some edibles. We'll have to stop that contraband. Time for a shakedown.

Check back tomorrow for more updates.

Almira Gulch

Chapter 11

August 16 (Sunday)

Amanda woke to Jason's shriek. "Amanda!"

She rushed across the hall and slapped at the guestroom light switch.

Jason was huddled in the small bed with his knees tucked tightly and his arms around his shins.

"What on earth is wrong?" It was 4:25 a.m.

"Panther! Panther... on me! Tried to... tear my... face off!"

"Don't be ridiculous. You were dreaming again."

"No! Real! Here!" Jason could only manage one or two syllables in his panicked explanation.

"Now, settle down and tell me what happened in your dream."

"No dream! Panther... here! Clawed my face!"

With exaggerated movements Amanda looked around the cluttered room. "Don't see any wildlife now. Maybe the light scared it off."

"I'm serious, Amanda!" Finally words with more than two syllables. "Panther on my chest again!"

"What size panther this time?"

"Same as last one. At least fifty pounds. Hard to say. He was breathing on me again, and then he started whacking my face with his claws."

"I don't see any bloody rips in your flesh." She yawned largely.

Jason felt for lesions. "Well, maybe not claws. It patted my face with its *paws*."

"So it's a friendly panther." It was difficult not to smile. "In dreams, animals can represent danger or friendship. This little panther wants to be your buddy."

"No! It wasn't a dream and he doesn't want to be friends. He tried to claw my eyes out!"

"Well, skip ahead to that part. I need to get back to sleep."

"On my chest, breathing into my nostrils, then he patted my face. I wanted to look, but I was too scared, so I kept my eyes shut." Jason shuddered. "Then he reached with his paws and raised up my eyelids! It was horrible!"

"Well, both eyes seem present and in working order. Maybe the dream panther didn't want to keep your eyeballs. Perhaps he was just counting them."

"Why would a panther count my eyeballs unless he planned to eat them?" He shuddered again and gripped his shins even tighter. "And it wasn't a dream!"

Amanda sighed and yawned at the same time. Her airway got confused and she nearly coughed. "Well, I've never heard of panthers — whatever their size — pulling up human eyelids for optical exams. Maybe that's his way of waking you up."

"He nearly scared me into a shock-seizure."

"What exactly is that?"

"I don't know all the medical stuff, but it's caused by being scared to death by panthers." He made it sound almost authoritative.

"Whatever. I'm going back to bed."

"Leave the light on!"

"Okay, but I'm closing your door so the light doesn't bother me." Amanda sighed and closed the guestroom door slowly. From the corner of her eye, she saw Diabla rubbing against the sofa in the living space. It looked like she was ready to go outside again. Amanda tiptoed down the hallway and stroked the long black fur for a moment. The huge feline hunched her back with every stroke. "Good job, Diabla, my little guest panther. Mission accomplished. You can go home now." She opened the front door quietly and watched the miniature black predator slowly melt into the darkness.

Amanda closed and locked the door, yawned again, and used the bathroom before she went back to bed.

* * * *

Amanda's provision of daily breakfast was becoming an exercise in imagination. With Christine's able assistance, Amanda had produced something differently awful for the past five mornings. So far, her favorites were the scrambled tofu on Day Four and yesterday's hemp granola. Today she had an added treat.

Jason dragged himself into the kitchen area and slumped into a chair at the table. He hit the seat just about the same time his sagging pajama bottoms slid halfway down his gluteus maximus. The chair was cool, so he squirmed enough to cover his exposed flesh with the faded, striped flannel.

"Were you able to get back to sleep after that panther dream?"

"Not a wink. I kept imagining him pulling up my eyelids with his paw-fingers." Jason shuddered again. "And it wasn't a dream. I found more black panther hair on my shirt."

"Like I told you, vivid dreaming. It can seem so real that you actually find real-world evidence of the situations you dreamed about."

"Not a dream. He wanted to suck out my eyeballs."

Amanda changed the subject. "Christine helped me locate something to go with your cereal besides that unsweetened prune juice you've been griping about."

"I bet it didn't come from a cow."

"Correct." Amanda pointed to the quart container. "It's dairy-free and gluten-free."

"What does that leave?" He leaned closer but refused to touch it. "Is it even liquid?"

"Well, it's sort of a pale cousin to milk."

Jason frowned. "Probably a third cousin, twice removed. What's this particular cousin made of?"

"Some sort of artificial soy protein base."

"Artificial? Even the natural soy crud tastes like horse pee. I can't imagine what the fake soy tastes like."

"Well, you're supposed to sprinkle this wheat germ on top." She held up a small bottle. "It cuts the bitterness of the artificial soy."

The look on his face revealed utter defeat. How had Jason lasted six days with hardly any palatable food? How stubborn does one have to be to remain in inhospitable circumstances even though he's perfectly healthy, except for low blood sugar from restricted intake of a remarkably odd diet? Why was he holding on to the illusion of illness when he could just walk out and go home?

Amanda didn't know. And today she didn't have time to dwell on it. "Well, I'll put the milk-cousin in the fridge if you want it. If not, there's still some prune juice left. I'm in a rush this morning."

"You're going to work *again*?" He looked like he might cry. "But it's Sunday! Doesn't King Louie realize he's running you down to a nub?"

"Like I told you yesterday, I'm way behind. The applications have to be duly considered and I'm the one who does that part. Besides, if I'm down to a nub, it has other contributing factors besides King Louie."

Clearly, Jason was oblivious to her point. "Any idea what time you'll be home? They have a great breakfast buffet at Shuney's."

"You can't eat all that greasy stuff. You're a sick man. We're trying to build up your immunities and clean out your system, not clog it up further."

He looked like his faithful dog had just died.

"Well, anyway, I can't stay and chat while you eat, but I also bought you a new cereal to go with that soy milk-cousin stuff, since the other breakfast meals have gotten a firm thumbs-down."

"Finally. Hope it's Sugar Crisp... or Cap'n Crunch. Something tasty."

"Here's the box. You decide. Bye."

As she exited the door, she heard him wail, "Flax? This stuff is for barn animals!"

Jason may have been partly correct, but it was also a legitimate healthy cereal for adventurous humans: organic flax plus granola.

Amanda went to the side of her duplex and turned off the breaker for the air conditioner. She had just enough time to get an egg and cheese biscuit — plus coffee — from Hardee's on her way to work.

* * * *

Amanda saw a few other employees in the lobby of her office building, but she had most of her own floor to herself. She recognized one accountant on the far end, but he belonged to a different county department which had a few offices in that corner. She didn't realize that individual ever worked on Sundays. Maybe he was a spy for King Louie.

In her own office, Amanda kicked off her sneakers and read the blog for Day Six.

Curing the Uncommon Man-Cold
Day Six

This was a riot. They weren't maids – one works in a local doctor's office – and they weren't Hispanic. Actually, it was two of my old sorority sisters who both took two semesters of college Spanish. They've each remembered only enough of the lingo to get lost in Juarez once and, on a different occasion, to nearly get arrested in South Miami.

With perfect timing, they arrived as *Marty* was about to consume a contraband candy bar. And they sprayed it! No, not real cleanser… just water with blue food coloring. [I insisted on that because I predicted there was a serious chance he'd try to eat something while they were present. Ha.]

Marty seems to be addicted to the toothpaste with three colorful stripes. He might need a special clinic for detox after he leaves *Missy's* apartment.

I wanted to nip this in the bud… cold turkey. I suggested we switch his toothpaste to that awful stuff they used to sell for sensitive teeth back in the 1960s. It tastes like psoriasis cream, I'm told. However, *Missy* insists we have to let *Marty* hang onto something of comfort. Good grief.

We've noticed some wagering threads which link to our blog. I can't offer any tips. *Marty* has already defied all the odds I could have imagined. He's one desperate individual. But not desperate enough to walk out the door to freedom.

Almira Gulch

Amanda checked the comments section of their primary blog. Betting was high in favor of *Marty's* imminent departure but a small percentage predicted he'd outlast their efforts to oust him.

She checked the tallies on the parallel blogs. Kick-Marty was at 54, Free-Marty was at 32, and Lighten-Missy was at 10. Amanda also spotted a new blog with a new running serial: *Burn the Witch.* That tally was already at five.

Amanda went to the staff lounge to brew some coffee.

She made good progress until 11:00 a.m., when her cell phone rang.

Annoying! Amanda was in the middle of a really boring portion of the grant application and that interruption would force her to read it again. She opened her phone with an aggravated flip. Christine. "Hey." Amanda squeezed in this next part before her older friend could speak. "Before I forget, have you seen the new shadow blog called Burn-Witch?"

"No. Which witch?"

"Well, obviously you, Brunhilda. I told you Jason has been calling you a witch."

"Yeah, you mentioned that. I think it began when I yanked a few of his chest hairs." She chuckled.

"Possibly before. Anyway, when I looked at our blog earlier today, I checked the tallies on the three shadow blogs we've seen so far."

"Right. I also checked them not long ago."

"Well, the new one I just saw today is *Burn the Witch* — 5."

Christine was briefly silent. "Okay, I understand that Jason says I'm a witch, but how did the bloggers figure out what Jason thinks?"

"Didn't you mention that in one of your early posts?"

"Not sure." Christine paused and likely tried to remember. "Anyhow, that's not why I called. I want to meet you at your apartment. Today... noon." She had not visited Jason alone again. "Grab something to eat before you get there. This is another unconventional remedy for Jason, and you might not have an appetite afterwards."

"You promised you wouldn't poison him..."

"No, not poison. The key is for him to think it *could be* poison." Christine started to hang up but then apparently remembered something. "Oh, I think I know how the bloggers figured out the witch reference."

"How?"

"From the blog name I'm using. You know, the *Wizard of Oz* character I told you about. Since Almira Gulch's alter ego in the movie is the Wicked Witch, the blogger must have picked up on that image."

"Maybe." Amanda wasn't convinced. "But I thought I saw it in your blog."

"Whatever. See you at noon."

"Okay. But remind me to tell you about the cat's panther performance this morning at four-something. Even better than we imagined. Diabla deserves an Academy Award." Amanda smiled into her phone. She realized Jason had been whipped.

"Yeah, I'd like to hear that. Noon... your place. Later."

* * * *

When Amanda drove up about an hour later, Christine was waiting outside.

"What's so important that I had to drop what I'm doing at work, on what should be my day off?"

"I shouldn't say. It'll be more effective if you don't know." Christine nodded once. "Just play along."

"That's about all I've been doing for the past six days." Amanda groaned loudly. "Okay." She remembered it was August. "Hold on a second. Let me turn the A/C back on for the next hour." She went to the compressor and flipped up the lever on the breaker box.

They entered together and found Jason on the couch staring at TV snow. This time he had the remote control upside down. It was not evident why he thought that might make a difference.

Since the air conditioning had been off all morning, the windows were wide open and the ceiling fans were at highest speed. Jason also had the HVAC blower motor running, which allowed additional warm air to exit the ceiling vents. He did not appear to notice the slight change in temperature of the air from above, but he turned and waved when they closed the door.

In the distance they could hear Mrs. Yodel in the midst of her unceasing practice.

"Does she do any actual songs? Or just practice Swiss-Austrian scales?" Christine wrinkled her nose.

"Not sure. But I think that might be a song. She probably even wrote it." Jason nodded like a music teacher keeping time with the composition. "As best I can calculate, it goes on like that for about forty-five minutes. Then there's about a ten-minute chorus. Then she returns to the verse."

"You're kidding." Amanda scoffed.

"Why on earth would I make up something like that? The really, truly stupid things of this world are too bizarre to make up." Jason looked both of them over and then addressed his girlfriend. "So, what's up? You off work finally?"

"No, this is kind of a lunch break and then I've got to go back and read more grants." Amanda turned toward her inventive friend.

"It's time for your holistic therapy session and Amanda didn't want me here alone with you. So we have a chaperone." Christine's smile was thin. "She apparently thinks I'm after your bones."

"Maybe so, if you plan to grind them up for a magic potion."

"You're not still holding a grudge about that poultice, are you?"

He lightly touched his right pectoral area. "I'll tell you in a few months when the hair grows back." He pointed toward the small bag Christine was carrying. "What's in there?"

"Are you familiar with that poor old woman who lives near the dump, north of town?"

"The voodoo woman?" He looked around quickly. "You didn't bring that old hag in here, did you?"

"She's not really that ugly." Christine to the defense. "She's just challenged... uh, facially and bodily."

"She's a bona fide hag if I've ever seen one. And she'd still be in jail if she hadn't made pin-cushion dolls of the warden and his wife."

"I understand they're both recovering reasonably well."

Though Amanda had not heard about any of this, she did not inquire.

"Anyway, the voodoo priestess is not here." Christine used her soothing voice. "No need to worry."

"What's in the bag, then?" He pointed again, with more vigor.

"Well, since we both knew a visit from that unfortunate woman would cause you some distress, I just stopped by her place to get something before I came here." Christine held up the small brown sack. It was the kind used for pints in retail liquor stores. "Something special for you."

"You didn't give her my name, did you?"

"Don't believe so. Why?"

"They say the voodoo hag collects names. She puts them in a jar and experiments with different kinds of magic. That's how Kevin's older sister got the shingles. Somebody left her name with the voodoo hag."

"Oh, you don't know that for truth." Amanda couldn't bite her tongue any longer. "Shingles comes from chicken pox virus or something. Anybody can get it, at just about any age over forty."

"Maybe so, but you get it faster if somebody gives your name to the voodoo hag."

Christine held up her hand. "Enough distraction. This has nothing to do with shingles or names. This is about getting you well again, so you'll be back on your feet and out of Amanda's hair. She's overworked, here and at her job. Not much we can do about her job."

Jason again missed the invitation to leave. "You could give King Louie's name to the voodoo hag."

Amanda was distinctly interested in that suggestion.

Christine pulled a small blue bottle from the paper bag. "Custom tonic. Certain to return you to the pink of health."

"I don't wanna be pink!" He sounded six years old.

Christine displayed the container as though it was special vintage.

Jason peered cautiously without touching it. "I don't guess you checked whether Madame Voodoo is authorized by the FDA to dispense medicine."

Christine shook her head. "You shouldn't make fun of her abilities. That kind old lady has cured many an ailing creature in this town."

Jason cringed at the word *creature*.

From her purse Christine pulled a gigantic enameled serving spoon. It was the size used around campfires to stir and serve baked beans to a full troop of starving scouts. Then she opened the small bottle.

"I don't think I can watch this part." Amanda left the couch area and stood near the front door, looking out the window to one side. One eye continued to monitor the drama, however.

On the couch, Jason crossed his arms and tightened his mouth.

"There are stronger remedies we've already discussed." Christine sounded slightly sinister.

"I am not doing that colon thing." His sphincter likely puckered involuntarily. "No way."

Christine switched back to her smoothing voice. "Well, if this works, perhaps the colonic bath won't be necessary, at least not at this stage of your illness." She waved her hand to get him refocused on the tonic. "It's supposed to lower fever, dry up sniffles, make you regular, and improve the constitution."

"My constitution is okay, but my Bill of Rights is in question."

"Well, you still need to be regular." She poured nearly three ounces into the bowl of her enormous spoon. "Shouldn't underestimate the importance of bowels moving in a timely fashion."

"Christine, you're way too concerned about my bowels and colon. Both are doing just fine, without oatmeal enemas."

She put down the bottle and moved the loaded spoon closer to his face. The liquid was dull, but bubbly, with slimy streaks of a greenish tint. *Interesting combination.* "So, basically you're either saying you don't want to get well, in which case you're just taking advantage of my dear friend Amanda." Then

Christine played her trump card. "Or you're simply not man enough to drink this little potion."

Not man enough? That was known to be one of his relatively few triggers. Jason's eyes shone brightly. "Bring it on, witch. I'll drink it with you toe to toe." That line obviously came out before he realized Christine was not there to consume... but solely to administer.

"Better swallow it quickly. Otherwise it sours on the way down." Her eyes sparkled. "Bottoms up." She poured the indescribable liquid into his mouth in one swift motion and then backed away.

Jason drank it in two slow gulps, with considerable revulsion. The defiant shine in his eyes dimmed to a dull glimmer. His face went pale. He clutched at his throat and made the *gerrh* sound a few times. Then he grabbed his lower stomach. He rose from the couch with what little dignity he could muster and hurried toward the hall bathroom.

His loose pajama bottoms fell below mid-crack just about the time he turned the corner.

Amanda returned from the front window. "What was in that potion, anyway?"

Christine smiled. "Cod liver oil, green food coloring, and Alka-Seltzer."

"You got that from the voodoo woman?"

"Of course not. That old hag scares me. I just made this up." Christine paused to listen for Jason's sounds from the bathroom. "Maybe I'll bottle up some more and sell it on the blog."

Amanda started to go check on Jason.

Christine shook her head and touched her friend's elbow. "If he heaves, you don't want to see how it looks coming back up."

Amanda shrugged and stayed put.

"You ever see the old movie *Bell, Book and Candle*, with Kim Novak?"

"Loved it." Amanda nodded.

"Jason's expression just now. He reminded me of James Stewart drinking that disgusting brew which was supposed to remove the spell."

"Good visual image. You should put that in your blog."

"Our blog." Christine's manicured fingertips pointed first at Amanda and then back at herself. "Remember?"

"Yeah, well, our blog — and this entire top secret project — has more potential security leaks than the U.S. Congress. Besides Sunny and Maria, who were needed to manufacture activities here at my apartment, you've evidently briefed at least six people who were involved in bogus service calls of one kind or another. I can't explain how much it freaks me out for that many people to know what we're doing… and blogging!"

Christine didn't bother to mention any other people she'd probably told — who might also play a specific role in their drama.

Amanda went to check on Jason. He had not vomited, but he hovered over the toilet as though he might have to dive in with no notice. Jason didn't see her in the doorway and she backed out discreetly.

Christine left the spoon, bottle and bag on the dining table, a subliminal threat for Jason. "He might need another dose this evening, if he doesn't get better quickly," she said, loudly enough that he could hear. Christine winked at Amanda and left the apartment. There was a bit of spring in her step.

Amanda leaned into the bathroom and told Jason she was leaving. Then she went to the outside compressor and flipped the breaker lever back down.

Chapter 12

Amanda returned to her office to finish at least two more grants on her donated Sunday shift. *Hell Weeks truly were.* Before she resumed reading, she phoned Jason's mother.

Following that call to Margaret and after wading through two more grant applications plus nearly halfway into a third, Amanda left her office and headed home.

She arrived at her apartment about 5:30, after nearly a full Sunday of uncompensated work. She was tired and disgusted. Her disgust had at least two triggers: Hell Weeks at the job and man-cold at her apartment.

Jason didn't even greet Amanda as he came down the short hall holding his left elbow. "You got an Ace bandage or something?"

"What happened now?"

"Banged my elbow."

"Where?"

He pointed to the back side of his elbow.

Her impatience was quite visible.

"Oh, you mean, how. Well, I guess I was lightheaded from lack of food or something. Anyway, I lost my balance on that narrow path from the door to the tiny bed, then I fell over and hit your exercise walker."

"You toppled onto my mom's treadmill? That's way over against the wall!" Amanda started down the hallway. "Come show me."

Jason followed behind, limping. "Well, it was a combination of collisions, actually. Tripped on the narrow path, tried to get my balance on some of those boxes stacked along the sides. Then fell over those and landed next to the tread thing. Tripped on some giant bricks and busted my elbow on the iron rail."

"I think that's aluminum. But I'm sure it hurt anyway."

"Did you know somebody's got bricks stacked in there?"

"It's come to my attention, yes." *Exactly who does he think "somebody" is?* Amanda reached for his arm. "Let me see the injury."

Jason groaned theatrically as she gently examined it.

"Well, it's not what I'd consider a fatal wound, but I do see some bruising. You're wanting to wrap it?"

"Yeah. It's throbbing and stuff."

"Wrapping an elbow just makes it stiff. That might not be the best thing…"

"Do you have a bandage or not?"

"Yeah, somewhere." She eyed him closely. "No reason to get testy."

"I'm in pain here, you know."

"Yeah. Plus the residual sniffles and that deadly temp that lingers around 98.7 degrees."

"And my—" *cough, cough* "—cough."

"Of course." She sighed. "I'll get the Ace thingy."

She returned shortly. "Hold it out." She wrapped his elbow fully extended, tight and stiff. "Can you wiggle your fingers?"

He wiggled. "Yeah."

"If your lower arm starts to turn colors, be sure to loosen that wrap."

Jason looked startled. "What colors?"

"Oh, I'd guess slightly red at first. Then white from reduction of blood flow. Then bluish-black, maybe. Probably solid black next, and then green, I think."

"Green?" His eyes got wide.

"Gangrene. Doesn't it turn green? Or is that a figure of speech? Maybe it stays black. Whatever. If it gets past red and white, just loosen the wrap."

Jason kept wiggling his fingers and watching for color changes.

That could entertain him for hours.

"I can't stay long. I've got an appointment. But I'll be back and then I've got a small committee meeting here around 7:30."

"Here? Another frazzlin' meeting? Does the entire city of Verdeville conduct its business from your apartment? Who is it this time?"

"Not that it's any of your business, Mister Uninvited. But my guests are Maria, Sunny, Christine. That's it."

"Do you realize that you four do everything together? Cards, crops, committees… and that expensive session selling makeup. I'd think you'd all be sick of looking at the same faces everywhere you go!" It came out with more intensity than he'd likely intended.

"Now you're insulting my friends? What next, Jason?"

He groaned and sighed at the same time. "I was hoping we could spend a little time together. You know, talk and stuff."

"We'll have time to talk after you recover and move out. Right now you need to heal and I've got important things going on. There are other circumstances in my life, you know, besides dealing with temporary invalids."

Jason had tuned her out. He was flipping through the paper from that morning. "Doesn't Penney's always have a sale flyer?"

"I've seen lots of their sales advertised."

"Did they stop putting them in the newspaper?"

"I don't figure they run every day. Maybe just Sundays." She was guessing.

"This is Sunday. Today's paper." He held it up as proof. "No flyer."

Her hand moved to her mouth to cover a growing smile. On Christine's advice, Amanda had extracted that mini-catalog sale insert before Jason got up that morning. "Uh, I hate to break it to you, but they stopped selling sporting goods and hardware when you were in elementary school."

"Huh? Oh, ha ha."

"I'm surprised you even noticed the mini-catalogs from that store. Just clothes and linens, mostly."

"Well, I like to keep up with current events." He obviously punted.

"In the realm of fashion and home decor?"

"Cheese Louise. Ask a simple question and you have to go through the Spanish Imposition."

Amanda didn't correct him. She figured his very lightly fevered brain, coupled with frustrated hormones, had skewed his word discernment. "I'll be back before 7:30. If my guests arrive, open the door and then dash back to the guestroom. I don't want them shocked by whatever shows above the saggy waistband of your jammies."

She left without waiting for a whiny reply.

* * * *

Amanda had met Jason's mother on several occasions and had visited in her home at least twice. She liked the 62-year-old widow who seemed considerably younger. Mrs. Stewart was attractive, slender, and nearly always dressed like she expected company. She tended flowers and other plants, both inside and out, and kept a clean house. Margaret had regular activities with friends her own age and participated in most of her church's functions. She also read a lot and possessed a considerable amount of common sense.

The Mayfield Avenue neighborhood was what is often called settled: established in the 1960s and nicely laid out with tall and lush trees on generously-sized lots. Amanda admired the pretty flower beds and welcoming porch of the ranch style, about forty years old.

Margaret opened the door before Amanda even knocked. "Come on in. You must be exhausted." She motioned to a living room chair. "It's been a full week now, hasn't it?"

Amanda nodded and sat. She was slightly surprised that Jason's mother was so sympathetic. "It's been pretty rough. A lot worse than his alleged illness in January."

"Is Jason behaving worse, or is it because of your stress at work?"

"Not sure. I guess Jason's about the same, but... this probably sounds awful, I guess, but I don't find him nearly as endearing as he seemed in January."

Margaret smiled. "From what I recall, his previous cold wasn't all that charming to you at the time."

"No. But we'd just gotten serious a couple of months before January. So our relationship was still pretty new."

"A honeymoon period of sorts. You had more tolerance then. More patience."

"Yeah, I guess I sort of enjoyed feeling needed then. But now it feels different, dealing with a needy man." Amanda stopped suddenly. "I'm sorry. I probably shouldn't say that to Jason's mother."

"That's okay. I know Jason pretty well myself. He can be very needy at times. He was my youngest, you know."

"Well, that's partly why I'm here, to get your input on some things. But first I need to tell you that I haven't exactly been Nurse Nancy, tending to his every whim. In fact, I've been more like Stern Stella — trying to make him miserable enough to go home to his own apartment."

"Oh, I already know. Christine called me early this past week and I've been reading her blog since the second day." Margaret chuckled. "That Jason surely is stubborn. Most men would've escaped by the fourth day, if not sooner. Even if they had to crawl out a second-story window. But he's already lasted six full days."

So Christine had also told Margaret... which brought the total to at least eleven people who knew about the secret project. "I didn't realize you already knew about the strategy Christine devised. You know, without her help, I'd have been the one jumping out of windows by now." Amanda sighed. "Christine's Scare-Cure is pretty comprehensive."

"Jason brought this on himself. When you first stated you didn't want him to stay over, he blew it by insisting. So, in my opinion, he's getting what he deserves. Men can be so dense at times."

"You don't think I'm being too hard on him?"

"Oh, I'd call it tough love of a sort." Margaret was thoughtful for a moment. "You know, I had to do that with his daddy."

"All this elaborate scheming of Christine's?"

"Oh, no. Not nearly this elaborate." Margaret's expression softened, as if with a fond memory.

"So what did you do?

"Well, a lot of these far-flung strategies of Christine's weren't even in play back then. You know, no Internet and such. So back then, I had to search for the simplest elements."

Amanda was imagining a leather harness or a muzzle. "What'd you use?"

"Hot water."

"You scalded your husband?"

Margaret smiled. "Oh, no. Just the opposite. I blew out the pilot light on our old hot water heater and told Henry it was broken. I flat out lied... said the technician was swamped and couldn't come until sometime the next week."

"Well, that sounds okay as far as it went. So he's got no hot water to shave or bathe." Amanda was puzzled. "How did that cure him of colds?"

"Well, you see, I stopped bathing, too." Margaret laughed. "No deodorant, no makeup... and I didn't shave my legs."

Amanda smiled broadly. "So guys with man-colds got horny in the 1960s and 70s also?"

"Of course. Even up through the 1990s. But I surely didn't want to get close to all that mucous and such, so I made certain he wouldn't want to be around me, either."

"Pretty drastic."

"Drastic times." Margaret nodded. "I needed him up and out, and back to work. Sympathy and sex weren't going to get him moving in the right direction."

"So your cold water strategy worked?"

"Henry was off the couch by the third day." Margaret's hand made a quick sideways *whoosh*. "By the way, there was a bonus in that little episode."

Amanda looked puzzled.

"I had a birthday later that same month. Henry got me a new water heater."

"Very thoughtful and personal gift." Amanda rolled her eyes.

"Oh, that was fine with me. We didn't have all that much money back then and I really wanted a new water heater. That old one was secondhand — only held about twenty gallons and the burner unit was on its last legs. You couldn't wash dishes and take a bath in the same evening unless you waited a couple of hours." Margaret chuckled again. "Yeah, my Henry realized he didn't ever want me looking and smelling like that again."

They talked a bit more about Jason and about flowers. Margaret offered to make some tea, but Amanda had to hurry home for the evening meeting Christine had scheduled.

* * * *

Curing the Uncommon Man-Cold
Day Seven

During the afternoon, we had a team supposedly shampooing the carpets in *Missy's* apartment. All they really did was wet the floor with spray bottles and then roll a noisy shop-vacuum over it. The result was that *Marty* had to tiptoe on paper towels spaced along the edges of the rooms and hall.

For the evening activity, *Missy* hosted a publicity committee meeting for an upcoming program similar to the national effort called *No Child Left Behind*. This particular session might have been called *no snacks left behind*, however, because we took everything with us, including the trash. I smuggled out the remaining oatmeal raisin cookies. [This Scare-Cure is frightening my diet as much as anything else!]

Yet he's not sick. All *Marty* has to do is walk out. What on earth is keeping him there? *Missy* and I both agree he's stubbornly holding out for some TLC, but surely it HAS to be more complex than that. Doesn't it?

All that evening and night, the apartment A/C ran again, but *Missy* had closed the vent in the guestroom back on Day Five. Ha!

Missy phoned me with some of today's developments. At present, *Marty* looks like an ambulance victim. I guess I forgot to mention that yesterday his right arm was in a makeshift sling. He just told *Missy* that he threw out his shoulder somehow, but we know it's because he was dumping that dissolved candy bar in the trash can!

The injury today involved his left elbow. Claims he tripped on a brick and careened into a treadmill. I'll probably have to rent a wheelchair before this case is over.

What an actor! Someday there might be an award for the best 'sick' performance of a cold victim. And *Marty* should win, hands down, since he's been clever enough to add the exaggerated injury spectrum. I predict, very soon, many of these victims will sustain such injuries and develop a limp just like *Marty's*.

He has seized on the previously missing component of the entire phenomena: *visually* manifested pain! Most of the rather uninventive man-cold sufferers of previous generations typically relied on manufactured sneezes and fakey coughs. But having Ace bandages and arm slings solidifies the sympathy factor. He's brilliant!

With his left elbow wrapped tightly — fully extended — and his right forearm in a pretend sling, I don't know how he manages the normal bathroom functions. But let's not contaminate our brain cells with such images.

By the end of today, Day Seven, *Marty* has survived six full days of this Scare-Cure. No sign of leaving yet.

Check back tomorrow evening for the report of my best gimmick so far.

Almira Gulch.

Amanda sighed heavily. Since this carpet cleaning team likely had two members, the new total was now at least thirteen individuals who knew about her supposedly secret project! That assumed the woman who conducted the make-over session was completely out of the loop.

Chapter 13

August 17 (Monday)

For the patient's breakfast Amanda brought out the hemp and flax granola cereal boxes, plus the artificial soy milk cousin.

Jason kept his distance from all three containers.

"So what are you going to do? Just suck down another half tube of toothpaste?"

"I thought I'd take a few swigs of that prune stuff. The nasty taste kinda grows on you. Plus, it's keeping my insides cleaned out, so your witch friend won't keep harping about colon sweeps."

"Whatever." She returned to her bedroom to finish getting ready for work.

Jason did not appear to notice the air was comfortable after the overnight cooling by the conditioning unit. In a few minutes, Amanda would flip the breaker again and the temperature would rise dramatically as the day went forward.

That day's strange remedy — carefully choreographed by devious Christine — was a morning treatment instead of midday, as the others had been. It was also the first therapy administered by Amanda without Christine's presence or apparent involvement.

Jason sat on the couch and looked for the TV remote. Perhaps he figured a few hours of snow and white noise might calm his starvation agitation.

"I have to leave soon, but there's time for today's alternative therapy treatment."

As she completed that sentence, Jason covered his right nipple reflexively. "No more chest hair yanking."

"Nothing to do with your chest."

Jason relaxed slightly.

"Christine discovered an Oriental treatment which focuses on the pelvis — the breeding ground for life, but also the landfill for germs. Especially the cold virus. So it's necessary to draw out the impurities. She said I'm supposed to ask if you agree to try this therapy."

If Jason had been listening to many of those words, he would have realized they were practically gibberish. But apparently all he heard was the noun *pelvis*. So his brain switched from thought activity to sensation processes. He clearly got excited and all of Amanda's explanation was likely a fog of yada-yada. He should have listened more carefully. Jason mustered only a single-word reply: "Agreed." And he nodded a lot.

"Stand up and pull down your PJs."

With the pitiful sprung-out elastic barely keeping his pajama bottoms up to his hip bones, all Jason had to do was shrug twice for them to drop to his knees. They did. He stood there looking at his uncovered pelvic region. "Boy, I'm glad we're finally getting to the root of the problem... my illness, I mean. Good thing your friend finally located that article about pelvis impurities. I saw something about that on the Discovery Channel last month, I think."

"Would you rather sit or stand?"

Jason's legs began to tremble. "Sit. Don't want to keel over, you know."

"Wait. Put this towel down. Don't want to get anything on the couch."

"Sure. Towel." Jason's vocabulary seemed limited to one- and two-syllable words and no complete sentences. It was similar to his state after the panther dream, though clearly prompted by passion rather than fear.

"Ready?"

Jason nodded eagerly. He'd obviously been ready for nearly eight days.

"Might ought to close your eyes."

"Okay."

"Let me hold your hand."

He nodded and extended his right hand.

From a mostly concealed container, Amanda extracted a large scoop of petroleum jelly and glopped it onto his hand.

"What?" Jason opened his eyes when the jelly hit his palm.

She clamped Jason's hand over his pelvic region.

The patient winced and groaned when his own hand made contact. "What the creepin' crud?"

"To draw out the impurities from that garbage dump for germs that's inside your pelvis. Just like I said."

"Wait a minute!" His eyes began watering. "Hey, this stuff burns!"

"It's mentholated, silly. You can't expect the regular kind to draw out any impurities."

"But my crotch is on fire!"

"That's just the ointment working." Very businesslike. "Now you can't touch that area for 24 hours." Amanda reached over to the table. "Here's some oven mitts to remind you. Hands off." She went to the sink to wash her hands.

"Hey! What about...?"

Amanda tuned him out as she grabbed her purse and departed. She wished she'd had a camera to capture the expression on his face. *If this isn't tough love... nothing is.*

* * * *

It was the beginning of Amanda's second horrid week of the annual Crisis Phase for her grant application evaluations.

The wall clock showed 8:11. Amanda was a few minutes late arriving at her office, but King Louie wasn't there to notice — he usually rolled in around 8:45. That gave her time to read the blog for Day Seven. Christine's Scare-Cure had indeed gone viral.

She read through the recently posted comments. Up to that point, bloggers either posted appreciation for sharing the info on this new treatment or they merely expressed pleasure at seeing *Marty* get what was coming to him. Of course, *Marty* had several defenders as well.

But with another day's comments, a subtle shift appeared. Bloggers were beginning to suggest that *Missy* and *Almira* had taken this project way too far. To summarize the views of the dozen or so new comments, it was clear they agreed with the initial concept, but thought it should have ended — one way or the other — after about three days. For it to stretch into eight days (and counting) was on the verge of pathological, they said. Nobody explained what pathological meant in this context. But it didn't sound good.

"Has it gone too far already?" Amanda pondered out loud. "Is it my fault for pushing? Or Jason's fault for resisting?" *Not sure.* Maybe both. Maybe it was all Christine's fault for originating the concept of curing the uncommon man-cold.

Some things in nature were not meant to be tinkered with. Perhaps this illness was one of those taboos. But why should Amanda suffer? *Indeed.* Related question: how much should Jason suffer? *Hmm.* How much would Jason endure? And why?

Amanda read a short piece of Christine's recent addition. It was difficult to concentrate on the central blog for some reason.

She clicked on the shadow blogs to check current tallies. *Kick Marty Out* — *85...* that had gained nearly thirty votes overnight. *Free Marty* — *46...* up more than a dozen. *Lighten Up, Missy!* — *22...* more than doubled since yesterday. Then she clicked on the Burn-Witch link. It had increased nearly six-fold overnight! *Burn the Witch* — *29.* Christine's persona was not exactly popular, but interest in her demise was showing the most dramatic vote increases.

Amanda logged off and went to the staff room to see if coffee was brewing. Two co-workers stood near the coffeemaker discussing the exciting new man-cold blog!

"Yeah, everybody's buzzing about it." Gayle yawned.

Joan lowered her voice. "My sister says she knows that guy Marty."

They'd both seen her walk in, but didn't immediately move from the appliance to let her have access. Was that a snub? *Not sure.* Amanda figured some of this section's women hated her simply because her office had a door.

"So who does your sister say that Marty guy is?" Amanda slightly raised her cup to communicate her peaceful intention. In offices, sometimes women formed momentary alliances to briefly exclude other females. Typically these would shift and vary, but there was always someone offending somebody, no matter how unintentionally. Often it was overtly deliberate. This particular episode seemed mostly a matter of them staking a temporary claim on the coffeemaker turf. Obviously, no encroachments were welcome while they were speaking to each other.

The co-workers parted to give Amanda access to the coffee. Evidently she was on their "conditionally accepted" list. For that particular day, anyway.

"Hi, Amanda." Joan waved half-heartedly. "Oh, Sis wouldn't tell me. Just said she's pretty certain."

"She's just guessing." Gayle contributed even though she didn't know Joan's sister.

"I've seen that blog." Amanda filled her cup halfway. "It could be in Colorado or Maryland."

"Or even in Nashville." Joan, eagerly.

"How could anybody tell who it is?" Amanda only pressed the matter because she knew so little about how blogs function.

Joan answered first. "Well, my sister says those computer wonks can run some sort of trace or something that backtracks to the originating hub."

"Hub?" Gayle winced as though the word were painful.

"Whatever you call the things that route Internet traffic. It's a weird number system with lots of decimals. I don't know. Like I said, only the computer geeks can do it."

"I didn't know they could track a blog." Amanda. "Somebody told me the FBI and CIA couldn't even trace it."

Joan chuckled. "Not without a warrant. But if you get cozy enough with a brainy computer geek, he'll hack you into the president's Twitter."

"I wouldn't want anywhere near his twitter." Gayle frowned.

Amanda's hand shook slightly as she took a half-hearted sip of coffee. "So, if you get really friendly with a geek and he does that tracking stuff, you could actually find out who runs those blogs? I mean, whatever subject any blog was about."

"Sure, I guess." Joan shrugged. "Only, you'd have to want to know really bad… to be willing to get that friendly with the wonk guy."

"I wouldn't," said Gayle. "Besides, it wouldn't be just any geeky guy who could unmask the blogger's Internet footprints. It'd be the creepy one with the most pimples, the hairiest warts, and the ugliest belly button."

Joan looked slightly astonished. "Would you have to see his belly button?"

"Nobody would want to know that bad." Amanda tried to smile, but it felt more like she was gritting her teeth.

"Well, no matter where this blog takes place, I hope they fix that Marty guy real good." Joan obviously had experience with man-colds. "This is the first website I've ever seen that gives us any hope at all."

"I don't know," Gayle added. "I'm hoping that poor man just leaves her apartment before they do anything else to him. He's suffered enough."

Amanda weighed in. "They've been pretty tough on him, but some people say he deserves it because he insisted on staying even though she told him it was Hell Week." *Oops!*

"They have Hell Week there, too?" Gayle looked puzzled.

Joan had answers for nearly everything. "I guess everybody deals with budgets or something about this time of year."

"Not to mention teachers," Amanda added, "heading back to the classroom about this time." *Nice save.*

"Yeah, Missy is probably a teacher." Gayle sighed. "I used to want to be a teacher, but I realized I can't stand children."

"Good thing you figured that out early." Joan nodded.

"Oh, it took me a couple years of teaching before I figured it out."

Amanda saw an opportunity to depart while they were established on a different subject, so she said her goodbyes.

When she got back to her office, Amanda closed the door. Icy sweat had formed in her armpits. Besides blabbing to so many other people, Christine evidently had overlooked that little loophole in the blog's security: if you sleep with the ugliest computer geek in Tennessee, he can hack the blog back to its source just to show off for you. *Danged witch!*

About midmorning Amanda's cell phone rang.

"You got a minute to talk?" Christine.

"Yeah, but first I got something to say. Your fail-safe security on the blog has even more holes... besides the dozen-plus people you've told or involved. Get this, Christine: I was talking to two women this morning who practically ran the Internet blog lines back to your house already."

"Impossible. They're bluffing."

"I don't think so. They said not everybody can do it, but it's a specialty of those ultra-turbo computer geeks."

"That's a gross generalization... they're pulling your leg. Besides, who'd be so curious that they'd cozy up to an ultra-nerd?" Apparently Christine satisfied herself on the matter. "Anyway, that's not why I called. We need to discuss this evening's plans."

Amanda wasn't through griping about security flaws, but her fatigue factor trumped the other complaint. "More evening plans? I don't think..." Amanda heard a sound and then looked at her cell phone screen. "Hold on, I've got another call. It's Jason."

"No! Don't take his call. Make him wait at least an hour."

"Why? Maybe it's an emergency."

"The only emergency with his supposed sickness is when he needs new batteries for the remote control." Christine always spoke with authority even when she had no idea what she was talking about. "This is no emergency. Trust me, he just wants to wheedle you for some food or booze or something."

"Okay, I'll keep him waiting for a bit. Now, what's happening at my place tonight? I could really use an evening off."

"We're going to carve a cushaw."

"A what-shaw?" Amanda was clueless.

"Cushaw. It's in the squash family, sort of. But probably the branch of the squash family that's used steroids for five generations."

"Huh?"

"Picture something like a yellow crookneck squash." Christine was probably looking right at it. "Now, the market lady said those usually weigh about three-quarters of a pound or so. Now imagine one about 65 times that size! They grow to be nearly four feet tall and can reach up to 50 pounds. Our bad boy weighs in at about 45 pounds."

"That's not a squash!" Amanda's voice was slightly too loud. "That's one of the pod people!"

"Whatever. Anyhow, we're going to carve it tonight, at your place."

"Are you sure it's even edible?"

"Of course." Christine's authority again. "People have been eating cushaw for years... from Louisiana, all over the southeast, and up here through Tennessee. Even as far as southern Kentucky."

"Why? Did they run out of the normal-sized squash?"

"Don't tell me you've never carved and cooked a cushaw." Christine spoke as though it was a routine requirement to pass high school home ec.

"The last time I had to feed a hundred hungry people, we just went to the pizza buffet. What use would I have for 45 pounds of cushaw meat? Or whatever you call the stuff inside it."

"You won't net out that much inside stuff because the rind is so thick and heavy." Christine paused. "Have you got a chainsaw?"

"Chainsaw? What?" Too loud again. "Are you planning to cut a big notch in the doorway to get this atomic squash into my apartment?"

"As if. The saw is to cut through his heavy old rind. These bad boys have really tough exteriors, or so I'm told."

"Well, you aren't bringing a chainsaw in my apartment." Amanda put her foot down. "The lease specifically prohibits any type of motorized logging equipment."

"Okay, I'll bring a camp saw and an axe. Chainsaws are hard to start anyhow." She spoke as though she used one every weekend. "One more thing — I'll need help bringing him in."

"Bringing who in?"

"The cushaw." Christine apparently strained to sound patient. "I'll need help to get him in from my car."

"You said *him* again. Does the cushaw type of titanic squash actually incorporate gender?"

"Very funny. No, I took a marker and drew a guy's face on him. With one of my old wigs on his green-and-tan head, he looks a bit like a crookneck hippy. And I named him, of course."

"Of course. So, what did you name this sacrificial victim, scheduled to expire at my apartment tonight as part of your sinister campaign to terrorize my allegedly ill boyfriend?"

"Well, his name is Jason, of course." Christine cackled like she was practicing for a role in *Macbeth* — *Double, double toil and trouble. Fire burn, and cauldron bubble.* "We're gonna scare your boyfriend right out of his cold."

"Scare *him*? Heck, you're scaring me!"

"See you at seven. Bye."

Amanda put down her cell phone and closed her eyes. Despite being apprehensive of her scheming friend's devious mania, she thought it would be nice symmetry for Jason to meet his own Cousin Cushaw tonight.

She rested her forehead on the desk. Amanda briefly considered pounding her head a few times in hopes of clearing up her confusion and exhaustion. But she didn't.

At that point her corpulent Yankee boss lumbered in and plopped down in her visitor chair with a loud whoosh of exertion. "Another nap?"

Hairy hell.

"You got those second dozen appraisals done yet?" His New York accent was especially grating when Louis demanded something.

Amanda sighed. "No, it usually takes a full hour or more to draft each evaluation, and that's after about three hours of reading. I'm not much farther along than when you asked me at 10:45."

Louis seemed unaware that thoughtful assessments actually consumed time. It didn't take him very long to sort Amanda's completed recommendations into three piles: yes, maybe, and no. He looked pointedly at the cell phone on her desk and shook his head. His toupee shifted ever so slightly. "We need at least a dozen more apps with preliminary sorting by my meeting tomorrow morning."

"Well, if somebody was helping me, it'd go a lot faster."

When the subject of assistance arose — even during the office's annual Hell Weeks — King Louie quickly lost interest. He just grunted.

Louis stared at her for a few moments, pried himself from the chair, and finally left her office. He turned the opposite way of his own refuge, so maybe there was another employee on his hourly circuit.

By the time her boss left, it had been about forty minutes since Jason had tried to reach Amanda on the phone. She called him back. "Sorry, I was tied up in a meeting. What's up?"

"Uh, this might sound strange, but have you seen my pants anywhere?"

"Well, you remember they were stained real bad, so you asked me to get them cleaned."

"Stained? How? When? Uh, I don't recall..." Suddenly, Jason sounded terribly old and very tired.

"Memory loss is fairly normal. You were probably light-headed at the time. You know, a half a degree of fever can play havoc with your mind."

"Oh. Yeah. Well, I kind of remember something about britches. I don't know."

"What do you need slacks for? Those ratty old jammies with the elastic all sprung out of the waistband — aren't they stylish enough?"

"Naw, I need pants."

"I can bring anything you need, if it's on your diet. You checked yourself in to Amanda Hospital, remember?" she explained patiently. "I'll get your pants from the cleaners when you're ready to go home. You won't need them 'til then. Unless you're ready to go home now. In which case, I'll drop what I'm doing here at work and drive straight over to the cleaners. Are you going home now?"

"Uh, no. I'm still sick, you know." He coughed twice as proof.

"Of course. Then no need for trousers. I don't want any more clutter to deal with in my tiny apartment."

"Yeah, this place is pretty small. It seemed a lot bigger before I got sick."

"That half degree of fever is distorting your perception." She smiled into the phone and wondered if he could sense it.

"I guess. Still, a man ought to know where his pants are."

"But if you're not leaving, why do you need them?"

"Oh, nothing. I just wanted to step outside for a minute. You know, speak to the neighbors for a bit. Be neighborly." He sounded so pitiful. "I thought it'd do me good to get some fresh air. Walk outside a few steps." He was a terrible liar.

"While you're getting your strength back, you mean."

"Uh, yeah. That's about it."

"So you saw a neighbor come home with groceries and you figure you can sweet-talk them out of a snack. Isn't that really it?"

He broke open like an overripe cushaw. "Amanda, I was prepared to jump Missus Yodel as she reached her stoop. If I didn't worry about becoming somebody's *girlfriend* in prison, I would have grabbed her right then and eaten the top half of the first bag I came to. I'm starving!"

"Well, we have a special treat for supper tonight. I think you can eat as much as you want."

"How about a rack of baby-back ribs, with baked beans, stuffed potatoes, Cole slaw, maybe an ear of corn, and some ice cream?"

She admired his persistence, as well as his optimistic appetite. "I'm afraid it's not quite that sumptuous."

"What? More acorn juice? More egg cousin tofu smushed crud?"

"Nothing of the kind. You've eaten squash before, haven't you?"

"Oooh, squash. Yeah, I can do squash. 'Course, I don't eat it when I have access to real food, but in an emergency situation like this, yeah, I could groove on some squash. Uh, how are you cooking it? Steamed, boiled... oh, fried in batter? That would be super. Absolutely turbo. Batter-fried squash."

"Now, I didn't say any such thing. I just asked if you'd ever eaten squash. This isn't my meal preparation anyway. Actually, I've never prepared this particular dish before. It's kind of a cousin to squash."

"More cousins?"

"This is a specialty handed down through generations in Christine's family."

Jason groaned loudly. "I should have known. If she's behind this, it'll probably be a squash made of hummus, or some gluten-free, organic sprout cluster. Maybe soy-generated squash... or worse. That witch!"

"Be careful what you wish for."

"Huh?"

"If you think Christine is a witch, it might come true."

Jason paused and likely considered the implications. "Uh, anyway, I can't find my credit cards or car keys, either."

"Why do you need car keys? You don't have any pants."

Heavy sigh... with a moan mixed in. "Never mind."

"Okay, bye." Amanda smiled briefly after she flipped her phone closed. Christine's harebrained Scare-Cure strategy might actually be working. Jason had no medical symptoms of a cold, not even a sniffle. Out of sheer stubbornness, he was hanging on to the notion of being sick. Maybe the upcoming cousin cushaw episode would cure him over the edge.

Chapter 14

After work, around 5:40, Amanda reached her apartment — dead tired. Mondays at her office were always arduous, even during regular weeks of the year. But during these crunch weeks, after toiling all weekend, a Monday was agonizing. Before entering, she went around the side of her duplex and activated the air conditioner, then kicked off her heels while closing the door.

Amanda dropped her purse to the floor with a loud *whump* and collapsed in the chair near the entry. Something was beneath her buttocks. She leaned left and reached under her bottom with her right hand. A flattened tube of toothpaste! "Jason!"

"What?" He had just arrived from the hall bathroom.

"Is this a subtle reminder that you need more toothpaste?"

"Uh, yeah. I was too weak from hunger to write a note." He coughed for punctuation.

"Oh, come off it! You're not too weak to click that remote for hours at a time!"

"Cheese Louise. Bad day at work?"

"Don't even get me started." It took considerable effort for Amanda to rise from the chair. "I'm going to nap for about twenty minutes. I'd suggest you don't even breathe too loud while I'm asleep."

— — —

Jason stepped aside as she walked past. *Mondays are her moody days.*

About thirty minutes later, Amanda emerged from the bedroom with tousled hair and badly wrinkled skirt and blouse. It was 6:15. Obviously still groggy, she initially trudged the wrong direction. Then she turned toward the guestroom, where she retrieved a pair of jeans from a small stack of clean, folded clothes on a large box. She returned to her own bedroom and soon reemerged in those jeans plus a tee-shirt which advertised a past county fair.

Jason recognized it as the sole honorarium for Amanda's efforts in securing federal grant monies for the fairgrounds last year. He hoped she was no longer as grouchy as when she'd first arrived home, and Jason ventured a tentative question to test the water. "Going somewhere?"

Amanda groaned. "No, it's yet another event *here* this evening. I think I'll have to move out of my own apartment to get any rest or peace."

"What other event could there be? You've had crops, cards, committees, plus Christine... and those are just the ones beginning with C. What else could you possibly do here tonight?"

Finally beginning to shake off her groggy exhaustion, Amanda surprised him by smiling very slightly. "Well, in fact, it actually is another C activity." She looked like she had a secret. "This one's a big surprise."

"I used to like surprises, I think. But now they scare the crud out of me, especially if Christine's involved. Will she be here?"

"Christine, Sunny, and I'm not sure who else. Maybe Maria." Amanda looked around the apartment's main rooms. "And I've got just about half an hour to straighten up." She started in the hall bathroom as Jason watched from a safe distance. At the lavatory Amanda found more tiny black crumbs — a small sprinkling near the edge of the counter. "Jason, what are these?" She pointed dramatically as he shuffled closer to the door and peered in.

Jason merely shrugged.

"No more B.S. about black mold creeping out of the air conditioning ductwork. There's no regular ducts in this bathroom. Just exhaust." She touched it again and sniffed it gently. "We've already established it's not black cocaine. And it's not ordinary house dirt."

Jason hadn't realized he'd left any crumbs — he'd been very careful. "Maybe it's ground-up acorn stuff, from that allshitz coffee you made." *Good answer.*

"Acorn grindings for ersatz coffee would be brownish, not black."

"I can't figure it out, either." He shrugged again, with extra movement for effect.

"Well, it wasn't here when I left for the office this morning. Has anyone else been in my apartment today? Anyone wearing clothing covered in tiny black crumbs?"

"No. Those carpet cleaners came in yesterday. But they didn't go in the bathrooms or kitchen... that's tile. Just the carpet areas. Oh, speaking of, they said they wouldn't clean that narrow path in the bedroom where I'm staying. Too hazardous, and not even wide enough for their machine."

Amanda's expression showed she was clearly tired of complaints about clutter in her guestroom. "Nobody else come inside today?"

He shook his head, thinking the motion might somehow prompt his brain to concoct an answer.

"Then what are these tiny black crumbs? And who's leaving them?"

"How about ants? You know, they carry grit and stuff. Maybe black ants carrying black grit to a black ant hill somewhere." It was a valiant effort.

"And their only path in this imaginary black universe is over my guest bathroom vanity counter?" She narrowed her eyes. "Nice try, Doctor Science." Amanda scanned the bathroom like she had x-ray glasses. "You know, I'm going to figure this out eventually."

Jason shrugged again, but with scarcely detectable movement. It was his attempt at nonchalance.

Amanda swept the tiny black crumbs into the wastebasket and moved on to straighten up the other public rooms before her friends arrived.

Jason did his best to stay out of her way. Difficult, with a female whirlwind in a small apartment. At about 6:55 p.m., he heard the first noises outside the apartment door.

Amanda instructed him to remain in the guestroom since he didn't have any trousers. He emitted a token whimper, shuffled down the hall, then shut the door and listened closely.

Jason didn't normally listen to girl talk — it irritated those microscopic hair-like antennae attached to the epithelial cells of his inner ear. But this evening, he tuned in carefully because he thought he might be able to tell which kind of cookie was being crunched, or what type chips being dipped. Could he identify a beverage by the sound of its sip? He intended to try.

Even over the distance of the short hall and through the guestroom door, voices from the main spaces were fairly loud and moderately clear. But he'd need to strain to discern the sounds of food and beverage consumption. Jason heard enthusiastic greetings from the front door. Then sounds like someone bumping against a wall. Also, maybe somebody stumbled. Some urgent breathing and grunting... like shoppers carrying the largest dog food bag from Discount World. Then distinct dialog again.

"Do you have a shovel?" Christine's voice.

"Didn't you bring one?" asked Amanda.

"Why do we need a shovel?" Maybe Maria... possibly Sunny. Funny how similar their voices were at times, especially from down the hall and through a door.

"To bury the innards." Christine again. "Too messy for the garbage can and there'll be too much of it."

Whoa! Jason began assembling the words *shovel* and *bury* and *innards.*

"How do we get inside him?" Definitely Sunny.

"That's what the saw is for, doofus." Christine the witch.

"This might take an axe," said Amanda. "With a real thick hide, you can't get a saw groove started."

Then something else which Jason couldn't quite make out.

Double dang! He'd put together more words, including *saw* and *axe*. Jason pinched the apprehensive skin on his forearm. It wasn't thick. What were they discussing out there? Uh, *who* were they talking about? *Well, whoever it is... he's about to be murdered!* Jason focused again on the kitchen voices.

"Who's that?" Amanda must have pointed to someone.

"Little Herman." Christine's voice.

Herman must be the victim!

"I thought we were doing Jason tonight," Amanda replied.

Did she say doing? Normally that word had a positive connotation for Jason. But with all this kitchen talk of saws, axes, shovels — not to mention burying innards — it was a drastically different effect than those words formerly conveyed.

Another comment Jason couldn't pick up. *Maybe Herman pleading for his life in muffled agony.* He was probably gagged!

"We do Jason later. Practice on Little Herman first." Christine's voice. "Once we get the cuts right, then we'll crack open Jason."

"Wha...?" Jason felt ice inside his intestines. All this time he'd been yakking about Christine being a witch who wanted to kill him. Now, in Amanda's apartment on this Monday night, his predictions had come true! *Christine IS a witch!* Would Christine really gut him and chop off his head? *Dang right she would!*

But would Amanda allow Christine to go to that extreme? While Jason considered that question, he heard more dialog from the kitchen.

"Keep him still!" Christine's voice.

"I've got his neck," said Maria.

"Don't let him roll over!" cautioned Amanda. "I don't want Little Herman's innards all over my floor! Keep him above the drop cloth!" That answered Jason's earlier question. Amanda was right in the middle of poor Herman's grisly murder. And they'd already announced their plan: once they finished off Herman, they were coming for Jason!

What could he do? How could he escape the apartment? Couldn't fit out that bedroom window even if he could squeeze through all the hazardous clutter to reach it. If he tried to run past the plotters, he'd probably trip on his pajama bottoms and those women would whack and hack him to death, right there in the hallway!

The carpet cleaners had come too early. Christine had probably intended to schedule them for *after* these brutal murders!

More sounds from the kitchen. Not voices. These were grunts and groans. Sawing and whacking!

Where were his pants? His keys? How fast could he run with one hand holding up his pajama bottoms? Was there any other escape route besides right through that gaggle of murderous females with sharp implements and a startlingly detached attitude about vivisection?

No!

Jason couldn't stand it any more. He dialed 9-1-1 and rushed out of the bedroom holding his phone in the air. "Don't kill Little Herman! I've called the cops."

The four ladies at the dining table stopped their strenuous activity and stared. Jason's pajama bottoms with the busted elastic were precariously close to revealing *his* "little Herman".

Amanda replied, "Called the cops for what? Supper?"

"Mutilation is more like it. I heard what you're doing to Herman. Where is the little feller?"

"I'm afraid your boyfriend's fever is back." Christine turned to Amanda. "Check if he's back over 99 degrees again." Then, to Jason, "You better give me that phone."

Jason always gave his phone to scary witches brandishing sharp knives.

Christine rolled her eyes as she took the device with her free hand. "Hello?"

Amanda pointed to the small crookneck squash named Little Herman and to the giant wigged cushaw named Jason.

Jason staggered at the sight of the entity bearing his name. "What the creepin' crud is *that*?"

"A cushaw," Amanda answered. "It's in the broader family of the squash. Sort of a cousin. Like I told you before." It was about four feet tall with a base roughly three feet in diameter. It had smooth skin like a watermelon — not rough like squash or pumpkin. Its color was a unique pattern of light green with light tan stripes.

Cousins will be the death of me! Jason nervously eyed the sharp implements. Four women… four weapons. He sputtered with no syllabication.

Amanda continued. "His rind is especially tough, so it sometimes takes really heavy duty tools to split him open and carve out his insides. I wouldn't let her bring the chainsaw inside."

"Uh, I thought you were killing somebody. Dismemberment. Herman. Cannibalism." He touched his midsection. "Then me."

— — —

Amanda monitored Jason's composure while Christine continued on the phone with the 9-1-1 dispatcher. "Yeah, it's just a mistake, Hazel. We're at Amanda's making supper. The guy who called? No, he doesn't even live here. Nope, I don't think we're in any danger. He just came down the hall with one hand on his phone and his other hand clutching his jammies. Those ratty things were on their way down to his knees. No… didn't really frighten us. Amanda knows him. Yeah, kind of a nut case, but we try to let him think he's mainstream. Nah, I don't want to file any charges. Not yet, anyhow." She rolled her eyes for the benefit of her companions. "Huh? We were trying to carve up a cushaw. C-U-S-H-A-W. It's like a really large cousin to the squash. Anyway, it takes a lot to get through his thick rind. Right, just like a man." She winked at her colleagues. "Well, anyway, the caller here… see, he's *off-work-sick*." Christine made air quotes with her free hand. "No, nothing fatal, but he's awful poorly. You see, he's got a man-cold. Yeah, I know. Completely out of commission for two weeks. Well, our patient is improving rapidly, just this evening. Might set a new standard. Yeah, I'll let you know how it goes with the cushaw. Bye."

Jason appeared stunned. "You know the 9-1-1 dispatcher?" In the movies, it was never anyone you knew.

"I know that one. Hazel and I used to play dolls together in grade school." Christine handed back his phone.

Jason received the device with two fingertips, as though it were radioactive... then shook his head. "I don't think she would've sent any cops even if little Herman had been a live person being slaughtered right here in the kitchen. I think you're all in this together."

"All... who?" Amanda was truly offended.

"Women. All of you. Together, all over America, you're starving men who are helplessly ill. No cable, no A/C, no freakin' food. Parties every night. And I'm reduced to eating toothpaste, choking down packets of artificial sweetener, and I even came real close to mugging Missus Yodel for a loaf of dry bread. Plus, somebody sic'ed a small panther on me that nearly ate out my eyeballs!" Jason moaned and felt his forehead. "Don't feel so good. I think I'll lie down."

"That's a good idea." Amanda tried to sound sincere. "I'll check on you in a minute."

"Don't bother. I'm locking the door until all the sharp-edged hardware leaves. When I hear you chopping off *Jason's* neck, I want to be certain I know which Jason is your intended victim."

They struggled not to laugh as he trudged down the hall.

It took all four of them nearly an hour to cut open the Jason cushaw and carve out his insides. They separated the edible components and double-bagged the heavy chunks of rind. It was a mess, but they didn't really need a shovel. That had been Christine's idea for a bit of seasoning on the scare. It did involve the axe and the bow saw, however, along with smaller sharp-edged utensils for all the inside work.

When all was settled, they had about twenty pounds of meat plus about five pounds of seeds and stringy pulp from the main cavity (about the size of a volley ball).

"You want to plant this in the back yard?"

"It's not even my yard, Christine! I just rent this duplex. Unless I get thrown out after all this commotion, that is."

"I'll take the seeds," offered Sunny. "My mom does all kinds of clever things with seeds."

"Be sure and clue her in that these ordinary-looking seeds turn into gi-normous squashes," Amanda cautioned.

"Oh, the bigger the better. If she grows one, she'll probably use the rind as a huge gourd-thing. If she can empty it without this much destruction and get it dried up enough."

"Whatever." Amanda washed her hands. "So who's taking this big pile of cushaw meat?" She looked hopefully toward Maria, who had a hungry fireman to feed.

Maria just shook her head.

"I thought you'd want to keep that, Amanda. You know, to bake a cushaw casserole or something." Christine could be a real smarty at times.

"I don't bake... you know that. And don't hardly cook any more, either. What are we going to do with that stuff?"

Ever devious, Christine had a notion. "We could form it in the shape of Jason's head on a platter — it'd scare him every time he walks by."

"That's evil. Plus, I bet it'll stink after twelve hours." Amanda the practical.

"We could leave it on the doorstep of the yodeling lady." Christine made it sound like a sincere donation.

"Oh, heck. Let me take that to my mom, too." Sunny clearly wanted to end the debate. "If she doesn't want it, she might know somebody."

— — —

Jason heard none of that exchange from the guestroom — his head was under a pillow. This evening's episode with his newly-departed cushaw cousin had been extremely unnerving. On one hand, he couldn't believe he'd actually called 9-1-1 because of what he overheard from down the hall. On the other hand, he couldn't believe he hadn't called authorities sooner — after the first mention of *saw* and *axe*.

He stopped to calculate: it'd been seven full days since last Monday evening. *How desperate do you have to be to spend that long in such primitive conditions?* No cooling, no food that was edible, no TLC, no positive attention of any kind. Not a whisper of sympathy for his illness. And his pants were missing!

Why was he holding on? Jason was aware he was no longer *sick*, though he still felt lousy. But why did he feel so rotten? Was it because of his lingering fake cough? Or because he'd not yet received any of the attention he properly craved? If so, why did he crave it so much? *Hmm. That's pretty introspective.* Jason didn't usually look that deeply within.

Chapter 15

August 18 (Tuesday)

Amanda rose early and left quickly for her office. She keenly felt the grinding crunch of the grant applications. *Jason can scratch around for his own dang breakfast.*

It was nearly the middle of the second Hell Week and she was totally exhausted — physically, mentally, emotionally. In the flurry of work-work and Jason-work, Amanda had not stopped enough to contemplate the possible effects of all this on their relationship. Her focus had been short term on both fronts: one, get the apps read and evaluated, and two, get Jason out of her apartment.

But what about the long run? Or even the medium run? After she'd finally blasted her boyfriend out of the apartment, what next? Would he just keep going in the opposite direction? Would he follow his buddy Kevin to hotel happy hours and cruise for desperate traveling business women? Would Jason just wash his hands of their entire relationship?

If so, would that be good or bad?

On good days, that would be *bad*... for their relationship to end. But on bad days, that would be *good*... to step back, get free, and start over. Maybe someone not as needy. Both Margaret and Christine had clearly indicated their expert opinions — except for the control freaks, almost all men are needy. Some reveal it in different ways. Was it so bad that Jason's manifestation was one or two viruses each year? She could do worse. What if she'd been attracted to someone like Kevin, who could be faithful for only about 24 hours at a stretch?

Nope. If she got mixed up with someone like Kevin, she might really need to handle him like a cushaw!

Later, in her office, Amanda quickly scanned the central blog for Day Eight. The comments seemed to be shifting. More bloggers were saying — in slightly different ways — *'You've gone too far just to teach him a lesson. End it, one way or the other.'*

She logged off and resumed the business of evaluating and ranking grant applications.

* * * *

At the apartment, Jason finally plotted his departure.

Step one: find pants. He searched everywhere. Amanda must have had a secret compartment or floor safe... perhaps a hidden attic hatch. After searching for nearly an hour in every nook and cranny, Jason was positive his trousers really were at the cleaners as Amanda had said. All this time he'd thought she was lying.

Having no keys and no pants complicated his escape logistics, but he thought it must still be possible. Guys in movies frequently escaped without street clothes.

Jason wondered how to start a car without a key. Hot-wire it. TV criminals do it in about fifteen seconds with no tools besides fingers. Could he do that? *Uh, probably not.*

What about walking or running? How long before somebody gave him a ride? Well, in his saggy pajamas with several days of whiskers and a stained shirt, probably no one.

Who else could Jason call to pick him up? His mom! No, she wouldn't come for him. That woman had no sympathy for his illnesses or the unbelievable situations he occasionally found himself in. No help there.

Kevin was his only hope. With trembling fingers, Jason again phoned his closest buddy. He waited seven rings. Voicemail. *Crud!*

He left a "mayday" message. But this was late August, so Jason wouldn't hold his breath for rescue. He knew his pal pretty well — Kevin probably wouldn't respond until next May 1st.

* * * *

At work, Amanda was drowning in grant applications. As arranged the previous evening, Christine brought sandwiches and they ate lunch in Amanda's office with the door closed. Amanda would have preferred the staff lounge, but they certainly could not talk privately in that space.

Their sandwiches finished, Amanda rose to put the empty wrappers and napkins in her trash can.

Christine plopped onto the newly vacant chair and logged in to the blog. "Just checking the latest tallies on Burn-Witch. I need to gauge my popularity." She clicked on one of the links.

Amanda returned and looked over her older friend's shoulder. "The most recent entry is *Burn the Witch — 37*. After yesterday's burst of activity, yours isn't growing as fast as the others."

"Hmm. Let's compare that to the Kick-Marty serial, which is the first one they started." Christine clicked a different link and her eyes scanned down the block of comments. "Uh, here it is. *Kick Jason Out — 119*. That's about three times the number wanting to burn me."

"What?" Amanda yanked the wheeled chair backwards — nearly causing whiplash for her friend — and peered closely at the screen. "You said Jason!" She touched that name on the screen like it contained an evil spell. "It *is* Jason! How did they get Jason's name? You said we'd be known only as *Marty* and *Missy* — never identified!"

Christine scooted forward again, partway. "Must be a lucky guess. Jason's a pretty common name." She looked like she was straining to remain calm. "Let's check another link." Christine clicked. "What the heck!"

"Not another Jason reference!"

"The Lighten-Missy link now has YOUR name!"

"Where?"

Christine pointed to the most recent serial. "Look! *Lighten Up, Amanda — 54!*" She pointed again, as though the first gesture didn't take.

"Move over!" Amanda looked where her friend had pointed. Then she shrieked. "Oh, no... they've got my name, too!" It had to be restated. She stared, stunned. "How?" Amanda yanked on the seat again and positioned her face near the screen. "How the hairy hell did they get my name?" When she swiveled the chair and put a hand on each of its arms, that effectively bracketed her older friend.

Christine looked pale, unusual for someone who made two weekly visits to the tanning salon. "I don't know. This isn't even our blog." She twisted away from Amanda's hold and scooted back to the computer. She clicked a link. "See, here's our blog. No real names here."

"Click back to the other one." Amanda barked the instruction like a riled police officer. "And pull over."

Christine rose hurriedly.

Amanda perched on the edge of her own office chair and read a few comments. Then she scrolled down and read a few more. Tears. "They're talking about me like I'm on reality TV."

Christine leaned in again. "Yeah, and some of them want to vote you off the show."

"That's not the least bit funny." Icy.

Christine pointed to the screen at the bottom of the comments. "This is what I call a shadow blog. It only exists because of our blog."

"So who's operating this shadow?"

"No way of telling. They can't find my name, as creator of our blog… and I can't find theirs. I mean, unless somebody cozies up to a computer geek, like your co-worker said yesterday."

Amanda scrolled back up to the top. "There, that's a name."

"Not a real name. All of us blog creators use pseudonyms. See, this blog was created by Simon-Sezz."

Amanda clicked back to one of the other links. "This other site doesn't seem to have our names yet." She pointed. "This one's been solely Free-Marty… and they're up to *Free Marty Now! — 61.*"

"I bet it won't be long. I'm sure the hardcore bloggers check all these other links sooner or later. If they're logging on to our main site, several are bound to be interested in the other comments and these tallies."

Amanda turned away from the screen and faced her clearly rattled companion. "You swore there was no way our actual names would ever be associated with this blog, but here we've already seen both real names. Who knows what else they've already discovered about us. Probably addresses and places of work." Amanda was getting louder. "How did these cranks get our real names?"

"Settle down." Christine checked that the office door was closed all the way. "Your boss is right around the corner." She returned near the chair where her dejected friend sat with head in hands. "Look, this blog of ours went viral, much faster and wider than even I predicted. We've had thousands of hits. There was always a very slim mathematical possibility that somebody just happened on our blog who also knows that Jason is at death's door with a cold and you're at wit's end trying to cure him. And maybe they put two and two together." Christine paused. "But this makes me think somebody actually did sleep with a turbo-whiz-bang computer geek just to bust this thing open."

Tears burned Amanda's eyes. "Why? Who? You said it was foolproof!" She felt like slugging somebody, beginning with the first tanned, large-bosomed woman she could reach.

"Amanda, I'm really sorry. I had no idea. I read all the stuff about blogs and it sounded secure enough to run the shipping schedules for Fort Knox."

"Evidently not! Not if some horny, pimple-faced computer nerd can figure it out! Unless one of your numerous confederates spilled the beans!" Amanda plopped her head on the desk and pointed weakly toward her door. "Just go!"

Christine muttered regrets as she grabbed her purse, opened the door, and scurried out of the office. She practically collided with Louis, who stood nearly inside Amanda's doorway.

Louis watched Christine hurry away and then turned again toward Amanda's office. He waddled in, plopped down in the guest chair, and exhaled loudly. "Catfight?"

Amanda looked up. "Oh, grizzled gonads!" She put her head back on the desk.

Louis just sat there. Unlike nearly 90 per cent of his other drop-ins, this visit by her boss actually had a point. "You're still going to the teleconference tomorrow, aren't you?"

She looked up, suddenly quite sober again. "Actually, I was figuring to pass. They're going to have a handout package anyway and I'm really swamped. So I was hoping you could go without me."

"I'm not going." Louis acted like everybody already knew this. "You're the only one we're sending."

"I thought we're both supposed to be there."

"Well, I've got this other thing…"

"Couldn't you send someone to take notes? June? Gayle?" Amanda was practically begging.

"No, we need someone there who's actually working with the grants."

"And you can't make it?"

When Louis shook his head briskly, his chin flesh waggled and the awful toupee shifted almost imperceptibly.

Amanda sighed heavily enough to rustle some papers on her desktop. She took a deep breath and counted to a zillion, very slowly. "Where is this dang conference, anyway?"

Two hours passed. Though Amanda had tried to refocus on her work, she suddenly realized she'd already read the budget section of the grant application in her hand. Maybe several times. *Not able to concentrate.*

Now that the identities of *Marty* and *Missy* had been discovered — somehow — and leaked out through several of the shadow blogs, Amanda figured it was time to pull the plug on the project. What was the point of going on? The entire scheme was more taxing on her than it had apparently been on Jason, and he showed no signs of leaving (even under all the duress).

Now that Amanda realized some of the blog readers knew her identity, she began to suspect most of the people she encountered also knew the truth. Wonderful to comprehend her co-workers had likely discovered she was the frantic, desperate woman with the pseudonym Missy.

But which co-workers? Gayle? Joan? King Louie? Others? It seemed as though all of them looked at her *funny* today. Was that because they knew? Or because she was acting paranoid? Or both?

The boss gave her the funniest looks.

That figured. *Louis Erie is probably Simon Sezz.*

* * * *

Kevin Haywood, Jason's buddy at GCEC, stopped in at one of the upscale hotels along Nashville's Fourth Avenue. The Nashvillage had the best lounge, with evening happy hour at 6:30 when a convention was using the facility. The hotel provided free drinks for its customers, and Kevin pretended to be staying there. It wasn't really all that artful, however, since the evening manager didn't care who drank up that huge facility's sizeable booze budget.

Bill, an also-divorced acquaintance, saw Kevin and they struck up a conversation while Bill waited for a female business traveler to return from the powder room. "You ever read blogs?" Bill kept his eye on the restroom door.

"Not much, unless somebody e-mails me a link to something particular. Why?"

"The other day at work, a buddy was talking about some guy somewhere who's really sick with something. So he goes to his girlfriend's apartment to recover. But instead of taking care of him, the girlfriend — and her best friend — conspire to make that guy's life a living hell. You wouldn't believe all the stuff they do to him."

"What stuff?" Kevin didn't really care. At work, he'd heard a snippet about a similar blog.

"Well, I don't remember everything, but they're starving him, for one. And they keep sending over cleaners and other kinds of technicians to interrupt his recovery. Plus, get this — they turn off the A/C during the day!"

"And the stupid schmuck puts up with all that? He deserves whatever they dish out." Kevin was distracted as another attractive female entered the drinking space. Happy hour during conventions was absolutely the best time to cruise.

"I don't know." Nearly a head taller than most of the men present, Bill scanned the room to see if anyone looked better than the woman still in the restroom. "At first I thought the same thing. But the more I read on that blog, the more I felt sorry for him, kinda. I mean, he's as stupid as a headless hen, but give the guy a break — he's sick."

"What's he got?"

"Well, it sounds like a regular ordinary flu. But the blog keeps calling it a man-cold… whatever that is. You ever hear of a man-cold?"

Kevin shook his head. "I've heard that mumps is different for grown men. But I thought viruses were pretty much gender neutral… you know, men and women get the same basic germs. Maybe this is new, like that weird version of swine flu or something."

"Not sure. Whatever it is, the girl — and her devious friend — are running this sap through the grinder. They might actually be trying to kill him."

"So where is this? Out in California somewhere?"

"Blog doesn't say." Bill rose up on his toes to look over the milling crowd toward the restroom. That made him temporarily about seven feet tall. "What the heck is keeping her?" He focused again on Kevin's question. "Could be anywhere. Could be right here in middle Tennessee for all I know. I guess this new man-cold virus could hit just about any ole guy."

"They give any names on this blog?"

"The guy's named Marty and his girlfriend is Missy."

Kevin smiled slightly. "Sounds like a real sweet honeymoon."

"Yeah, but when I saw it this afternoon, there's a link to a different site. On that other blog, somebody claims they figured out who Missy and Marty really are."

"So what I.D. did those other bloggers come up with?"

Bill briefly closed his eyes to think. "Uh, the girlfriend is Aretha, Amelia… no, uh, Amanda. And the poor stupid schmuck they're terrorizing is named, uh, Jared, Jacob… no, uh, Jason. I think. Yeah. Amanda and Jason."

"Well, good luck to both of them. They probably deserve each other."

The taller man's attractive female acquaintance finally approached from the restroom and Bill bade a hasty farewell to Kevin.

Kevin sipped his drink and spoke to himself. "Stupid slug. Imagine letting a girlfriend keep you holed up in her apartment with no food and no A/C. That Jason guy is an idiot. Pure-D idiot." Kevin absent-mindedly scanned the lounge area again. "Jason!" He pulled out his phone and listened to voicemails, including Jason's from that morning. His eyes growing larger, Kevin grabbed a new drink and hustled down the hall, past the exercise area, to the wireless Internet room. Two work stations and only one was occupied.

He did a hurried blog search with keywords *Marty*, *Missy*, and *man-cold*. There were nine hits. One was about cartoon characters.

Kevin remembered enough of what Jason had previously explained that he fairly quickly put it all together — the Missy and Marty of recent blog fame really *were* Amanda and Jason!

Now that he was finally aware of what was happening to Jason, Kevin was in a quandary. Should he sit back, scan the blog, and just briefly enjoy monitoring his buddy's misery? Or should he jump into action to help his beleaguered friend? He debated silently. *If I was being terrorized by fanatics and lampooned on the Internet, I'd want my buddy to come rescue me.* Kevin decided to rescue…

But the woman at the next computer looked up and smiled. Kevin smiled back. *What the heck… Jason can wait 'til morning.* Pretty nice looking and her drink was in the same kind of plastic cup he had from the happy hour lounge.

"How you doin'? Welcome to Nashville! Can I get you a refill for that?"

She smiled again and nodded.

Kevin forgot he even had a friend named Jason. He hustled to the lobby, got two more drinks, and briskly returned to the hotel's computer room. He handed her one of the cups. "I'm Kevin." He put his free hand in his pocket for the 2x3 schoolchild photo. Then he assumed his well-rehearsed sad expression.

"Sandy." She sipped the remainder of her first drink and picked up the new one. She looked into Kevin's face. "Something wrong?" Sandy nodded toward the computer he'd recently logged off.

"Oh, no. Well, it's just I really miss my son." He pulled out the photo with a practiced movement. "He's with my ex in Memphis. If it wasn't for e-mail and Facebook, I'm afraid we'd lose contact completely. His mother doesn't want me in his life at all."

"Aw, that's not right. A boy needs his daddy. Let me see." Sandy reached for the photo.

That nearly always hooked them. Once they touched the picture, they *belonged* to Kevin. He didn't respond verbally; the sad face always worked best.

"He's so cute. How old?"

"Oh, he was about six when that was taken." Kevin just picked a likely number. It wasn't even his child, of course. He'd swiped the picture from Lost and Found at work last spring.

Ever since, that little photo had become his ticket *home* at many hotel happy hours.

Chapter 16

August 19 (Wednesday)

Amanda watched as Jason stared at the morning's food possibilities: flax, hemp, and hummus. Obviously averse to those selections, he might have to default to celery again (with a dab of toothpaste for flavor), but it had become limp and turned light brown. It would take some otherworldly additive to make that palatable.

In any case, the unwelcome patient would have to mope and moan about breakfast without Amanda's company. Downtown's parking would be intense as people jockeyed for court cases, meetings, and other city/county business. She was already behind schedule.

Amanda was about to leave when Jason resumed whining about his elbow. "Could you give me a hand with this Ace bandage? It's too tight, but I still need some support."

She dropped her purse and keys with extra obvious aggravation and approached the injured patient. "Only you could hurt your right shoulder *and* left elbow while recovering from a cold without even leaving my apartment."

Standing very close, Jason shrugged. *Whew!* He needed another shower — badly. Many men seem proud of their generated smells, like dogs that roll in rank roadkill. However, Jason didn't seem boastful — it was more like he was totally oblivious.

Amanda removed the wrap and took off his homemade bandanna sling. Then she re-rolled the bandage so it would be easier to dispense. "Now hold both arms where you want them to rest." Nurse Patience.

He experimented with different positions. "Okay, like this."

"You sure?" When he nodded, Amanda rigged a double sling, one loop slightly higher than the other. It was actually quite creative and reasonably effective in taking the pressure off both arms. However, it made him look a bit like an amateur double for a low-budget mummy film.

Jason headed toward the bathroom to look in the mirror. "Thanks," he called over his shoulder.

Amanda was too irritated to reply as she rushed toward the door.

"What's the matter?" Jason stopped and peered around the bathroom door frame.

"Well, now, on top of everything else, I'm late for a mandatory seminar at the Greene County courthouse that I shouldn't even have to go to if King Louie would get off his fat Yankee butt and do even a sliver of his own job!"

"I'm sorry. I didn't know..."

She didn't hear the rest of Jason's apology. She trotted to her Jeep Wrangler, backed out of the space quickly, and sped toward the old state highway, which, at that part of town, had become merely a frontage road for I-40. The old highway also went through the center of Verdeville and right past the 1930s courthouse building.

It normally took around ten minutes to get to the courthouse from Amanda's duplex apartment. But when she reached the edge of downtown, she was blocked by the longest freight train she'd ever seen. The trains across the border in Kentucky usually went whizzing by, but these in middle Tennessee seemed to be looking for a shady spot to pause for a picnic.

No cabooses any more, but the last freight car finally cleared the intersection. Long lines of vehicles from both sides began creeping across the double set of tracks.

After another mile, Amanda circled the courthouse looking for an empty spot on the street. Not surprisingly, nothing was available, so she headed for the newer lot on the south side of that large facility. Three or four slots were left, if she could reach one in time. She was already fifteen minutes late for the 8:30 meeting.

One other vehicle moved among the rows, probably looking for a spot, which meant Amanda had at least two chances to park in this lot. The small truck in front of her had just turned into the lot and seemed intent on the space straight ahead. For no apparent reason, unless he simply changed his mind, the pickup driver slammed on his brakes to move left instead of going straight.

But Amanda had already begun her turn off the main street when the truck started into the lot, so she was immediately behind him. She quickly stomped on her brakes also, but the tail of her car was still out in the old state highway.

Crash! Amanda's small vehicle was thrown to the side like a discarded soup can. She felt sharp pain in her foot, her head smacked into something hard… and she blacked out.

* * * *

Kevin left the hotel at about 8:45 on the morning after he'd won the temporary heart of the empathetic bank examiner from Knoxville. In his vehicle, he remembered his mission to extract Jason from the Internet-publicized mess he'd gotten into unawares.

Close to 9:00, Kevin arrived at Amanda's apartment on Melrose. He knocked on the door for about five minutes before a nearly unrecognizable male finally unlatched and opened it.

"Jase? Is that you? What's with your arms? You look like a freakin' mummy who can't keep his britches up!"

"Thanks a bunch. That's nice, coming from the friend who refused to rescue me over four days ago."

"Well, better late than never." Kevin took a closer look at his friend. "Phew! You smell like a street bum." He tried not to inhale.

"Wasn't expecting company." Jason moved aside so his rescuer could enter.

In vivid contrast to all of Jason's other offensive smells, Kevin noted that his breath was minty fresh.

"What made you decide to finally show up? Slow day at *Gee-keck*?" GCEC was the Greene County Electric Co-op where they both worked.

"I'm on the late shift this month. Remember?" Kevin looked around. "But hustle up, we gotta get you out of here."

"What's the rush? I've been here for nearly nine full days."

"The rush is that your name's plastered all over the Internet. Amanda and her booby friend have been making a sucker out of you."

"I don't doubt the sucker part at all, but what's that got to do with the Internet?"

"You mean you really don't know your story and name is all over cyberspace?"

"Like I told you before, they took away TV, computer, food... everything. I've been imprisoned and left to die." His exaggeration skills had survived so far.

"Yeah, well, that's over now. Your buddy Kevin is on... the... job. And we're getting you out of here." He quickly scanned the rooms again. "Uh, Amanda's busty friend isn't lurking around here, is she?"

"Not as far as I know. But go back to the Internet part."

"Okay. One of them — I'd guess Christine — started a web thing... blog. Not sure when, but probably right after you moved in here. They've been yakking about how they're doing this and causing that, just to blast you out of Amanda's apartment."

"Why didn't they just ask me to leave?" His expression resembled a lost and lonely child.

"According to the blog, Amanda asked you several times, but you flat out refused. Is that just propaganda?"

"Oh, I don't know... I'm weak from starvation. You got any food?"

"Food later. Escape now. Get your freakin' pants on."

"Can't find 'em... or my car keys."

Kevin surveyed the space. "Well, grab that tablecloth and wrap up. We're outta here."

"Hold on. Let me get my toothpaste." Jason dashed to the hall bathroom.

Kevin watched as his friend removed a safety pin from his waistband and hurriedly wrapped the tablecloth into a Dorothy Lamour sarong. He looked like a cross-dressed street bum with no eye for color.

Jason inhaled deeply at his armpit and seemed satisfied that it smelled okay. He stopped at the kitchen and penciled something very brief, obviously for Amanda. Then he affixed the pin to the note. Jason grabbed up half a dozen containers of something odorous. "Potpourri," he explained. As they passed the dumpster next to the wash house, he ceremoniously tossed them inside. It was reminiscent of the brash ensign throwing overboard the captain's precious plant in the *Mister Roberts* movie. Jason clutched his friend's elbow. "On the way to the nearest drive-through food place, tell me why the whole cyberspace knows I've been sick."

"They know everything, buddy-boy. Abso-freakin' everything. Hop in and I'll brief you."

Squinting at the sunlight, he resembled a dazed prisoner finally released from solitary on Devil's Island. Jason looked even worse wrapped in Amanda's floral tablecloth than he had in the saggy pajamas. Those were not his colors. He limped on his way to Kevin's vehicle.

"You've been set up, Jase. From the day you walked in that apartment, every freakin' thing's been rigged." Kevin explained the rest of what he knew and how he'd found out.

At first, Jason seemed unable to believe all the deprivation had been deliberate, but Kevin's new information, added to what he already knew of Christine, apparently convinced him. Still, Jason obviously struggled with Amanda's complicity. "Amanda must have been deceived nearly as much as I was."

"Sorry, buddy, but she was totally in on it." Kevin shook his head. "So, which drive-through do you want?"

Notwithstanding his emotional trauma, Jason was already drooling on the tablecloth. "Closest one."

* * * *

At about 9:30 a.m., Amanda slowly regained consciousness in the hectic emergency room of Greene County Hospital. A youngish male doctor peered into her eyes, shone a small flashlight, and asked several questions. What day was it?

How old was she? Name? Birth date? *Complicated stuff.* She'd have to get back with him later. She closed her eyes again.

Shortly, the doctor and a nurse got Amanda to sit up. Somebody rubbed her right hand. "Ow!"

"Good. Now tell me about your hand."

Amanda was in a narrow space with curtains on either side. The front was open and people scurried back and forth. "Something... squeeze... hurts..." Slow and groggy.

"That's a good start. Let's go back to the other information." The doctor ran through the series of questions again.

She answered most, several correctly, but missed two: Amanda messed up her birth date and guessed the day was Tuesday.

"No, today is Wednesday. Do you know the date?"

"*Your* date?" Amanda pointed to the nurse. "You're dating Nurse Ratchit? She's too old for you. I think I'm more your age." Still groggily, but not as slowly.

In the adjacent stall, a man complained loudly about his underwear being confiscated. No explanation as to who took them, or why. Amanda's temporary neighbor on the other side of the heavy drapes was an elderly woman who released loud and putrid flatulence.

"Pee-yuu! Did you do that?" Amanda was awake again.

"Next door, honey," explained the nurse.

"You mean the man with no undies?"

"No, honey. Your other neighbor." The nurse pointed.

"They oughtta change the feed for that horse."

"I thought that pain medicine would keep her out even longer." The nurse addressed the doctor.

"The ambulance crew evidently missed the concussion possibility and just treated her pain from the broken toes."

"Toes? Who broke toes?" Amanda hadn't yet taken inventory.

"What did they give her on the ride over here?" The doctor squinted at the chart quickly.

"The medics radioed in for permission to give her something for pain because it looked like it would take half an hour to extract her from the vehicle." The nurse sighed as though she'd explained this before. "The E.R. doctor nearest the dispatcher gave the okay."

"Bad order. Who was it?" He couldn't find any notations in the chart.

"New guy." The nurse rolled her eyes.

Part of Amanda's brain dozed for a few moments, though she continued talking. She also moaned and responded, but not really in a lucid fashion.

A bit later: "...do I need to take off her bra?" Nurse's voice.

Amanda zoned in on the tail of that question. She wondered what they were about to do.

"No, I think she might fight us." The doctor.

"What are you doing to me?"

"Good, she's awake again. Sit her back up."

"The doctor is checking your ribs, honey. Sometimes the steering wheel can crack a rib or bruise it."

"You don't see under my bra without an expensive dinner first."

"Awake and with a sense of humor." Doctor.

"She might not be kidding." The nurse nodded wisely.

Amanda pointed her forefinger at the nurse. The meaning of that gesture was unclear to any of the three present.

"No exterior signs of trauma on the ribcage. Have the films come back yet?"

"Backlogged, Doctor. One of the machines is down, so the tech has to walk the plates all the way over to pediatrics to develop them."

"Wonderful."

"You've got a nice bedroom voice... uh, manner." Amanda's throat was dry and the words needed more tongue movement to get out cleanly.

The nurse cleared her own throat. "I think that's bedside manner." She turned to the physician. "Normally, we'd walk her around a bit, wouldn't we?"

"Typically, but she can't hold weight on that foot. However, I don't want her dropping off again, so help me keep her talking." He looked around. "If the medics hadn't given her that dosage, it would be fairly easy to establish concussion one way or the other."

More from Amanda's neighbor: "Why'd they take away my skivvies? Everybody else in here got to keep their skivvies!"

Amanda wondered about her own underwear. It had always been stressed as such a big deal to have clean underwear if you ended up in an accident. She knew she'd begun this morning with fresh panties and wondered vaguely if they'd remained clean after her wreck. She struggled to check with her uninjured left hand, but it felt tethered. After a difficult examination, she discovered the IV tubing which terminated in the back of her hand.

While the medical personnel were talking about keeping her awake, the non-talking part of Amanda's brain drifted off once more.

A few minutes later, Amanda came to again as the nurse gently squeezed the fingers of her uninjured left hand.

"...I'm more worried about the concussion." The doctor had been in the middle of explaining something. "The foot pain can wait."

"You wouldn't say that if you had to walk on this baby." Amanda clutched toward the doctor's forearm, but missed him completely. "I want a second opinion. Somebody who knows how to give pain meds. My foot hurts."

"She's evidently awake again." The nurse. "That last talking nap was nearly fifteen minutes."

Amanda remembered only two words of her most recent conversation with the doctor and nurse: *concussion* and *X-rays*. She was aware of three distinct, throbbing pains: head, right foot, and right wrist. Plus her body ached all over.

The doctor peered at her again and asked more questions. Evidently Amanda passed the test this time, because he gave the nurse permission to start splinting the injured toes.

Amanda was out of it again briefly, though she continued to talk for those ten minutes. Then she came to a third time. Her mouth felt like she'd been chewing unprocessed cotton. Her breath tasted funky and she wished she had a mint. "What happened?" Her eyes were clearing and Amanda finally got a good look at her attending physician.

"We hope to learn more about that from you," said Doctor Handsome. "What do you remember?"

Amanda tried to squirm to a more comfortable position in the bed, but gave up with a heavy groan. "Uh, driving to the courthouse for a meeting. Running late. Trying to turn into the parking lot right behind a pickup truck... but then he stopped suddenly. I slammed on my brakes... that's all I remember."

"Well, the medics said another vehicle crashed into your rear. It seems you hit your head. Likely on the side window. And your right foot has trauma. Probably a few fractured metatarsals. There was some confusion — it looked to me like you'd had a concussion. But the medics evidently didn't think so, because they gave you something fairly strong for your foot pain. That's hampered my diagnosis here."

"Did I have a concussion?"

"I thought possibly, but can't be certain because those meds interfered with your responses."

"My wrist hurts."

He examined it again. "You've been talking a lot about that. I just see minor bruising... no appreciable swelling. Can you move it?"

"Hurts, but it moves."

"Possibly you hooked your hand in the wheel and overextended the wrist. Watch it for a day, wrap it if you want to, and see what your regular physician decides to do. You'll need to see him or her tomorrow. The nurse will book an appointment."

"Where's my car?"

The doctor shrugged and started to move away from her bed. "If you feel up to a visitor, there's a friend outside waiting to see you."

"What kind of friend?"

"Female, tanned. Can't sit still." He smiled.

"Christine. Yeah, send her in!" She'd thought maybe it was Jason, whom she did not want to see. *Not that he'd come to the E.R. to check on me anyway.*

"Okay, I'm off my shift. Another doctor will check on you soon."

"Wait. Am I going to stay here tonight?"

"Really don't know. I was mainly following up on the concussion part. Another physician's on duty now and she'll decide about your foot. We've straightened and secured your toes with splints and bandages. The X-rays are slow coming back. I don't think the damage is extensive enough to keep you. So they'll probably put you in a boot and send you home. Can your friend drive you?"

"Yeah, sure."

"Okay, I'm off. Good luck with all that Jason stuff."

"Huh?"

"You've been talking about Jason. I figured he's your boyfriend." He'd obviously noticed she wasn't wearing a ring.

"What did I say?"

"I'm not a therapist." He smiled like a television doctor. "But assuming you weren't hallucinating during that chatter, I'd say you ought to give Jason something to eat and let him have his pants back."

"Uh, how much did I tell you?"

"I don't think you left out very much." Doctor Handsome smiled again. *Nice teeth.* "Tell Jason I agree with him about the hemp and flax cereals… those should be on the farm animal aisle at Tractor Supply."

"I'm really embarrassed, Doctor."

"Don't be. Even if you were kind of out of it, we needed to keep you talking — in the sense of the concussion possibility. And it was fairly enlightening as well." He started to leave again. "By the way, what is a cushaw?"

"You don't want to know. Believe me."

"Okay." He shrugged. "Bye."

"Thanks, Doctor."

He was already gone.

The man in the next stall evidently saw him pass and shouted, "Hey, Doc! Did you take my skivvies?"

The nurse watched him leave. "Honey, I'd hang on to your Jason. Or give him another chance… whatever the situation is. It was hard to make out exactly what Jason did. But it's obvious you really love him."

"What was I talking about?" Amanda was finally able to focus on the nurse's nametag and realized it was Rachael, not Ratchit.

"In my experience, people in the hospital who are out of it — but able to speak — usually talk about regrets or about things they love. In some cases, that's the same topic. I don't think you want Jason to become a regret."

"What the heck did I say?"

"Oh, people also talk about things they hate. Speaking of which, who in tarnation is King Louie?"

"You don't want to know."

"Well, I've got other patients. Bye."

"Thanks, Rachael."

The woman in the other adjacent stall passed gas again and the stench made Amanda's eyes water. It was about 10:10 a.m.

Chapter 17

Jason salivated during the entire ride — his initial eight minutes of freedom from Amanda's apartment — and whapped Kevin's arm when they reached the first fast-food establishment. After Kevin turned in, Jason ordered the largest burger available and super-sized the fries and drink.

Kevin pulled over and watched as Jason swallowed his first real meal in over nine days. There was not much actual chewing. When Jason signaled he could process aural sensations, Kevin began explaining what he'd learned about the blog and how Amanda was certainly complicit. "I'm not saying Amanda cooked up all that stuff, but she certainly went along with it."

"That witch Christine cooked it all up. Did I tell you she nearly tore off my right nipple?"

"That's pretty kinky. What was she wearing?"

"No, it wasn't sexual." Jason had mustard on his mouth. He tried to lick it off but didn't get everything, so he just wiped his face with the tablecloth sarong. "It was punishment. Torture. Witch stuff."

"I think I'd let Christine hurt me a bit, if she was wearing a black leather corset and high-heeled boots."

When Jason sighed, a sesame seed flew from his mouth and landed on the driver's forearm. Kevin reacted like he'd been shot.

"No, you're missing the whole point. There was no sex, no comfort, nothing good at all. This was all deprivation and it's like they were punishing me for something."

"Now you understand what I've been trying to explain about that blog. They *were* punishing you — all because you had what they call a man-cold."

"I think I heard that mentioned before. What's a man-cold?" Jason frowned. "Don't we get the same colds that women have?"

"It's beyond me. Bill didn't know, either."

"Who's Bill?"

"Guy I know. Saw him at the lounge last night."

"You're picking up men now?"

"Funny, funny. Bill was there for the same reason I was: a convention of bank employees. I ended up with a cute examiner for the FDIC."

"Wait a minute. You mean you found out last night that I was being deliberately abused by evil women for over a week, and my name had recently been transmitted all over the World Wide Web… but you waited 'til this morning to come rescue me?"

"Sandy was lonely and pretty. What can I say?"

Jason just shook his head. "Well, swing by my place. I need some clothes and my other set of keys. Then take me back to Amanda's so I can get my truck."

"Sure. And while we're at your place, log on to this blog real quick so you can see what I'm talking about." Kevin paused. "You need to understand, I didn't know you were the victim 'til last night. For the first week or so, when I heard people talking about this blog, I thought it was a different schmuck that was being terrorized and starved."

Jason nodded. Impaired perception was about all he could expect from Kevin.

When they zipped over to Jason's apartment for his spare keys, he quickly changed into street clothes. Then he scanned the blog and related links for about ten minutes. Finally it sank in — Amanda had been a willing participant in the entire drama and some of the abuses were even of her own invention! He felt like he'd been gut-punched.

"Let's go, Jase. If you still want to get your truck before I head to work."

"Yeah, sure. I'm ready." He logged off and scrambled toward Kevin's vehicle. "We got time to drive through the chicken place on the way? I still feel kind of weak."

Kevin checked his watch. "Okay, but I better not be late."

They set a speed record picking up his chicken.

Jason was furious and mortified at what he'd learned from the blog. But the greasy fried chicken helped settle his nerves slightly. It didn't help his stomach much, however.

Kevin dropped him in front of Amanda's apartment and sped away.

The no-necked boy was near Amanda's front door, whacking the laundry room wall with his tennis ball. "They fine-ly let ya out?"

Jason nodded.

"What was ya in for?"

"It was all a big misunderstanding." Jason started to turn, but stopped. "Free advice, kid. When you grow up, don't ever get sick."

Jason unlocked his truck; it took four tries to get the engine started. Sitting idle for nine days does funny things to fuel injectors. He lowered his window and took in one final earful of yodeling before he drove away.

If he hurried, he could make the breakfast buffet at Shuney's.

He made it.

Jason left Shuney's before the lunch crowd arrived. He went home, drank a beer, and sat down with his laptop. He scanned more of the blog and adjunct links and chaffed considerably at the sizeable tally for *Kick Marty Out*.

Jason finally comprehended what he'd endured for over nine days and he took none of it gracefully. Felt betrayed by Amanda, of course. But he was also humiliated by all the blog attention, where he was mostly depicted as an immature brat and spoiled wuss, or a momma's boy who'd spent too much time breastfeeding. *Where did that come from?* He made a mental note to ask his mom how long he'd accessed her milk.

With his pride heavily damaged, Jason sent Amanda a final e-mail. Thus officially broken up, Jason intended to have no further communication with his newly *ex*-girlfriend.

In fact, he might even join Kevin at the hotel happy hours after his digestive system stabilized. Right now he had a huge stomach ache — the beer didn't set well with the buffet's scrambled eggs.

* * * *

Still in her original E.R. bed, Amanda felt like she'd been trampled by wild goats.

Immediately after the nurse left, Christine bustled into the curtained area. "How are you feeling? Was that doctor cute, or what? You need anything? Gawd, what's that awful smell?"

"Uh, too many questions. Let's see. Broken toes, sprained wrist, and maybe concussion." Amanda pointed to her own head. "Yeah, he's a dreamboat. Uh, I need some pain meds for my foot."

"Which foot?"

Amanda motioned toward her right.

"That's the same foot you hurt in that rain accident at the Centroplex, wasn't it?"

Amanda nodded. "And the smell is that old lady next door." She pointed. "Keeps tooting. Smells like rotten cabbage."

"Oh." Christine pulled back the curtain slightly and studied the other patient for a moment. It was not like her to resist the temptation to investigate someone else's post-operative privacy, despite the applicable HIPAA laws. She covered her nose.

"Do you know anything about my Wrangler?"

"Wrecker took it to their impound yard. Told me it was totaled. I also talked to the cop on the scene."

"How'd you get there so fast?"

"It wasn't all that fast. It took them nearly fifteen minutes to get your door open. The passenger door was crumpled over by the impact to your right rear corner. Your door was jammed when it hit the edge of that concrete wall. Wonder why they need a wall around a parking lot?"

"Okay, whatever. But what were you doing there?"

"Eating breakfast with my lawyer. The dreamy one. We're thinking about taking Daniel back to the cleaners."

"You just happened to be downtown near the courthouse at the same time I'm being rammed by an 80-ton tank?"

"It was only a Cadillac from the mid-1980s. But those things were built like tanks."

"Who was driving? A terrorist?"

"A little old lady who'd come downtown to pay a parking ticket." Christine chuckled. "Now she's got a new ticket to pay — failure to yield."

"What actually happened?"

"I got this from the cop, who got it from the other two drivers and some witnesses. When you began your turn into the parking lot, the old lady in the Caddy accelerated in the lane she was in. When you stopped short to avoid hitting the guy in front of you, the Caddy smashed into your rear, which was still out in the main street."

"All because the guy in the truck couldn't make up his mind." Amanda groaned. "Any idea where my purse is?"

"Right here." Christine held it up. "Tow truck guy had it."

"Was it my cousin Pete?" Pete was a son of a cousin to Amanda's mother. Amanda found it simpler to call him a cousin than to differentiate which number and whether removed.

"I don't know your cousin, but this guy's nametag said Norm, I think." Christine lowered her voice slightly. "Did you have much cash with you?"

"Oh, I guess about fifteen bucks. Why?"

"All gone. Not sure if the towing guy took it or maybe a bystander. But they cleaned you out."

"Credit cards?"

"I saw some cards, but I don't know what you carry. You'll have to check that when your head gets clear. Your phone's still in the pouch. Hopefully they just took your cash."

Amanda struggled to shift position again. Still unsuccessful — she couldn't put enough weight on her right wrist. "You think I should notify Jason or something?"

"Well, that's the important news I have for you." Christine moved closer.

"What?"

"He's gone." Very solemn.

"Jason's gone? Are you sure?"

"Positive. On my way here, I drove by your place to get him. I figured he'd want to come if we could find his pants. His truck was still there, but Jason was long gone."

"Well, his keys were in his pants."

Christine shrugged. "I checked next door. Missus Yodel said a man drove up and banged on your apartment door. In a few minutes Jason came out wearing your floral tablecloth wrapped around like a sarong. I don't think those are his colors, by the way. He left with that other guy."

"Probably Kevin or Big Ernie. I doubt anybody else would've come for him, except maybe a cab driver."

Christine nodded. "Jason also left you a note." She held it up tentatively.

It was a scrap of shopping list paper with a safety pin clasped at an angle. "This is what I used to take up the slack in Jason's jammies." Amanda examined the pin wistfully. The note was merely three penciled words: *Thanks for nothing*. She cried.

"Hey, Lady Doc! What did they do with my freakin' skivvies?" That loud question from next door signaled the new arrival.

A female doctor entered while scanning Amanda's chart. "Nothing definitive on the concussion, but if so, it was apparently mild. However, if you develop any dizziness or headache beyond that lump you already have, come back immediately."

"What about my foot?"

"Three middle toes are fractured, maybe broken. Have to wait 'til the specialist reads the films. You may have heard there's a delay getting the X-rays processed."

"What did you see?"

"They look fractured to me. Which means you wear this ugly boot," she pointed to a clear plastic bag containing a wooden shoe sole with a blue canvas upper, "for a couple of weeks and keep those splints around your toes. They should heal just fine. Start wiggling those toes in about a week, but just a bit at a time. Don't overdo it."

"What about the pain?"

"Here's a prescription for three days of pain pills. Enough to last until your own doctor decides on a course of treatment." The physician looked around like she wondered if she'd left any personal possessions. "We're backed up in E.R., so I've got to go. The nurse can answer any questions." The doctor left the draped partition quickly, picking up a new chart from a rolling cabinet on her way out.

"Hey, Lady Doc! Where the heck are my skivvies? I can't get out of here with my privates waving around!"

Christine peeled back the curtain slightly. She probably hadn't seen any privates waving in quite a while. Then she sighed. "He exaggerated."

Nurse Rachael returned through the curtains with a small stack of paperwork and some older style wooden crutches. "They're sending you home. I thought they might hold you until the films came back, but there aren't any beds available and we're stacked up back here. They're even using some of our units for post-op." She inclined her head toward the woman with intestinal gas. Rachael handed Amanda a slip. "Here's your appointment with your regular doctor. Can you get transportation tomorrow?"

"I can take her." Christine grabbed the slip.

"How'd you know who my doctor is? My purse was with the tow truck."

"Your friend here told us. Plus you already had a hospital chart from last year sometime." The nurse had Amanda sign several papers and told Christine to drive around to the E.R. entrance. As an orderly prepared to wheel Amanda out to Christine's car, Rachael quickly covered her final briefing. "Your bill includes a week's rental on these crutches. If you bring them back within seven days, you won't owe anything extra. That gives you time to borrow some or rent 'em at a drug store. You might not even need any after the first week."

"Uh, Nurse, does anybody have that man's underpants?" Amanda pointed at the curtain. "He's been festering about them for at least twenty minutes."

"His wife has all his clothes in the waiting room." Rachael sighed heavily. "He's been told several times already, but it never sinks in. So we've given up. When the meds clear out, we'll tell him again."

The orderly chattered as he took her out but Amanda hardly responded.

Christine drove Amanda home, stopping only at the drive-through pharmacy for a three-day supply of pain pills. Otherwise, both were silent as Christine obviously monitored Amanda's composure.

When they arrived at the complex's parking lot near Amanda's duplex, Christine reached over and touched her friend's left shoulder. "I also need to tell you, Jason knows about the blog."

"What do you mean? How could he know?" Amanda sputtered. "How do you know he knows?"

"I'm sorry. It appears that Kevin spilled the beans... or maybe Big Ernie." Christine pointed to the neighbor's door. "When Missus Yodel told me earlier about the man picking up Jason, she said they were also talking loudly about his name and reputation being ruined by the Internet. She didn't understand most of it, but she heard enough to convince me the friend was briefing Jason that he'd been outed on the blog."

"No way to mistake Big Ernie for Kevin. She didn't mention the man's height?"

Christine shook her head.

"Must have been Kevin, then. How on earth did Kevin find out about the blog, or about Jason's real name appearing recently?"

"Don't know. That's a question for Jason, if he ever talks to either one of us again."

Amanda started to cry again. "What have I done?"

"Well, I think we cured his cold, in case that's any comfort."

If looks could kill.

Christine went around to the side of the duplex and flipped up the breaker handle on the A/C compressor. Then she returned to the car and helped Amanda into her own apartment.

The crutches were set for someone several inches shorter than 5' 6", so Amanda had to slump quite a bit. With considerable difficulty, she made her way to the kitchen and put her purse on the table.

Christine remained near the front doorway, likely to give her friend a few moments and a little space.

It was difficult to move with short crutches since her right wrist hurt so badly, but Amanda hobbled down the hallway and looked into the guestroom. Even though she already knew Jason was long gone, she still had to check.

The small, cluttered apartment seemed quite empty. Also very quiet — except Mrs. Yodel's incessant practice radiated from their shared wall and the HVAC ducts groaned from the reactivated air movement.

Christine closed all the apartment's windows. "I can stay here with you tonight, if you like." She looked around the living room and apparently had second thoughts. "Or you could come over to my house."

"No, thanks. I want to be here. And I don't need any company." Amanda's shoulders sagged. "If you'll take that Q-tip thingy out of the cable connection, I think I'll just watch TV a while and..." She broke down again. Too much all at once: office workload, wrecked car, busted toes, broken relationship, and King Louie had probably already left several demanding voicemails.

Christine fixed the coax connection and did not appear to watch her friend's tears.

A few minutes later, Christine touched her shoulder lightly. "You're positive you won't let me stay?"

Amanda shook her head. "I think I'll just nap a while or watch old movies."

"Can I bring you something to eat later?"

"Yeah, that'd be wonderful. Supper."

"Anything in particular?"

"Surprise me. Only don't make it *healthy* stuff." Amanda tried to smile, but it turned into a choked sob.

Christine hugged her for a moment and then departed. It was nearly 2:00 p.m. and she probably hadn't had a chance to eat lunch yet.

On short crutches, Amanda hobbled around her empty apartment and wished she had someone taking care of her. She swallowed a pain pill with slightly less water than it needed. *Kahh!* Then she phoned her auto insurance agent and answered as many questions as she could, despite possessing no information on either of the other two drivers. Those details would have to come from the police report.

After watching the end of one movie on the Lifetime Channel, she snoozed through the beginning of another film. Amanda saw the rest of that movie and a portion of the one which followed. Each story made her weepy.

Mainly, after the pill kicked in, she snoozed.

When she woke again a couple hours later, Amanda was hungry but there was nothing available to eat besides rice cake crackers and a small can of tomato paste. She briefly considered sampling her own dental product.

Her toes throbbed horribly.

About 4:50 p.m., she phoned her office and left a detailed message for Louis. She knew he'd be gone by then.

When Christine reappeared around 7:00 with supper soup from the grocery deli, Amanda was on the couch sniffling at a movie with the volume very low.

"Have you been crying all afternoon?" Christine looked into her eyes.

"On and off. I was going to check my e-mail and Facebook, but I remembered my laptop's still in my Jeep."

"Well, you might as well write that off. Part of your vehicle looked like a mangled accordion." Christine paused. "Well, your computer might've survived, depending on where it was. I can drive by the impound yard in the morning and check."

"Thanks. In the meantime, could I borrow your laptop?"

"Don't have it with me, but I can run it by tomorrow, if yours is definitely busted."

Amanda muted the TV volume completely and put down the remote. "Thanks for helping me today."

"You're welcome." Christine cleared her throat softly. "Uh, you know, I feel really bad about all that stuff we did to Jason. In hindsight, I guess we should have pulled the plug on about the third or fourth day."

"Yeah, hindsight." Amanda's eyes clouded again.

"Should I stick around a bit?"

"No. Go." Amanda's hand made a sweeping motion toward the door, but her tear-stained face didn't turn.

Christine set the front door so it would lock behind her and left quietly.

By the time Amanda got to her deli soup, it was cold. She nuked it for a minute and then ate. She tried dunking a rice cake cracker, but it soaked up so much liquid that it simply collapsed under its own weight.

About 10:00 p.m. Amanda finally checked her phone messages: one from Maria and one from Sunny. Three other messages were from Louis at work, but she'd have to wait until morning to listen to them. It would upset her too much to hear King Louie's New York accent that late at night.

Chapter 18

August 20 (Thursday)

Jason was up before 8:00 so he could phone in sick.

His supervisor asked if he was feeling any better at all, since he'd already missed eight workdays. He made his voice sound a bit huskier and coughed a few times. "How much sick leave do I have left, Mizz Grunion?"

"You will have used nine if you can't work today. You earn fifteen days a year, but ten days were taken in January, so you'd already be in the hole. Lucky you were able to carry forward five days from last year. Five plus fifteen, minus ten… and minus another nine. You've got one day left for the rest of this year."

"Well, I might have to use that one tomorrow—" *cough, cough* "—'cause I don't think I've got this thing licked yet."

"Yeah, I understand those man-colds are pure hell." Ms. Grunion probably rolled her eyes at the phone. "While you've been off, the new girl has had to handle all your calls plus her own. A person can process only so many billing complaints, you know."

"I know. I'm sorry I got sick and everything. Maybe I'll bring the new girl some M&Ms when I come back on Monday."

"Well, you should bring her more than a 75¢ bag of candy. And you'd better be here Monday morning, because I'll have to dock you otherwise."

"Okay." *cough* "Thanks, Mizz Grunion." *Dang, what a grouch!*

Over the past 22 hours, Jason had refueled his belly and carefully collected ten newspapers from the prickly holly bush near his front door. Several were soaked from the apartment complex's automatic sprinkler system.

He toasted some frozen waffles and drowned them in syrup. Then he ate Cocoa Puffs out of the box for a couple of hours while he clicked through his 98 channels and licked his wounds of the past ten days.

It felt good to again have cable TV and a remote that functioned properly. Jason was especially pleased to note that *his* neighborhood was keeping digital cable, instead of retrofitting to analog.

Later, Jason logged on to Christine's blog, where he read a few more entries. He licked the cereal residue off his fingers and posted his first and only blog comment. Then he logged off that site, intending never to view it again.

* * * *

Amanda heard a foot kick at the bottom of her apartment door and guessed it was Christine with both arms full. Since it would take her a while to reach the entrance, she called out, "I'm coming." Amanda's eyes were red from tears and lack of sleep; she'd been up most of the night watching sad movies. It was a bit after 9:00 a.m.

"I didn't know if you'd eaten yet, so I brought some breakfast. Egg and cheese biscuits — one with sausage and one with bacon."

"I might take both. Only thing to eat here is a can of tomato paste. Last week, when I cleared the pantry — which was already very slim — I really cleaned it out."

"Well, these biscuit things will fill you up. Got any coffee brewing?"

"All the coffee left with you over a week ago. Where's that black bag?"

"Oh yeah, in my trunk. I'll go get it. In the meantime, here's a laptop you can borrow. It's Daniel's. I didn't get to the wrecking yard yet to check on yours." Christine handed over the computer. "I'll get that food bag while you're logging on." She hustled back out the door.

Amanda winced when her right wrist tried to support half the weight of the laptop. Once on the couch, she managed to open the computer and quickly logged on with the built-in wireless connection.

E-mail first, because she hadn't read hers since Tuesday night. It was the usual spam, plus two messages from Louis and one from Maria. Another from Amanda's sister Kaye. Also one from her mother in Arizona… which brought to mind that she really ought to tell Mom about the wreck. Something from Sunny with a subject line "cushaw guts". And a message from Jason! She opened it. Scarcely a dozen words. Amanda began crying again.

Christine came in huffing slightly with the weight of the food-filled trash bag. "What's wrong now?" She put the sack down with a thud.

Amanda pointed to the screen. "Jason broke up with me… by e-mail!"

"He couldn't even man-up enough to call it quits in person?" Christine sat on the couch and put an arm over her friend's shoulder. From that position, she could likely also read Jason's short message but she properly remained silent.

Shortly, Amanda closed that message and lowered the lid until the laptop clicked softly, and then she stared at the device on her lap.

Christine broke the silence. "He wants you to send his pants and keys over to his mother's house. You want me to take them to Margaret?"

When Amanda nodded, a few tears dropped onto the computer's lid.

Christine didn't appear to notice. "So, where did you hide those britches, anyway?"

Amanda sucked up significant nasal drainage and dabbed her eyes with the heel of her hand. "Where he'd never look — in plain sight."

"Not plain enough." Christine scanned as far as her head could turn in both directions of the living space. "Where?"

Tears usually dampened her appetite, but Amanda realized she was quite hungry so she opened one of the breakfast sandwiches. "The whole time Jason stayed in my guestroom, they were hanging on the left rail of the treadmill."

"Good place. It's a lot more level since you added those bricks." Christine scurried down the hall, retrieved the slacks, and hurriedly returned to the couch.

Amanda's face was blank. "I can't believe I got dumped by e-mail." A biscuit crumb fell to her lap.

"Well, you're probably better off, Amanda. I don't think Jason was the right match for you anyway."

"He seemed pretty right, until he decided to invade my apartment despite my protests." She took another small bite.

"A man's true colors are revealed during a crisis, no matter what type or size of crisis." Christine pointed toward the former site of Amanda's tablecloth. "And you can wrap a man up in bright floral colors, but underneath... he's just brown burlap."

Though Christine apparently liked the sound of her metaphor, it didn't make much sense to Amanda, who paid little attention to the brief philosophy lesson. "Uh, I don't think I can read any of your blog right now." She took another small bite of egg, but her heart wasn't in the nutrition. "But I was curious about the buzz."

"No more buzz... it's dead. Took it down this morning, right before I came over here. Wrote my final post. Told everybody I'd unintentionally turned a minor illness into a major catastrophe, and explained about your wreck. Announced I was donating the money we'd collected to the local displaced women's center. Somebody else had already posted something about the breakup."

"Even our *breakup* is on the Internet now? Blistered butt-rash! I guess that was probably Jason's post."

"Yeah. But I wasn't going to say." Christine sat next to her friend on the couch. "I didn't post anything on Wednesday, because of your wreck and hospital and everything. So the bloggers were buzzing, asking if anybody knew anything about *Missy* and *Marty*." Christine sighed. "Since you last saw it — Tuesday, I guess — there'd been a new undercurrent. We'd already seen several bloggers urging us to drop the entire project. But this new thread was encouraging *Marty* and *Missy* to reconcile. It's ironic — I guess they saw the break coming before Jason made up his mind on..."

"He sent the e-mail yesterday afternoon." Amanda's eyes filled again.

"In the last comment I read this morning, somebody wanted to pitch in on some flowers to be sent to *Missy*."

Tears resumed.

Christine let her cry on the couch and then briefly shoulder-hugged her friend. "I guess we ought to get moving. Your doctor's appointment is for 10:30, isn't it?"

"Yeah, glad you remembered." She sucked up the drainage. "Let me take a spit bath and wash my hair in the sink. Give me fifteen minutes."

* * * *

Amanda's regular doctor — plus several new X-rays — confirmed everything the E.R. doctors and nurse had said. Possibly a mild concussion, likely with no bad effects. Right wrist was strained but not sprained. Ribs bruised but not fractured. Three toes on right foot were fractured, but not broken. The doctor examined each toe — excruciatingly — and had her nurse re-splint them.

Amanda struggled to put on her ugly blue canvas boot with the wooden plank sole. "I still don't understand how these three toes got injured from a rear-end — or right rear corner — collision."

"I'm guessing you really stood on that brake pedal — a natural reaction when the vehicle stopped in front of you. When the other car hit you, it put even more pressure on your braking foot than those toes could withstand. So they cracked." The doctor's chin jutted out slightly. "I see lots of broken feet in car crashes."

"Didn't know that."

"It gets worse as women age, of course. Bones lose density and strength. But you've got plenty of time before you need to worry about osteoporosis. Not too early to take calcium supplements, though." The doctor waggled a forefinger as she handed Amanda a prescription for a week's worth of pain pills.

"How long do I wear this boot?"

"Hard to say. Maybe a week or so. Take off the boot for your shower, but wrap a freezer bag or something around your foot so the splint bindings don't get wet."

That sounded awkward. Maybe she'd have to skip showers for a few days. *Ha.*

"Come back here in a week... next Thursday. The nurse will take off the splints. You can show us then how much movement you can stand. Pain isn't visible, but those toes won't let you walk on them until they're ready. No need to rush things. Take care of your toes — you'll need them in good shape when you're an old lady."

This doctor is obsessed with old age.

On their way from the doctor's office, Christine drove to the pharmacy again to fill the new prescription. She also stopped at a fast-food place and got a bag of roast beef sandwiches, plus curly fries and two gigantic diet drinks. "This ought to keep you going until supper."

"All that?" Amanda pointed.

"As if. Half is yours."

"Not sure I can eat that many little sandwiches. Let me have two and you take the other four." Amanda sorted. "Oh, I've been meaning to ask you: what about your book?"

"On hold. Maybe we should proceed more slowly. I shouldn't have expected to fix several generations of man-cold problems in two weeks."

Now she becomes cautious!

Getting from the car into the apartment was still quite awkward. People say you don't get accustomed to temporary crutches until you don't need them any more. Christine helped as much as possible, but she was mostly in the way.

"If you wrap that wrist, it'll be easier to grip the crutch handle." Christine pointed. "Do you have an Ace bandage?"

Amanda nodded and then got misty again. It was the bandage she'd used for Jason's alleged injuries. He'd left it wadded up on the bathroom counter.

After Amanda calmed down again, Christine hugged her briefly. "I've got to abandon you this afternoon. I have another face-to-face with my delicious lawyer downtown."

"Be careful entering the parking lots." Amanda smiled slightly, despite the drying tears.

"Ha, yeah. Well, Bruce works for a firm with its own private parking area, thank you very much." Christine started to leave. "Are you going to be okay for supper? I mean, with the stuff in that big bag?"

"I don't remember what's in there, but, yeah, I'll be fine. You go ahead. And thanks, Christine, for helping me yesterday and today."

Christine just waved… then left.

Amanda spent a few moments thinking about Christine's several kindnesses these past two days. In contrast, she reflected on how horribly she had treated Jason when he came to her for help. The injured patient turned on the television and cried through part of another movie.

The doctor had said Amanda should stay home for at least three days… during her crunch weeks! The grant cycle process couldn't survive with her missing *any* days. She figured everything was ruined: her job, her relationship, and her car. She blamed Louis for sending her to a meeting that *he* should have attended.

Amanda also blamed Jason, who'd made her late and indirectly caused the wreck. But mostly it was his fault for moving in despite her protests.

She additionally had every right to be furious at Christine, for too many reasons to mention, but mostly for escalating everything. The entire matter could have been settled quicker and with significantly less collateral damage if she'd never asked her older friend for help. Curiously, however, though she felt wounded *by* Christine, Amanda was not actually angry *at* her. At least Christine had tried to help. Her methods were far afield, but her motives were unselfish... more or less.

Amanda brooded, limped to the bathroom and kitchen a few times, and cried at the television some more.

— — —

In early afternoon, her phone rang... a work number. Louis! She knew she had to answer.

"Didn't you get my voicemails and e-mails?" He couldn't be bothered to ask how she was feeling after her wreck. *Dang Yankees.*

"Sorry, I got tied up with hospital, insurance, drug stores, and doctor visits. But my laptop was in my wrecked car, so I couldn't read any e-mails you sent." That was a truth variant — no way could Louis know she'd had access to a borrowed computer.

"When are you coming in?"

"Doctor told me to stay prone for at least three days."

"When did those three days start? Yesterday morning when you collided with that other vehicle?"

"I didn't collide with anybody. Some old lady ran me down!"

"Whatever."

"Louis, I'll be back on Monday. Okay?"

There was a short pause on his end. "How about I send over the rest of these apps, so you can read while you're relaxing?"

"I'm not relaxing! I was in a car wreck!" She was just about to scream.

"Well, I could send some over tomorrow, then. That'd give you the weekend to catch up."

"Louis! I already worked my entire Saturday and Sunday *last* weekend, with no extra pay and no hint of appreciation. Plus, I'm allowed paid sick leave like everybody else on the county payroll. Nobody else works while they're sick."

"But you're not sick. It's just your foot."

"And concussion and wrist. Look up *injury* in the county manual, if you want. But I'm not reading any dreary grant apps until I get past this pain medicine. I'll be in the office early Monday."

"But who's going to prepare the recommendations?"

Amanda sighed heavily. "I've left notes and evaluation forms on each app as I've read them. All they need is to be typed up."

"What about the ones you haven't read yet?"

"If you can't wait, Louis, *you* read them. I'll be there Monday. Bye!"

After she folded her phone, she wondered if she'd even have her job by Monday. *Hairy hell!*

Monday would be the 24th, which meant six more work days before September 1st. If she could keep Louis out of her office for that period and wrangle even one hour of clerical help for each of those shifts, Amanda could still pull this grant cycle together. *Possibly.* Hobbling around on broken toes certainly wouldn't help things, but she could survive.

Amanda was, if anything, a survivor.

And, now that Jason had clearly exited her life, she was also solitary again — no distractions at home. Well, except noisy kids and a yodeling neighbor.

Amanda realized she was looking in the direction of the television but not actually watching the program. Her mind had wandered. How could she have let things go that far? Why hadn't she just asserted herself more vigorously at the beginning and chased Jason away with a broom handle?

Would the repercussions of a physical ejection have been any worse than the fix she was in presently? *Couldn't be.* At worst, Jason would have sulked for a couple of weeks and then one of them (or both) would have looked for opportunity and means to make up.

Why had she let it go so far?

It hadn't been just the manic overconfidence of her domineering friend — though surely that remained a driving force. It had not been merely curiosity at how long Jason would endure the deprivation — though she had been captivated by that question.

While not aware of this during Jason's stay, Amanda was now convinced of an element distinct from all these others. She realized she'd been given a unique opportunity to learn more about her lover. At his nadir, to be sure, but information to weigh when considering if Jason was a viable long-term mate. It sounded rather clinical as she reflected on it now.

The January episode had been difficult and exhausting, of course, but it had lacked the intense work pressure of Amanda's annual crunch at the office. Plus, that had been only about ten weeks after they'd first become lovers, so there had still been something of a honeymoon aura.

In January, she'd thought his saggy, rumpled pajamas were kind of cute. In August, they'd just looked sloppy and rank. What a difference those few months had made!

Did such awareness signal that — if eventually married — their relationship would continually slide downhill away from love and attraction? She didn't know. But surely this recent crisis was a test of all that "richer / poorer... sickness / health" mumbo-jumbo.

Amanda watched the Lifetime Channel with one eye and listened to incessant yodeling practice with one ear. Incredibly, she was still able to nap briefly on the couch. *Love those pain meds.*

— — —

Though unsteady and slow, Amanda was up at about 6:30 p.m. when her doorbell rang. It took nearly five minutes to hobble to the entrance on her too-short crutches. Though aware she looked awful, she had no inclination to check a mirror, so she just sighed heavily and opened the door. Jason's mom. "Hi, Margaret, come on in. The place is a mess." Amanda moved aside clumsily.

"I'm sure it's typical of a place where a sick man has held forth for a week and a half and an injured woman has just come home."

It was. "I was about to scratch around for supper. You're welcome to join me."

Margaret smiled. "Well, let me see what you're offering. If it's any of the dishes detailed on Christine's blog, I think I'll pass."

"No, this is fairly ordinary stuff as best I can recall. I haven't even opened the bag Christine brought back." Amanda pointed toward it.

"Let me give you a hand." Margaret hoisted the sack onto the table and began removing things. Suddenly she stopped and looked around the dining area. "Where's your tablecloth?"

"Your son was wearing it when he vamoosed. Bright floral design... should be easy to find him."

"Florals aren't usually his colors." Margaret sorted items as she unloaded the bag. "Looks like soup is the best possibility of this array. Would you like me to heat it?"

"Please." Amanda sat at the table and leaned her crutches against the next chair. "When was the last time we talked? Saturday?"

Margaret nodded. "You stopped by to ask if you were being too harsh on my Jason. I didn't think so at the time, but under the present circumstances, I guess you were." A slight pause while she located a saucepan and opened the soup can. "How's the foot?"

"Toes. They hurt... throb."

"Your head is better? The concussion, I mean?"

"Yeah. Did Christine fill you in?"

Margaret nodded as she stirred the soup. "She called this afternoon."

"Well, my wrist also hurts, especially when I have to hold those crutches. But what really hurts... is in here." Amanda pointed to her chest and choked up again. "I'm sorry. I've been doing a lot of that for the past two days."

— — —

Margaret kept tending the soup. "It's okay, Amanda. It's natural for your feelings to kind of flood out right now."

"One reason I feel this bad is that I was so awful to him. I mean, I told him I couldn't handle any company and I made several direct suggestions that he leave, like *'Maybe you should go to your own apartment, Jason.'* And I gave him plenty of other hints."

"Too vague, for a man," Margaret interrupted.

"Probably." Amanda nodded. "But mostly, for the time he was here, I just kept making snide and sarcastic remarks." She shook her head. "Does Jason not *get* sarcasm?"

Briefly silent, Margaret smiled softly. "I used that with Henry, too — for years — with little measurable result. Finally, one evening in the middle of an awful argument — no idea what it was about — I just flat-out lost it. I said, *'Don't you know when I'm being sarcastic?'* He had this shocked expression on his face and then he said, slowly, *'No, I don't.'* So I said, *'Well, what the blazes did you think all these years when I've made comments like that to get you on the same page with me?'* And he said, *'I just thought you were in a bad mood.'* That cured me of sarcasm. I realized he'd managed to ignore some 90 per cent of what I thought I had clearly communicated... by attributing it to my supposed moodiness." She stirred again, leaned closely to gauge the steam, and took the soup pan off the stovetop.

"I've heard Jason say something about moods, too."

Margaret looked in three cupboards before locating two bowls. "If you just want to zing him while impressing yourself with your own cleverness, then keep up the sarcasm."

"Ouch, that hurts."

"It was meant to. I learned... and now you." Then Margaret softened. "But if you're trying to communicate some nugget of information or thought, or attempting to explain what you're feeling about something... just say it plain. Straight and simple. Men aren't stupid — well, some are." She smiled slightly and selected two spoons from the second drawer she opened. "Okay, most men are pretty darn dumb. But some are perceptive enough to get the simple things. If what you say is likely to be dismissed as moodiness without any substance, then you haven't accomplished much besides hurt his feelings with the nastiness behind the sarcasm." Margaret thought for a moment to determine if she'd left anything out. "Plain, straight, and simple. Add loving, if you can muster it under the circumstances of the moment."

Amanda's eyes clouded. "I feel rotten — being so nasty to him, on top of everything that I let Christine do. Poor Jason."

Margaret ladled soup into the bowls. "Don't beat yourself up, Amanda. I read a lot of the blog before it went down this morning. Sure, some of your friend's ideas were pretty harsh, but sometimes a grown man does need a whipping, so to speak. If I'd had Christine's imagination back when my Henry went through this phase, it might have been easier to cure him of his colds."

"You mean besides the broken water heater gambit." Amanda tried to taste the soup but it was obviously still too hot, so she just stared into her bowl.

Margaret recognized a stalemate: neither one of the ex-lovebirds wanted to make the first move. She was only about 70 per cent sure Jason was still interested in salvaging the relationship. But she was now certain Amanda really wanted things to mend, so Margaret would nudge a bit. "Something else is bothering you." Not a question.

Amanda's eyes clouded. "I'm afraid Jason won't… won't ever come back. That I've really wrecked things and I'll never see him again."

Margaret took the already-opened sleeve of saltine crackers, partly stale, from the table and crumpled half a dozen into her soup. "Now, settle down. Men are prideful and can't stand people laughing at them. With Christine's blog, Jason's heard a lot of laughter. That hurts, sure."

"I know. They were ridiculing me, too."

Margaret nodded. "Look, Jason's a stubborn man. Nearly as mule-headed as his daddy. But I was always able to smooth Henry's feathers. Because he had just a tad more love for me than he had stubborn pride for himself. So he always came around, eventually." Margaret gingerly tasted her soup. "If Jason loves you as much as I think he does, he'll come to his senses. You might need to gild the lily, so to speak, to help patch things up. But he'll come back."

"Gild what lily?"

"You know, cook his favorite meal, bake him some brownies…"

"I don't bake." Amanda blurted it out quickly. "And his favorite meal is the entire steakhouse buffet. I'll have to gild something else."

"You didn't let me finish. I was starting to explain that you can smooth over about ten times as many ruffled feathers on a man if you just give him special attention."

"Attention? Like holding the lug thingies while he changes a tire? Watching him play golf? What?" Amanda must have been so distraught that her mind was on a completely different track.

Margaret eyed her closely. Surely Jason's girlfriend wasn't that dense. "In the bedroom, for Heaven's sake!" Margaret sighed heavily. "Good grief. Do I have to write it down?"

"Oh, that kind of special attention." Amanda rolled her eyes. "Well, I can think of several possibilities."

"Thank goodness. For a minute, I thought I was dealing with an idiot." Margaret resumed eating her soup.

Amanda only fiddled with her spoon and then sighed with a lot of shoulder movement. "It's probably just as well that we're broken up right now, because of all my work stuff. But I don't want to lose Jason forever. I'd like to get him back after September 1st."

Margaret started to speak, but took another breath and waited a moment. "Amanda, a good relationship has to be able to survive the bad weeks as well as the rest of the year. You can't just put a husband, or boyfriend, on hold for two weeks when work is at crunch time. If the relationship has any substance, it doesn't go on hiatus when external pressures are high. You can establish temporary boundaries, of course, but real love continues through the crisis phases." Margaret went on to clarify that everything she said also applied to the male involved.

— — —

Amanda felt distinctly rotten. Those were things she already knew, but she'd allowed herself to forget them. It made her seem shallow and self-absorbed. "I don't know what's next, Margaret."

"You succeeded in running him out, though it wasn't the way you'd envisioned. The blog magnified everything. He responded to the public ridicule by breaking up with you. So, the ball's in your court." Margaret watched the patient's face briefly and then looked toward the window. "I need to leave soon... don't like to drive after dusk." She finished her soup quickly, rinsed the bowl and spoon, and put them inside the dishwasher. "Amanda, loving partners can't completely avoid critical periods, but you can't suspend the relationship during a crisis. If you and Jason had anything more than a fling, it needs to harness enough steam to get *through* the crunch times."

Margaret left before Amanda could formulate a reply. She'd still only consumed a third of her soup.

Later, after she finished eating, Amanda picked up her phone. Jason was on speed dial number two. She pressed it. The phone rang six times and went to voicemail.

"Hi, Jason. It's Amanda. It's seven-something on Thursday night. I'd like to talk... about everything. Give me a call back if you'd like to talk, too."

It wasn't exactly the apology opportunity she'd envisioned if she had reached him *live*. But hopefully he'd be interested enough to call her back.

When Amanda last checked her phone around 11:00 p.m., there were still no return calls from Jason. *Maybe his battery's too low.*

On the borrowed laptop, Amanda logged on to e-mail. Perhaps a different medium would get through to him. Her text was succinct:

Lots of mistakes in the last 10 days or so.
I'd like to talk it over.
Please acknowledge.

She sent it with a *read receipt* requested. If Jason opened it but didn't respond, at least she'd know he'd seen her message.

Chapter 19

August 21 (Friday)

Since Jason had already told Ms. Grunion he wouldn't be at work that day, there was no need to rise early and phone in. This was the final day of his two-week sick leave *vacation*. A very strange time — absolutely nothing had gone as he'd hoped.

Now, his entire balance of paid sick days had been wasted and his relationship with Amanda was busted. *Destroyed... wrecked... whatever*. Whose fault? Mostly Amanda's. Sure, Jason sent the e-mail formalizing their breakup, but she was the one who'd trashed their *whatever*.

They'd been steady lovers for nearly ten months — a very odd time, as Jason looked back on it. Amanda had always been the one setting parameters and he'd agreeably let her do so. She'd seemed to need an analysis of their togetherness. Jason had just wanted to share in their time together. He hadn't wanted to think so much — just to enjoy it.

And he had enjoyed those ten months... mostly. There had been that awkward experience around the beginning of June, another example of Christine's explosively meddlesome involvement. But once that confusion had settled down, Jason had resumed his normal default setting: hang out together, make love with Amanda, and chase off the other guys who'd be only too happy to take her away from him. *Well, they can have her now.*

Since he'd listened to Amanda's voicemail yesterday afternoon, Jason knew she'd received his break-up e-mail from Tuesday evening. But he had no intention of responding to her call. He would have already taken Amanda's number off his speed dial if he knew how to program his phone.

Jason surfed his 98 cable channels for about an hour. Though he'd never stopped to figure the exact percentage, he only liked about a third of them. Of course, he had to click through all the others to get to the ones he liked. So, two-thirds of his brief stops were on channels he didn't want and the rest of that hour was distributed among the 30-plus channels he appreciated enough to pause upon. His time on each varied with the content: if a commercial was on, he zipped away immediately. But if it was regular programming on those *good* channels, he might spend as much as a full minute assessing each before moving on to the greener pastures up or down the numbering sequence.

Amanda had acted like his television M.O. was irritating. What about her watching pattern? Park on one of three channels for hours and watch chick flick after chick flick with no variety? What a waste of thirty other good channels.

Jason put down the remote and logged on to e-mail. Kevin had sent another conquest story from a recent happy hour — an adventurous school teacher from Missouri. True to that state's motto, she had insisted that Kevin "show me"... so he did. *Ha!* Kevin was hopeless, but he surely had a lot of female enjoyment without all the confusing hassles.

The other e-mails were not nearly as inspiring. Three spams: delete, delete, delete. L.L.Bean wanted Jason to buy a jacket. *Nice, but too pricey.* Something from his middle brother: *blah, blah.*

E-mail from Amanda! *What else does she have to say?* He opened it. More of the same from her previous phone message… she wanted to talk. They'd had plenty of potential time to talk during his ten days of neglect, deprivation, and Internet ridicule. But on those awful days, Amanda had spent considerably more time with Christine than she had with him.

Now she wanted to talk. *Fat chance.* Delete. That e-mail was history, their relationship was history, and now… so was Amanda.

A very strange history indeed.

* * * *

Christine intuitively realized she and Jason's mom needed to get their heads together, but Margaret beat her to it.

Earlier that morning, Margaret had phoned and instructed Christine to meet her at the new coffee shop on the I-40 frontage road, north side. Normally, Christine was more accustomed to giving instruction than following, but she deferred to Margaret, one of the few women Christine allowed that tribute.

Each arrived within three minutes of 10:30 a.m. They were seated quickly since the breakfast rush had already cleared out.

"Jason's pants are out in my car. He left word with Amanda to get them to you. His keys are in one of the pockets."

"I'll get them as we leave." Margaret smiled slightly. "Sometimes it's useful to have a man's trousers."

When the waitress ambled over, they ordered.

Christine was accustomed to being in the driver's seat. Since she was not certain of Margaret's specific reason for this called meeting, she was intensely curious for it to begin. So Christine broke the ice. "You know, I feel so responsible for this breakup."

"I agree, you are."

Christine had hoped for sympathetic reassurance that she wasn't really at fault. But clearly, Margaret didn't play such games. "You shoot pretty straight, don't you, Margaret?"

She nodded. "Helps me reach the target more often."

Their coffees arrived. The smallish shop was a perfect marriage of coffee, tea, and fresh-baked croissants. It smelled heavenly.

"Amanda's life is a mess right now." Christine sprinkled sweetener, about half of a pink packet. "I'd like to do what I can to make it right."

"It's really between them." Margaret took only cream. "And should've been to begin with." She sipped her coffee reflectively. "However, I think there's still hope for salvage. I have a strong hunch Amanda's injuries have set the stage for this relationship to come back together, eventually." Margaret dabbed a napkin to her lips. "Wounded pride is the biggest barrier. But a good outcome partly depends on how perceptive Jason is."

"Not so much, from what I've seen." Christine shrugged very slightly. "Since we're talking straight and plain here."

Margaret nodded agreement. "I used to think Jason's crayon box didn't have a built-in sharpener. But later, I concluded he was just too lazy to use it."

"Too spoiled, maybe?" Christine continued stirring and didn't meet Margaret's eyes.

Most likely Margaret felt the barb but did not appear offended. "Perhaps... he was my youngest." She took another sip. "So that's an obstacle. Plus, whether Amanda's love is stronger than her pride."

"Another big factor might be whether she still has a job, come Monday." Christine finally tasted her coffee and paused before continuing. "Is there anything I can do to help patch things up?"

Margaret traced her ring finger around the edge of the cup. "I'm pretty sure Jason doesn't yet know about the wreck. Amanda said she hasn't told him and doesn't intend to. So, up 'til the time Jason finds out, it's important for you to continue helping her. Especially for things like transportation."

"What about after Jason finds out?"

"Once he learns about Amanda's injuries, you need to exit the scene — back away, disappear completely. Let the two lovebirds reconnect without an audience. Couples need space to work out their problems. They don't need friends or relatives — or bloggers — butting in and trying to sway them."

"Uh, aren't we butting in? I mean, we sit here plotting what to do about their relationship. And we're trying to influence the outcome."

"They're young; they need a nudge. Besides, this is different. You're Amanda's best friend and I'm Jason's mother. We both have an interest to protect." Margaret's smile was so tiny it seemed like most of it remained inside. "But we've both got to vanish as soon as Jason finds out about the wreck and Amanda's injuries."

Christine closed her eyes while thinking. "So we do the advance work — set the stage. Then we're invisible."

"Stage play is a good analogy. You know when the crew in black outfits changes the sets between acts? Think of us as the women in black outfits. They need us to move around the furniture and maybe even adjust a few walls."

Christine remembered looking very good in tight black outfits, so she smiled slyly. "But Jason and Amanda won't know the walls have moved until they bump into a few."

"And stumble over the chair we moved from here to there." Margaret pointed vaguely to the adjacent table.

"Pretty devious." Christine grinned. "Wish I'd thought of it."

Margaret sipped more coffee. "You went straight to high-tech with your previous involvement. To get them back together, my approach is low-tech. From talking with Amanda last evening, I'm pretty sure she's since tried to reach Jason to reopen dialog. Right now I believe it's up to him."

"You think he'll take the cue?"

"He might need a little direct prompting."

Christine leaned a bit closer. "What have you got in mind?"

"I'm leaving here with his trousers, so I'll summon him. When Jason comes over for his pants, I'm going to help him make up his mind that he and Amanda need each other."

Christine was quiet for a moment. "So you're going to tell him about Amanda's accident?"

"Not to begin with. I'll save that for the final hand. I want to see his cards first."

"I liked the stage play metaphors better."

"Me, too, but I couldn't think of one to keep it going." Margaret shrugged. "Here's the bottom line: Amanda's injuries are a blessing in disguise. This will get them back in that apartment together and either their relationship will mend... or end."

* * * *

Amanda was miserable. With a plank-soled boot, short crutches, and a hurt wrist, she felt like a prisoner in a dreary, noisy, and cluttered jail. So far, she'd served roughly 48 hours on her post-injury *sentence*. It was about midday Friday and she couldn't think of anything to eat besides soup. All she'd had for breakfast was stale toast and a single serving of instant coffee which she'd saved from a motel in Vicksburg, Mississippi two years before.

Jason still had not returned her call from Wednesday evening.

She checked her mailbox again. Amanda could tell from the electronic receipt that Jason had received and opened her e-mail from the previous night. But no reply. Nothing new from Jason since his break-up message.

She'd made two attempts to meet Jason halfway and he had not responded to either. Her brief window of willingness to accept him back had not been open very wide to begin with, and now it was barely a crack. If Jason did not reply very soon, Amanda figured that window might slam the rest of the way down and she'd turn the latch.

Maybe this was the way it was meant to be. In the crucible of this ordeal Amanda finally got to see Jason's true colors: he was a selfish and inconsiderate wuss, and a momma's boy (too long at the teat). *Christine was right all along*.

Amanda was embarrassed and also proud — a burdensome combination. All the attention and ridicule from bloggers had provided added pressure to stand her ground.

If Jason made no contact by suppertime, a two-day window, it was goodbye and good riddance. The confused flicker of love remaining in Amanda's heart seemed overwhelmed by the one-sided, incredibly high maintenance Jason evidently required.

— — —

Amanda couldn't handle soup for lunch. Maybe some tasteless rice cake crackers would keep her from grinding her teeth. Those crackers had such insignificant flavor, she couldn't tell if they were fresh or stale.

She turned on the television and watched a tear-jerker movie in progress. During the afternoon she napped some and cried a bit. She also took another pain pill. *Kahh.*

* * * *

Margaret phoned her son about midafternoon. There are invitations to visit and there are summonses to appear. This was the latter. She told Jason to be there around 6:30. "No meal."

At 6:00 p.m., Margaret put a single frozen entree in her microwave.

By the time she'd finished her supper, rinsed and tossed the plastic tray into a recycling bin, Jason had arrived, three minutes late.

As he entered, Margaret pointed to his trousers hanging on the hall closet doorknob.

"Is that what I had to drop everything for?"

"I can't have a man's pants decorating my front door. What would the neighbors think?" She quickly realized he didn't get the intended humor — just as dense as his daddy. "I wanted to see how you're feeling now that your cold should have run its complete course." *Thank goodness he'd shaved and showered.*

Jason tried to manufacture a cough, but couldn't quite pull it off. "I'm better now. But I didn't go in to work today because my stomach system is still so weird from ten days of no food."

"And you didn't want to go back on a Friday, anyway." She smiled. "Well, that enforced diet was probably good for you. I think you slimmed down a bit." Margaret patted his belly. "Good idea to keep it off."

"Okay. You've inspected my stomach and I've got my britches." He squeezed the pocket to check for his keys and also located his credit cards. "Still not sure why I had to rush over here."

Margaret needed some time to give him a course correction back to reality. "Sit for a minute and let me tell you about when your father got sick with a man-cold."

"The stinking man-cold thing again! What's so different about colds for men versus the ones for women? Same germs, or virus... whatever. Isn't it?"

"Oh, I suppose the causes are about the same. The effects differ a lot, though." She patted the sofa. "Sit down and I'll explain."

Jason sighed heavily and sat.

"Now, you know that I loved your father, deeply."

He nodded.

"Well, my relationship with your father was ever so much better after he lost the dangerous illusion that a stuffy nose would get him a long vacation, being waited on hand and foot."

"I don't remember Dad ever being sick."

"Precisely. I'd already cured him by the time you were in kindergarten. I couldn't take care of the house and three boys *and* a sick husband." Margaret paused to see if her son was on the same page. "Once or twice, when your dad was really ill, I was by his side almost all day and night. But it's important to separate a rare true illness from frequent gold-bricking. The man-cold is about 10 per cent sick, maybe 40 per cent gold-bricking, and 50 per cent drama."

"I never associated Dad with drama."

"Okay, think of it this way: with a horse, you have to break him of excessive wildness before he can be useful. Similarly, some men have to be broken of certain excesses. Milking a man-cold is an excess and it needs to be broken."

"What did you do to Dad?" Jason looked retroactively worried.

It was slightly embarrassing to do so, but Margaret told her son about the cold water cure she'd used on Henry.

"That's why you always patted the water heater when you passed it in the utility room?"

Margaret nodded and smiled.

— — —

Jason sat back on the couch and took in all this new information. "So you're telling me that milking a whatever-cold at Amanda's expense was wrong." Jason admitted, silently, that he'd already realized that. He understood, now, that he'd mainly been thinking of himself. "But, hey, it feels good to be coddled a bit, now and then."

"Sure it does." Margaret placed a motherly hand on his arm. "The key is in timing and motive."

"Motive?"

"If your motive is sex…"

"Mom!" He couldn't help lurching backward.

"Sorry, Jason. I'm speaking plainly for a reason." She cleared her throat softly. "If you're motive is sex, just bring Amanda some flowers, or take her out for dinner, or both. Try being romantic. But don't use a pretend illness to get her into bed with you."

"It wasn't pretend. The doctor said I had a cold."

"I know the cold was real. But you blew it into a full-scale tragedy. A cold is a cold. Drink juice, take vitamin C, rest as much as you can, and then get over it. Don't use it as a bludgeon on somebody else's life."

"Okay." He digested that, though it was not the least bit tasty.

"Now, when Amanda held you at her door that first evening and said she couldn't handle company, that meant *bad timing* — *not now*. But more importantly, she was saying *no*.

When you hear *no*, it means exactly that. It doesn't mean *maybe*. Your charm can't cancel the *no*. It was wrong to impose on Amanda when she clearly said *no* and even explained why."

"Lots of times people say *no* but don't really mean it."

"Wrong — they still mean it. But some will nearly kill themselves trying to accommodate you anyway. You were being bullheaded. Jason, when a woman says *no*, that's the end of the conversation... not the beginning of a debate."

They talked for another ten minutes.

Jason softened, a little. His heart wasn't in the breakup anyway, and he knew he truly did love Amanda, despite all of the recent neglect and abuse... which was how he viewed it.

Margaret broke a short silence. "Has Amanda tried to reach you yet?"

Jason nodded. "She left voicemail, uh, Wednesday night. E-mailed me yesterday."

"How did you respond?"

"I didn't answer." He was surprised his mother would expect him to. "I'm not going to make the first move."

"Jason, if she's sent you e-mail and tried to call you, then she's made the first moves. Now it's your turn."

"I don't know if you're aware of all the horrible things she and Christine did to me while I was there."

"I have a pretty good idea. You deserved some of it, you know."

He was shocked to hear his mother agree with the wicked witches. "But they also published everything on that Internet site and now everybody knows all of it, including my freakin' name."

"I know. That's probably the most unfortunate aspect of the whole debacle. There's no privacy or confidentiality in cyberspace and anyone who uses it with that notion is just plain stupid."

"Including Christine."

"Including her, yes. She was trying to help Amanda, but Christine botched things badly by involving the Internet. She should have privately offered coping suggestions to Amanda and then bowed out."

"Did you hear what they did to that giant pumpkin thing?"

Margaret chuckled. "Yes, I know about the cushaw. I'm sure it was a frightening experience for you to overhear, but it actually was a pretty clever ploy. I'll give that one to Christine."

"She's a witch, you know."

Margaret thought for a moment. "Almost all women are witches... a little, I think. The important thing is, what are we like the other 90 per cent of the time?"

Jason was antsy to leave.

Margaret touched his arm again. "What do you plan to do... about everything?"

"Look, I know you like Amanda and apparently you wish we were back together. But Mom, I just don't think there's enough left between us to put back together." Jason's head fell forward as he sighed. "A woman who really loved me couldn't treat me like that."

"A man who really loved Amanda wouldn't barge in on her after she told him *no*."

Jason shook his head. The equation didn't quite match up for him.

— — —

Margaret gave her son a moment. Then she realized it was time to play her trump card. "If you'd been injured in a bad wreck, even though you two were still broken up, would you want Amanda to come see you?"

"Of course!" No hesitation. "Wrecks even out things. The argument or whatever has to be on hold when somebody's hurt bad."

Margaret nodded wisely and added a dramatic pause. "Would you feel that same way if the wreck happened to Amanda?"

"Same thing, exactly." Then it registered. "What happened? Is Amanda okay?" He looked around his mother's living room. "Where is she?"

Margaret explained about Amanda's courthouse wreck and injuries. She revised the diagnosis considerably, however. In this retelling, Amanda had suffered a major concussion and fractured ribs; a wrist was terribly sprained and one entire foot was shattered. Of course, by the time Jason sorted out those discrepancies, the degree of Amanda's injuries would no longer be the main issue.

She watched her son closely. No one could fake the worry on his face or the fear in his eyes. Jason still adored Amanda… no doubt about it.

— — —

Jason was stunned like he'd banged his head on a low beam.

Besides worry and fear, he felt distinctly guilty over the simplified cause-and-effect: if he hadn't invaded her apartment, Amanda wouldn't be injured. More specifically, if she hadn't helped him with the Ace bandage that morning, Amanda probably would have arrived before the parking lot became so crowded.

All that guilt aside, Jason wanted to rush to Amanda — he was drawn to her. When somebody's injured, all the arguments are on hold.

"Amanda's at home?" Jason pictured all those injuries cited. "Not in the hospital?"

"Overcrowded. Had to send her home, despite her terrible condition."

He rose abruptly, kissed his mother's cheek loudly, and said goodbye.

Jason was already on the road before he remembered he'd left his pants, cards, and extra keys.

Chapter 20

On Jason's hurried drive to her apartment, he tried calling Amanda, but she didn't answer her phone. He envisioned her in traction on an adjustable bed with thick white wrappings around her head and tubes in her arms. *Maybe she can't even reach the phone.* He drove faster.

It was only about three miles from Margaret's house to Amanda's apartment, but it seemed like thirty. On top of everything else, he was stopped by a slow-moving Tennessee train apparently looking for a picnic spot.

In this medical emergency, Jason realized how much he adored Amanda, despite the awful things she'd put him through. He was still baffled why she'd treated him so badly, but since Christine was assuredly a witch, maybe Amanda had been under a nefarious spell. He put that out of his mind, however, because he knew Amanda needed him now and Jason was positive she'd be eager to see him. He tried calling again but still got no answer.

When he reached her complex's parking lot, he halfway expected to see medical teams bustling in and out of her doorway.

Nope. All was quiet, except for No-Neck flinging his tennis ball against the bricks and Mrs. Yodel diligently practicing.

He knocked eagerly. Jason didn't expect to see Amanda, of course. Most likely an attending nurse would manage the door.

Nobody answered.

Jason knocked again. The kid stopped flinging his ball and came over to watch.

After a few moments, a curtain moved at Amanda's front window. Still no answer at the door.

"Amanda! It's Jason. I've come to help."

"Jason who?" Through the door.

He turned to No-Neck. "She's just kidding. She knows me." Jason hated feeling that he owed that kid an explanation.

The boy eyed him carefully. "Ain't you th' one that tole me never git sick?"

"Yeah, that was me. Why?"

"Well, yer girlfriend got sick. Cain't walk."

"Paralyzed?" Jason banged more urgently on the door. "Amanda! Let me in!"

The yodeling stopped next door. A few moments later, Mrs. Yodel appeared beside him. "Last week you couldn't get away, and now you can't get back in?" Even in ordinary conversation, her pitch repeatedly changed between two distinct vocal registers. The obsessive woman couldn't stop yodeling!

Other residents of the nearby duplexes began to congregate and soon, a car stopped on the shoulder of Melrose and the driver got out, just to see what was going on. Perhaps he thought it was a murder scene.

Jason knocked again. "Amanda, I need to see you. If you won't let me in, I'll just sit here on your doorstep and wait."

Still no reply, but the curtain moved again. Members of the crowd peered over each other's shoulders and murmured their predictions.

"We need to talk." Loudly. Then, in scarcely more than a whisper, "Uh, I need to be inside, away from all these people." He was getting jittery with the assembled crowd. Jason had seen a B-movie where such a crowd suddenly tore into a man who'd been trying to get through someone's door.

"Amanda, please!"

The door latch clicked.

The crowd gasped.

Jason waited apprehensively, his hand craving to turn the doorknob.

Just when Jason thought someone might scream — and it might be him — the door opened about three inches. A bronzed security chain stretched across the expanse at roughly eye level.

Amanda looked awful, but she was standing. *Maybe not paralyzed after all.*

"Can I come inside?" Very plaintive.

Her sigh was so heavy, likely the entire crowd heard it, except for the old man with double hearing aids. The portal closed, the chain made a scraping sound, and the door slowly opened... a bit less than halfway.

Several in the crowd clapped.

Amanda reached her arm through the doorway and waved, obviously with no enthusiasm. From the scattered and muted cheers, she might have been a semi-popular crown princess waving from the palace balcony.

She hobbled to the side and Jason was able to enter.

Amanda closed the door and hissed, "I only let you in to avoid any further embarrassment with my neighbors."

Yikes. Jason had expected a warm welcome. He'd hurried to aid and comfort the woman he loved and she acted like he was selling cemetery plots in a swamp.

Amanda wasn't buying. She looked out the window and saw the crowd had not yet dispersed. Perhaps some expected to see Jason come flying back out. "You might as well sit for a minute, until that gaggle breaks up out there."

Jason tried to imagine how to ask why she was so hostile, without making her even more so. Since he couldn't formulate the words for that question, he shifted to a statement. "My mom just told me about your wreck. I didn't know, or I would have come by sooner."

"Why?"

"Uh, so I could help out and stuff."

"I left you a phone message and an e-mail. You didn't return either. What have we got to talk about now?"

Jason stammered a bit. "I thought maybe we could put our fight on hold until you get over your injuries. By the way, you don't look nearly as beat up as my mom seemed to think."

"I guess that's a left-handed compliment of sorts." Amanda hobbled over to the couch and let herself down with considerable effort.

"What's wrong with your back?"

"Nothing. Why?"

"How come you're all hunched over?" He squinted to aid his own diagnosis.

"Crutches are too short."

"I can adjust them." Jason quickly examined the bolts on the crutches: standard slot on one end and very tight wing nut on the other. "Have you got a screwdriver?"

"Yeah, I guess. Maybe next to the silverware drawer."

He found it on the fourth try and returned. "Stand up again and let me see how far off they are."

— — —

Amanda assessed Jason like he was a total stranger. She'd had no idea her ex-boyfriend was handy. She stood and held the crutch under her arm. The well-used pad lined up roughly with the middle of the side of her breast.

About four inches too short. Jason examined the holes. "Four ought to do it." He removed the carriage bolts and slid the foot piece down four holes. Then he reinserted the bolts and threaded the wing nuts. He did the same with the other crutch. "I won't make them as tight as before in case we need to adjust them again."

He said *we*. *Hmm.* "Uh, thanks." There was a long pause while she studied him further. "Jason, what are you doing here?"

"Helping you."

"I don't need help."

"Yes, you do." He nodded as though he thought it might convince her.

"What can you do to help me?"

"Bring you stuff. Drive you places. I can even heat things up." He paused briefly. "Plus, I can straighten up and clean."

"Ha!" It came out with more emphasis than she'd intended. "How is it you think you can clean up now, when you were a certified slob in here for ten solid days?"

"Because you need me now."

"I needed you before, but I just needed you to be somewhere else."

"Well, now I'm here again, but it's for a pacific reason." Yet another word Jason mangled. "It'll be completely different." He nodded. "Now, you're the patient."

"And you're going to take care of me?"

He just smiled. It might have been sincere, but it also looked the slightest bit dopey.

Who is this guy? And what did he do with Jason? "Whatever."

Jason looked around the living space and raised his hand toward the ceiling. "I see they've already fixed your TV and air conditioner."

She wondered how much to reveal. "Uh, I'm not sure how to say this, but all that was lies."

"What about the panther sitting on my chest?"

Amanda thought for a second. Sometimes when a person comes clean, it clears the slate and everybody feels better. But occasionally the truth is so fantastic that it's better to perpetuate the legend. "Vivid dreaming, like I told you." She hoped Diabla didn't reappear while Jason was around.

He didn't seem convinced about the panther hair, but Jason dropped that part of his inquiry. "Well, I've read some of that blog, so I know everything else was rigged to run me off."

"Then why are you back?"

"Because you need me even if you don't realize it yet."

There wasn't much point to this nearly circular conversation, so they simply agreed to be in the same space together through the weekend. It was a truce of sorts: Amanda would allow Jason to stay and help, but she refused to appreciate it.

Responding to his earlier question, Amanda revealed the correct diagnoses of her injuries. It lacked all the hyperbole attached by Margaret. She could imagine wise mothers might add fibs to their exaggerations.

"If your toes are fractured," Jason pointed, "how can you sleep under the covers?"

"I can't. I've just slept here on the couch with my foot sticking out from under a sheet. Can't have anything touching my toes at all."

"I can fix that. Have you got any big boxes? Sturdy cardboard?"

"Lots of boxes in the guestroom."

"True, I even fell over some. Forgot." He rose from the couch. "Okay if I empty one and modify it a bit?"

"Uh, yeah. One near the door is big and sturdy. Just has a couple of enormous comforters inside. You can stack those somewhere on the junk pile."

"You mind if I cut up that box?"

Amanda shrugged and sighed.

He found a bread knife after checking two kitchen drawers and then disappeared down the hall. Amanda could hear grunting, sawing, and even *"Ouch, dang it!"* once or twice. About twenty minutes later, wiping sweat from his eyes, Jason appeared and beckoned her to come look.

She moved much more gracefully on her adjusted crutches and made the distance in record time. In her room, the foot of her bed looked like a small lean-to. The sheet and spread were draped over the box, which was cut away at the bottom, with a tail hanging over the edge of the mattress. Large notches steadied it to the footboard. The sides had enough of a corner remaining for extra support, but still provided an opening of over three feet in width.

"This should give you some maneuvering room. This way, your toes don't have to touch the covers but you can still lie in your own bed."

Amanda was briefly speechless. "Why are you doing this?" She was still searching for motive.

"I want to help. If I had fractured toes, I'd want somebody to build me a foot box to keep the covers off."

"I've never even heard of a foot box." She pulled back the covers a bit and peered inside.

"Well, maybe it doesn't have a name. But it's a box and it protects your foot."

His logic was undeniable; his project was clever and practical. And he'd done it without being asked. *Who is this man?*

"Are you ready for bed now? Or do you plan to sit up a while and watch TV?"

"Why?" She was quite logically suspicious.

"Just wanted to know if you need me to clear off that footstool in the living room so you can prop up your leg. Or, if you're going to bed now, I can see how the foot box works."

"It's just now about 8:00. I think I'll stay up a few more minutes."

"Okay, I'll go clear things up in the TV area." Then, from down the hall, "You want anything to eat or drink?"

"Uh, maybe a cup of juice would be nice. But you don't have to…"

"No problem. I'm here at the fridge anyway." He'd evidently spotted the beers from the black bag and, with noisy clanking, placed them in the refrigerator again.

Jason was a whirlwind of helpfulness. Once Amanda was situated in front of the television, Jason also sat on the couch and handed her the remote control. *Wow.* She'd never before touched the remote while he was in the room.

"I've been catching up on some movies I haven't seen in a while." Amanda looked over at him. "That work for you?"

"Sure. Movies. Whatever. Maybe I'll check e-mail or something. Or read."

Did he say read? "That laptop's borrowed from Christine. Mine's still behind the seat in my vehicle, I think. We presume it's busted. I don't know if I have anything here you'd be interested in reading. Maybe a trashy novel or two. Some magazines." She pointed toward the small end table with a decorative rail surrounding its small lower shelf.

Jason selected the trashy novel on top. He spent more time on the cover than the text. He did actually start reading it, but soon he was watching the movie instead. It was a standard chick flick without a single car crash or chase scene. No guns blazing, either.

At first Amanda figured he was just pretending to be interested, but when he began asking questions about why Mr. X was so mean to Miss Y and why the bank was foreclosing Miss Y's mortgage, she knew Jason was actually watching the film. *Extraordinary*. Also aggravating, of course — because his questions ruined her own viewing experience.

— — —

Jason continued to monitor his patient and by about 10:00 p.m. she was obviously sleepy. He helped Amanda to her room and waited outside the doorway while she changed clothes, brushed her teeth, and used the bathroom. When she got into bed, Jason was present to witness the foot box in use. He smiled with the satisfaction of an inventor and then turned out her light. "Good night, Amanda."

"Uh, yeah. Thanks, Jason." It sounded like the words stuck in her throat a bit.

Jason watched television for just over half an hour. His thirty good channels probably averaged about 45 seconds apiece.

Later, he got ready for bed; with no extra change of clothing, he just stripped down to his shorts and tee-shirt. On his way to the guestroom, he grabbed the trashy novel and read for about fifteen minutes before he dropped off.

Chapter 21

August 22 (Saturday)

Jason was up and moving before Amanda emerged from her closed bedroom. Though he couldn't know for certain, he assumed she was awake and likely reading in bed. He figured Amanda would prefer some distance between them, since she hadn't even wanted him inside her apartment the previous evening.

Amanda needed assistance, but Jason realized she was too proud to accept. So he decided to treat her like a patient instead of a girlfriend. He was determined to help even if it killed her. But how? The only logical possibilities were inside the apartment, the place he felt least adept. So, he took a deep psychic breath and decided he'd defy all odds and try to wash dishes and clothes... maybe even attempt to cook.

He looked over the sorted food items still arrayed on the table. The plastic coffee container was easy enough to locate, but he didn't see any filters. Jason wondered if Kleenex would work and cautiously tested a sample under a steady drip from the tap. *Nope. Won't hold up.* Maybe a paper towel. Experiment successful.

He lined the coffeemaker basket with two paper towels — better to be double-safe than sorry — and dumped in coffee until the basket was half-full. *Looks about right.* He filled the carafe with water and poured it into the reservoir. Switch on.

While the coffee machine sputtered, Jason looked for bread. *Hmm.* Just three slices: two heels and a squashed inside piece. The date stamp indicated it was already old. Gingerly removing them, he examined each slice as though he were chief bread inspector at the Verdeville Bakery. With his thumbnail, he scraped two green spots off the crust of the inside slice. Otherwise all seemed okay — a little stiff, but they still smelled like bread rather than penicillin. Into the toaster oven.

He figured he wouldn't begin looking for eggs until Amanda emerged from her bedroom.

In the meantime, hot water began spewing out over the top of the basket. *Weird.* He quickly pulled it out part-way. It wasn't filtering; hot water just collected in the basket until it spilled over the edges. Action required! He searched in the utensil drawer for a sharp implement. *Ice pick… perfect!* Slid the basket back out and stabbed the bottom several times. Near-scalding water splashed over his hands and fingers. *Ow!*

Slowly, the water began to drain. Of course, that also let a quantity of grounds slip through. *Creative science often includes compromises.*

While he was solving the thick-filter problem, the toast began burning. Before he could deal with the toaster, rising smoke activated the ceiling detector and a terrible piercing beep commenced. Fortunately, he put down the ice pick before he covered his ears.

Find stepstool! Hall closet.

Anyone who's ever silenced a smoke detector knows two hands are needed to cover the ears and both are also required to disable the alarm. Since few humans come equipped with four hands, fundamental decisions must be made. First logical choice was to cover one ear and use one free hand to rip out the battery. *Nope.* Battery connection harnesses are manufacturer-certified to require two dexterous hands to remove them. Sacrifice both ears!

Amanda had begun moving down the hall on the alarm's first painful shrieks. Now she tried to whack the detector device with the foot of her left crutch, since her injured right wrist helped steady her stance. All she actually accomplished was to bludgeon Jason's knuckles, but she apparently felt the need to remain involved.

It was no use yelling at her to stop whacking, because neither of them could hear anything but the piercing alarm. Jason finally wrestled the battery out of the detector and then slumped down onto the stepstool. Amanda kept her crutch poised in case the device reactivated itself.

Jason rubbed his ears and moaned softly. Then he massaged his bruised knuckles, realigned his karma, and nonchalantly greeted the patient. "Morning. Coffee coming right up." *Alarm? What alarm?*

— — —

Amanda took stock of the kitchen. Three pieces of burned toast and a puddle of brackish hot water around the brewing machine. Small streams of coffee already dripped over the edge of the counter to the floor.

Noticing her look of horror, Jason got up slowly. He tossed some paper towels to the floor and tamped them with his foot. Then he did the same on the counter with his hands. "Have a seat and I'll bring it over." After trying several cabinets, he located two cups and began pouring coffee.

Amanda couldn't see his activity because he faced the other direction, but she heard paper tearing a few times and a spoon stirring noisily.

Jason brought Amanda's cup to the couch where she'd just gotten settled. "It might be a little dark."

He was modest; it was triple strength. When Amanda took a sip, it drew in her cheeks. She made the *kahh* noise twice.

"Oh, and I already sweetened it."

"How much *sweet* did you put in?"

Jason had to close his eyes to remember. "Two of the yellow packets."

That's enough to sweeten the entire pot! But she didn't say anything. Amanda took another sip. *Kahh!* "I might need to add a skosh of water in mine, to take the edge off a bit."

"Want me to do it?"

"No, thanks. But would you mind getting my left slipper from the bedroom? My bare foot's in a draft."

"Sure. Where?"

"Probably my closet."

Jason went to her bedroom suite to search for the solo slipper.

While he was gone, Amanda poured her coffee into the soil of the potted plant near the television. The rising steam looked a bit like a gauzy mushroom cloud from a miniature atomic bomb. She left one sip of liquid in the cup, along with about half an ounce of grounds which had escaped filtration.

Jason actually produced the right-foot slipper, but its broad-toe design would also accommodate her other foot. It just looked odd — like she was about to turn a corner. "Thanks."

"You want me to add that water to your coffee now?"

"No thanks, I already finished it." She held up the nearly empty cup.

He took it. "Want some more?"

"No! I mean... no, it feels like I've already had three cups. Plus that smoke alarm kind of woke me up anyhow."

"Yeah, that was awful. Probably a defective battery." He pointed to the source of the smoke. "You want any toast?"

"No, thanks. I'm trying to cut back on my charcoal intake."

Clearly, he still didn't catch her sarcasm. "How about a scrambled egg with cheese mixed in?"

Normally that would tempt her, but Amanda pictured at least one egg on the floor, some raw egg sloshed on the burner, and a solid clump of cheese being added too late. "No, thanks. I've developed a yen for those rice cake crackers. Maybe I'll chomp on those for a while."

No doubt Jason remembered those crackers only too well. "You sure? I don't mind cooking."

"Yeah, I'm sure." She was totally certain. "Thanks anyway." It was only later that Amanda remembered no eggs or cheese were even present in her household.

Jason poked through the items which had been on the dining table since Thursday. The partly stale saltine crackers evidently seemed most promising of that lot, so he finished the entire sleeve.

The remainder of the morning went similarly, though without additional smoke alarms.

With apparently sincere motive of helpfulness, Jason ascertained the contents of the dishwasher were clean by smelling the inside of every single glass — a redundant test Amanda had never found necessary.

Putting away clean dishes is usually considered helpful, but *help* is a relative term. Everything involving any cabinet seemed to involve nearly *all* of them. Evidently Jason had a concentration deficiency. If he'd just seen the location for glasses about twenty seconds before, he immediately forgot that portal if he'd held a bowl in the meantime. Yet he didn't catch on that all the glasses could be put up within the same short time span and then he could move on to bowls.

By the time Jason finished putting away the dishes, Amanda figured she'd scream if she ever again heard, "Where does this go?"

Once the dishwasher was empty, Jason ran the hot tap full blast for nearly fifteen minutes as he rinsed the few dishes in the sink. A single swipe of the sponge would have dispatched whatever he'd identified in or on each dish, but he apparently figured several minutes of full-bore scalding water was a better solution.

After their torturous rinsing, those few dishes were dumped into whatever portion of the dishwasher struck Jason's fancy. His single pattern seemed to be no pattern, since no two similar items ended up anywhere near each other. It goes without saying that several top rack items were tossed into the bottom. Amanda made a mental note to rescue them later if the *Tasmanian Jason* ever went to sleep.

When the kitchen activity finally ceased, water soaked the counters and had splashed to the floor all around the dishwasher. No doubt Jason observed those conditions but evidently concluded it was a natural state for water-related kitchen areas to have *standing* water.

He got another cup of coffee and sat on the couch next to Amanda, who was watching yet another movie. Jason took a sip. *Kahh!* "Maybe I should've made that allshitz acorn stuff. This is a little stout."

"No, I'm all out of acorns. This was okay. Next time, though, you might hold back a bit on the sweetener." She didn't want to sound too critical. "Uh, maybe not as many grounds, either..."

— — —

Jason felt pretty validated. All that kitchen drudgery had been mildly therapeutic and it brought to mind a serious topic he'd wanted to discuss with Amanda. He looked in the direction of the television without observing any programming content whatsoever. It was the archetypal scene where the strikingly handsome man realizes he's wronged the gorgeous woman and urgently wants to make up. "Is this show at a crucial part?"

She rolled her eyes and sighed. "Not really. I've seen this movie. They're just about to kiss and jump into bed together."

"I think they all have that scene." He shook his head briefly. "Had a question about all that cure-scare stuff Christine designed — I read about it on the blog. Everything was a pack of lies, right? Flax and hemp and cushaw?"

"No, those are legitimate foods."

"What about the cable guy, analog conversion, maids, therapies…" He paused to remember everything. "The A/C glitch, Greek funeral, and the back-order part they loaned you. All that was baloney?"

"All fabricated, Jason." She shrugged. "Did you actually believe any of that?"

"I didn't have any reason to think you'd lie to me."

"I'm sorry I lied. That was totally wrong. But some of it was so preposterous that we figured you'd just have to realize it was a sham."

Jason shook his head. "You two really had me going. I believed everything, even the stuff that was completely unbelievable. I guess I'm about the dumbest guy in Verdeville."

"No, you're not dumb. You had no way to know I'd been convinced to conspire to make you miserable." She faced him but didn't meet his eyes. "Everything that happened was designed to jar you out of causing me all that extra stress during my Hell Weeks. But you never seemed to catch on. It was astonishing."

Jason felt wounded. "It would have been easier to run me off by just being direct and honest."

She delayed her reply to lessen the residual anger. "I tried direct and honest. I told you I was swamped at work and you should stay in your own apartment."

"But I didn't think you meant it."

"I guess that's part of our relationship we should've worked on: clear speaking and plain understanding." Her delivery had more tenderness than the words themselves conveyed.

"I'm sorry I was so dense. It just never occurred to me that you'd deliberately make things awful just to get rid of me." He sighed heavily.

"I really am sorry. It was cruel. I see things more clearly now. At the time, I was swept up in the momentum. Christine can be a powerful force sometimes. Like a tornado."

"More like a witch. At one point I thought she had you under a spell."

"No, I was just being selfish." Amanda's eyes watered. It may have been the guilt that she'd allowed him to suffer so much... or the pain in her toes.

Jason tried to comfort her, but he felt self-conscious with his arm hanging over her shoulder. So he put his hand on her thigh, but that was awkward in a different way. Finally he just held her uninjured left hand. But he couldn't hold her hand very long; it seemed odd not to touch other parts of her. So, shifting physically and topically, Jason offered to wash Amanda's clothes.

— — —

Amanda nearly shrieked. After a brief panic attack, she gently talked Jason out of laundry duty. Amanda could imagine the effects of wrong cycle and hot temperature on her best wash-and-wear garments, and it gave her chills.

Jason must have thought she was cold, because he retrieved a clean bath towel and draped it over her shoulders.

Though Amanda had begun this reversal with a rather stony attitude problem, she had already witnessed that Jason truly was compassionate — though he expressed it clumsily — and not nearly as shallow as she'd thought. He was still considerably inept around the household, but those were skills which conceivably could be acquired with dedicated tutelage. Jason's newly-manifested compassion was an innate quality, however, and one which Amanda suddenly realized she valued highly.

At about 10:45 a.m., noting the cupboard was bare of almost everything besides a few staples, Jason volunteered to make a grocery run.

"Are you going to punish me with the same kind of awful garbage Christine fed you?"

"I wouldn't do that to you, Amanda." Jason hugged her left side briefly. "No human, vegans included, should have to eat hemp and flax… and tofu."

Amanda squinted into his face. She suspected he would just purchase his own favorites. "I think I'll tag along."

"No need to. Just tell me what stuff you like."

"I need the fresh air anyhow. I've been cooped up here since I left the hospital Wednesday, except for that visit to the doctor's office."

Jason sighed so heavily Mrs. Yodel probably heard it next door. He likely figured this grocery run was about to slow to a crawl.

Amanda ignored his furrowed brow. "I just need to use the bathroom and I'm ready. Will you grab my purse?"

Since she hadn't shaved her legs in three days, she really wanted to change from her cargo shorts to jeans, but there wasn't time and it would hurt her toes. Plus, she didn't figure anybody would notice her at Verde Grocery anyway. Since her hair was ratty, Amanda grabbed a baseball cap, gratis from a local veterans' group which had received a grant due to her recommendation.

She made it to his pickup just fine — much easier with the crutches at the proper height. Partly because of her injured right wrist, it was awkward getting into the truck, so Jason helped. Amanda buckled up and began writing her shopping list as soon as her driver backed out of the parking slip.

Clearly, Jason noticed her list was growing quite long. He sped up. When he drove faster, she wrote faster. When he slowed for traffic, she wrote slower.

Parked in the grocery lot, Jason seemed about to bolt from the car, but Amanda clutched his forearm. "Before we go in, we ought to talk about expectations."

"Huh?"

"I've never been grocery shopping with you before, so I'd like to know what your expectations are."

"Expectations?" Perhaps he'd never heard that word in the context of groceries. "Simple. Zoom in, hustle to the racks with whatever I need, and zoom back out. Stop and pay, of course."

"Of course. Well, I kind of figured you'd have the commando approach. So, I wanted to brace you. Shopping for nearly two weeks' worth of groceries and supplies involves strategy, scheduling, and maneuvering."

"Why do women have to make everything hard?"

Amanda ignored his obviously unintended double entendre. "It's not about being difficult. It's about practicality and economy, saving time and gasoline. With the commando method, you have to shop nearly every day and sometimes twice in the same day. With that mad dash approach, a shopper tends to forget things or overlooks components of a particular meal."

"Like getting buns and Sloppy Joe mix, but forgetting the meat?"

"Good example. That was your contribution to our July 4th dinner, as I recall."

Jason nodded with no apparent embarrassment. "I think I comprehend what you call *scheduling* if that means getting the frozen stuff last."

"Yes, it does! Good." She almost felt like she was helping her young niece answer homework questions. "Now, maneuvering is mostly getting around the unintentional and inconsiderate blockers who clog the aisles and slow down the flow of your shopping experience. It takes skill."

"Like zipping around to the other end of an aisle to get from behind the old deaf couple who stand on both sides of their basket?"

"That's one example. Another is those triple-length carts with the huge plastic kiddie cars on front."

"Okay, got it. What was the other part?"

"Logistics. Basically planning and forethought." Amanda nodded sagely. "So you only have to make one trip along each aisle with no doubling back across the store for something you forgot. Of course, the cornerstone of a solid plan is a thorough list."

"Amanda, I think you're the one with the wrong approach. It doesn't have to be that complicated. With my method, you zero in on the aisles with the good stuff and you grab what looks tasty."

"And you end up with chips, snacks, and beer."

"Right. Primary food groups."

Amanda shook her head. "You've got to have a list." She held up the one she'd been writing since they left her apartment.

"That's a store inventory sheet!" he sputtered. "We'll be here all day, trying to find that much junk!"

"Not if the list is in logistical order by aisles."

"Hold on. You fully intend to go limping in there on crutches and hit the full length of every single aisle?" Jason seemed aghast. "That's nuts!"

"They have motorized carts with little baskets. I'll ride."

"You'll need a lot more than a little basket for that warehouse full of stuff."

"Good thing you're here. Everything on this list should fit into one regular shopping buggy."

He sputtered a bit. "I didn't come here for an *experience*. I buy stuff to eat because I'm hungry. I don't want to think about it, or draw out maps, or write marching orders. Three steps. In-grab-out."

That description resembled Jason's occasional approach to other aspects of their relationship, but Amanda was focused on groceries at the moment. "Let's just try it my way this one time. If you don't like it, we won't have to shop together again."

"Aw, man!" He sounded like a third grader told to sit still in church.

Chapter 22

Amanda waited while Jason used antibacterial wipes on the seat and handles of the one battery-powered scooter nearly always available — the oldest of its type from that chain's entire eastern division, and the only one to have been locally modified. Some of the employees called it — with absolutely no affection — Ole Crotchity.

Jason helped her get situated and then placed the crutches in a regular shopping cart. The feet of those crutches stuck out in front of Jason's cart by nearly twelve inches and it almost looked like he was ready for a joust.

With a chorus of wobbles and creaks from Ole Crotchity, Amanda began to drive toward the far right edge of the store.

Jason caught up. "What's that horrible noise?"

"Uh, I think my scooter squeaks. Must be one of the wheels."

"I think it's all three wheels. That's piercing!" He leaned down to examine Ole Crotchity's underpinnings. "Move forward a few feet."

She did, and Jason signaled a prompt stop.

"It's just the back two wheels squealing." One had a slightly higher pitch and clashed with the other in precisely awful discord. "But get a load of that front wheel!"

Amanda leaned over and peered toward the bottom of the yoke. "I can't see anything. What?"

"It looks like a wheel from a shipping dolly, or a mechanical mule like the movers use to haul pianos and stuff."

"What would a dolly or mule wheel be doing on my scooter?"

"Well, steering, ideally. But that wheel has a gouge out of it, kind of a flat spot." He examined it more closely.

A four-inch hard rubber wheel has a circumference of approximately twelve and a half inches. Through some horrible misfortune, Ole Crotchity's jury-rigged front wheel had roughly eleven inches of a circular shape, interrupted by an inch and a half of flatness. The result, when it rolled, was a jarring bump while the vehicle's momentum struggled to overcome the resistance of the wheel's flat spot.

Jason's face was nearly on the floor. "Move it forward again, just about a foot."

She did, but nearly two feet.

"Whoa! You've also got a bad shimmy in that wheel."

Amanda looked at him with restrained impatience. "I think you're just stalling because you'd rather not have me tag along for this shopping experience."

He shook his head slowly. "No, I'm telling you that wheel is busted and I don't think it even belongs on that scooter."

"Okay, so the front wheel wobbles and thumps and the back wheels squeak a bit. Let's just shop."

He sighed. "I'm just trying to warn you, it's going to be a noisy and bumpy ride. But I can't stand that squealing. I'll be stark raving mad before we get through the first aisle. Hold on a minute." Jason left his buggy and returned to the place with the moist towels. He pinched off two pieces approximately an inch square, rolled them roughly into small cylinders, and squeezed out the excess juice. Then he plugged each ear. The towel pieces extended about half an inch outside his ears and looked a bit like the electrodes on the Frankenstein monster.

Besides the piercing wheel squeak, her borrowed scooter had a decidedly slow turning response. After twisting the very stiff front wheel yoke, there was at least a two-second delay before the machine began moving in the indicated direction. Plus, Amanda could only steer with her left hand, the weaker of the two when both wrists were functioning normally. She could pull on the yoke to turn left, but she had to use an extended push on the handle to veer right. That was her weakest motion while temporarily impaired.

That model of scooter had another alarming idiosyncrasy: no brakes! To slow, the driver had to release the throttle switch and simply coast. Depending on speed, slope, and terrain, it typically took a couple of extra feet to stop. Amanda had seen no speed limits posted, so she'd just reached full throttle by the time she neared the fruit section.

A frail man at the apple bin saw her approach and stared like a confused squirrel on a county lane. Amanda mistook his gasp for an attempted greeting, so she waved as she got closer. His eyes were large — he likely recognized Ole Crotchity and possibly had experience with that defective machine.

When Amanda figured her speed had frightened the man, she released the throttle button. Her momentum still took her past the fruit bins and nearly to the lettuce heads before the buggy finally rolled to a stop. The fragile-looking man had lurched back out of her way and accidently bumped the stack of oranges, which had once been a beautiful partial pyramid. But oranges, Amanda quickly noted, are so symmetrical that they'll roll nearly indefinitely unless stopped by the wheels of a nearby customer's grocery cart. Much to the surprise of that particular shopper, one wedged under her wheels.

When Amanda tried to back up, she realized her jury-rigged front wheel's flat spot was lodged on one of the sticky floor drains near the vegetables and wouldn't move. She tried pushing backwards with her left foot. *Nope.*

The escaped oranges had attracted the attention of the male fruit-tender, who alerted the woman who stocked and moistened vegetables along the wall. She, in turn, signaled the meat man, farther along that wall at the butcher shop. His apron spotted with blotches of fresh blood and related gore, the meat man lumbered over. Looking burly and distinctly surly, Mr. Meat picked up the front of Amanda's scooter and pivoted it on the back wheels until she was pointed away from produce altogether. Then, without words, he pointed toward the main aisle. A dab of pig intestine landed on Amanda's forearm and she recoiled in horror.

It was her inaugural occasion to be pelted with flying butcher gore. Also the very first time a bouncer had tossed Amanda out of the fresh food section. She realized she'd been banished to canned goods, boxed meals, beverages, and snacks. *Oh, hairy hell.*

Slowly regaining her composure after that mortifying eviction, Amanda noticed a young girl complaining to her mother that she was thirsty. To get the child to shut up, her mom reached in the top of her basket and tore open a ten-pack of fruit-flavored punch pouches. She handed a pouch to the girl and resumed her own obviously frazzled shopping experience.

The child ripped off the attached mini-straw and began stabbing at the designated spot on the top of the pouch. To Amanda, it resembled the homicidal maniac from the movie *Psycho* during the classic shower scene. The straw finally made it inside, as a considerable amount of punch jettisoned from both the opening and the straw. The child's eyes lit up with investigatory excitement.

Scientists have established that this particular model six-ounce pouch is capable of squirting over eleven feet when firmly squeezed by an adult grip. In the hands of an eight-year-old girl, it went roughly half that distance. The juice reached the rear thighs of a hefty woman wearing spandex shorts that were considerably strained by the flesh they attempted to encase.

That woman turned and glared. The mother promptly chastised the girl, who automatically put on her totally innocent mask and loudly slurped the remaining two ounces of juice from the pouch. The entire exchange had consumed only a few moments, but it further rattled Amanda's composure and momentum.

Once the parties to the juice episode had moved away in separate directions, Amanda resumed her own interrupted shopping experience.

After maneuvering Ole Crotchity along the far side of the first aisle, Amanda concluded it was like trying to drive a recalcitrant bathtub. In the close quarters of a crowded grocery store after 11:00 a.m., a tub with a two-second turning delay and two extra feet of stopping distance could lead to disaster. Not to mention the flat spot in the jury-rigged front wheel.

Through superior mental discipline, Amanda was able to tune out the awful, grating, squeaky noise from the two rear wheels and the wobble-thump feel of the front one, but she didn't realize the double-whammy significance of the other scooter flaws until she'd completed one full loop and reached the front end of the second aisle. She was distracted because Jason's focused speed had him already halfway along the third aisle.

Hurrying to catch up, Amanda tried to effect a sharp right turn around the front end of the shelving which currently separated them. But the checkout lines ahead extended nearly back to the end caps, so there was precious little space available to maneuver anyway. When she saw her turn was developing too late, she automatically tried to overcorrect, with only her weaker left hand. By turning even harder on the yoke, the front wheel happened on its flat spot, then bounced up, and the scooter trembled like it *wanted* to tip over.

But with no brakes, she was still moving! Partly forward and partly to the right. What she'd intended as a 90 degree turn to the east actually became a 45 degree tendency to the northeast. With no brake to press, instinctive reflexes slammed her left foot onto the scooter's worn and stained floor pad. In the absence of any pre-trained verbalization, Amanda hurriedly yelled, "Fore!"

She wasn't even a golfer, so it was a mystery why Amanda selected that word. But the nearby shoppers instinctively understood its meaning and several scattered. One old woman, not as quick to react, was shoved backwards into the rack of quick-sale items which stuck out in the middle of the main fairway. Nearby, an enormous, prissy-looking man nearly tripped on the tall basket of four-dollar DVDs.

Amanda was already apologizing profusely before Ole Crotchity finally came to rest on the foot of Mr. Priss, the flustered heavy man with ugly leather sandals. He looked like he'd selected several words to invoke, but managed to restrain himself for the moment.

Jason appeared around the front end of the fourth aisle. He'd obviously heard none of the commotion because of his earplugs, but he could now see Amanda's scooter had been involved in multiple collisions so he hurried over. "What happened?"

"Excuse me!" blurted Mr. Priss, nearly beside Jason.

Jason didn't hear.

"Excuse me!" Louder. The persnickety man tapped Jason's shoulder like he was touching a dead animal.

Jason turned that direction.

"Your wife is on my foot!" He pointed.

Jason didn't hear his words, but he saw Amanda also pointing at the front wheel. So he lifted the front of the scooter and freed the fleshy foot. "Sorry."

"You both ought to be. Menace!"

"What?"

Mr. Priss repeated himself and added invective.

"What?" Jason could not read lips, but he could tell the petulant expression included anger.

Checkers had stopped checking and baggers had stopped bagging. Several customers gathered and other staff appeared, including a young woman handing out samples of fried shrimp. Jason took two, which seemed to anger Mr. Priss even more.

The little girl, still holding the nearly empty punch pouch, stood very close to Amanda and began staring at her limbs. "Mommy, what are those little black things all over her legs?" Speaking loudly, as all eight-year-olds do when observing personal flaws in others, she pointed with great flourish.

The mother tried to shush her. "Hush, honey! Sometimes crippled ladies can't shave."

Suddenly Amanda realized that changing into jeans would have been worth the temporary pain.

At that point, the assistant manager zipped onto the scene. She tried to calm the effete Mr. Priss while also tending to the elderly woman with unwanted quick-sale items scattered in her cart.

Amanda tried to advise Jason on a joint retreat, but he still couldn't hear. Finally she motioned for him to come closer. When he leaned way forward, she plucked out his ear plugs with a loud *smop* sound and said distinctly, "Get me out of here!" She pointed toward the back of the store.

After a long aisle of Ole Crotchity's squeal-wobble-thump noise, Amanda coasted to a delayed stop in a small recess among the freezer units along the back wall. She shook her head in complete disbelief. What she'd intended as a structured teaching moment for Jason had turned into a major debacle. It was probably the single worst scooter collision in Verde Grocery's nine-year history.

— — —

Jason felt right at home in the rear of the facility, because — he quickly realized — more shrimp were being deep-fried back near the seafood cooler. The table was temporarily abandoned, so he snatched two more samples on the fly.

As he returned from the beer section, Jason stopped to chat with a second shrimp woman — who handled the actual deep-fat frying at the temporary table — and obtained yet another sample.

A small crowd had formed in the near end of the pet food aisle, and all watched intently to see what would happen next.

Jason screeched his push cart to a stop next to Amanda's idle scooter. "What's up?"

"Everybody's watching us," she hissed.

Jason looked up. He figured they were actually watching Amanda individually, but he wisely didn't point out that distinction.

The assistant manager also monitored the situation, from the seasonal candy section. She spoke quietly into a cell phone and pretended to fiddle with large bags of marshmallow peanuts. The entire scene resembled a movie version of a very amateur stakeout.

Jason noticed Amanda's concern. "She can't mess with you — you're handicapped. That old lady got some expired bread she didn't want and the fat guy has another bruise on his ugly foot. No harm, no foul." He sounded a bit like a verbose NFL referee.

Since Jason's former earplugs were now tightly clutched in Amanda's fist, she was able to whisper. "I don't think I'm in the mood for a shopping experience after all." She looked back toward the spectators in the pet food area. "I'll just try to sneak past that lynch mob and wait in the front near the ice machine." Amanda apparently didn't fully realize it, but *sneak* was overly optimistic.

"What about all that orderly row-by-row stuff?"

"Let's just use your in-grab-out method today."

"Commando. Cool." He smiled. "Uh, you want me to wrestle with that list?"

"No." Her lips overformed that word. She then folded the page with theatrical deliberation and tucked it in the bottom of her purse.

Jason felt distinctly relieved.

"Just get four things: bread, milk, tuna, and chicken."

"Chicken? You don't mean a complete hen, do you?"

"Grocery stores don't sell them with feathers any more, Jason." Amanda gave him a look. "I just need some canned chicken."

"You mean they squeeze those huge suckers into a can?"

— — —

Amanda's stern expression was already so fixed that her attempt to count to ten only reached five. "Small portions of chicken meat are canned. About the size of large tuna fish cans, and probably on a shelf near the tuna."

Jason closed his eyes. "Okay. Be-my-total-candy. Got it."

"What did you say?"

"Be-my-total-candy. It's a pneumatic device to remember bread-milk-tuna-chicken."

She was too weary and disheartened to point out that air-powered equipment had nothing to do with memory, so she merely nodded. Big-mouth-total-cluck.

Jason watched her for a moment. "Are you waiting on me to leave first? Like in the movies?"

"Yeah, like the movies." This particular film was probably *Weekend at Bernie's*. She felt like Bernie.

"Okay, I'll get bread-milk-tuna-chicken and meet you in front after I check out." As he left, he repeated, "Be-my-total-candy."

On his way to the bread, Jason veered again toward the roving fried shrimp samples. That young woman saw him coming and tried to scramble away with her platter, but Jason practically pinned her against the toilet tissue rack.

Amanda wondered if Jason's zealous quest for free seafood would distract his mnemonic device from remembering the four items she wanted. She steeled herself for the short drive through the store to the front. *In-grab-out, Jason.* That would be the last time she ever spoke those words, even to herself.

Realizing her exit was bracketed, Amanda saw she would have to pass either the cluster near the pet food or the manager on her phone near the candy. Fearing the animal aisle with the clustered spectators, Amanda chose the manager's direction and gently pressed Ole Crotchity's throttle button. She covered the short distance quickly and didn't even slow down. "Sorry... leaving... never drove these before... always looked so simple... sprained wrist." Her words came out like an unrehearsed telegram as she sailed past.

The manager nodded warily and continued to narrate into her phone.

Amanda could only imagine who was on the other end of that call... perhaps the Tennessee State Czar of Grocery Security.

Every face turned as Amanda navigated Ole Crotchity toward the front of the store. It could have been because of the incredibly irritating squeal-wobble-thump noise, but she imagined they all expected her to collide into a cluster of unsuspecting nuns.

Having allowed two extra seconds for each turn and two additional feet for each stop, Amanda managed to arrive at the ice machine without injuring anyone else. From her vantage point, she could see outside as Mr. Priss obviously explained his delay to the prune-faced woman in his car — most likely Mrs. Priss. As he narrated the tale, he pointed several times to his fleshy foot.

Inside, Amanda could also see down two of the centermost aisles.

— — —

Jason was actually enjoying his shopping experience after all. He found the bread easily enough, but made three additional sweeps of the complete store width to locate milk, tuna, and chicken. *Be-my-total-candy.* On each pass, he collected another shrimp from the cute female with fine samples. On one of his circuits, the other young woman cooking the shrimp actually ducked behind the table and pretended not to be there. But Jason stood for a moment and shuffled his feet, which that employee could easily see below the edge of her stained white tablecloth.

Then he knocked on the tabletop like it was a horizontal service door. The harried teen rose slowly and smiled sheepishly. "Would you like to sample our fresh fried shrimp, sir?"

"You betcha." He took three more. "Thanks."

— — —

Amanda was definitely *not* enjoying her experience. By her rough tally, Jason had eaten enough seafood samples to represent a complete dinner at the local fish house. *Might be some method to his madness.*

She also noticed a moderately attractive woman was *accidently* goosed with the feet of the crutches, which extended like lances beyond Jason's buggy front. Amanda monitored as Jason addressed the woman. Both smiled and they chatted for precisely 53 seconds before the vixen moved on.

Amanda watched as Jason finally made his way to the checkout line, waited his turn, and paid for the purchases. It was considerably more than his beer and Amanda's four items. He'd also found several snacks which she knew were his favorites.

Jason approached looking completely satisfied with his shopping experience. Then he noticed Amanda's consternation. "What?"

"Who was that hussy who backed into your buggy?"

"Oh, that's Sally, from work. She's a buddy."

"Fairly attractive buddy. Did you have to impale her bottom with my crutches?"

"That was just a nudge. A little payback 'cause she pinches me on St. Patrick's Day."

"You don't wear green?" Amanda didn't like knowing other women pinched Jason.

"I don't even own any green clothes." He grinned. "Besides, I don't mind her pinch once a year."

"I'm about to pinch something clean off, if you don't get me out of this store."

"All right. What's the rush? I'm going for the total experience today. Got to see a buddy from work and ate a dozen shrimp."

The true count was closer to eighteen. "Plus, you cleaned out the snack aisle. I thought you were going for be-my-total-candy. This array looks more like be-my-total-candy-and-meet-me-in-Memphis-the-next-time-you're-in-Tennessee."

Jason looked over the selections as he silently mouthed her version. "Nah. Some of those letters are wrong."

Before Amanda got off squeaky Ole Crotchity, she carefully drove the short distance to the customer service desk and announced loudly, "This scooter is terribly defective. It nearly killed two citizens inside your store and I may have whiplash. My attorney here was a witness to the entire unfortunate experience."

Having formally shifted accident liability to the grocery chain, Amanda dismounted the scooter and accepted the crutches Jason held patiently.

On the way out to the car, Jason the new attorney pushed the cart slowly behind her and made no effort to disguise his study of Amanda's derrière, which she could tell moved very nicely even with crutches under her arms.

On the way home, Amanda was mostly silent. She calculated how many months she ought to wait before returning to that store.

Jason asked if she would mind a short detour to his apartment for a change of clothes, since all he had at Amanda's was a toothbrush. Amanda said she didn't but sighed heavily to clue him to her actual aggravation.

He managed the entire transaction in less than seven minutes. *In-grab-out*. As he got seated in his vehicle, he announced, "When we get to your place and I get stuff situated, I'll rustle up some lunch in the kitchen."

"What exactly do you plan to rustle?" She worried about his decidedly narrow culinary range.

"Maybe a sandwich of some kind." Jason seemed deliberately vague.

Amanda pictured him trying to fry bacon for a BLT or grill a cheese sandwich. *Simplicity is best.* Besides, she didn't have bacon, lettuce, tomato, or cheese. "Uh, how about tuna sandwiches?"

"Sounds simple enough." He repeated his *be-my-total-candy* mantra. "We just bought some tuna fish."

Amanda groaned heavily as she wondered what kind of wig would disguise her sufficiently to ever again shop there for groceries.

Arriving home, she preceded Jason into the apartment and went directly to her bedroom to lie down. Amanda's shopping experience had been exhausting.

Chapter 23

Jason put the milk inside the fridge and situated his snacks. Everything else landed on the table until he could get Amanda's particular guidance for proper destinations. He figured her closed door meant she was napping.

He went to the kitchen and leaned against the only dry expanse of the horseshoe-shaped counter. "Tuna sandwich — I've... got... you... covered." Jason squinted at the small print on the squatty can. *Hmm.* No instructions. He picked up the canned chicken. No instructions there, either. "Guess they figure everybody's a home ec teacher."

To ascertain Amanda's door was still closed, Jason peered around the corner down the short hallway, then flipped open his phone and called Margaret. "Mom, how do you cook tuna fish?"

"Speak up a bit. Are you whispering?"

"Uh, sore throat, I guess." A bit louder. "So, how do you cook tuna?"

"Cook it?" Margaret acted like she'd never heard this question before.

"Yeah. It's raw in the can, right?"

"No. Already cooked. They pre-cook it before they even completely clean the fish... right at the dockside processing plants. After they filet it and seal it in the cans, they heat it again — for several hours — and sterilize it. It's called retort cooking. When you open the can, it's basically ready to eat."

"Okay, let's see. Ow!"

"What's the matter?" asked the concerned mother.

"Cut my finger on the dadgum lid!"

"You'll want to hold the can down low, so the lid doesn't nip you."

"Now you tell me. Thanks a bunch." Jason sighed heavily. The can was only an inch tall. *How do you hold it* low? "Okay, thanks. Bye."

In slightly less than two minutes, Jason called his mother back. "Doesn't look right." He whispered again.

"What did you do?"

"I dumped the fish onto a slice of bread and slapped the other piece on top." He shook his head while holding the phone stationary. "Doesn't look right."

"Did you drain it first?"

"You didn't say to drain anything. How does that work?"

"You still have the can?"

"Uh, pretty much." Jason hedged on full disclosure — it was already in the kitchen trash, but on top of everything else.

"Put the tuna back in the can. Have you still got that lid?"

"Nah, threw that sucker away. Dangerous."

"Okay, you can use your fingers as a sieve."

"A what?"

Margaret didn't even attempt to define it. "Rinse the tuna under a thin stream of water, while it's still in the can, and then pour out the excess oily liquid. Keep your fingers over the opening of the can so the tuna doesn't fall into the sink."

"Oops."

"What happened?"

"Some of the tunas escaped."

"Well, leave them in the sink. You don't want to mess with all that bacteria."

With his mother still on the phone, Jason dumped the remaining freshly-rinsed tuna onto a new slice of bread. "Still looks funny."

"Did you mix it first?"

"Mix? With what?"

— — —

A few miles away on Mayfield Drive, Margaret wondered how specific she'd need to be to talk her son through this experience. She felt like an exasperated air traffic controller aiding a frantic passenger who'd just assumed the controls of a damaged plane. "Some people use mayo. Put three tablespoons of mayo into the tuna and mix it up thoroughly." She strained to hear his actions. All she could make out was vague slapping sounds. She wondered if her youngest son had ever identified a tablespoon.

He cursed. "It tore the bread all to pieces."

"You're supposed to mix it in a *bowl!*"

"Good grief. Why do you reel out these instructions one inch a time?" Jason noisily extracted two more pieces of bread. "It's taking the entire new loaf to make one stinking sandwich." Cabinet doors slapped, pans clanged, and bowls clinked. "Okay, found a bowl. Now I dump in the tuna and mayo together... right?" He didn't wait for her reply. "Dadgum!"

"What's wrong now?" She imagined several possibilities.

"More tunas escaped."

"Where now?" For all she knew, they might be on a train to Oshkosh.

"Floor."

At first, Margaret did not intend to specify the following, but then she thought better of it. "Jason, throw away the part that fell on the floor. You're not allowed to invoke the three-second rule if somebody else has to eat whatever you're fixing."

"But there's new research — most guys agree now that you have at least five seconds to reclaim stuff that fell on the floor."

"Absolutely not! I won't bother to debate your pseudo-science, but here's the overriding law: do not apply the floor-time rule — no matter how many seconds — unless it's something you intend to consume all by yourself. Understand?"

"Yeah, just jump all over me next time."

She ignored his complaint. "Now, scoop the rest — from the counter only — into the bowl and mix it up really good." She waited a moment as the noise at his end seemed to match her instruction. "Okay. Now add some celery."

"Hold on."

Margaret heard the fridge opening. Several things clanked, two inside drawers slid out and in. Then the appliance door slammed.

"Okay, got the celery loaded. Next step?"

She briefly closed her eyes to visualize. "You just stuck that entire celery stalk in the bowl, didn't you?"

"That's what you said."

"I meant to say, 'Chop... up... the... celery... and... mix... in... the... *pieces*.'" There was a pause and Margaret heard three drawers open and close. Then it sounded like somebody was trying to saw a huge rubber tube in half.

"This celery is too limp to chop. Plus, it's mostly brown."

She groaned. "Toss the celery, Jason."

Over the phone, the celery sounded like an empty banana peel as it obviously hit the growing trash pile.

Margaret tried to think of other components which would provide some flavor and color to a tuna fish sandwich. Maybe fresh grapes with crumbled pecans or sliced almonds? No. If Jason tried to slice almonds, he'd end up in the E.R. She drew a blank. "Most tuna fish has celery chunks to give it some green."

Jason knocked over several items as he rustled in the cabinets. "She's got a can of green peas. Would that work?"

"Never mind, forget green. Just serve it plain." Margaret realized she'd better check. "Now describe what you have so far."

"A really slippery spot on the floor to clean up, an empty bowl I'll have to wash, and four pieces of soggy bread in the trash can... underneath the brown celery. Oh, and two new bread slices on a paper plate with tuna on one of the pieces."

"You did mix the mayo with the tuna?"

"Of course! Plus, it has a few clumps of that soggy bread from my earlier attempts." He sighed. "But bread is bread... right?"

"In many cases. But I'm sure this will be an interesting surprise for Amanda." If Margaret were making this sandwich herself, the ordeal would have ended twenty minutes ago. At the very least, it should have some garnishment. She tried to imagine something Jason could handle without dumping out the entire container. "Check if Amanda's cupboard has onion seed or celery salt."

"Where?"

"Little tins or jars, wherever she keeps spices."

Seven cabinet doors opened before Jason said, "Oh, spices." More clinking and scraping sounds. One container fell noisily to the counter. "Okay, here's the celery stuff. What was the other one?"

"Onion seed."

After more noise, "Okay, got them both. Little can and small bottle. How much of each?"

"No! Do not add them in. Just put those little containers on the side of the sandwich plate — or a tray would be better — and let Amanda season it to her taste."

— — —

After ending the phone call, Jason assessed his devolving situation. Since so much tuna had been lost to the sink and floor, there was only enough material to make a sandwich and a half. He gallantly took the half. Rolling up the bread slice like a burrito, he ate the entire thing in two bites. Good thing his grocery experience had featured two generous, attractive shrimp girls and included several thoughtful purchases from the snack aisle.

Finally exiting her bedroom, Amanda hobbled down the hallway on her crutches. Jason proudly presented her with his carefully prepared tray. She seemed puzzled about the two spice containers until she peeked inside the sandwich.

Amanda got situated on the couch and lightly dusted the tuna with celery salt and onion seed. She tasted it and made the *gerrh* sound. She turned on the television, which Jason had reset to her favorite movie channel.

Jason stepped outside the front door and sat on the porch steps, hardly aware of No-Neck banging two tennis balls against the laundry house wall. Suddenly Jason realized he'd been taking care of someone else, being protective, for the first time in his life. He'd never needed such an instinct before, so this was new for him.

Being youngest of three boys, Jason had always had somebody looking out for him. He'd never really been expected to look out for himself, much less take care of anyone else. Being the baby, he'd been babied. Somehow he'd continued as the indulged one for most of his 32 years.

It probably explained why his college sweetheart had broken off their engagement two months before their scheduled wedding eight years ago. Karen had kept expecting Jason to grow up but Jason thought he'd already advanced as far as anyone should expect. In fact, that was Jason's capsule identification: most people expected very little of him and he rarely disappointed them. Karen had finally realized Jason was not the proper raw material for her to mold into a suitable husband.

He hadn't thought about Karen and his old engagement for a long time. Why would that come up now? And why was he being introspective? Actually thinking!

When the no-neck kid was called back to his pen somewhere along the row of duplexes, his irritating, unsyncopated rhythm mercifully ceased and he dropped the tennis balls next to the wall before he departed.

While that golden opportunity presented itself, Jason retrieved both balls and hid them behind a potted plant on Amanda's stoop. As he sat again on the concrete threshold for a few moments of silence, he became acutely aware of his fatigue. That entire day so far, Jason had helped Amanda. He'd bumbled a lot and was basically helpless around the household, but he'd tried… and, in the process, worked himself to exhaustion.

He went back inside the apartment, sat on the couch near his patient, and fell asleep during the emotional climax to a dreary movie Amanda had likely already seen four times.

* * * *

Amanda had a shard of tuna stuck between two teeth. As Jason napped, she got up quietly and made her way on crutches to her bathroom for some floss. Then she shut the bedroom door softy and called Christine. "Where have you been? I think I'm banned for life from the Verde Grocery."

"What on earth for?"

"I'll fill you in later. I'm starving! Jason cannot cook. You should have seen what he produced as a substitute for tuna sandwich—" *kahh* "—it had rolled-up bread-pills inside! He had to call his mother for tuna instructions! He must've thought I was asleep. I only overheard his side of the conversation, so I don't know what she told him. But it took him 45 minutes to put tuna and mayo together."

"Even blindfolded and one-handed, that ought to be five minutes, tops."

"I know." Amanda barely took a breath before changing the subject. "I can't believe you abandoned me!"

"I didn't. Margaret *suspended* me! I'll explain that part later. Right now, tell me how it's going. I mean, besides being thrown out of grocery stores and eating his tuna surprise."

"This is a new side of Jason."

"I've seen his backside. I'd guess this must be his front."

"Seriously. He's being sweet, in a clumsy way. It's kinda humorous and also a little scary."

"Scary?" Christine probably needed clarification because she'd previously admitted the entire Jason relationship was spooky to her.

"Yeah. In a horror movie, he'd treat me nicely for about 72 hours and then stab me in the heart with sharp scissors."

"No, he wouldn't! Scissors are a girl's weapon. Jason would probably use a jagged hunting knife."

Amanda ignored the cutting facetiousness. "But this new Jason is gentle and helpful, or at least he tries to be."

"He's actually taking care of you? Wow, I'm impressed. Never thought he had it in him."

"Me, either, actually. I guess maybe I've never given him much of a chance. I was too busy taking care of him."

"Amanda, he sure doesn't need another momma."

"No, and I don't need a 32-year-old child, either. I'd just like my boyfriend back... only I'd prefer him to be healthy again."

"Margaret said you're supposed to take the richer and poorer, in sickness and health."

Amanda pressed the phone closer to her face. "I sometimes wish I had that much steel in my backbone."

"Something's different, Amanda." Christine seemed very puzzled. "You sound funny when you talk about Jason."

"Different? Funny?"

"Funny... like you talked when you first got so goofy about him back before Halloween. Different, like you've just now fallen in love."

"Nah. Well, maybe." Amanda giggled. "It's been really strange... these last 24 hours. Jason's a different man."

"That can only be a good thing."

"Seriously. He's a lot deeper than I realized. More considerate, more caring. Less selfish."

"I'll call Margaret." Christine's voice became a whisper. "Maybe you've got temporary custody of the *good* brother."

"No, he's got enough of old Jason's clumsiness that I'd recognize him with my eyes closed. But now there's something extra."

"Exactly what? You also sounded gaga about that Washington big shot not too long ago. Remember?"

"That was so different!" Amanda smiled as she savored that memory. "He was only an infatuation. Elegant man with expensive haircut and tailored suit. Those Cary Grant types just sweep me off my feet."

"Isn't that what this new Jason is doing to you now? Sweeping you up, with kindness and attention?"

"Could be, but I don't think so. I really think Jason has truly changed."

"Men don't change, Amanda. They temporarily turn different shades, like those garden lizards do. But men never really transform."

"I think Jason has."

"No, he's acting unusually nice and you're falling for it." Christine lowered her voice a full octave and spoke very distinctly. "I already told you about that special school men go to, where they learn tactics on how to get women into bed." She resumed normal voice. "This is just a ploy. Jason isn't different. You're the one who's changed."

"Explain."

"You're falling in love with him all over again. Only this time, he has more hooks in you than merely east Nashville charm, boyish good looks, and tight jeans."

"Nah." Amanda giggled like a sixteen-year-old with a crush on the football player in tight jeans. "You know, over this past *very* long day, I've realized something: it does feel nice to be babied a little." She didn't tell Christine she'd even found herself milking her injury, just a little bit, for the extra attention it received from Jason. An additional groan when he was watching would prompt a consoling touch of his hand.

"Yeah, everybody needs to be babied a little, every now and then. Even me." Christine sounded surprised that she'd said it out loud. After a pause, she griped a bit about how tight her clothes felt lately. "You know I weigh every Saturday at my sister's house. She has one of those fancy-schmancy electronic scales."

Amanda nodded into the phone.

"Well, I weighed today and I've gained eight frazzling pounds!"

"I don't get it. I thought you've been holding steady." A white lie.

"Gained! It was all those extra treats I ate just to keep Jason from getting them. And now they're stuck on my hips!"

It took a while for Christine to stop sputtering about that stressful topic.

"Christine, can you do me a favor?"

"Nothing involving Internet blogs. I've learned my lesson."

"No, this involves the party supply store… tomorrow, as soon as it opens." Then Amanda explained what she needed.

They spoke for a few more minutes, until Amanda heard Jason stirring in the living space. "Got to go. The new Jason is awake."

"Don't let this new Jason doppelgänger near your bed. Be warned. Bye."

It was close to 7:00 p.m. and Amanda's stomach was grumbling. The nutrients from that slender and plain tuna sandwich had run out long ago. "What are your plans for supper?"

Jason stretched on the couch and yawned. He appeared still groggy from his nap. "Don't know. That beer's probably cold by now. How about some delivered pizza?"

"Ooh, that's sounds lovely. I'll take the works on my half."

"Okay, but I'll have to use your phone."

"How come?"

"Last week when I was here, I tried ordering pizza. They said my phone number didn't match your address so they wouldn't take the order."

"I thought they stopped checking that stuff years ago when everybody still had landline phones."

"Well, it probably didn't help when I told the chickie that I was in prison." Jason scrunched up his face. "I guess she took it too literally."

"Most people would."

"Or maybe there's been a rash of prank pizza deliveries. Anyway, they stiffed me… even blocked my number!

Otherwise, I would've had plenty to eat while you and Christine were starving me."

Amanda cleared her throat softly and touched Jason's hand. "Something I still don't understand is why you continued to stay here and put up with all that misery Christine and I were dishing out."

He looked thoughtful for a moment. "You know how you're sometimes watching a really awful movie, but you keep on watching? Can't quite bring yourself to turn it off?"

"Yeah, you keep thinking it *has* to get better." Amanda nodded earnestly.

"I think it was partly that. Plus, there was a shock factor. I came here expecting things would be as good as the way you treated me when I was sick last winter. I liked having you take care of me, you know."

She looked down toward her lap. "I know, now."

"And when that didn't happen, I just kept thinking, surely it's got to get better."

"We did terrible things to you. While it was going on, I convinced myself that I was just a bystander and it was really Christine's doings. But I think I knew even at the time... I was involved also."

"Kevin said it was punitive."

"Not really. I think part of it was temporary insanity — a frantic couple of weeks at a crazy job with a lunatic boss. I went a little nuts, I guess." Amanda thought for a moment. "But there was also an element of curiosity. You know, whether Christine's strategy would actually work." She rolled her eyes. "We could never figure out why you put up with it. You could have left at any time."

"I kept thinking some tiny villagers would pour a bucket of water on Christine and she'd melt into the castle floor. With the evil witch destroyed, I figured you'd come to your senses and comfort me, a little."

"I'm sorry I didn't comfort you. But I felt I had to blast you out of my apartment since you wouldn't leave on your own. Nursing a sick man is very high maintenance." Amanda went silent for a moment. "I feel positively awful about being so rotten to you. 'Specially with the way you're taking such good care of me now."

He looked around like a mysterious light had just turned on. "Am I taking good care of you?"

"Yes, you are, and I really appreciate it." Amanda searched his face. "Speaking of... why *are* you treating me so nicely? I mean, since you got here last night."

Jason gave her a long look. "I've always wanted to treat you real nice, but usually you've already decided what's going to happen, or you're busy with something, or dashing off somewhere. What's different now is that you can't run away."

Amanda's eyes filled. She stroked Jason's tousled hair and rested her hand on the nape of his neck. "Your mother said the only reason you stuck it out was your mule-headed stubbornness."

"Mom said I was mule-headed?"

"Among other things."

"What else did she tell you?"

Amanda considered how much to reveal. "She suggested I bake you some brownies."

"Do you bake?"

"Here's my phone. Order the pizza."

— — —

After supper they both watched television.

Jason took a long sip of his beer. "You know, I probably would have starved to death if it hadn't been for those Oreos." He clearly struggled to suppress a grin.

"Oreos! Finally an explanation for the mysterious tiny black crumbs I kept finding." She turned and faced him. "Where the heck did you get Oreos?"

Jason chuckled. "In a corner of your garage, in a grocery sack. Along with a dozen eggs, a quart of milk, and a loaf of bread."

"Impossible! Christine swept my garage with a fine-tooth comb."

"Well, she must have walked right by that bag. It was in the corner, in plain sight."

"So you dined on eggs and milk and bread, and Oreos?"

"Nope, just the Oreos. Bread was moldy, green and black. Milk was rancid and clumpy. And eggs without refrigeration spoil really fast. Sam-and-ella, you know."

She winced at his pronunciation. "I don't remember missing any of those groceries." Amanda closed her eyes briefly.

"There were twenty-something items listed on the receipt, but only those four in that particular bag."

"Wonder how long they sat there?"

"Receipt was dated middle-June." Jason took a final swig of his beer.

"Middle of June. Oh, that's when my sister was here with two of her husband's nephews. The Oreos were to keep those boys from climbing my drapes. I wondered what happened to those other items. I figured the bagger just screwed up and gave them to the customer behind me." Amanda winced. "They stayed an entire weekend with me and nearly drove... me... out... of... my... mind."

If Jason wondered how much trouble it could be to entertain and feed three people for two days, he wisely remained silent.

"So the milk, eggs, and bread were inedible. How were the Oreos after two months in that corner?"

"Pretty bad, actually. Summer... hot garage. The white centers had mostly melted and the black wafers had wallowed apart. The half which kept most of the remaining melted white stuff wasn't too bad, though awful chewy."

"Yeah, I'd expect *crisp* would leave that hot bag after the first week." She looked around. "So, where'd you hide them?"

"Well, I gave that considerable thought. If I'd been at my own apartment, they would've gone straight to the underwear drawer of my dresser."

"I can imagine they'd be relatively safe there."

"But since I was a stranger in a strange land, so to speak, I couldn't think of any hiding places. So, I left them in the bag in the corner of the garage. You know, hide in plain sight. You'd been overlooking them since mid-June and the evil witch Christine didn't find them in her sweep. I figured they were safe right there."

"You left the whole bag of Oreos out there?"

"Well, I ate nearly half the bag that first day I found them. Then I got to thinking I might ought to ration them out a bit. So I ate five cookies a day over the next four days. Then I ran out. Nearly cried."

"I've read that prisoners form attachments to certain things."

Jason shrugged.

"But at least you've trimmed down that waist a little. You're looking very fit, after your crash diet."

"That's what my mom said. I didn't realize everybody thought I was so fat before."

Amanda struggled with the proper response. "You're not fat. But all your snack choices go to the same spot." She poked the area of his former paunch.

Jason just looked down at that area of his body like he'd never noticed it before.

Chapter 24

Amanda got up on her crutches and hobbled toward her bedroom. "I really need a shower."

Jason rose from the couch and followed her. "Need any help?" He sounded tentative.

"The doctor said I can't get these bandages wet." She pointed to her right foot. "Could you get this boot off? I can loosen the straps, but I can't pull it off without brushing against my toes." She sat on the bed and extended her right leg.

Jason went down on one knee like he was about to propose. He gently cradled her calf with his forearm and carefully removed the boot. In truth, he did lightly graze one of her injured toes and Amanda struggled to keep from yelping.

"Okay?"

She let out her breath. "Yeah, thanks."

"What else do you need?"

"Could you bring me a gallon freezer bag and some tape?"

"Sure." He jumped up and hurried down the hallway, but returned immediately. "Where are the freezer bags?"

"Drawer next to the fridge."

"Makes sense." He dashed away and came back with two bags. "In case the first one doesn't fit."

Two identical gallon freezer bags would be exactly the same size, but she didn't mention that minor detail. "Did you find the tape?"

"Oh, tape. Where do you hide it?"

"Drawer next to the silverware."

He sped off.

Amanda heard him turn in the hallway and she called out, "Silverware's to the left of the sink. Tape's in the next drawer over." She heard the silverware drawer open, so he evidently had to establish a point of reference. Then the other drawer opened and closed.

"Got it," he hollered from the distance.

Amanda's drawer held at least four sizes and types of tape. Jason came back with the largest: duct tape, two inches wide. "I figured a quart bag would use the small tape, so the gallon bags probably need the big stuff."

"Wise choice. Thanks."

"You want me to put the bag on?"

Not totally certain it was a good idea to involve him, she still replied, "Please."

When she extended her leg, he cradled it again. Amanda liked the feel of his arm under her calf, and she yearned to feel his touch higher on her legs. Much higher. Of course, she'd want to shave first — right now she had three and a half days of stubble. She closed her eyes.

He obviously took great care to keep the bag from touching her toes. "How's that?" Jason gently let her leg come to rest against the side of the bed until her heel barely touched the floor.

She opened her eyes and examined the temporary transparent bootie. "If I hold the edges over, could you run a bit of tape around it for me?"

"Sure. How many wraps?" He probably envisioned the ankles of NFL linemen... with perhaps a dozen layers.

"Uh, I think one will be sufficient. Thanks." She liked having him hover around her legs and wished she could think of another related chore. She couldn't.

Jason did, however. "Can you get into the shower okay? Need help stepping over the ledge? I don't think you're supposed to take the crutches in there... might slip. Plus the wood could warp and those wing nuts can rust."

Good thinking. "You're right, no crutches in the shower. Yeah, I could use a hand getting in and out." *This could be dicey.*

— — —

Jason scanned her bedroom. "Uh, what are you wearing after you dry off?"

"There's some cotton nightdresses in that drawer." She pointed.

He reached toward the dresser and then looked over his shoulder. "This one?" He'd been taught never to look inside a lady's drawers.

"Yeah, that's the drawer. Nightdresses on the right. I'll take whatever's on top."

"It's pinkish."

"Pink's fine." Amanda closed her eyes as she mentally walked through the process. "Let me get into the bathroom and I'll take off my things." She wore cargo shorts and panties, plus tee-shirt and bra. "Then I'll call you to help me get in the shower."

"Okay." Jason rubbed his palms on the sides of his jeans and waited.

Unless that was a crutch hitting the wall, Amanda bumped her elbows as she disrobed. She yelped once —

panties probably snagged on the toe splints. The toilet flushed. Then she announced, "Okay, I could use some strong arms now."

Jason approached her bathroom with as much nervousness as the first time he'd made out in high school. "Should I close my eyes or something?"

"Only if you want to smack into the doorframe." She giggled. "Jason, you've seen me naked before."

"I know, but that's only been right before we..." He strained for the remaining words.

No matter, she certainly understood. "Well, I'm injured now, so just think of me as a patient. You won't even notice my body."

Jason knew that was a lie. He began moving with his eyes closed, but smacked into the doorframe. When Jason reopened his eyes, his mouth fell open as well. He definitely noticed her lovely naked form. It was as though he'd never before seen her in the flesh. Amanda had goose pimples over 80 per cent of her body, and Jason could see nearly 60 per cent of those.

"I'm ready to get in now."

"Huh?" His brain couldn't process any possible activity besides caressing her skin and kissing her lips. But somewhere, somehow, he found an override switch. "Okay, am I holding you or are you gripping me?"

"Let's try it both ways before I get in. We'll see which seems more steady."

Jason reached his left arm behind her back and that hand brushed against the side of her breast before he found her upper arm. His right hand held her near forearm. "Okay, that's with me holding you." He was perspiring and could feel a very slight tremor in his limbs. "If we both move sideways about two feet, you'd be in the shower."

Amanda acted like she didn't want his arms to move, and she sighed heavily. "Okay."

He figured that was the signal to drop his arms.

"Right. So, now I'll hold onto you." She leaned into his left side, with her right arm around his back and her left hand clutching his belt buckle. "I don't think this works as well. It has me backing into the shower. Let's use the first one."

"Amanda, we better get your nekkid body in that water before I jump in there with you. This is agony."

"I'm sorry." She probably wasn't, but she touched his shoulder softly. "Okay, the first position was best. You hold onto me and we'll move slowly to my left."

It was not elegant, but their movements eventually got her into the shower where the water was already running. Jason closed the curtain, backed out of the bathroom, went down the hall, and washed his face in cool water at the kitchen sink. Amanda was a beautiful woman and Jason found it difficult to witness her wearing nothing but a freezer bag... without taking the next logical steps.

After drying his own face on a dining napkin and locating clean towels in the hall closet, Jason returned to her bedroom. He sat on her bed with two large towels in his lap and waited.

Amanda took her time in the shower. She'd said it was her first full wash since Wednesday morning... not counting the spit baths on Thursday and Friday.

Jason heard Amanda humming something, but couldn't quite make it out. Parts of it sounded like Carly Simon's *Anticipation*. But other portions resembled Mitzi Gaynor's shower song in *South Pacific*. When the water stopped, so did Amanda's medley.

She pulled back the curtain and called out, "Sorry it took so long. I had to wash my hair twice and shave my legs. My heel kept slipping with this plastic bag on my foot." She tapped on the wall. "If you're nearby, I'm ready to dry off and get out."

He jumped up and reached into the bathroom. The steam and herbal shampoo aroma was nearly overwhelming. "Here's two clean towels. Call me when you're dry."

"Uh, wait. I'm going to need some more help. I've only got one drying hand. I have to hold on to this rack to steady myself." She returned one of the towels. "I think I can get most of my front, but I need you at my back."

Jason groaned, but competitive sports had taught him to keep going when the going got tough. He dried her neck, shoulders, arms, and upper back. *Alrighty*. Then he toweled her ankles, calves and knees. He paused before touching her mid-back, buttocks, and thighs. "This is the red zone, Amanda. Once I get inside the 20-yard-line, I usually want to score."

"Injury... patient. Remember? A doctor shouldn't score with an injured patient." She seemed to enjoy this too much; it clearly pleased her to know she still excited him.

Jason closed his eyes and rubbed her posterior, from mid-back all the way to mid-thighs. Sweat poured from his forehead and he held the damp towel near his belt buckle. "That dry enough? Let's get you out of there."

"Okay." She turned and faced him.

His eyes grew large and there was another slight tremble in his hands. "Me holding you, or you holding me?"

"Coming out, I think I can hold onto you. If you'll come a bit closer, that is."

He moved slowly. She reached behind his back with her right arm and clutched his belt buckle again with her left hand. As she did, the damp towel fell away and Amanda could see why he'd held it there.

Very awkwardly, he helped her step over the shower ledge and take two more short steps to the center of the bathmat. "Here's your crutches and your nightie thing. I need to step outside and get some air."

Amanda's smile had a dreamy look about it and she kissed his cheek lightly. "Thanks for all your help."

"No problemo." He left hurriedly, but his gait was affected.

— — —

Looking into the large mirror, Amanda realized she had not felt that alive in years. As she slipped the cotton nightdress over her damp hair, she thought she heard a tennis ball banging into the wall of the laundry house. Surely not the no-neck kid, not at that time of evening! She hobbled to her bedroom window and peeked out. Jason was taking out his frustration on the unsympathetic bricks.

He banged on those bricks for a good ten minutes while Amanda dried her hair and found her left slipper. She was seated on the couch when Jason came back inside.

"Thanks for your help, Jason. I'm sorry if it was awkward." She wasn't really.

He panted from the outside exertion. "I just want to ask you one thing."

"Shoot."

"When your foot heals up, we're both going to get in that shower, together. Okay?"

It was more of a declaration than a question, but she nodded. "Sure."

"And then you dry me off — back and front."

Amanda just smiled slyly.

Jason pointed to the gallon bag still covering Amanda's foot, and she nodded. He knelt down and gently peeled off the duct tape. After carefully removing the freezer bag, he softly dabbed a dishtowel around the top of her foot where some moisture had crept in.

"Did my bandages get wet?"

He leaned way over and peered closely. "Looks dry to me." From that same position, he looked up at her face. "Do you have to put the boot back on?"

She nodded again. "Supposed to."

"I think we left it in the bedroom. Be right back." He returned with the blue canvas plank and very carefully placed it back on her right foot. He cradled her newly shaven calf for a few moments before apparently realizing his boot task was already complete. Amanda didn't mention it.

They settled on the couch and watched the very end of a dramatic romance; then Amanda handed him the remote. "I think I'll read for a bit. Anything you want to see?"

"I think there's a pre-season NFL game this evening. Maybe the Titans are playing. No college football 'til September 5th." He reached for the remote slowly, as though he thought she might jerk it back at the last moment. She didn't. "You sure you don't mind me changing?"

"No, I want you to change." She'd answered a different question. "I mean… it's fine. Go ahead and watch the game. I like watching you watch ballgames." White lie.

"You do?"

"Sure. It's interesting to see you get so riled up at the refs." That part was true.

Jason surfed until he found the game. It took two complete runs through the entire sequence because a commercial was playing the first time he hit the correct channel.

By 10:30, Amanda was ready for bed. It had been a very long day.

Jason followed her down the short hallway and carefully helped her into bed.

"Ow!" She reached down toward her right leg. "Cramp!"

"Where?" Jason hurriedly sat on the bed beside her and pulled her leg straight. Then he placed her right ankle on his left shoulder and began massaging her calf. "Here?"

She groaned. "Yeah. Oh. Ow. Ow. Oh." She lay back on the bed. "Sometimes when I... ow... can't move my arch, it cramps up to my calf. Ow! Hurts like the devil."

"Need some potassium. I'll buy you some bananas tomorrow." Jason continued kneading her muscle with strong and assertive hands. After a while he slowed his rhythm. "Still hurt?"

"No. It's okay now, I think. Thanks."

He gently lowered her leg to the bed but his hand remained under her calf. Amanda figured it seemed so natural there, Jason might not even realize he was still touching her. "Well, into the foot box." There was disappointment in his voice. He helped guide her legs even though she didn't really need the assistance. Jason leaned way down near her knees and peered into the box. "That ought to be enough room in case you need to move around a bit." Her nightdress had ridden up her thighs and he stared for a moment before discreetly pulling down the hem. "Uh, if you get another cramp, just call out. I'm only 42 inches across that hall."

"You've been a terrific help today, Jason. Thanks."

As he adjusted her pillows, he leaned way over her face and it seemed — for a moment — they might kiss. She certainly wanted to. Jason looked deeply into her partly-closed eyes and surely could see her desire. His face moved slightly closer and, at the last second, his lips shifted to her forehead instead. "Doctor can't kiss injured patient."

She realized she was hungry for a real kiss... and more. Who was this new Jason who suddenly seemed so desirable? Whoever he was, he'd stirred up yearning in a way she hadn't felt in a long time. This was a very different man leaning over her pillows. She wanted to explore and discover the new world of Jason.

"Good night, Amanda."

What a time for Jason to develop restraint! *Blistered butt-rash!*

Chapter 25

August 23 (Sunday)

Amanda slept restlessly, in and out of light slumber. She kept thinking about the caring, new Jason who had emerged from the ashes of selfish, man-cold Jason.

Yesterday. Despite all of Jason's clumsy attempts to help, their incredibly embarrassing grocery experience, and the awkwardness of her shower — Amanda wished that seemingly endless Saturday had never ended.

Whatever was presently going on, she wanted more of it. Had Jason changed? She thought so. What if Christine was correct that the changes really had occurred mainly in Amanda's own mind? *Doubtful.* Whichever individual had transformed — or if, perhaps, both had done so — the results were fantastically positive. Amanda saw him differently, yes. But Jason had shown alternate sides of himself which had never been viewed before. At least not by Amanda.

Jason's own mother seemed unaware of such positive potential in her son. Could everything about this new Jason be attributed to his concern over Amanda's injuries and his eagerness to assist? *Not likely*. Relatively minor injuries are insufficient motivation for a grown man to shift so abruptly and significantly. What had been the genesis of Jason's caring attention, tenderness, and befuddled-but-sincere help around the apartment?

Amanda didn't know. Jason wasn't likely to explain, either, because he probably couldn't discern it himself. As far as she comprehended, Jason didn't do all that much thinking, especially not introspectively. So this change (whatever had happened) had to be the result of an instinctive shift, related to baseline emotions rather than mental analysis.

But what? Which emotion? To answer *love* was corny and not completely believable... yet it had to involve Jason's reawakened awareness of his affection for her. If instinct, what type? Surely not *nurturing* — men don't possess those genes. Not as far as Amanda had heard, anyway.

Protectiveness? *Perhaps.*

— — —

The lighted digital clock indicated 3:16 a.m. when Amanda woke suddenly.

She climbed out of bed and hobbled toward the bathroom without getting her crutches. It wasn't very far and there were furnishings and walls to hold onto. The room was pitch black except for the clock display. Normally the edge of the window shade would reveal a sliver of illumination from the security light in the parking lot. Maybe that bulb was out; she'd have to call about it in the morning.

The dim display was enough to orient her; if she got up from the left side of her bed and the clock was presently behind her, then the bathroom was straight ahead. What happened to her boot? She couldn't feel the hard plank sole. Had she removed it during her previous restlessness? *Don't remember taking it off.*

But something else seemed unusual. It was as though someone had rearranged her few pieces of bedroom furniture. In the dark, those furnishings seemed to shrink back from her grasp. It felt like there was additional space in the room — a greater distance between her bed and the sides of the bathroom and closet. As though someone had relocated those walls.

Things were very different when Amanda was in the dark.

There are people who move forward into blackness simply because they can't be bothered to flip a switch only a few feet away. But there are times people stumble in the dark because no light is available. Amanda couldn't locate the light and didn't understand why.

She took two tentative steps, placing very little weight on her unbooted right heel. She reached with her left hand for the chair between her bed and dresser, but didn't find it. One more tentative step and she nearly lost her balance. Surely the dresser was just over there. *No dresser.* She turned to her right, where she should encounter the antique highboy which stood against the closet wall, right next to a light switch.

Her arms moved in front and beside her as she took two more short, limping steps. *Nothing!* Empty space. How strange for her room's dimensions to be so distorted merely by the absence of light. Her window had to be straight ahead, because she'd turned that direction after losing contact with the foot of the bed.

She pivoted to the right again. Best to head back to her bed and start over. A lamp was not far from her pillow. Another short, halting step. Hands out in front and to the sides… aimed low to find the bed's footboard. *Nothing!*

Amanda was becoming frightened. She took another short step and bumped her fractured toes against something. She yelped in pain, then stood in that spot and trembled. Tears flowed as she called out the name of the person she knew would rescue her: "Jason! Jason!"

Amanda awoke with his name still in her throat, and abruptly sat up in her bed.

Jason burst into her room and switched on the ceiling light. "What's wrong?" He looked around like he'd expected to find a lurking panther. "You okay?" He landed on the edge of her bed and hugged Amanda tightly. Portions of her nightdress were soaked with sweat and she shivered. "What's wrong? What happened?"

Amanda couldn't form the words, but she now realized it had been a dream. With the room light on she could clearly see the chair, dressers, and walls were all in their proper alignment. Her tears soon stopped but her heart kept pounding under the thin cotton gown. "Dream... nightmare, I guess. Dark... couldn't get oriented. Things weren't where they belonged. Lost in my own room." She hugged him tighter and shuddered again.

"You're okay, Amanda. Everything's all right." Jason looked around as much as he could without turning his head, which was nearly fused to the top of Amanda's. "I'm here. It's okay."

Yes, it was okay. Partly because it had only been a dream, but mostly because Jason was there to comfort her.

He hugged her very tightly and then released. "Let me up for a minute and I'll be right back."

She was reluctant to loosen her intense grasp, but Amanda nodded and noisily inhaled the contents of her sinuses. *Where'd the tissue box go?* With large eyes, she watched him closely.

Jason went to her closet, turned on its lone bulb, and closed that door about three-quarters of the way. Then he turned off the overhead light and returned to her bed. "Scoot over a bit and I'll lie here with you for a minute."

Had she heard those words prior to Friday evening, Amanda would have assumed it was a clumsy maneuver to generate some comfort sex, but she knew the new Jason wouldn't take advantage of a situation like this. And that was the key she'd been searching for: she could *trust* this new Jason! *Imagine!*

He lay on top of the covers next to her and put his right arm under her neck. "Everything's okay, Amanda."

She melted into his right side and rubbed her tears onto his tee-shirt. With her head on his upper chest, she slowly relaxed and her heart stopped pounding.

After about ten minutes, Jason was sound asleep.

Amanda, however, was wide awake.

For another fifteen minutes, she tried to fall asleep, but couldn't. With considerable difficulty, she extracted her feet from the cardboard foot box and slid out of her bed's right side. With the light from the closet, she easily located her crutches and left slipper. She used the hall bathroom and then hobbled to the kitchen.

It was just now 3:10 a.m., several minutes before the time featured in her dream.

When sleep is elusive, there are always household chores needing attention. Amanda rescued the top rack dishes from Jason's indiscriminate tossing to the dishwasher's bottom section. Next, she sat at the table and segregated all of Jason's snacks and treats. Then she merged the few new actual groceries with those from Christine's large bag, which Margaret had unloaded, and put sticky notes on each sorted clump. With more sticky notes, she numbered each cabinet door which held foodstuffs.

Jason had good intentions, but his help was littered with four tiresome words: "Where does this go?"

Yawns finally overcame her nervous energy and Amanda fell asleep on the couch.

* * * *

Jason arose before Amanda and it took him a moment to realize he was in her bed. *Hmm.* He rewound those scenes from early, early morning. *Oh, yeah.* Bad dream and Amanda couldn't sleep. *So where is she now?* He checked the guestroom. *No.* Then the living room. Yes, curled up on the couch and looking a bit chilly. He found a large beach towel in the hall closet and draped it over her trunk and upper legs.

After a brief visit to the bathroom, he dressed, sat at the only clear spot on the dining table, and opened the borrowed laptop. Jason logged on to his e-mail account and strained for the right words to transmit to the beautiful woman dozing a few feet away. It took him ten minutes to write three sentences.

Though Christine had pulled down *her* blog, the parallel sites were still up and running. Jason located the serial he wanted, and then scrolled down to a section he remembered from Wednesday. He carefully transcribed it on a piece of tablet paper from the cupboard behind the table. He folded that page and tucked it in his back pocket.

Once again seeing his names — real and fabricated — in cyberspace was a reminder that he still had no idea how several bloggers had learned the true identities represented by those pseudonyms. Then it dawned on him that the bogus maids, carpet cleaners, insect sprayers, and cable guy — plus whoever else Christine had involved in the bizarre caper — would have told *someone* about their participation in a secret scheme. Perhaps each had told several someones. Nothing makes tongues wag faster than a juicy secret. Even his own mother had seemingly been aware of the blog, though she hadn't admitted it outright. Kevin had known all about it and he was about as discreet as a billboard. Even Kevin's friend Bill had been in on it. By that point, Jason figured probably 20 per cent of Verdeville knew at least something of the bizarre drama of *Marty* and *Missy*.

Jason went out to the front stoop and let the rising sun shine on his face. It was already very bright and he had to close his eyes tightly.

He'd gotten up earlier than normal because a lot was on his mind, which was rather unusual — Jason's mind was typically uncluttered territory. But his entire view of Amanda had changed dramatically in the past four days.

On Wednesday, their relationship had gone into the toilet when he'd seen Internet proof that Amanda had deliberately conspired to make him miserable over those previous nine days. But Friday, when he'd learned of her injuries, he'd almost forgotten all about his own deprivations and wanted only to be with Amanda to help her.

Then yesterday. *What was that all about?* All of her tantalizing and... whatever? Since they'd begun sleeping together after the Halloween party last year, they'd had sex reasonably often; in fact, whenever they got physical it almost always turned into sex. But last night he'd been physically all over her, yet it didn't lead to anything... except his own pent-up frustration. Revving the engine so much without being able to pop his clutch was very unsatisfying. Yet, there was something about all their contact which gave him a warm feeling. Not just the warmth in his loins, but something deeper. Maybe warmth in his heart?

Jason couldn't be certain, but he might have just felt tenderness for the first time since grade school, when he'd gotten his own tiny puppy. Boys weren't taught a lot about tenderness; it was off the approved curriculum. But whatever they'd done last night had actually felt good. Of course it would have felt a whole lot better if sex had followed it. *Danged Hypocritical Oath!* Being her temporary doctor was the pits.

Good thing Amanda was not inside his head right now, because she'd once said he had that oath confused with something else. *Nah.*

He went back inside the apartment quietly in case Amanda was still asleep, but she was no longer on the couch so she'd probably gone to her bedroom.

Actually she'd washed her hair in the kitchen sink, where the shampoo bottle remained open on the counter. With hair still damp, she appeared in the hallway a short time later. The morning sun shone through the front window and backlit her shapely figure in the pinkish cotton gown.

My, my, my. What a vision! And so early in the morning. Jason had to blink.

She hobbled over to the couch, where Jason sat with the remote in his hand and the television not yet on. She leaned way over and kissed his cheek. "Thanks again for all your help last night. I hope it wasn't too hard on you." In that position, her nightdress fell forward enough that Jason could see a considerable portion of her breasts. She obviously knew it and smiled slyly.

"If you don't get some clothes on, it's going to be hard on you!" Jason didn't know how much more teasing he could stand.

"Hey, let's skip all this meal preparation business here and just hit a drive-through." Amanda hadn't even sat down yet. "Sound okay?"

"Uh, sure. Any particular place?" Jason was always ready to eat, and any drive-through would have better coffee than he'd made yesterday.

"You pick one out while I shuck this nightgown and put on some street clothes." She hobbled on her crutches down the hallway.

Jason heard lavatory water running and several drawers opening. Amanda soon emerged wearing basically the same items as the day before, but different colors: khaki shorts and light blue tee-shirt. On her left foot was a sneaker. "Ready?"

"Uh, I need my wallet and keys, and some shoes."

— — —

Amanda touched his lips with her fingertip. "Go ahead and brush your teeth while you're moving around. Makes the food taste better."

Jason complied and emerged from the hall bathroom with a boyish grin. He'd even combed his hair.

Amanda threw her arms around his neck and kissed his mouth deeply. One of the crutches fell to the floor. *Who is this guy?* And how had he turned Amanda into a high school girl again? She realized she had a different appetite than could be satisfied at a drive-through window. Amanda was hungry for this new Jason. The one who tenderly looked after her, bashfully dried her naked body, and then went outside to cool down. The person who'd comforted her after the bad dream. The man who'd exhibited restraint for possibly the first time since she'd known him. Tenderness plus restraint. *Wow!*

Jason broke the kiss. "What's that for?" He was out of breath.

"That's the kiss you stiffed me on last night. Bet you thought I'd forgotten." She smiled. "So, let's eat. I'm starving."

On the way to his pickup, Jason listed half a dozen fast-food places with good breakfast menus. His well-known favorite would have been the Shuney's buffet, but Amanda couldn't handle that venue on crutches, so it would have to wait. For now, they settled on the drive-through of the nearest Golden Arches.

After receiving their order, Jason drove slightly over a mile southeast of old downtown, to Verdeville's City Park. It was about 9:00 a.m. and relatively deserted. He parked near a large oak tree and they set up their fare at a concrete picnic table with a few leaves and acorns scattered about its stained and chipped surface.

Amanda was getting better at exiting and entering his truck with the crutches. She'd be an old hand at it by the time her toes healed.

The acorns probably reminded Jason of "allshitz" coffee, because he thumped them, one by one, with his middle finger. Each flew several feet away from their sturdy table.

With little conversation, they finished their breakfast sandwiches and fried potato cakes. Jason had purchased a third large coffee which he then divided between both empty cups. As they sipped their refilled coffee, a slightly dusty minivan drove up and parked about 60 feet away. First to exit were a girl and her younger brother; both raced to the nearby swing set. Then Dad from the driver's side and Mom from the other front seat. Mom was obviously pregnant and even from that distance she seemed radiant.

Amanda looked on with longing. She wondered if she'd ever have a minivan and three kids. And she wondered what kind of father Jason might eventually be.

— — —

Jason also watched the family, but his attention focused on the mother with beautiful legs. He'd never really looked closely at pregnant women before. It was an instinct mechanism: pregnant women were off limits and out of season. *Ignore.* But he noticed this one, even from 60 feet away — she was lovely.

Then he turned to Amanda. That's how she would look when pregnant — lovely with beautiful legs. Desirable even with a baby belly. Funny thing was, Jason had never before studied Amanda while his mind held any image associated with motherhood. Whenever he gazed at Amanda, Jason saw beauty and felt desire, but he'd never done much thinking beyond deciding what clothing article came off first.

The family of four and a half moved farther away, toward a fort built of weathered landscape timbers. Jason actually wanted to join them, but neither mentioned it nor moved in that direction. It looked like Amanda felt the same way.

"Jason, you know that Christine is my closest friend."

He nodded. *Why'd she have to mention Christine?*

— — —

Amanda had wanted to broach the topic since the previous afternoon, but it had not yet come up in conversation. In fact, it probably never would, so she just blurted it out. "It's important to me for you two to get along." She inhaled and let it out slowly. "How do you feel about Christine now?"

"Like I said, melt her to the castle floor with a bucket of water."

"Hmm. A little bit of grudge still simmering."

"I'd at least like to pour some glue on her boobs." Jason pointed to the shirt covering his hairless right pectoral.

"Oh, the poultice. Or maybe you just like Christine's chest."

Jason shrugged. "Well, they have a certain volume that appeals to me. But no, my gluing process would be purely revenge. She nearly ripped off my nipple. So, tit for tat."

"Quite apropos. But I'm not convinced this is about glue and gauze. I think you want to check out her girls."

"Her rack has impressive dimensions, to be sure. Other things being equal, I could admit a certain clinical curiosity as to their consistency." On vary rare occasions Jason spoke like an alliterative instructor, yet didn't seem to be aware of it. *Weird.*

"Clinical? You want to feel up my girlfriend!"

"Solely in the interest of science."

"I don't think Christine is presently sponsoring that particular field research." Amanda touched Jason's knee. "But will you try to forgive her and get along? For my sake?"

Typically, Jason was not one for long pauses, but he seemed to let this one linger to give his noble sacrifice more impact. "If anybody else asked me for Christine's clemency, I'd let that witch burn at the stake. But for you, I'll make an effort to get along."

"A sincere effort?"

"As much as I'm able to muster."

Amanda wasn't certain how to quantify that, but she let the matter drop. He'd try. *Good enough, for now.* So she hugged him.

Near their picnic table, a few birds lit on the lower oak limbs; the sun — very slowly — moved higher in the sky. In the distance, they heard parent voices and childish laughter.

Since Amanda had already mentioned Christine, it was not surprising that Jason turned to her with a follow-up. "You and Christine kept talking about that so-called *man-cold* like they're all exactly alike. I don't even recognize the *syndrome* she described on that blog."

"You wouldn't. You're a man." Amanda's eyes still monitored the family in the distance.

"No, I mean I did have a little fever, my head was actually hurting, and I couldn't breathe much. That's sick. At least according to my doctor."

"Who's also a man." She patted his hand.

— — —

Jason realized it was time. He reached into his back pocket and unfolded the notebook page. "Look, I wrote this down before you woke up this morning. Maybe it'll give you some understanding of what I was going through. Here goes." He read it out loud.

When you get that first fuzzy feeling in your head, it's usually the beginning of the warning signs. And you begin checking your body's systems for other anomalies. It's like you had this really primo muscle car: powerful engine, sleek design, cool wheels, and great paint job. One day there's a slight hesitation when you accelerate. Hmm. That's unusual. Then you hear a ping here... a rattle there. Maybe a tiny grinding noise. Warning signs. Could be you're nearly out of fuel, tires nearly deflated, low oil pressure. Or is it more serious? Maybe the compression's off or timing's not right. What it really needs is some time in the shop for a complete diagnostic by a qualified factory-trained technician. You hope it just involves a tune-up... but you never know if it's going to require a valve job, new brake pads, piston rings, tie rods, universal joint, or front wheel alignment.

Amanda probably didn't know much more about cars than ignition keys and steering wheels, but she didn't interrupt.

"So that's kind of my perspective." He folded the paper and placed it on the picnic table. "I felt lousy and I wanted a chance to slowly check out all my systems."

"Why didn't you explain any of this before?"

"I didn't even think about it at the time. I mean, I felt bad and just figured you knew that I needed to be in the shop for a while. I didn't think I had to wrap words around it."

"So you wrote this out to explain." Amanda pointed to the paper.

He shrugged. It was true Jason had written those words on that page, but he hadn't composed the essay. It was somewhere on one of the parallel blogs. Right now he banked on Amanda never discovering that original post.

Amanda took a thoughtful sip of her cooling coffee. "Well, I feel awful for everything we put you through. I just thought you were being a big baby and wanted to regress to when you were the center of attention and the entire world revolved around you and your needs, or whims."

Lame smile. "Yeah, that, too."

Amanda whapped his hand.

"It's not always easy to separate what's described here," Jason tapped the paper, "from the way you just stated it. But a man needs, occasionally, to shut down his systems and run a complete…"

"And the little boy wants Momma to hug and coo and comfort him at her breast."

"Is that so bad?" Jason shrugged again. "Anyway, it's not so easy to differentiate. All those needs rolled up together and the body has signaled it's time for a diagnostic."

"Runny nose, headache, and half a degree of temp."

"I didn't say I was Code Blue on the E.R. crash cart. Look, it might not seem justifiable, but I'm at least trying to describe it. I do want you to understand that it's not just manufactured. The cold really happened."

"And then fabrication clicks in, so you can stretch it out." Amanda made that motion with the fingers of both hands.

"Well, once we shut down for the checkup analysis and receive a bit of extra attention or comfort… it feels good. So, if it does drag on, it's because we feel so at home that we don't want to leave."

"I guess I can't blame you for wanting that. But it's still unfair, off balance — most women just have to keep going. Cooking, cleaning, working, handling children, et cetera. When do women have this little vacation in the diagnostic shop? When do females get a reprieve from responsibility, obligation, accountability, whatever?"

Jason shrugged. He started to mention PMS and menstrual cramps, but since he didn't understand a single thing about either one, he wisely kept his mouth shut.

Chapter 26

Amanda watched as the distant relaxed family returned to their minivan; all got inside except the young girl, who needed a few final swings before leaving. She was probably about eight and looked like a tomboy. About twenty years before, Amanda had been just like her.

The mother called several times, with increasing volume. The girl finally left the swings and, distinctly disgusted, entered the family vehicle.

Their minivan drove away slowly, the girl gazing toward the swing set.

Amanda watched the vehicle disappear around a tree-lined curve and then turned to Jason. "Thanks for sharing your essay. And since you've decided to bring up colds again, let's establish some ground rules, just in case either one of us should ever get sick again."

"Hold on. Just to make sure... these are rules for each of us. Right?"

She nodded. "Number one, it's a lot easier to visit a sickie and bring him meals… so stay at your own apartment unless you're truly at death's door."

Jason frowned. He likely thought he'd just recently experienced that dire status.

"Number two, if you absolutely *have* to be in somebody's else's dwelling, shower every day and comb your ratty hair. At least every other day, you shave."

"That includes legs, for you." He stroked her thigh, still surprisingly smooth from last night's shave.

Amanda smiled as she nodded. "And burn those nasty jammies."

"What do I have to wear? Prison uniform?" Jason looked down and possibly imagined garish stripes on coarse gray wool. At the moment he wore a tee-shirt, jean shorts, and sneakers.

"I'd settle for decent looking sweatpants with an actual waistband, and a clean shirt each morning."

"So, what's your sick apparel going to be? Sexy negligee?"

"Dream on. Probably warm flannel jammies with the feet sewed on." She touched his upper chest. "But they'll be clean each day." She closed her eyes to think of other components. "Oh, and brush your teeth, morning and night. Plus, clean up after yourself."

"Not crazy about having to endure my illness in solitary confinement, but I think I can hold up the rest of that contract. Is that it?"

"We'll have to work out something about food — maybe the sickie brings his or her own food as long as it doesn't inhibit recovery or cause extra mucous." *Hmm.* Food and diet would need additional study. "Biggie: no channel flipping TV marathons in the middle of the night. I need my rest since I have to work the next day. Oh, and I require at least an hour to chill after I get home from work."

"Sounds fair enough." Then Jason grinned cheesily. "What about the kindly nurse fluffing my pillow and other stuff."

Amanda recalled how much she'd wished for someone to take care of her during those first three days after her accident. "Okay, tit for tat. If I'm the desperately ill sickie, on the day I get well enough to leave your apartment, you're the cabana boy who gives me a full body massage."

"No problemo, *señorita*."

Amanda thought for a second about reciprocation. "Your next cold better not be during the remainder of this decade. But the next time you're truly ill, I'll try limited participation in your attentive nurse fantasy. But only on the day that you leave my apartment."

"So, that's my incentive to get well quicker? No sex 'til I'm walking out the door?"

"Not walking out *per se*. But, you know, I'd need a certainty you were heading the direction of the door." She smiled.

"Like a parting gift."

"Maybe a departure celebration."

"So, how would that work? Would I be in actual departing motion?" Jason's fingers mimicked walking. "Or would a bed be involved?"

"I don't know. Bed, couch, floor, gurney. Whatever's convenient." She smiled fondly. "Remember that time we made love on a dining room chair?"

He nodded vigorously. "It was so good, I nearly passed out." Jason seemed to like the turn of their conversation. "Well, we could do the nurse thing even if I don't have a vicious cold. You know… practice, so we could work out the kinks."

"You want to be sure we're on the same page…" Her fingertips touched the inside of his forearm.

"Received the same memo…" His hand returned to her thigh.

"Attended the right briefing…"

Somehow their list transitioned to a close embrace. Then they kissed.

When her fractured toes touched the broad cement base of their massive picnic table, Amanda groaned and pulled away. "Let's head back to my place." *Breakfast sausage is not tasty enough to revisit in a kiss.*

— — —

Jason did not want the kissing to stop, but he figured Amanda's apartment held promise for other delights.

For the moment, however, he was using restraint. He'd seen pain in her eyes and she probably needed another pill.

His natural urges would have pressed the issue, but somehow his rational brain and newly empathetic heart kicked in instead. So he waited and watched. And drove.

When they arrived at her apartment, Jason hurried to the kitchen cabinet to bring her the pain pills. She only took one.

After they got settled in, Amanda propped her right leg on the hassock and watched portions of two different sappy movies. She leaned against his side with her shoulders under his right arm, until Jason nearly dozed off.

Apparently tired of television, she accidently roused Jason as she got out from under his heavy arm. Then Amanda repositioned her footstool and moved over on the couch nearer the lamp. She gave him the remote and resumed reading the paperback she'd left the previous evening.

Jason surfed for a few moments. As usual, with over 30 good channels, it was difficult to make up his mind. It was only late morning and the pre-season football Sunday games hadn't started yet. So bored with television at the moment that he actually felt like talking, he put down the remote. "The other day my mom was telling me stuff I'd never heard before."

"Like what?" Amanda marked and closed her book.

"Mom said Dad had a couple of suspicious colds, sometime before I started school, I guess. She was at the point with him that she actually felt like leaving my dad if she couldn't break him of the alleged man-cold syndrome."

"Sounds pretty serious. And…?"

It was painful for Jason to phrase this. "But she said she loved him too much to leave him."

"So she broke him instead."

"Uh-huh. And early this morning… I was thinking."

— — —

Amanda sat up straight. *This is new.* "Thinking about what?"

"I figured…" He started hesitantly. "If you loved me enough… to do all that stuff… to break the cycle of what you call man-colds… then you probably loved me enough… not to leave me." Jason appeared relieved that he got all those words out.

She snuggled into his side. "I'm not going to leave you, Jason. But I sure was ready to throttle you."

"But you do love me?"

"Yes, Jason, absolutely. Even at your grungiest, even with that awful breath and those pitiful jammies. Even with all the whining, I never stopped loving you." She kissed his cheek. "But I didn't *like* you very much, not last week."

Jason scrunched his brow. "How do you tell the difference? How far can it go — not liking someone — before the love is gone, too?"

"I don't know. I guess that's what Margaret found out with your dad. There must be a point when the weight shifts over and you *could* stop loving someone, but I don't know what it is." Amanda touched his wrist for emphasis. "I've seen old married couples who didn't seem to like each other at all any more, but somewhere deep inside, a core of mutual love remained."

"My mom said love was about the person, but liking was about the behavior. She said when me and my brothers were kids, she sometimes hated what we did, but never stopped loving us."

Amanda nodded. "That's maternal love. There's a lot of primal instinct and other stuff involved with motherhood. Part of that's about *you've got my blood in your veins and you came from my body*. That's different from romantic love."

"I guess I'd agree, but I'm not sure I could explain that difference."

She thought for a moment. "Romantic love is about attraction, passion, bonding, and whatever, but it begins with two people who have no blood ties. So whatever grows out of that romantic love doesn't have the blood to back it up." She wondered how well she was explaining her grasp of the difference. "The love of partners has to do with commitment that involves, at least to some extent, a series of choices. I think."

Jason looked into her eyes. "What are your choices?"

Amanda didn't answer. She'd only recently realized that, until yesterday, she'd never truly been in love, even though she'd convinced herself at those other times that she was. Whatever she'd experienced with her sleazy college professor had certainly not been love. And her attraction to that Cary Grant executive had been little more than inflamed infatuation.

Jason watched her for several moments and probably guessed she didn't have a response. So he sighed quietly and resumed channel surfing.

Nobody could imagine how many times Jason had zipped through sequential channel numbers during the past hour. Though he seldom reviewed the programming guide for the locations of interesting shows, he now checked that screen for the time. Nearly noon. "You feel like any lunch?"

"Depends on what you have in mind." She was not willing to try tuna again.

"I was thinking simple... like cereal. We got milk at the store yesterday."

"True, but I think the only cereal I have here is flax, hemp, and those large shredded wheat bricks you complained about."

He frowned. "How 'bout I make another grocery run and get some good cereal?"

"Define *good*."

"You know, tasty, sweet. Regular stuff. Real cereal."

Amanda eyed him skeptically. She suspected this was some kind of guy maneuver but couldn't imagine his motive. Men don't eagerly rush to the store to pick up cereal. Nonetheless, she nodded slowly.

He checked his pockets for keys and wallet. "This'll be a commando mission: in-grab-out. Twenty minutes, tops."

"Okay, but get me some ordinary generic raisin bran. I don't think I can handle Fruity Pebbles or whatever you're likely to come up with."

"Okay, red-bunny."

"What?"

"Red-bunny. That's my pneumatic for raisin bran."

Mnemonic. But she didn't correct him. "If you can remember red-bunny, surely you can remember raisin bran."

"But the brain holds onto it better when you substitute something. Saw that on the Discovery Channel."

She was surprised Jason's quick surfing thumb had allowed him sufficient exposure to any one channel to absorb an entire segment of anything. "Okay, red-bunny. Bye." Amanda waved without turning around.

Jason started out the door. Then he came back, walked around to the front of the couch, leaned way over, and kissed her lips lightly. "Be right back."

Her lips were still slightly parted when the front door closed. "He kissed me goodbye." *Who is that guy?*

While Jason was gone, Amanda logged on to her Facebook account to check recent posts and then read her newest e-mails. One each from Maria and Sunny, one from sister Kaye, two from Mom, one from King Louie, three from Christine, and a new one from Jason! She checked the time stamp. Why had Jason sent her an e-mail at 6:17 a.m.? At that point, she'd been still asleep on the couch less than eight feet from where he'd been typing.

The last e-mail she'd received from Jason was his break-up memo. Her fingers trembled slightly as she clicked open this new message.

> *Please disregard my previous transmission. It was intended for a different woman I used to know. I apologize for any inconvenience and assure you your account will be properly credited.*

Amanda shook her head. Jason couldn't write three sentences without defaulting to the schpiel he was required to say at his job. But she smiled. The sentiment of the first portion was lovely.

She wrote back:

> *I used to be a different woman, so maybe we met before, in passing. Since we're both apparently transformed now, let's see how these two new people get along.*
>
> *P.S. Apology accepted.*

She transmitted and then opened that same message in her sent mail folder. She left it up on the screen so Jason could see it as soon as he returned. On an afterthought, she went to the laptop's tools menu and reset the screen display to ignore sleep. If it took that long for him to notice it, her message to Jason would stay on the screen until doomsday. Or until the laptop's battery fritzed out.

* * * *

Jason was back from the grocery within thirty minutes.

He brought an eager smile and two plastic bags to the couch where Amanda sat watching another movie, on a different channel than her usual networks.

"Two bags?" She tried to peer inside, but he kept them closed. "You only went for one item."

With great flourish, Jason produced four greenish bananas. "Potassium. For your leg cramps."

"Uh, thank you." Possibly no one had ever brought her green bananas before. "What else have you got in there?"

He pulled out his Frosted Mini-Wheats. "These have good, sweet taste out the wah-zoo." Jason peered into one of his sacks and then put it behind him.

"What's in that one?" She pointed toward the bag he'd moved.

"Uh, I remembered to get a few snacks for the game this afternoon."

"For example." Amanda rolled her eyes.

"Pretzels, nuts, chips, dip. You know, essentials."

She sighed heavily. "Right, essentials. So, where's my raisin bran?"

"Huh?" Jason briefly wondered if someone had switched the script.

"Raisin bran. You know, red-bunny — the actual reason you went to the grocery to begin with."

"Oh, that's what red-bunny was!" He chuckled. "I kept repeating red-bunny, but by the time I got to the grocery, I couldn't remember what it stood for."

"So, what's in this bag you're holding?" She reached for it. "Not a dyed rabbit, I hope."

Jason tightened his grip on the sack. "Naw, they were out 'til Easter." He paused briefly for the drama, and then reached into the bag and pulled out a flower.

— — —

Amanda gasped. "You brought me a rose?" Her eyes teared. "You've never gotten me a flower before." It was not exactly a grandiose arrangement; simply a single blossom, just barely opening its petals. At the end of its stem was a tiny, slender plastic reservoir of water. "Why'd you bring me a flower?"

He looked sheepish. "When I forgot what red-bunny stood for, I tried to think of something else with the same initials. All I could come up with was rose-bud."

She threw her arms around his neck and kissed his mouth. The sudden impact of her hug pushed Jason back on the couch. Two snack bags popped open with a loud simultaneous *whoosh* and his butt crushed most of his pretzels and chips. His nuts apparently sustained only minor jostling.

When he could finally catch his breath from their kisses, Jason apologized about forgetting her cereal.

Amanda drew back just enough for his face to be in focus. "Jason, you can forget my cereal any time if you're bringing me flowers. That's a standing ordinance."

If Jason had expected a brief mini-lecture about the reasons for taking lists to the store, he was pleasantly surprised.

Amanda nearly itched to remind him why lists were important, but she didn't want to ruin the moment. It was not every day a woman received a rose from the new Jason.

They both ate cereal for lunch while Jason watched a pre-season NFL game. Amanda tried his Frosted Mini-Wheats and actually liked them. They were sweet enough to fill her sugar quota for a full week, but that was okay. He'd brought her a flower!

"You want me to get a glass or something to put that in?" He started to get up.

"No, I'll just hold it a while." She leaned over and gave his cheek a sugary kiss. "It's lovely, Jason." She slowly twirled it a few times until one of the remaining thorns nicked her finger.

— — —

Jason pondered the complexities of the universe.

Who would have thought that noticing the pretty teenaged girl filling helium balloons at the front of the store would have led to his purchase of a flower for Amanda?

Who would have guessed Jason could forget what red-bunny actually represented?

Who could imagine that he'd manage to think up a pneumatic match for red-bunny in the flower/balloon department?

Not Jason... that's for sure.

On very rare days, the Man-Gods sometimes smile on even the most bumbling of the earthly male specimens. For Jason, this had to be that day.

During the remainder of the afternoon, Jason snacked a lot and dozed a little. That evening, the Nashville Titans played in a different pre-season game. Amanda read her novel on the couch, but she napped in her bedroom because Jason's crunchy snacks were too loud.

Chapter 27

Amanda hobbled back along the short hall on her crutches while Jason dozed during the second half of the Titans' game. She heard scratching noises high on the front door and then the sound of a car driving away. Amanda checked again to be certain Jason was still snoozing and then opened the door. Smiling as she looked inside the small shopping bag, she took it to her bedroom and then returned to the living space.

With difficulty, Amanda maneuvered around the sprawled-out Jason and sat at her regular end of the couch. The jostling awakened Jason.

— — —

Yawning, Jason went to the kitchen during a beer commercial to refill his snack bowl with another handful of tiny chip fragments. They tasted almost the same as the intact chips, but Jason couldn't dip the shards without getting salsa all over his fingers. It was unseemly to keep licking his fingertips and it made them too sticky to surf the channels properly during the game's numerous commercials. He even tried skimming a forkful of fragments into the salsa, but it was a bit like trying to eat green peas with a butter knife. So he gave up on chip shards and focused on shoveling pretzel crumbs with a spoon. At least his nuts were intact.

On one of those kitchen visits, his eye caught the laptop screen. Not wanting to appear overtly nosy, Jason glanced sideways as he passed, but couldn't quite make it out. On the return trip, he paused and actually looked directly at it. Amanda didn't seem to notice.

He read her apology-accepted message and smiled. Yes, this was the day the Man-Gods smiled down on Jason. He was now officially un-broken-up. A loud cheer from the stadium spectators caught his attention — the Titans had just scored! And, Jason thought to himself, he might also.

"Uh, thanks for the... e-mail." He almost stammered. Normal protocol training didn't exactly cover the method of thanking your girlfriend for sending an un-break-up e-mail in response to your e-mail apology (for sending a break-up e-mail). Check the index of any etiquette book. In the absence of any other conceivable action, Jason sat next to Amanda, lifted her hand, and kissed it.

— — —

Another first for Amanda — the new Jason kissed her hand! What next? If Jason kept evolving at this speed, he would probably even be able to remember to put the toilet seat down after completing his business. (If she ever decided to use the solvent which Christine had brought over Friday to remove the thoroughly bonded Super Glue.)

On Amanda's part, she was not sure how to respond to the new Jason who'd just kissed her hand. That might happen two or three times during the entire lifespan of a typical female, unless she was involved in a theatre troupe. People in stage costumes do a lot of hand-kissing.

In the absence of any other conceivable action, Amanda hobbled down the hall on her crutches to use the bathroom, brush her teeth, and take a quick spit-bath.

— — —

Jason could hear the tooth-brushing sounds and figured that was an indicator of good things to come. He cupped his hands and exhaled heavily. *Yikes!* Tiny, broken pieces of chips and pretzels seemed to cause worse breath than the large, intact ones did. So Jason hustled into the hall bathroom and brushed his own teeth with the triple-striped toothpaste. While he had that familiar taste so near his mouth, he also consumed another inch, since he'd grown so attached to it during the recent unfortunate business.

Amanda made her way back to the living room and sat again on the couch.

Jason's hands were sweaty and he couldn't get his legs comfortable.

"Let's say things are stabilized between us and we have good prospects of moving forward together." Amanda's introduction sounded awfully formal.

"Does that basically mean we're making up?" *Sounds promising.*

"I suppose…" She paused so long, it seemed she might not complete that thought. "Although if you're expecting this to… go anywhere, I should warn you I haven't shaved my legs since last night."

Jason gently lifted Amanda's left leg and cradled it in the crook of his left arm. His right hand slowly and thoroughly inspected the skin surface from her toes, past her knee, and under the wide cuff of her cargo shorts. "You have the most beautiful legs I've ever seen, Amanda. Even with a few extra hours since your last shave." Again, his hand slid under her cargo shorts. "Plus, your thighs are smooth as silk." There was extra heat behind his grin.

— — —

Amanda, warmed by his touch and his words, wanted to feel more and hear more. "You seem to be an expert on lower anatomy. How versed are you on upper portions?" Amanda arched her back and thrust out her chest theatrically.

"I love those also." There was a long pause as he refreshed his visual recollection of her bosom and, with his forefinger, outlined a figure eight on her tightened tee-shirt. Jason looked deeply into her eyes. "And I love *you*, Amanda."

She straightened her upper body. "Despite the awful way I acted?" Amanda tended to poke bruises better left alone.

"Love is stronger than the cold virus."

It didn't sound like Jason, so he'd probably heard it from somebody. Still, he'd remembered it… and at the right time. "Aw, Jason. You're so much deeper than I ever suspected."

Jason shrugged and grinned.

"Hey, I've got a surprise for you." She smiled slyly.

"No bizarre treatments from Christine's witchcraft scrolls."

Amanda chuckled. "Nothing to do with Christine whatsoever. This involves Victoria."

"Who?"

"I've got a secret from Victoria. It was kind of your mom's idea."

— — —

Those two images in Jason's brain, at the same time, were so conflicting that he couldn't think of any words. But he needn't bother — he figured he was about to get lucky. Finally.

"It could be a tad awkward with crutches and this boot, but I'm willing… if you feel up to it, that is."

"Oh, I'm up to it, all right." *Whatever* it *is*.

She kissed his mouth and certainly tasted the striped toothpaste still on his tongue. "Okay, wait here for a minute and I'll go try it on." She steadied herself by gripping his upper thigh and rose from the couch.

Jason's thigh still tingled from the touch of her hand as Amanda, on crutches, moved toward her bedroom. He couldn't sit still but didn't know what else to do. Jason also suddenly realized he was hungry, but that would have to wait. *Don't live by bread alone.*

Amanda was gone for much more than one minute and Jason figured the boot was getting in her way of… whatever. That gave him time to consider some of the delectable fashions he'd seen in the spicy catalog before Christine had whisked it away. Lots of possibilities and most had very skimpy portions of lace, nylon, or silk. In fact, all the fashions in Victoria's catalog left hardly anything secret.

Her bedroom door opened and Amanda's crutches made their unique thump and creak noises down the short hallway.

Jason rose when she entered.

Amanda wore a white cap and a very tight white minidress, open partway down the front. There was a red cross on her lapel and a plastic stethoscope around her neck. A nurse! A white fishnet stocking encased her left leg and two empty garter straps grazed her right thigh.

If Jason's brain-mouth connection had been working, he might have said something clever and in character, like, *Oh, Nurse, thank goodness you've finally arrived. I thought I was a goner.* But all he could manage was, "Wow…" Among all the other visual stimuli, the empty garter straps fascinated him.

"I didn't even try to pull the other stocking over my boot." When she shrugged, the unbuttoned part of her dress revealed considerable curving flesh and her hem rose above the top of the single stocking.

Jason hadn't even touched her yet. He was fundamentally a visual learner. Tactile would soon follow. "You look gorgeous, with one stocking or none, Nurse... uh, what's your name?" He was finally able to get into character.

"Call me anything but Missy." Then she leaned over and whispered into his ear. "I wouldn't normally put on a get-up like this... except, after all I put you through, I decided to go all out. This once."

Jason didn't hear words. He went crazy when she whispered in his ear.

— — —

After a total of about forty minutes since Nurse Nancy arrived, the patient achieved a miraculous recovery. Both were briefly giddy.

Amanda finally removed her nurse cap, which was all she had on by that point, except her blue canvas boot. Jason wore nothing but socks and a very satisfied, sleepy smile.

The beach towel Jason had used to cover her that morning was over the back of the nearby chair. Amanda spread out the towel on the couch and lay down with her right leg on the hassock.

He found a very narrow spot next to her left side, laid his head gently on her chest, and listened to her heartbeat.

Amanda's heart continued to beat rapidly for another ten minutes or more.

Jason kissed her mouth softy. "That costume didn't come from Victoria. I've got her catalog memorized and that's not one of her secrets. So, where'd you get it?"

Amanda grinned. "You know that party supply store down past the chicken place?"

He nodded.

"Last week I saw they had their Halloween stuff out way early. I called Christine last night and asked her to swing by today and pick this up."

"Today? I didn't see her."

"You were snoozing during one of the games." She poked his ribs. "Your team was losing."

Jason lifted his head slightly. "Oooh. Do you suppose they have any witch costumes?"

She pulled her hand away from his chest and gently whapped his lower belly. "I thought you were scared of witches."

"Only scared of evil witches, not good ones." His hand roamed tenderly. "And I've got a feeling you'd be a very good witch."

Delicious sensations resulted from his touch. "I'm not saying I'm ever going to wear any more silly costumes for you." She paused as she searched his eyes. "But if I ever did do the witch thing, I'm sure I'd be… wicked."

Then Amanda smiled and kissed the new Jason again.

-30-

Author's Note

It's long been an accepted part of American female lore that men allegedly handle illness quite unlike women — so differently, in fact, that (at some point) scientists isolated the cold virus itself... and men now contract their own species of that ailment.

My first *exposure* (pardon the pun) to this anomaly was seeing a male actor's portrayal of a minor cold in a scene near the end of a 1970 movie*. I asked myself, "Do some women really view men's illnesses that way?" When the affirmative answer came back, I asked, "Do some men really act that way when they're sick?" Over the years since, I've seen or read several little scenes in which similar views were expressed.

I've always loved screwball comedies — whether on film or in novels — but that was not what I set out to write in this case. Originally, I'd intended to have the alpha male character in my Somerset Series suffer from a man-cold for part of a novel... and the heroine would have to put up with his whining and exaggerating.

But as I began writing the dialog in one of those scenes, I realized the topic was much too important to be merely an additional plot thread. The infamous man-cold needed its own novel!

And the next logical step soon became clear — the tragic epidemic of man-colds surely needed a cure.

— — —

Diary of a Mad Housewife, with Richard Benjamin and Carrie Snodgress.

Acknowledgements

This manuscript, written mostly in September of 2009, got shoved aside by a flurry of publishing, promoting, editing, and other writing. All during these four years since, I've worried that the contest judges, agents, or editors who'd seen part (or all) of my story would somehow beat me to the punch and publish something on this topic — *man-colds* — before I had the opportunity. Doesn't seem so, however.

I'm extremely grateful to my friend, Gunnar Grey – owner of Dingbat Publishing – for letting me in on the ground floor of her developing company. And I'm especially pleased that she has allowed me to work again with two very talented and personable professionals whom I know from another publisher and who also do freelance work elsewhere. They are Traci Pollitt, the perceptive content editor, and Elaina Lee, the creative cover artist. I am also indebted to John Grey for his thorough proofing of this manuscript.

I would be remiss if I neglected to mention that Theresa Thevenote's Facebook discussion of the cushaw — the awesome monster cousin in the crookneck winter squash family — inspired me to write a particular scene in this novel. Everything I know about tofu, I learned from my wife's second cousin, Blake J. Williams; my knowledge of hummus comes from my wife's niece, Sharon Lenox. Also thanks to Renita Godby for her anecdote of the cat lifting her eyelids… and to Carla Lynn Shurr Hostetter for her story of the missing necklace pendant.

Special thanks to my brother, Charles A. Salter, who provided helpful, detailed feedback on the early draft he read, and to my wife, Denise Williams Salter, who read an early draft and assisted in several other ways.

My list of early readers is a long one. Those who not only read my novel, but offered helpful feedback, were: Nanette D. Scott, Sona Dombourian, Kathleen T. Smith, Theresa Thevenote, Trudy Patterson, Sharon Pullen, and Renita Godby. Other readers were Rita Roudebush Williams, Dottie Robinson Salter, Jackie Choate, Madeline Carbon, Katherine Cavendish Gibson, Linda Rushing Gill, and Sharon Warner.

I also appreciate the interest of Richard Jasper, Bella Fitzgerald, Caroline D. LeBlanc Wolf, Pamela Picard, Rebecca Salter Rod, Julia Salter Moers, Carol Ann Goin, Susan Wise, and Christine Witthohn.

About the Author

My newest novel is *Curing the Uncommon Man-Cold*, a screwball comedy released by Dingbat Publishing in December 2013. My published novels (with Astraea Press) are: *Called to Arms Again* (May 2013), *Rescued By That New Guy in Town* (Oct. 2012), and *The Overnighter's Secrets* (May 2012). Also released through AP is a short novella, *Echo Taps* (June, 2013). Romantic comedy and romantic suspense are among eight completed novel manuscripts.

I'm co-author of two non-fiction monographs (about librarianship) with a royalty publisher, plus a signed chapter in another book and a signed article in a specialty encyclopedia. I've also published articles, book reviews, and over 120 poems; my writing has won nearly 40 awards, including several in national contests. As a newspaper photo-journalist, I published about 150 bylined newspaper articles, and some 100 bylined photos.

I worked nearly 30 years in the field of librarianship. I'm a decorated veteran of U.S. Air Force (including a remote tour of duty in the Arctic, at Thule AB in N.W. Greenland).

I'm the married parent of two and grandparent of six.

Books by J.L. Salter

From Astraea Press
The Overnighter's Secrets
Rescued by That New Guy in Town
Called to Arms Again
Echo Taps

Coming Soon from Dingbat Publishing
Scratching the Seven-Month Itch

Chapter One

Drank way too much punch before I realized it was spiked — right before I passed out Saturday night...

Coming to in total darkness, my foggy brain ached and my eyes strained. Nothing but the sensation of immense space. Pinched my forearm to rule out a bizarre dream. Ouch! Final recollection before everything went black: exhausted and still desperately thirsty.

My tentative hands groped enough to establish I was still on the hard plank bench. No telling how long I'd been there — everything hurt when I sat up. Stretched out my arms. "Ow!" Splinter. Yeah, the fund-raising jail with square wooden bars. But why was I still there?

"Hey!" Ghostly echo. Completely alone in the dark. The Greene County Halloween Festival was obviously long over and the spooky former armory building clearly abandoned.

As I struggled to my feet, I also realized I'd selected a terrible outfit for a jailbreak: low-cut satin blouse almost covering the bustier which threatened to squash my innards. Plus a tight high-hemmed skirt, patterned hose, and one remaining shoe with a four-inch heel. No telling where the other one was. Yeah, I'd had the terribly original notion to come as a sexy witch — including a pointy hat and hand-made broom. Sure wish I'd worn sneakers and a sweatsuit.

So, how on earth did I get left behind? And exactly how would I get out?

"Hello?" I knew it was too tentative, but somehow it seemed yelling into that vast darkness could make me feel even more vulnerable than I already did.

Dilemma.

One of the big festival fund-raisers was to lock up attendees until someone donated enough money to bail them out. At first I was steamed to be imprisoned since I'd spent two weeks working on that stinking event. Then I figured at least I was off my feet for a few minutes. Once I sat down exhaustion took over, plus the spiked punch, of course. But that didn't explain why I was still there in the dark with everybody gone... all alone.

At least I think I'm alone. "Hey! Hello?" Louder. "Anybody here?"

Silence could be good or bad. But I wished somebody would come turn the lights on and get me out. Plus, I need a restroom. Why did I leave my cell phone locked in the car? Not that there was any point waiting on a rescue. When you wake up behind wooden bars in real life, no handsome stranger comes to your aid.

My forefinger hurt but I couldn't extract a splinter in the dark. Took off my right shoe since I couldn't walk in the dark with one high-heel. Better find the other one. Maybe later. Stood up. Oh, still a bit woozy from that long nap. Fumbled my way from the back of the jail. Straight ahead should get me to the door. Tripped on something. Oh, my other shoe. Thank goodness, those heels were way too expensive to leave behind.

Just a few more steps. Yikes! Bumped my head on something hanging from the top of the wooden jail. Maybe a light bulb! Checked. No, just something with a disgusting spider web attached that I didn't want to touch again, or think about, ever. Hate spiders!

One more step. Fingers brushed the bars of the front wall. Good. Door couldn't be far away. Sideways to the left. Nope. Other direction. Ah, door frame. "Do you remember which way it opens, Kristen?" No, I didn't. And I was talking to myself again. I put both shoes on the floor, reached one hand through the bars, and felt the mechanism. Angle was wrong. In order to flip this latch, my entire forearm (past my elbow) had to get through.

What kind of latch? Metal. I felt a handle… it moved. But the door didn't open. "What did the latch look like, Kristen?" I asked myself. A freezer door? No. Gate hasp? Nope. It was like those rental trailers. Have to lift something and swing something else to the side, or vice versa. Tried that. Okay, I could lift or swing, but couldn't do both with one hand.

"Hey! Anybody here who can help with this latch before I wet myself?" Multiple echoes. I'd forgotten how big the main armory space was. When the Tennessee National Guard used it, dozens of cargo trucks fit in there. After the local unit was combined with the battalion in nearby Nashville, Uncle Sam donated the facility to the county. "Thanks a lot, Sam. Now I'm stuck here." Needed to stop talking to myself.

Tried the latch again from the other side. Ouch. Tight fit. My left elbow must be thicker. Wished I hadn't drunk all that punch earlier. I should have known somebody spiked it because I'd seen lots of folks got tipsy. But I'd just said, "Whatever" and drank another cup. That's how I slept through the abandonment by my former friends and the people I'd worked with on the community extravaganza. "Memo to Kristen," I muttered, "don't ever nap in a bustier. It pinches the girls and probably leaves bruises." Ha. Not that anybody would see them. Wally the Weasel was out of my zip code and my life. Nobody else in my rented house besides Elvis the neutered feline. Even that cat was probably more romantic than Wally, AKA Walter-who's-now-ancient-history-and-I-hope-he-dies-before-I-ever-see-him-again. Hmm, sounds awful. Not a good time to scare up bad karma with another curse on the Weasel. The last curse I put on Wally had to do with shriveling up his—

Okay, it was up to me. If I flipped up that gizmo, the handle pulled the thingy out of the what's-it. Great theory. Still needed two hands. "Hey! Anybody in this stinking armory who'll let me out?"

What was that noise? Something fell over! Somebody fell over? Better be a "good" somebody. "Hey! Over there... out there. Who's there?"

"O-o-ow!" From the left of me somewhere. But what? It must have been near the refreshment area not far from my prison pen. "Who's here? If you can speak, you'd better say something real quick, 'cause I've got a big ole magnum gun pointed right at your head!" Bluff 'em, Kristen.

"O-o-ow! Stop yelling! My head's about to explode." Closer. Man's voice. Could be good news... or bad.

"Well, you'd better show yourself. And get some light over here." Take charge, Kristen.

"I don't know where the stinkin' lights are. And stop yelling." Closer... I could almost smell him.

"Don't you have a lighter or something? I thought all guys carried lighters."

He groaned a bit more. "Only the ones that smoke."

"Terrific. The one non-smoker in Verdeville has finally arrived to let me out."

"Out of what? Where are you? Ow! Crud! What is this?" He'd finally found the left side of my cage.

"I'm in the fund-raiser jail. Quit stalling and get me out. I need a restroom. Come around to the front and watch out for the..."

"Ow! Splinters!"

"...splinters."

"Thanks for the warning." He sighed so heavily I could smell his breath. He'd drunk the punch too.

"Come around and let me out."

"Where's the door?"

"Just follow the splinters and turn to your, uh, right when you run out of bars."

With a few stumbles, another splinter, and some uncreative curses, the mystery man finally reached the door. "Okay. I'm here."

I already knew that because I smelled his breath again as he panted from the exertion. "Can you un-do this latch thingy?"

"Where is it?"

I realized he couldn't see my hand pointing directly at the latch. "I'm holding it. My arm's through the bars and I've got the thingy in my hand." I realized that could sound, um, unusual if overheard by anybody. I heard his hands roam over the outside of the cage door. He was too high. I sighed heavily and gave back a whiff of punch-breath.

Suddenly his fingertips touched my forearm. He yelped and recoiled.

It startled me too, but I wasn't going to act like a sissy. "That's nearly my elbow. Go the other way about a foot or so and my hand's on the latch dealie."

"Okay. It threw me a bit to touch flesh. My fingers expected wood." Yeah, mine too.

This stranger was tall — I could tell from the source of his breath, which surely needed a mint. His hands gently explored my forearm to re-establish the location of my elbow. Then he walked his fingers the other direction, toward my hand and the latch. If he intended to grope me like this, he owed me dinner. Large hands and long fingers. Short nails. Some calluses on his fingers and the pads of his palm, but not like a lumberjack. Just a man who knew how to work with his hands but probably didn't rely on those skills for his paycheck.

"Will you get on to the latch?" I truly needed a restroom. I would have been hopping by then if I weren't worried about that spider web above.

"Well, let go of it and give me a chance at the mechanism." A slight bit of spittle when he sighed again. Not sure I wanted to share spit from a tall stranger in the dark. "Okay, I have it in my hands, but I don't understand how it goes."

I thought men could undo anything except left-handed buttons. "It felt like a doo-hicky that latches the overhead door on a rental van or something."

"Oh!" The light came on — in his head, that is. "One of those. Okay. No sweat." Two smooth movements and it was open. Of course, it took two hands like I said before. Humph.

I reached down for my shoes, quickly found them, and then pushed on the door, apparently before he'd moved away. It caught him somewhere on his trunk.

"Ooof!"

"Sorry. Like I said, I need a powder room."

He made noise backing up. "Okay, take off... for wherever."

"Where are you going to be?" Didn't want a strange man lurking in the dark.

"On your tail or as close as I can, without tripping."

"I don't want a stranger following me."

"I need to use that same facility."

There wasn't much I could do about that. "Whatever. Well, the door ought to be way over there where that exit sign is." It was the kind with three or four small bulbs normally, but that particular one had only one dim lamp glowing. The signs over the other doors must have burned out completely. They didn't spend much on maintenance in abandoned armories.

"Oh, yeah. Switch by the exit door. Makes sense."

So the tall man also had some cognitive powers. Wonder what he looks like? "Do you remember what's between us and that door?"

"Nope. Never been here before. I'm new in town. Plus, I don't know what part of this place we're at right now." His feet made a shuffling sound as he changed the subject. "So how come nobody let you out of that cage?"

"Karla was supposed to call my brother, but I guess Eric couldn't be bothered to drive over here from Marrowbone. I can't believe Ellen didn't double-check with Karla and both left me locked in that dark cage!"

"Who's Ellen?"

"Used to be my best friend. But now, she's made the top of my hit list." I'd moved forward a few careful paces as we talked. "So what are you doing here, if you've never been in the armory before?"

Another heavy sigh, from slightly farther behind me. "Long story." His lengthy story also sounded like it might be sad.

I focused on the dim, distant exit light and the restroom not far beyond it. "Yeah, well, I'd like to hear it sometime. But for now, we need to speed up before I bust open a bladder gasket." I held one shoe in each hand as I stretched my arms forward. I remembered a dunking booth against one wall and a huge overhead door nearby. Several small booths around the perimeter. A large inflatable castle dominated the middle of the space.

Whap. The shoe in my right hand grazed something. My fingers felt coarse rubberized fabric. "Found the castle. I think the area right around this is clear, unless somebody stacked something on the floor. We'll bear left to reach the corner." I sped up a bit, figuring we had a good forty feet after turning the corner of the inflatable.

Suddenly his hand touched the side of my neck and gripped my shoulder! "What the…"

"Sorry. I'm a little dizzy and my head's pounding. Just had to steady myself a bit."

"Well go steady with that castle wall. I don't want strangers groping me in the dark." Actually his touch made my heart beat faster, but the extra adrenaline didn't help my bladder any.

He'd pulled his hand away quickly. "Good grief. You act like I grabbed something."

"You did. My neck and shoulder."

"I meant something else."

Hmm. Interesting conversation. But I'd need to see his eyes before I let him anywhere near my else… or my others. "Look, buddy, I appreciate you opening that latch thing, but you don't go grabbing women in the dark." Actually, that's precisely when most men do grab women.

He didn't respond.

When my hand ran out of castle wall, I knew it was time to turn right and head toward the distant door. I focused on the incredibly dim exit lamp, slightly nearer with each tentative step.

My left foot struck something which my outstretched hands didn't detect. Must be low. Checked it out. "Uh, there's something like a big trash can here, right in front of me."

"Where? Ow!" He found it.

What a baby. I'm the one with no shoes. But I was ruining the feet of my patterned black hose — another seven bucks down the drain. Sheesh. We were probably within thirty feet of the door now, and I struggled to remember where the registration tables were. Slowed down and reached lower. There. "Table here. Just to the right of me. We'll scoot along the edge of this and ought to be right at the door."

"Well, hurry. If you know what I mean."

I knew. My eyeballs were sloshing. Both leather pumps in my outstretched hands reached the cinderblock wall at about the same time with loud clacks. Don't know why I did this — reflexive, I suppose — but I clutched both shoes in one hand and tugged up my bustier with the other. Modesty? Vanity? Then I groped for the light switch.

He did too, around to my left. "Okay, I'm in the doorway. Where's the light?"

"Can't be far. One side or the other." I felt his hands on my left arm as we both groped blindly for the switch.

"Oh. Sorry."

"Okay. No sweat." I lied. His touch was electric. I wanted to think about it some more, but my kidneys had short-circuited my brain. "Switches are about chest high on me. It's got to be here somewhere."

I heard one of his hands whap against the wall as the fingers of his other hand grazed my bustier. Yep, that's chest high. "Hey, buddy!" As I spoke I found the switch and flipped it vigorously. It was just for the entryway. The rest of that huge space would have a whole bank of switches, probably not far away. The bright light immediately overhead made both of us shut our eyes reflexively.

His must have opened first. "Uh, you're a witch!" He gasped as though that notion actually frightened him.

When I opened my eyes, he was staring at the goose-pimples among the décolletage created by my bustier. "Well, you're…" It took me a second to identify someone in a brightly striped shirt, breeches with a sash, a dagger — hopefully not real — tucked in his waistband, and a disheveled headscarf. Plus, a black eye patch dangled from his left ear by a strand of cheap elastic. "…you're a pirate!"

"Aarrgghh." He dashed away toward the nearest buccaneer's room.

Chapter Two

I clicked the light switch on the other side of that door and passed the pirate in the hallway. I practically had my panties down by the time I reached the toilet in the ladies' room — first door on the left after turning into the intersecting hallway. No time to put down paper and I didn't even think about whoever had used it before me. When your bladder has been chanting for half an hour, you can't be obsessive about hygiene.

After I'd dealt with my primary emergency, I had enough focus to wonder about the pirate guy. He'd groped my arm, touched my neck and shoulder, and even — supposedly on accident — grazed my bustier. I looked into the mirror. Hmm. This witch costume did reveal a good bit of flesh. I made some quick adjustments to the girls. Slightly more comfortable, but it was still a punishing outfit.

Checked the bottoms of my feet. My hose weren't completely ruined, but all that traipsing and scurrying had taken a toll. I'd have to rotate those to back-up status and get a new pair. Not that I wore black patterned hose all that often; I tended more toward soft gray or suntan shade for work at the bank. I put my heels back on. Ow.

For a moment I fritzed with my short hair — which I charitably called honey-brown — before I realized it was beyond hope. Also, my eye makeup had streaked. What a mess. I exited the restroom and stood at the corner of the intersecting hallways.

"Oh, I thought you'd gone." The brigand approached from the direction of the men's room door. He still couldn't keep his eyes off my visible flesh. "You look… taller."

I pointed to my shoes and finally got a good look at his face. Nice — under the greasepaint beard and overdone eye makeup someone likely copied from a bad pirate movie. Strong jaw, Roman nose, steel gray eyes. He was probably about six-two. The gaudy horizontal stripes of his tight shirt revealed an expansive chest. Not like a competitive body-builder, but a man who'd been physically fit most of his life. Hmm. Wondered how old he was. Hard to tell with buccaneers. Maybe a hair over thirty.

"Guess I'm heading out. Which way is the parking lot?" He turned his upper body three directions without pausing very long at any.

I pointed over my right shoulder. "The main lot's out there. Feeds into a ginormous overhead door they used to need for the trucks that pulled in the big space."

"Deuce-and-a-halfs."

"Huh?"

"Two-and-a-half-ton trucks. There's room in that truck bay for two full-size basketball courts. I had a cousin with a different Tennessee guard unit but most of these armories are pretty similar." The pirate rubbed his head and looked surprised, likely just then realizing he still wore the scarf. He grinned as he pulled it off. His movement also dislodged the thin elastic strand from his ear and the eye patch fell to the thick tile.

I wondered why he hadn't seen that in the mirror. Maybe he hadn't even looked. Some guys don't. Nice smile. Not movie star caliber, but just right for a real man. I eye-balled his dagger again. "So, you came here expecting trouble?" I pointed to his waistband.

"Oh, borrowed that from a nephew. Hard rubber." Another smile. "Didn't want to cut anything off."

No, indeed. "You said it was your first time at the Halloween Festival. So how'd you get left here?"

"I'm still wondering that myself." He shook his head. "Long story."

Whatever. "At least explain why it took you so long to come help me get out."

"First time I heard your voice, I thought I was still asleep and just dreaming or something. My head hurt. Drank too much punch. What'd they put in that junk?" He rubbed the back of his neck. "Anyway, I was ticked off..."

"Because of that long story you haven't told yet."

He nodded. "...and I drank a lot more than I usually do. Got real tired and just kind of slumped against the wall off in a corner. Not sure which corner. But not too far from where you were, apparently."

I liked the way his mouth moved when he spoke. A bit like Sean Connery when much younger — extra mobility in his lips.

He continued. "Well, anyway, I tried to make my way over to your voice, but I don't see so good in the pitch-dark, so it took a while to reach you."

"Why didn't you say something so I'd know you were coming?"

"I didn't know who you were. Plus, you'd threatened to shoot me! A disembodied voice yelling, 'Hey!' was all I knew."

"I'm a little surprised nobody tripped over your big feet as they were leaving."

"Yeah, you'd think people cleaning up would've noticed at least one of us."

"I was lying down on that shelf-bench so they probably didn't see me. And I don't think they did any cleaning-up. I was on the committee and everybody said the county jail convicts would clean up Monday morning. No need to do anything but turn out the lights and leave, which apparently is just what they did." Would've been nice if they'd checked for live bodies first, however.

The buccaneer shrugged and headed toward the door I'd previously indicated. "Okay. Guess I'm outta here."

"Hold on. You said you were new in town. Who are you anyway?"

"Just your run-of-the-mill pirate." He grinned. "Who are you?"

"A witch who puts nasty spells on rude pirates." I didn't grin. Why'd he dodge my question?

He turned again to leave.

"Hey, I'm not staying here by myself." I'd had my quota of being alone in large dark buildings near Halloween.

He took another quick gander at my chest and his gaze clearly wanted to linger. "Might be chilly outside in a witch costume."

My leather jacket was something else I'd left locked in the car. I sighed heavily and followed him toward the door. It seemed like I was forgetting something, but nothing clicked.

"It's been… interesting." He looked like he might shake my hand or something. But he just winked clumsily and pushed open the heavy door.

Brisk night air swirled into the wide hallway and I shivered. Wondered what time it was.

The newcomer stepped outside and clasped his arms around his chest; I stayed pretty close so he could be a windbreak of sorts. Right as I heard the massive door slam behind us I remembered my purse was still tucked under the bench inside the wooden cage. "My keys! My purse!" I tried the door. Locked tighter than my Aunt Tilly's coin pouch.

"Locked?"

Before I could nod my head, I started sniffling. The new guy stepped closer, tentatively, but stopped short of hugging me. You can't let a strange swashbuckler embrace you even if he is compassionate enough. As I shivered from the cold breeze, it made my sniffles sound even worse. Don't let strangers see you cry!

"Uh, is there something I can do to help?" He also shivered, but not as much as I.

I'd spent the last thirty minutes being strong. "Not unless," I sobbed, "you have a key to the armory."

He shook his head. "But I guess I could give you a ride." He didn't sound like he wanted to.

And I wasn't certain it would be a good idea anyhow. "Don't ride with strangers" had been ingrained in me since kindergarten.

Vehicle brakes squealed in the parking lot and we both turned just as a piercing bright light temporarily blinded me. "Stop right there! Verdeville Police! Hands in the air and don't move too fast."

***

Another funny read from Dingbat Publishing

UNEMPLOYED PUBLIC TELEVISION
Vampire Hunters

by Rob Marsh

A soul-exploring voyage into the mind, intended primarily for Fine Arts majors, featuring a rip-roaring adventure, a trenchant analysis of public television, and plenty of happy little vampires, zombies, robots, aliens, clowns, and other exhausted genres.

Myles is Interrupted

It all started one rainy day, deep within a muggy public television studio, somewhere in Glendale, California. Myles

371

Kieffer, an unassuming young man in his early thirties, sat at his desk and tapped idly at the keys of his computer. As director of programming at the local public television affiliate studio, it was his responsibility to complete the task of keeping the programming interesting, a task virtually impossible considering the mediocre content available.

Myles scratched at his shaggy blond hair and stared at the screen, exhaling deeply. He loosened his tie and studied the figures before him. Station ratings had been plummeting, and the latest fund-raising blitz had been a complete, abject failure. Myles glanced at the stack of bills on his desk, several emblazoned in red ink with vicious demands to pay, else have the power cut, the water shut off, and various other acts of brutality committed against the studio employees and their family members.

But all things considered, Myles thought, gazing out the window, his job wasn't too bad. Most of his day was spent behind the desk, arranging and rearranging program schedules for his crew of aging public television celebrities. Indeed, for some strange reason, straight out of college Myles had landed the job directing the one affiliate with the largest collection of old and irrelevant actors and their programs, but he didn't mind, for the most part. He did his job well, and was happy to be able to put his Communications major to work. For many years, perhaps too many, it had been his profession, and he nobly did his best, considering the situation.

The young executive left his office and headed to the break room, where he opened a brown bag and extracted a bland sandwich, an apple, and a mug of herbal tea. Outside of the room, two bearded figures debated with great animation the value of British television, particularly ones involving characters in powdered wigs. Myles grimaced and, ignoring them, opened his newspaper and sipped at his tea while his eyes scanned the classified section.

Suddenly, out of nowhere, an alarming figure sprang into the room. Garbed in a lab coat, a tinfoil conical helmet, a frenzied beard, and wild, rolling eyes, he grabbed at Myles' shoulders and shouted at him. "Myles Kieffer! YOU are the chosen one! Only you can save us from the inevitable destruction and annihilation of all mankind!!!"

Myles smiled politely, put down his tea, and calmly said, "Ah, this is about that unpaid gas bill Listen, I..."

The raving lunatic suddenly sat down across from Myles, silenced him with an open hand, and proceeded to produce a bundle of papers. Hastily removing a rubber band, he spread the pages across the table and began to explain, in frantically elaborate details, the years of research that he had done on ancient Mayan prophecies, Sumerian pottery inscriptions, Egyptian mummy dust samples, and endless charts, maps, hieroglyphics, and strange architectural structures, all emphasized with wild waving of his hands. Myles simply sat and listened patiently.

"What it all boils down to is that there's an evil mastermind who, aware of the ancient calendars, is harnessing evil energy to help bring about conditions to end all life on earth. We aren't sure who exactly it is, but we know where... somewhere..." a pause and a cold shudder, "...in New England!"

Myles continued to listen calmly, slowly drinking his herbal tea.

"He has a device or something that is drawing explosive, and colorful, space rocks to earth," the lunatic continued, "and as each impacts with the surface, it has a distinctive effect on the population, bringing about horrific transformative and destructive effects."

Myles studied the pages on the space rocks, each rock carefully illustrated by hand and colored apparently in crayon. "But what does this have to do with me...?" Myles asked.

Suddenly even more frenzied, the conspiracy nut grabbed Myles by the edges of his shirt and shook him frantically. "Public television is the catalyst of the destruction of the world!" he screamed, and sprang to his feet, the table toppling over and papers scattering everywhere. "It's not just dull and irrelevant television programming... it's about life-draining creatures. Myles, take the papers and no...!!!!" Suddenly a pair of unfamiliar men, dressed completely in black, stepped into the room, grabbed the loony, and proceeded to haul him away.

"Nothing to see here. You didn't see anything or hear anything," stated one of the two shadowy figures. Myles nodded silently and took another sip of tea.

"Myles Kieffer..." yelled the loony as his voice faded down the hall. "You must be the one to stop this... the prophecies have said so... nooo..."

Some doors slammed, and Myles heard the distant sound of an engine starting and the squeal of tires, then suddenly there was silence, broken only by the hum of the refrigerator behind him. Myles finished his tea and shook his head, resuming the boring review of his business reports.

Unexpected Mass Termination

His break finished, Myles gathered his business reports, as well as the loony's papers, and headed back to the office. However, his trek was interrupted by the arrival of another unexpected visitor.

Senator Hugo McCashglut, the wealthy and powerful politician, strode into the studio, trailed by an assortment of aides and political action flunkies who tenaciously reached out to stuff bundles of bills into his coat pocket. Senator McCashglut, a big, beefy man, held out a chunky hand to halt Myles, while with his other hand he brandished a massive cigar into his substantial mouth.

"Mister Kieffer," he began.

"S-S-Senator," Myles stuttered. "To what do we owe this unexpected..."

"Spare me your pleasantries," the senator grumbled, his voice deep and reeking of expensive, tax-payer funded booze. "I'm here to see to some changes. It turns out that my posh, leather upholstered furniture in my Washington office is out of date by a few years, and I need it all replaced immediately."

Myles nodded and squirmed nervously.

"So, to cover the cost of new furnishings, I've decided to terminate you and every employee of this location. In two weeks time, you are all out of work and this studio is to be closed and turned into an IRS office. Thank you. Good night."

And with that, Senator McCashglut strode and departed the building, his trail of followers carefully following behind him. As the door slammed shut, Myles stood and stared in bewilderment.

Myles staggered in a daze back to his office and set the papers down on his desk. He cradled his head in his hands and pondered the dark news. Not only was he out of work, but everyone in the studio was as well. How would he break the news to so many people?

His eyes drifted to one of the conspiracy nut's pages and he examined it more closely. These strange papers were a fair distraction to take his mind off the situation of mass terminations. Examining the first page, he saw what appeared to be the rocky wall of a Peruvian temple, showing a strange series of shapes: some figures of humans, some animals, some exotic fruits, and…

Myles held the picture more closely. The photograph was a black and white image with a figure circled in red. The figure appeared to be that of a puppet, one of the infuriatingly irritating puppets from the morning television line-up. Could it…?

Nah, it couldn't be, he thought.

He scanned through more of the pages. One crumpled, thickly folded document opened up to reveal a carefully annotated map of the United States. His public television station was noted with large letters saying "START HERE," and from that location a crimson line was scrawled across the map that stretched across the country, from west to east, doing a couple circular loops for no apparent reason, then finally reaching the coast and crawling north, to an enigmatic location heavily circled and noted with strange symbols, cryptic notations, and a coffee stain. Myles furrowed his brow and studied the final destination of the line, deep in New England, and shook his head as he considered the details.

What did this all mean? Why did so many of these images, symbols, and locations seem so oddly familiar? And that final destination… could it be…?

Myles bundled the conspiracy papers into a big manila folder and was about to toss it aside when he let out a mighty sigh and reluctantly tucked the packet under his arm. Perhaps reading it later would help him fall asleep. He had a dark job ahead of him, telling the entire staff about their sudden unemployment, but he would leave that for another day. Grabbing his jacket, he headed for the door.

***

Thanks for reading! Dingbat Publishing strives to bring you quality entertainment that doesn't take itself too seriously. I mean honestly, with a name like that, our books have to be good or we're going to be laughed at. Or maybe both.

If you enjoyed this book, the best thing you can do is buy a million more copies and give them to all your friends... erm, leave a review on the readers' website of your preference. All authors love feedback and we take reviews from readers like you seriously.

Oh, and c'mon over to our website:
www.DingbatPublishing.Weebly.com

Who knows what other books you'll find there?

Cheers,

Gunnar Grey,
publisher, author, and Chief Dingbat

δ
Dingbat Publishing